# C I T Y
# I N
# E M B E R S

THE COLLECTOR SERIES BOOK 1

**STACEY MARIE BROWN**

**Copyright © 2015 Stacey Marie Brown**

All rights reserved.

978-0-9890131-6-1

Cover Design by Jay Aheer (https://www.simplydefinedart.com)

Edited by Hollie (www.hollietheeditor.com)

Formatting by www.formatting4U.com

# ALSO BY STACEY MARIE BROWN

## Contemporary Romance

*Buried Alive*

**Blinded Love Series**
*Shattered Love* (#1)
*Pezzi di me (Shattered Love)—Italian*
*Broken Love* (#2)
*Twisted Love* (#3)

*The Unlucky Ones*
*(Má Sorte—Portuguese)*

**Royal Watch Series**
*Royal Watch (#1)*
*Royal Command (#2)*

*Smug Bastard*

## Paranormal Romance

**Darkness Series**
*Darkness of Light* (#1)
*(L'oscurita Della Luce—Italian)*
*Fire in the Darkness (*#2)
*Beast in the Darkness* (An Elighan Dragen Novelette)
*Dwellers of Darkness* (#3)
*Blood Beyond Darkness* (#4)
*West* (A Darkness Series Novel)

**Collector Series**
*City in Embers* (#1)
*The Barrier Between* (#2)
*Across the Divide* (#3)
*From Burning Ashes* (#4)

**Lightness Saga**
*The Crown of Light* (#1)
*Lightness Falling* (#2)
*The Fall of the King* (#3)
*Rise from the Embers* (#4)

**A Winterland Tale**
*Descending into Madness* (#1)
*Ascending from Madness* (#2)
*Beauty in Her Madness* (#3)
*Beast in His Madness (#4)*

**Savage Lands Series**
*Savage Lands* (#1)
*Wild Lands (#2)*
*Dead Lands (#3)*

## Note for my readers

This book takes place after what Ember does at the end of Darkness of Light Series and shows who she has affected.

I hope you enjoy this series as much as I've enjoyed writing it.

Thanks for riding this crazy rollercoaster with me.

# ONE

The pavement came up, slamming against the soles of my shoes. My legs stretched farther, leaping over a garbage can. Trying to slow me, the entity I ran after hurled another container to the ground, which crashed loudly in the narrow, grimy lane. My breath held in my lungs as I sailed over the bin, keeping my pace through the dark, shadowy maze.

"Zoey!" I heard Daniel call my name. My head swiveled to see his outline point down an alley, splitting off from the one we were in. I gave a nod and turned my focus ahead. We had been working together for almost three years, and I knew even by the lift of his eyebrow what he meant. We knew every inch of the alleyways in downtown Seattle by heart. The one he went into now eventually turned and intersected this one.

Breath pumped radically in my lungs as I sprinted after our target. This one was faster than most. He slithered around a dumpster, veiling his position. My fingers wrapped around the grip of the gun harnessed on my right side when the guy came back into my view.

It was a dart gun, filled with a high dose of chloroform. The real gun loaded with special fae-designed ammo was attached to my left side and was only used in emergency cases. In my three years, I only used it a handful of times. Hopefully, tonight was not one of those occasions.

The long, lean body cut around a corner, disappearing from sight once again. I rounded the bend and down the alley in pursuit when a trash lid came hurtling at my head like a Frisbee. With a squeak, I threw myself onto the uneven terrain. The metal rim grazed my head, hitting the wall before it clattered to the pavement.

The man's lip twisted in a scowl as he took off running. Scrambling up, I tore after it. It. Him. Whatever. In reality, he was fae. And fae meant vile, threating, loathsome creatures.

"Dammit," I mumbled as the figure hopped onto a dumpster and bounced up to grab the building's escape ladder. Aiming my dart gun at his back, my fingers twitched on the trigger. I only had one dart. If I missed, it would be all over, and Daniel was too far away. Our target would slip through our fingers. Shoving the weapon back into my holder, I scrambled up the bin. My jeans tore on a bent piece of metal, slicing deep into my knee. Sucking in a hiss of pain, I jumped for the fire escape, climbing the rungs to the roof.

A massive element came rushing toward my head. *What the hell? First a trash lid. Now a satellite dish?* This guy really wanted to decapitate me. I dipped below the building as the object skimmed my hairline, tumbling to the ground with a loud crack. Pieces of plastic, metal, and wiring scattered.

I peeked over the ledge. The spot where he had been standing was empty.

*Hell...*

My arms pulled me onto the roof, my feet scaling over the last two steps. I had barely landed when something sprang at me, knocking me down. A fist came for my face. I twisted, his hand grazing my ear, hitting the surface.

"I know what you are." His voice was more high-pitched than I expected. A forked tongue darted between his front teeth. The canine teeth had grown into long, spiky points, dripping with venom. *Great. A snake shape-shifter.*

No wonder Dr. Rapava was anxious for us to collect this fae. It was a rare find. Being close, I could see his eyes were a bright golden brown, his nose was stumpier than a normal man's would be, and his skin had a smooth, scaly look to it. His hair was black on top and tan on either side of his head. A tattoo of a cobra was inked on his neck.

"And I know what you are, too. Awesome. Introductions are over." I kneed him in the groin. Snake or not, he was still a man. He wilted, contorting, giving me time to scuttle back onto my feet. He spit on the ground and curled up, striking out for me. His mouth open, his teeth ready to sink deep into my skin. Why couldn't he be a cute garter snake?

I ducked, hitting him in the stomach. A long hiss broke from his lips. He spun and lunged for me, his knuckles contacting the side of my mouth. Pain burst up my jawbone, traveling behind my eyes. I stumbled back, my ankles knocking into some piping, and I fell on my butt. His tongue darted, venom seeping out of his mouth. "This should be extremely painful." He snapped his teeth and jumped for me, aiming for my neck.

A whoosh sound disturbed the air, resonating in my ears. Snake-man's body stilled before crumpling onto the roof, revealing Daniel standing on the building across the narrow alley, his dart gun pointed in my direction.

"About time." I smiled coyly, trying not to show the relief sliding off my shoulders. I got to my feet.

Daniel tilted his head and shook it slightly. "How many times have I told you not to engage without backup?"

"Today? Or a general roundabout number?" I blotted at the blood pooling on my lip. A strand of my long chestnut brown hair escaped its ponytail and clung to the wet matter.

"Zoey, I am serious." Daniel holstered his weapon. "You are young and think you're invincible. We aren't dealing with normal humans here. They're fae. They have powers and strengths we don't have. Some we might not even know about yet. You can't simply take them on by yourself."

My eyes rolled as he lectured me. I'd been hearing this type of speech since I began training with him. I wasn't very good at listening, but I'd gotten much better. I used to be extremely resistant and hot tempered, but those qualities didn't work in a business where those behaviors could get you killed. In the moment it was hard for me to remember. "I know. I'm sorry."

"Let's get him out of here before someone discovers

us." Daniel walked to the ledge of the building where the ladder hung. "I'll get the van and back it up below you. He should stay unconscious..."

"Yes, Daniel, I know the drill." I grinned and waved for him to go.

A smile stretched across his handsome, clean-shaven features, his blue eyes catching mine. My heart fluttered in my chest. This man had me so twisted inside I didn't know which way was up. The fact he was almost twenty years my senior didn't alter my feelings for him. If anything, it made me like him more. Experienced in life. I usually got along with people older than me.

My life hadn't been easy. I'd been raised in foster care, growing up tough and fast. My experiences made me relate to people not in my age group. I never dated guys who were my age. They always were five to ten years older.

Daniel didn't seem to feel the same. From the beginning he shut down any advances I made. He stressed our age difference or commented on my youthful twenty-two years. He could discourage me till he was eighty, but it was too late. I was already in love with him.

I watched his body easily scale down the fire escape and jump to the ground. At the age of forty, he was more fit than most twenty-year-olds I met. With his military background and present training, he cut a nice figure. He was about five-eleven, but his trim muscles made him appear taller. Perfect for me since I was only five-five.

A groan came from near my feet and broke my attention away from Daniel and back to our captive. We referred to them as the collected. For the last three years, I worked for a secret branch of the government, the Department of Molecular Genetics—DMG. I also called it HQ for headquarters.

During my first semester at college, we were given a test in my psychology class. To the teacher and most students, it looked like a quiz on social behaviors and mannerisms. Pictures were flashed on the screen, and we were asked to describe what we saw. I learned later the government was testing us for "the sight" and to see if we were sensitive to the paranormal—humans who could see through the veils of glamour fae put around themselves to blend in.

Seeing creatures was always something I could do. When I was a child, I thought it was normal. It wasn't until I was seven when I found I was different. People around me never experienced what I saw. I blocked it and turned away when I saw a glow or a creature. I got so good at obstructing my sight I started to think I made it all up—that my imagination, in desperate need to escape my own reality, caused me to see things. With my past, it was believable I would make up another world.

Over time, I let my walls slip. It was probably why I hadn't obstructed my sight during the test in class. When they showed a woman sitting on a lawn, I saw a leopard with glowing brown eyes. I didn't know till later when I was brought in to the DMG I was the only one who saw it—a shape-shifter. Fae.

Fae was the general term for them, like calling all of us human. There are different races and species under the fae umbrella: shape-shifters, fairies, demons, incubus, leprechauns, gnomes, sprites, and the list goes on and on. There were the Dark side (Unseelie) and the Light (Seelie). They once lived among humans until the world turned against magic, saying it was the devil's work. Some fae went into hiding in the Otherworld, but other fae inhabited the Earth, as they needed humans to live. Humans were a buffet to the Dark. They stole our life forces through sex, dreams, sins, and other ways humans expended energy. There were even some who ate us. We were nothing more than food to them.

Learning of fae and their existence had not been a simple switch but probably easier for me than most because I'd been seeing things since I could remember. It was like finding out *The X-Files* was really a documentary, and the government really had been hiding the existence of another species. Fae were not aliens in the way people thought. They were not from outer space. No little green men with large eyes poked you in the butt, although there was a fae species that had a green tint to their skin. If caught without glamour, they could easily be mistaken for aliens, which is how I feel the whole alien thing started.

Understanding the information I acquired about fae was important. I needed to know what I was dealing with to collect them. The more I learned, the more I hated them. They treated humans like nothing more than cattle and used us for their own benefit. We were an endless Mickey D's drive-thru to them. Easily discounted and tossed aside. Their disregard for us made me feel the same about them, if not stronger. What the DMG performed benefited humans. We captured fae to test and research.

Dr. Rapava, the director of DMG, had made a discovery fifteen years earlier that showed the value of fae cells in helping humans. Our testing had advanced finding a cure for things like cancer and birth defects. Imagine someday no child would die from cancer or suffer from a birth defect.

Like my sister.

Lexie wasn't my real sister. She was a fellow foster kid, but the closest thing I could ever imagine to having a sibling. The thought of her stuck in a wheelchair the rest of her life made me crazy. It was not her fault her mother was a druggie, which may have been the reason Lexie had been born crippled. If there was a chance I could help her walk someday, there wasn't anything I wouldn't do.

Tires crunched as Daniel backed the nondescript, black windowless van down the passageway. As I watched him, I thought how much my life had changed. Three years ago I would never have imagined I'd be hunting and collecting fae, going to college, and working for the government. Actually earning money legally.

It had taken Daniel a long time to break me of old habits and reactions. Stealing to get by was normal to me. It was an adjustment to butt heads with an ex-special ops military man who didn't look kindly on breaking rules. When you grew up on the streets, it was hard to see beyond what you knew. But he made me look at life differently. Want more. I could escape the harsh world and free myself from poverty and the dark events from my past.

The brakes squeaked as he halted the van next to the ladder. Daniel quickly got out, his short dark brown hair streaked with silver glittered under the streetlight. He jumped onto the dumpster, climbing his way toward me. His arm muscles flexed under his black sweater. *Damn.* I shook my head, looking away. I turned and gazed down at the body at my feet. The thin, lengthy form stretched out. Getting this fae back to ground level was not going to be easy.

Daniel's head popped over the rooftop. My foot tapped, peering angrily down at the creature. "Yeah. It would have been nice if he stayed below. If we could only throw it over the side." He sighed, climbing over the wall. "But you know Dr. Rapava would be mad as hell if we brought the specimen back damaged."

"It will heal." I shrugged. I was only half joking. It was true. Fae could mend wounds and broken bones in a matter of hours.

Fae were virtually immortal. They weren't immune to death, just *extremely* hard to kill. If you wanted to exterminate a fae, and make sure it stayed that way, it was safest to slay it with a special fae-welded metal, like the bullets in my gun. Goblin-crafted weapons were the best. They were poison to them. I heard rumors that at certain times of year, when the layer between our worlds was at its thinnest, fae were susceptible to both human and fae ways of dying. I also heard beheading, breaking their necks, or continuously cutting them so their skin never has a chance to heal and they bleed to death, were others.

But our job didn't entail dispatching them. We were here to collect.

Daniel frowned as he squatted next to the creature. "Don't tempt me."

"Whatever we do, let's do it quick. With the racket this guy made, I'm sure someone called the cops."

Three years after I left my shady lifestyle, my name was still on many police lists. At the age of nine, I was recruited to be in a group who liked to unburden people of their personal items: wallets, phones, credit cards. I was little and cute with big eyes. No one suspected me until it was too late. Pickpocketing was my introduction into the unethical world I became a part of. It was survival of the fittest, and I had to work extra hard because I was a tiny sweet-looking girl.

The police never caught me, and I didn't want them to now. Avoiding the cops at all costs was still a mantra I lived by. The DMG would get me out, but I still had a natural fear and avoidance of law enforcement.

Daniel nodded at my comment. He sucked in a deep breath and slung the fae over his shoulder. "Good thing this one isn't too muscular. Tall but thin." His voice still strained under the weight.

"He's a snake-shifter. Be careful of his mouth," I warned.

Daniel frowned with disgust at the fae. Keeping the shifter's venomous fangs away from his skin, he lifted himself and the fae over the wall. With a grunt, he slowly moved down the metal rungs. With one last look around the rooftop for any evidence left behind, I swung down, following close behind Daniel.

# TWO

Dr. Boris Rapava looked up from his desk as we entered his office housed far below the city streets. "Mr. Holt. Ms. Daniels." He gave a curt nod. "Excellent job, as usual. The specimen you retrieved tonight was one I have been hunting for years."

Dr. Rapava was born in the territory of Georgia, but his family moved to Russia when he was young. When he was twenty, he came to the States to further his education in genetic science. He had always done research in the unknown and unexplained, basically *X-Files* type of exploration. Twenty years ago, when a secret branch of the government discovered his work in fae mutant genetics, they came to him to officially ask him to head the DMG in Seattle.

For some reason, Seattle had continuously been a hotspot for the fae. Dr. Rapava once explained to me about these doors or windows connecting our world with the Otherworld. It was how the fae traveled between realms. I didn't understand the nuts and bolts of how they worked, but the gist of his statement was Seattle, Sedona, and New Orleans had the highest number of these "doors" and magical presence per square mile than New York had rats. European cities, like Prague, Edinburgh, London, Paris, and all of Ireland had the greatest quantity in the world, but in America, Seattle ranked extremely high.

When they recruited me, the DMG only had thirty employees, but something changed in the last year. Rapava heavily recruited anyone with the sight. Like me. He never told me what had made the government so nervous, but I sensed if they were recruiting and expanding, there was a larger level of threat coming from the fae. My mind kept picturing *Independence Day,* and we were being invaded by these creatures. The ones I'd come in contact with thought themselves superior to the human species. Their arrogance was probably how we captured a lot of them. Fae didn't believe we could match them.

I'd been trained to treat them as creatures and beasts, to see past the human form some portrayed. They were not sweet fairies but threats to humans. Very few people could see through fae glamour. Fae come in all shape and sizes. Some created animal illusions like rats or mice to hide in plain sight. Some had human forms. Some were shape-shifters. But there was something making them different from humans—eyes, hair, horns, something that would tip me off. Most of the time it was their aura. Fae auras are extremely different than those produced by humans. Humans have a simple mix of colors. Fae not only glinted with magic but were substantial in heaviness, and they released colors and energies not existing here on Earth. When I first started, it took me more than six months for my eyes to get used to experiencing their images and understanding them.

"Kate would like your brief on the collected on her

desk tomorrow." The doctor clasped his hands and leaned back in the chair. His dark skin contrasted with his white lab coat. He was in his mid-fifties with silver-white hair and hazel eyes. He was lean and tall and looked to be in good shape, but I knew he probably didn't own a pair of running shoes. He practically lived at DMG. He had to. There was not one time I came in he wasn't here, usually in his lab, testing and studying.

"Of course." Daniel nodded, which made me smile. He knew I hated doing the reports on our collections. He usually gave in and did them. His excuse was I already had enough papers to write for my college classes, and I should focus on those. I understood he did the reports to limit my stress so I could get an extra hour of sleep. I studied his profile as he continued to talk with Dr. Rapava. My heart twisted in my chest when his eyes flickered to mine, feeling my stare.

"Check with Kate before you go." Dr. Rapava dismissed us. He was efficient and to the point. He didn't dally or make small talk.

Kate, on the other hand, liked to chat.

Both Daniel and I groaned as we stepped out of the doctor's office into the hallway. It had to be nearing dawn.

Kate Grier was also in her fifties. She had gorgeous long snow-white hair and sparkling brown eyes. She was short and more on the round, curvy side. In personality she was Dr. Rapava's contrast. She was a brilliant scientist, but when she was out from behind her microscope, she was flighty and hyper, like the absentminded professor on espresso shots. She was often getting distracted mid-sentence and constantly losing things, like her reading glasses, which were usually on her head. She was sweet, but sometimes I wanted her and Dr. Rapava to take notes from each other. He could stand to relax, and she could get to the point quicker, especially at four in the morning.

As we walked down the hall to her office, a man called from behind. "It's the Daniels." Only one person seemed to take pleasure joking about my last name and his first. With a sigh, Daniel and I both swiveled to face him. Liam and Sera stood down the hall. They were another collector team. Liam seemed to have some kind of complex and thought of Daniel as a threat. Liam was constantly trying to one-up us or brag about their collection of the night. You know—those people who have to be the best and try to outdo everyone else? That was him, and Sera was even worse, instigating Liam's teasing. They had to let everyone know they were better and faster than the rest of us.

"Butch Cassidy and the Sundance Kid. How did your night go? We collected *two* fae tonight." Liam tried for a good-natured smile but fell short. He was African American and in his early thirties. Fit, trim, tall, and looked like he should play for the NBA. He spent five years in the military before he came here. He kept his hair close to his scalp and wore the tightest T-shirts known to man. He had an incredible body, and he did not shy away from showing it off.

Sera was in her mid-twenties and barely reached the middle of his chest. She said her ancestry was Siamese (now called Thai), but she was born in America and raised here in Seattle. She was petite with dark hair and almond-shaped eyes, pretty but cold and unfriendly. I knew if I were as small-boned as her, they would have teased me about it. But any negatives they found in other people were pluses for them. She could get in and out of tiny places and surprise fae when she took it down. My developed frame was a hindrance. The difference between Daniel's and my age was also a constant target for them as I was the youngest seer, and Daniel was one of the oldest hunters.

There were currently eight of us. There used to be more, but not all came back after the last group hunt. We were paired off: Daniel and me, Liam and Sera, Hugo and Marv, Peter and Matt. Each pair had one with the sight, a seer, and one with military training, a hunter. We were called the collectors.

Marv and Matt had the sight, but Sera and I were the dominant seers. Women and children tended to be stronger and more open to the sight, but Sera and I possessed above normal sensitivity. Because of this, we were usually the ones they called on to work.

"We got our job done, Liam." Daniel was not one to brag. Secretly Daniel wanted to punch Liam most of the time, but he never let it show and never gave in to their taunts.

On the other hand, I had trouble disguising my dislike for them. My fists clenched at my sides, begging to be introduced to their faces. Daniel's hand lightly touched my back, trying to ground me. It wasn't working. These two seemed to trigger my well-buried violent nature.

"Looks like it." Sera smirked as she nodded toward my swollen lip and ripped jeans. Her meaning was clear. She was evidently too good to get beat up by a fae, but I wasn't.

Daniel's hand pressed harder into my back as my body grew tight with anger. Liam's brown eyes glinted when he watched me tense up.

"Think the kid needs a timeout. Did she miss her nap today?" Liam smiled, his perfect teeth shining under the fluorescent lights.

My foot only took one step toward them when Daniel grabbed me around the waist, spinning me to face the opposite way. "We have to check in with Kate. We'll see you guys later."

Laughter broke out as Daniel forcibly guided me toward Kate's office.

"Why do you let them get to you?" Daniel spoke low as we turned the corner of the extensive underground headquarters. I'd yet to find the end, or maybe the beginning, of this building. It looked like how you would picture a secret government building: no windows, fluorescent-lined hallways, and offices with cheap linoleum flooring and stark white walls. The only areas where I forgot it was deep underground were either in the training room or the cafeteria. That was only because my mind was solely on kicking ass or getting mine handed to me or food.

"How do you not?" I growled.

He took a breath. "Zoey, you need to learn more control. You cannot go off and hit people, especially coworkers, because they upset you."

"Why not?" I snorted.

Daniel's head slanted to the side. "Because there are rules. They are not our enemy."

"Could've fooled me."

"We need to save our energy for the *real* threats."

His voice constricted in an odd twinge. I stared at him, but he kept his eyes forward.

"Well, I think it would do Sera some good to show her what 'the kid' can do." My lips curved up in a smile as I imagined kicking the shit out of her. She was excellently trained in karate and other forms of combat, but she didn't grow up on the streets. I could take her.

Daniel opened the door for me, his free hand still on my lower back, and ushered me into the office. His touch was the only thing leveling out my temper, but it accelerated my heartbeat.

"Daniel... Zoey!" Kate sat on the floor, books and notes spilling from the cupboard and fanning out on her lap and the linoleum. "I was looking for the notes on the specimen you caught back in November. He has similar qualities to the one you got tonight... or so I thought. Can't seem to find the paperwork."

Daniel breathed in. "You are looking at November from three years ago." He pointed to the binder label, displaying the month and year.

"Right." She waved her hand. "Silly me. Now where is last year?" Her head went into the cupboard, knocking more binders onto the floor. She hummed as she searched, seeming to forget we were in the room.

My shoulders drooped in frustration, my lids growing heavier. The struggle to keep them open and maintain my patience was getting harder. Daniel sensed my weariness and touched my arm in compassion.

"Kate? Dr. Rapava said to check in with you before we left," Daniel said, reminding her we were there.

"What?" A thud rammed the shelves. "Ow." She sat back, rubbing her head.

"Kate." Daniel's tone was firm.

"Oh, right..." She turned to us, her hand still on her head. "I only wanted to let you know we've been getting a lot of calls about fae being spotted around Belltown. The activity has tripled near there. Olympia also has had a rise in sightings. We feel something is happening. Have your phones close. You will be on call and need to be ready to go on a moment's notice until we figure out what is going on to stir up these goings-on."

We were pretty much always on call, but it had worked out I could continue school and take care of Lexie. Her latest test results had detected something in her blood. The entire next week was filled with doctors' appointments and tests, and I was the only one to get her there.

Daniel's fingers clutched my wrist comfortingly. He was the only one who knew what I went through on a daily basis. He caught my gaze, his expression telling me, *Don't worry. We'll work it out.*

Kate had already returned to searching her cabinet. We let ourselves out and traveled up to the surface. Luminosity loomed at the edge of the horizon, highlighting the east and flushing Mt. Rainier in a soft glow. It had been a long night. I already felt dirty and exhausted, and the day was only beginning.

Daniel pulled to the front of my house. Okay, house was an exaggeration. It was a mobile home with a chipped, feeble, white picket fence and a tiny AstroTurf lawn, things that made sure you knew this was the closest you were going to get to the "American dream."

My neighborhood was one step above being called a ghetto, and his car was like a parade float going down an empty street. The pristine BMW screamed to be carjacked, stripped, and sold for parts. It had taken a while to let Daniel see where I lived—part embarrassed and part wanting to keep my two lives separate. Having him enter my reality felt wrong. Nothing about him fit here. I'd been raised most of my life in rundown environments. His world was across town in a high-rise condo. My origins might be poor, but I wanted nothing more than to escape the chains keeping me here and soar to his world in the sky.

"I know later this week you have to take Lexie to her doctors' appointments." The car idled silently. "If we get a call, we'll make it work. She's your first priority." He looked at me. "Okay?"

It was a beat before I nodded. "Okay."

"Now, get your butt in the house and get some sleep." He smiled.

I opened the car door, sliding out of my seat. "Good... night?" The rise of the sun taunted this term.

"Good night, Zoey." The words were simple enough, but there was something behind his expression that gave me pause. I couldn't quite decipher it, but it caused my heart to pound. I shut the passenger door and went straight for the front door, giving him a last wave before he pulled away.

Entering the small two-bedroom, one-bath house, the familiar odors of stale cigarette smoke, flat beer, and coffee hit me. Jo usually went outside to smoke, depending on how drunk she was. The TV flickered in the dark living room. Jo was passed out in her recliner chair, where she normally slept. She worked the night shift as a fish deliverer. She would pick up the fresh fish, pack them in ice, and truck the load to different locations around town before the markets opened around 4 a.m. On her days off, she had trouble sleeping and usually drank and watched infomercials till she passed out.

My gaze rested on Jo. Her frizzy gray hair stuck out of her ponytail like it had been electrocuted. Her face was square shaped and creased with wrinkles. One look told you she had a hard life. Joanna Wilcox was not a warm fuzzy or that nice, but compared to some of the foster situations I'd been in, she was all right. She never laid a hand on me. She yelled a lot, but I could tune out her hurtful words. To make ends meet and probably in hopes someone would fetch her beer out of the refrigerator, she took in foster kids. Several had passed through the doors, but Lexie and I were the only ones who stayed. I had no doubt I would have been one of those kids who ran away thinking life would be better on my own, but Lexie ended any notion I held about leaving. Our bond was instant, and my internal need to take care of her kept me here—even after I turned eighteen.

Lexie was four and I was thirteen when Jo took Lexie in. I'd been with Jo less than six months. Lexie brought in extra cash because she was born with a disability that confined her to a wheelchair. Her mother had been a druggie and had Lexie out of wedlock. Lexie had been left at a gas station at the age of one, probably right after the mother learned there was a reason her daughter had yet to crawl.

At twelve, Lexie already had a tough life. I tried to

do whatever I could to make it easier for her. I became her mother, her sister, her best friend. I took her to school, made her lunch, and got her to medical appointments.

Walking to Jo, I picked up the blanket off the floor and covered her. She grumbled and shifted to face the other way. I actually felt like the mother to both. Trapped. Even though I was old enough to live on my own, I wouldn't leave Lexie, and I couldn't afford to take her with me yet. So I stayed. And because I brought in money, Jo let me.

With a sigh, I collected Jo's empty beer cans and the TV dinner off the floor next to her chair and walked to the kitchen, throwing them in the trash. The microwave clock read 5:23. *Ugh.* I only had an hour before I needed to wake Lexie for school. Since she turned a preteen, it felt like my mission was to get her up and out the door on time. Sleep was probably not in my cards. I flipped on the coffee maker and decided on a shower while I waited for the caffeine I desperately needed. Tiptoeing into the room Lexie and I shared, I crept to my dresser.

"You just getting home?" Lexie's sleepy voice drifted from her bed.

I whipped around. "Sorry. Did I wake you?"

Lexie shook her head as I treaded to her small twin bed and sat.

"What happened to your mouth?" She glanced at my face.

"Oh, boxing class." I waved my hand, disregarding my swollen cut lip. Cuts and bruises were easy to explain. People tended to use their hands or a weapon instead of words in this neighborhood. I never wanted Lexie to think violent behavior was right, so I said the wounds were from my self-defense classes. I didn't want her to think it was okay for anyone to hit her. If you got hurt when learning to defend and stand up for yourself, it was different.

"I was worried. Why were you out so late?" She sat up, rubbing her eyes. Then her hands dropped to her lap. "Oh... ohhh!"

My head moved back and forth. "No. It wasn't like that. Daniel and I had to work."

"Work... right." She smirked. No one knew exactly what I did. Keeping the fae secret was a big part of our job. The government wanted to keep the public ignorant of the threats surrounding them daily. They felt the mass hysteria caused by people knowing would stop the world in its tracks. Sometimes it was cool to think of myself as a secret agent, and other times it got exhausting keeping the lies straight. Jo and Lexie thought I worked as an organ transplant coordinator, matching and delivering fresh organs to patients in need. It made a good cover as to why I needed to go at a moment's notice at any time of the night and day. Lexie had met Daniel a couple times when he picked me up. Of course, she thought he was old, but loved teasing me about my crush on him. She assumed most of the time we went to an office and squabbled over who got which organ.

If only.

"Believe me, I wish it could be more." I ruffled the mass of coarse dark curls hanging past her shoulders. Lexie was half African American and half Puerto Rican. She was stunning with huge eyes, dark creamy skin, and the mop of wavy hair. Her face was like an angel. It wasn't till you glanced below her waist the illusion broke. Her legs were like grotesque, twisted tree branches. Lifeless and dead. Kids at her school had a hard time dealing with the contrast. She kept a blanket over her legs when she could, but her wheelchair could not be hidden. School was a harsh place, even when you didn't have obvious disabilities. Her guarded, tough nature also kept people away. Neither of us was any good at making or keeping friends. She had a few she hung with, but they weren't close. She never went to their houses, and she would never invite them here.

Being a foster kid, you learned to depend on yourself and not need anyone because most likely the person would disappoint or eventually leave. In my case, get rid of me. There were only two people I let in—Lexie and Daniel. She had been young enough to accept my love and help, but I was the only one. We were tough to the outside world. But in this room, we could let our guards down.

"I think you should go down on him at one of these all-night meetings. That would get his attention and definitely change his mind."

"Lexie!"

"What? You think I don't know about that stuff?" She shrugged. "Oh, right. You've gotten all prim and uppity now with your new fancy job and a classy man to try and impress."

"Uppity?"

Lexie leaned her back against the wall. "You used to say things like *sucking dick* and *coming*. Now you're too proper."

"Lexie, I'm not proper. I simply don't think you should be saying those things. Not at your age."

"You did."

"Yeah, but don't follow in my footsteps. Be better."

Her lids narrowed, studying me. "Someday I will escape this hellhole and won't look back."

"I hope so." I rubbed the blanket over her legs.

"And I'm not a kid anymore. I know more than you think I do."

"Tell me it's from overhearing, not doing."

"Okay," she responded coyly. I knew she was trying to aggravate me. Gossip in this area was rampant, and I had yet to hear of Lexie doing anything with any boy or girl.

I rubbed my temple. "At your school and in this neighborhood, topics like *going down* are more common than discussing the weather."

"And there is a stiff chance of a semen shower."

"Lexie..." I put my head in my hands.

She only giggled mischievously.

I was trying to keep her as innocent as I could, but you grew up fast in our situation. I was put into the foster care system as an infant and moved from home to home. Some were okay; most I never wanted to think about again. A few still gave me nightmares. All I was told about my parents was they were dead. By the time I got old enough to start asking questions, the system had lost my files. All I possessed was my name, Zoey Daniels. No middle name and no record of any kind. I went through the Internet, the phone book, and the obituaries. Do you know how many Daniels there are? All led to dead ends. Eventually I gave up.

"Did Jo feed you last night?" I turned back to Lexie.

She tilted her head, her expression saying, *What do you think?*

Rubbing my face with irritation, I suddenly felt years older than I was. Maybe this was why I was so drawn to Daniel. I was actually a forty-year-old in a twenty-two-year-old body.

"Don't worry about it." Lexie nudged me with her hand. "I rolled my ass down to McDonalds. Went through the drive-thru again. The manager didn't like it, but Raphael finds it hilarious. He always gives me extra fries."

Another groan came from me. "You know I hate when you do that. Not going through the drive-thru, but the going out in this neighborhood by yourself at night."

Lexie shrugged, a defiant grin on her lips. She was bold and said and did whatever was on her mind. But I'd seen some of the guys around here start to look at her differently. She was growing up, and they couldn't help but notice she was stunning. The wheelchair made her a perfect candidate to take advantage of. She was at the age where she would brush me off by saying, "I can take care of myself," and not fully grasping she couldn't. Not if they wanted to do something to her.

She was also unaware it wasn't only humans who could prey on her.

"I'll get the shower going. Might as well get up and get ready for school. We can work on the homework I know you didn't do last night." I pushed myself off her bed, my brow hitched.

She grinned. "You know me too well."

After I placed her in the shower on her specially built seat, I went back to the tiny kitchen. Coffee gurgled in the pot, the aroma masking all the nastier smells. Pouring a cup, I leaned against the counter. The sun shone faintly through the window, warming my back.

The sound of Joanna's snores rolled over to me, interrupting my moment of peace. I loved Lexie, but sometimes I wanted to run. Far away. And leave it all behind. There had to be more to my life than this. More to me.

My hand ran over the fogged mirror, wiping at the condensation. My image stared back at me. Dark circles spread under my large green eyes. My wet hair fell to the middle of my back. At a very young age, I started getting a lot of attention from the opposite sex. In my neighborhood, it was never the good kind. It annoyed me, but it made me tougher. The combination of my short but curvy frame, heart-shaped face, light green eyes, and long brown hair was like a neon sign: *Prey here. Make lewd comments, sounds, and grotesque hand gestures, please.* But I was far from a victim. My innocent features had been a curse and an attribute. When shit went down, and before the teachers and cops got to know me, they would doubt I was at fault. How could a sweet-looking girl rob an entire house? Or shoot a man in the leg? Or start a fight with a person three times her size? It had to be someone else. I got out of a lot of fights at school—until the teachers realized I was the cause, not the casualty.

The curse part was a given. Foster dads and men in

the neighborhood seemed to consider it my fault for looking the way I did. I was "asking for it" when my full chest and round butt developed. My fists had met with a lot of jaws in retaliation. It was why I stuck around for Lexie. She would be targeted because of her looks. The wheelchair only made it easier. I never wanted her to go through the things I experienced.

The image in the mirror came back into focus. Red liquid dripped down onto my lip. "Dammit." My fingers automatically went to my nose, keeping the blood at bay as I reached for a Kleenex. It was the fifth one this month. In the last couple years I got bloody noses frequently, but lately they were getting worse and were usually followed by a migraine. DMG doctors checked me out and said I was fine. Since Sera also suffered from them, I knew it was most likely a seer thing. Our eyes saw things differently and caused a lot of strain. Stress only aggravated it, which was something I possessed in abundance. Keeping my multiple lives straight and the lies accurate to the right people was a constant dance.

I went into my bedroom and sat on my bed, waiting for the bleeding to stop and the migraine to begin. The nosebleeds were manageable, but the migraines were harder to deal with. They ripped away my eyesight, blurring everything into glowing rings and squiggles. I popped open the subscription bottle the DMG doctors gave me for the headaches and swallowed a few. They were the only things that helped. Over-the-counter drugs no longer abated the nausea and pain. I descended against my pillow as a stab of pain shot through my brain and between my eyes. I wanted to close them and sleep for the rest of the day, but the final in my psychology class weighed on me. I hadn't started studying for it, and it counted for half our grade. I also had to set up a few of Lexie's clinic visits and pick her up from school later. But the throbbing ache sucked me under before I knew it, guarding me from the sharp pains that drank the energy out of my body.

When I woke, it was only an hour later. My damp hair dried in a tangled mess, and my towel was still wrapped around me. I got up and dressed, drying my hair before deciding it was going into a ponytail anyway.

My stomach growled, pointing my feet and attention toward the kitchen. Jo was still asleep in her recliner. The woman could sleep through a bombing. I reached in the cupboard and pulled out a cereal box and went to the refrigerator. No milk. Of course. With a rant, I slammed the door. With the cereal box in hand, I walked back to my room.

"You're not going to eat in your room, are you?" Jo's husky voice crackled. She had the voice of a thirty-year smoker, which she was, so it was well deserved.

"Yeah." I kept walking.

"You'll get bugs in there, and I'll have to pay to get someone out here to exterminate them."

I stopped and turned back. Was she kidding me? She left her food and empty beer cans all over the house. I cleaned up after her.

She twisted to look down the hallway at me. "Show some respect. I *let* you stay here. At any time I can kick you out."

I rolled my jaw. "Then who would pay for your beer?" I whirled, going to my room, slamming the door.

"You li'l ungrateful bitch. I have done nothing but sacrifice to feed and clothe you," she screamed at me through the door.

I scoffed. She hadn't done a thing. Before I turned eighteen, the system gave her money to feed me, most of which went to her beer and cigarette fund. I first got into robbing houses so I could get proper food and clothes. It later turned into a game. Something I did for the high and to be revered by others in my crowd.

I was used to her threats. They were a weekly occurrence. She wouldn't do anything. I brought in money and did everything for her, especially when it came to taking care of Lexie. She would be lost without me. She knew it, and I knew it, but we still played the game. One thing I could count on with Jo was she was all talk. In its way, it was comforting. If it stopped, I'd probably lose my footing. In my very turbulent and unstable life, it was the little things you counted on that you attached to for dear life.

My box of cereal next to me and my book on my lap, I tried to study. It wasn't long before Jo burst in the room demanding that if I were going to be a leech, the least I could do was get some groceries. At the top of her list were beer and cigarettes.

Shocker.

# THREE

At three o'clock, Lexie came rolling out of the front doors of her school, her expression a mix of relief, irritation, and hardness. When she spotted me, it became all annoyance. "I can get home by myself, you know? I'm not a baby."

"I know." Lately, some girls at school noticed she was becoming beautiful, and even with the wheelchair, she was gaining notice from boys. Before she hadn't been a threat, but suddenly she became one. The girls who didn't like the competition were trying to put her in her place. I started to retrieve her from school after one tipped her out of the wheelchair into the mud, then punched her.

Let's just say I was slightly livid.

She made me promise—several times—not to do anything. It was hard to keep, especially when I saw the group of bullies hassle her again after school. One look at me approaching stopped them. I was little, but the expression on my face must have shown I meant business.

Lexie hated when I came to get her, claiming it made her appear weak. I didn't give a shit. She was my sister, and I would protect her. I knew if I actually did anything, they would probably pick on her more. I was waiting for one of the girls to start something with me, thinking she could take me on. Oh, how I would love to show them how fast they would taste the dirt embedded in the concrete.

"Actually, you're my excuse. Jo is off today, and I wanted to get out of the house." I walked alongside, letting her push herself until we were far enough from other students before I took over.

"Whatever." She rolled her eyes.

It wasn't till you were out of your teens did you realize how annoying and vexing you'd been at that age. Actually, I'd been worse—stealing, fighting, drugs, alcohol. Lexie was full teenager, but she was a good kid.

My phone buzzed in my pocket. I smiled when I saw the caller ID.

"Ohhh! It's Daaannniieell," Lexie cooed.

"Shhh." I shot her a look before hitting the talk button. "Hey." My grin only widened.

"Hey." Daniel's voice caused my heart to pick up pace. "I know you needed to study and watch Lexie, but Kate called."

"Okay."

"Ohhh, Daniel. You're soooo hot. I loooovvveee you," Lexie yelled. With one hand, I covered the bottom of the cell and swiped at her with the other. My eyes big with a "shut up" look.

"It's an emergency, and all the groups are going out. I couldn't get you out of this."

"It's fine." I made contact with Lexie's head as she continued to carry on.

"Yes, Daniel. Anything for you, *Daniel*," Lexie teased.

Little sisters... you sure it was illegal to kill them?

"Shut. Up." I seethed at her as Daniel filled me in about the case.

"Have sex with my sister, please? She needs to loosen up."

I tried to smack her on the arm, but she wheeled out of my way, laughing hysterically.

"Lexie with you?" Daniel finally took notice of the commotion. My cheeks burned with the knowledge he probably heard every word.

"Yeah. Be lucky you don't have a little sister." I glared at Lexie. She continued to giggle.

"I actually wanted one," Daniel replied.

"You want mine?"

Daniel chuckled. "I'll pick you up at five, okay?"

"Okay. See you then." I hung up before Lexie could say anything else. "I am *so* gonna kill you."

She howled with laughter and took off down the hill. Her wheels carried her a lot faster than I could go. But I tried. I chased her all the way home. I would at least make her arms burn and ache as she pushed her chair to get away from me.

Staying mad at Lexie was impossible. She would bat her lashes at me and say something sweet, and I was under her spell again. She was good at wrapping me around her finger. I prepared her a snack and got her at least pretending to do homework.

On Jo's nights off, she usually went to a casino,

local bar, or stayed home. Unfortunately, tonight was the latter. She sat in front of the TV watching a game show, a beer in her hand. I didn't think Joanna would ever physically strike Lexie, but verbal abuse could be as harmful as hitting. I hated leaving Lexie alone with her, especially for the second night in a row. Normally, Jo would be heading to work by now for her night shift, but the company was trying to save money and cut a few of their employees' shifts. An idle, pissed-off Jo was not a pleasant person to be around. She took her life and money frustrations out on us.

This meant I wanted to leave with everything taken care of for Lexie: dinner, homework, and anything else Jo might find a nuisance.

"You goin' out again?" Jo grumbled from her recliner.

"Yeah. It's an emergency."

Jo snorted. Deep down she must have thought I was making up excuses to go party with my friends or something.

"I couldn't say no. We need the money."

Jo's head twisted, her lids narrowing on me. I was tapping at a weak spot, and I knew it. We were all aware I brought in a good chunk of the money, but we didn't talk about it. Jo's mouth opened to say something, but instead she took a swig of beer and turned back to the show.

Lexie sent me a *what are you thinking?* look.

I shrugged and rolled my eyes. Pulling out a frozen pizza for Lexie, I set the oven low, so it would be hot when she was ready to eat. "Don't forget to take this out."

Lexie followed me to the bedroom, watching me get ready. "I wish you didn't have to go."

"Me too." I tugged on a tank, black sweater, and dark blue jeans. I sat on my bed and pulled on my black boots.

"Where are you really going?"

Her words snapped my head up. "What do you mean? You know where I'm going. I have to work."

"Retrieving body parts. Right." Her mouth pinched together, and she nodded, staring at her lap. "If any of those people have extra legs to donate, send them my way."

I stood, walked to her, and squatted in front of her chair. Her tone and demeanor created a sour feeling in my stomach. "I don't like when you talk like this." I brushed her hair from her face. "What's wrong? You seemed fine a minute ago."

"Nothing."

"Lexie."

"It's only... I feel like I'm always being left behind in some way. I hate these things." Her fists hit her motionless legs. The mood swings had been happening more lately. The doctor said it had to do with her hormones and the medication she was on. She went from happy and carefree to violently depressed in a moment. Sadly, we all knew the truth. What the doctors found in her latest blood work was more bad news. Her condition was worsening. Eventually, she would be completely paralyzed. Maybe die.

"Hey." I tipped her face with my fingers. "Don't you dare hate anything about yourself. You are amazing, and I love every bit of you."

I was being a hypocrite; I detested her legs, too. I disliked anything that caused her so much pain and agony. They compelled her to feel different than everyone else. There were a lot of things she would never experience nor be able to do. No, I didn't hate her legs; I despised the woman who made her this way. Heroin had been worth more to her than her baby's health.

Her eyes glistened with tears. "Promise me someday I will walk."

Words caught in my throat.

"I don't want to live like this..."

"Lexie, you're scaring me."

A honk sounded from out front. Daniel.

She brushed a tear away and flipped her hand, waving me off. "I'm fine. Go."

I bit down on my lip and stood. "I'll be back as soon as I can. Okay?"

She nodded.

"Lexie, I promise you this—I will do everything in my power to find something to help you walk." I wished I could promise her more. I leaned over and kissed her forehead.

"You better get going. *Daniel's* waiting." She wiped her face and forced a smile. "I'll be sending out 'fuck me' vibes for you."

I took a deep breath, shaking my head. "Go do your homework."

I climbed into the government-issued van, scooting onto the nylon seats. Daniel pulled away from the curb, the vehicle coasting down the street. He nodded down at the cup holder. "Caramel latte."

"You are my hero." I reached for the coffee.

"Well, I figured with arriving home at dawn and getting Lexie to and from school, you didn't get very much sleep."

"That's an understatement. I got an hour."

"An hour?" Daniel's head jerked to stare at me before looking back at the road. He was dressed in his usual hunter attire—black pants and sweater. Knives and guns were strapped around his waist.

"I wasn't even planning on sleeping at all, but I got another headache."

Daniel's brow clenched in concern. "Another one?"

"Yeah. Used to them." I waved my hand, brushing off his worry.

"You are getting them a lot lately." He looked in the rearview mirror, his lips thinning into a set line. "I'm worried about you."

"What you should be worried about is me passing my psychology test tomorrow. Think I'm going to have an all-nighter studying for it."

A slow grin curved his mouth, crinkling his eyes in the corners.

"What?" I sipped my latte.

"Youth. I remember when I would get only an hour of sleep and still be ready to go again."

"Oh, come on. You're not so old." I rolled my eyes.

"In twenty years, come back and say it."

"You're forty, not eighty."

"Sometimes this job makes me feel eighty." He

winked. "But you keep me young." I felt a blush cover my cheeks. Daniel had been my mentor and trainer since the day I joined the DMG when I was nineteen. It was clear at the beginning: Daniel thought of me as no more than a kid or little sister. We'd had three years of being paired through the training, hunting, and collecting. We'd had meals together, confessed secrets in the late-night hours, and laughed and talked about everything. But it wasn't until the last couple months I felt the slightest change in his behavior toward me.

For more than two years I'd been in love with him. It wasn't long after the awareness of my feelings for him I foolishly conveyed them. He was kind and tactful in my letdown. He didn't let me quit or switch partners, telling me I would get over him and find a guy who was more suitable and my age. Neither of those things happened. I only fell more in love with him. Most days I could act like I didn't feel anything, but other days it was torture. I could see how good we'd be together. How amazing our future could be.

My world revolved around him and my sister. I'd constantly taken care of myself. I had to. But when Daniel came into my life, I didn't realize how much I needed someone. He took care of me and made sure I was all right. I had this fantasy he and I would take Lexie and get away from Seattle. Leave this whole world behind. Start a program to help disabled kids, especially in the foster system. Have kids of our own. Grow old. Maybe travel the world.

It was merely a dream... until lately. His glances remained on me a little longer, his touch lingered. Every moment, hope bloomed in my chest. I wanted nothing more than to feel his lips on mine, his experienced hands caressing my bare body. I had sex before, but it had never been with someone I loved. Because *he* was that person. He always would be.

"Hello, Zoey? Are you listening to me?"

"What?" I glanced at him. The late afternoon sun glittered off the silver streaking the sides of his temples. *Sexy.*

"I asked what you are doing for your birthday."

"It's not till next month."

"Technically, it's in twenty-four days." He shifted in his seat, keeping his attention on the motorway. The flickering of streetlights glimmered against the windshield in a rhythmic pulse. "Curious if you have plans with any of your friends or maybe a boyfriend taking you out."

"You know I don't have either." Feeling a moment of boldness, I stated, "Besides, *you* are taking me to dinner."

His eyebrows hitched up. "Oh, am I?"

"Yes." I forced back my fear, biting my lip. "Someplace I have a reason to wear a dress and heels. Where there is a beautiful view."

"Sounds romantic."

Twisting my neck, I peered at him through my lashes. "Exactly."

His head turned to look at me. He didn't say anything, but a smile hinted at his lips. I grinned in response, our eyes connecting. Charged tension occupied the space between us and lessened only slightly when his attention went back to the road, slowing the car as we reached our destination.

"Kate said her source hinted a group of fae had been

spotted throughout this area a couple of days ago and then earlier today." Daniel pulled the van into an empty parking spot along the street.

"Not an obvious change in conversation." I smiled into my cup. The sweet and acidic smells wafted into my nose.

He turned off the engine and sat back in his seat. "Zoey, what do you want me to say?"

"That you're taking me to dinner," I exclaimed, turning my body to him.

He leaned against the headrest and rolled his head to gaze at me. "Zoey, you are twenty-two, and I am forty. I'm too old for you. You need to date boys your own age."

"Exactly—boys. I don't want a boy. I want a man." I swallowed, my voice going low. "I want you."

He tipped his head back, closing his eyes. Pain flickered across his face before a heavy sigh bounded from his chest. "I have tried so hard to dissuade your feelings for me, hoping you would find someone more suitable." His lids lifted as he peered over at me. "But you're not, are you?"

"No." My determination was one thing I was sure of.

He was quiet for a long time. I pursed my lips, waiting for his response. He glanced out the side window. "Not sure I could handle seeing you with some young idiot, anyway."

My chest locked. No air moved in or out. "What?" I sputtered. He didn't respond. "What are you saying, Daniel?"

"I don't know."

"Yes, you do." My tone was unflinching.

He shifted in his seat. "If... *If* we cross this line, there is no going back."

"I don't want to," I uttered. "And there is no *if*."

"Even *if* we ruin what we have? I know how I function. I will not be able to stay partners with you if it doesn't work."

"You are worth it to me." I swallowed. "I'm willing to take the chance."

He chuckled. "It's because you're young and think everything lasts forever. Love will conquer all. My ex-wife will tell you differently."

"It will if it's with the right person." There was not a doubt in my mind. Daniel was the right person for me.

He turned to face me and reached out, his hand cupping my cheek. "You are a persistent one."

"I know what I want." Being a poor foster kid and knowing no stability till my teens, I'd learned things weren't given to you. You needed to go out and get them.

He stared at me for a long time before his gaze dipped to my lips. Air stuck in my chest with nervous, excited energy. Slowly, he moved in, leading my face to his. *Finally.* I had wanted this for so long.

His lips were only inches from mine.

Millimeters.

*BOOM.* A hollow bang shook the car.

Both of us jerked apart to see a man standing on the hood of the van. My eyes shifted, my sight perceiving what he really was. His complex aura and glowing eyes showed me he was no ordinary man. He was fae.

The man was so substantial it took me a moment to notice there was a girl beside him, holding his hand. She was tall; her hair was past her waist and a bright plum color. With every move she made, the color flickered and changed under the light. Her eyes were dark and sharp.

But he was the one who captured my attention. A large battle axe stuck up over his shoulder, harnessed across his back. The blade was so sharp it glinted under the streetlight. His dark blond hair looked long, but lines of tight braids were snug on either side of his head, causing the top to look like a Mohawk. His face was thick with stubble and hard cheeks and bones. He had a tattoo on one side of his neck, disappearing under his shirt. Scars lined both his eyebrows, causing me to wonder if they were on purpose. The man had to be at least six-three and two hundred pounds of solid muscle. He was harsh and terrifying—a modern Viking.

The man turned, his pale eyes stared through the window and locked with mine. Breath halted in my lungs. His irises were so light blue they looked white. The pinprick of the black pupils secured the middle of the stormy sea. His focus caused me to shiver, and I closed my eyes under his intense gaze. When I opened them, the couple was gone.

# FOUR

"What the hell?" My lids blinked to clear my version. Emptiness filled the space the man and woman had taken up a moment earlier.

Daniel leaped out of the car and spun in every direction, his trained eyes searching for the vanished threat. His hand grasped his dart gun, his fingers twitching to respond. I jumped from the van, mimicking Daniel on the other side.

"You saw them, right?" Daniel touched the dent on the hood. "Where the hell did they go? I've never seen fae disappear like they did."

I saw the Viking man briefly, but it was enough to imprint deeply in my mind. The outline he left was still in my sight, the fae magic thick and overpowering in him. With my familiarity of fae and different levels of magic each one held, I had never experienced anything close to him. It almost hurt to look. Not in the way it hurt to peer at the sun, but that he almost couldn't be held within my vision. It was a strange pressure. Visually, I had seen scarier creatures, but something about this man terrified me. He was not one you wanted to mess with.

The girl held magic, too, but compared to him, hers appeared dim. It was her beauty that sucked the air from you. She had worn skintight black pants and a long black sweater, which hung slightly off her shoulder. Her over-the-knee black boots only added to her sleek model frame. Even though she looked toned, she was tiny-boned, giving the appearance of being fragile. She seemed a little taller than me, but I had a lot more substance to my build. I was in shape and healthy from training, where a gust of wind might have knocked her over. She looked like she could be from someplace in the eastern block of Europe. She was exotic and beautiful, and I felt very ordinary in comparison.

An unsettling feeling wormed its way into my gut, and I reached into the car and grabbed my phone out of my bag, stuffing it into my pocket. We always kept them on us in case of emergencies or if we got separated. My feet led me away from the van, an impression telling me to head down an unlit alley.

"You sense something?" Daniel called. Sometimes I felt like a trained bloodhound. *"You got their scent, girl?"* I was waiting for him to pat me on the head.

With my dart gun ready, I nodded and followed my seer intuition. We reached opposite walls before peering down the gloomy lane. Clouds were rolling in, covering the light from the moon. Extra energy crackled in the air, hinting at rain and a possible thunderstorm. A dim light above the back door of a closed store at the end of the lane gave a little depth to the passage. It was empty, but something told me to venture in. Without question, Daniel trusted my instincts and followed. We crept slowly down the way.

The hair on the back of my neck prickled in warning the farther we advanced. We were more than halfway along the alley when my skin tingled, the feeling of magic enveloping me. I had denied my sight for so long. But now that I had let it out, it was like floodgates. It would never go back in.

I stopped.

"What?" Daniel whispered.

I bit on my lip and shook my head as I searched for the source of all the magic. My focus shifted to the wall we had been following. Something was off. My vision zeroed in on it, and slowly the wall broke away, evaporating into air. There was another small alleyway leading at a right angle from this one.

"Glamour." My hand reached for the wall, going through it.

Daniel's eyes widened. He blinked several times and shut his lids to rub them.

"Extremely powerful." Glamour was magic fae used to influence a person's mind. Other humans would not question the dead-end alley. Their mind would trick them into trusting what they saw. But if you had the sight, you could see through it. Once you stopped believing it was there, it broke the spell. One word from me put doubt in Daniel's mind, and now the illusion was broken for him, too.

"That will always disturb me." He stepped into the space where the wall used to be. It was disturbing to be so certain of something, then find you were wrong, and your senses were misleading you.

We moved together down the narrow passage. Everything in me was on high alert. The energy in the air and our surroundings unsettled me. It twisted in my gut; the feeling was not right. I was about to suggest we abort the mission and go for coffee and a slice of cake at the diner near the Space Needle when I heard voices—a lot of them.

Daniel touched my arm, taking a step in front of me. His protective civility kicked in when going into unknown territory—part special-ops training and part him. As the voices grew closer, their tone sounded angry and low. Slowly, outlines appeared.

Fae had better sight and hearing than humans, so it was difficult to sneak up on them. With so many of them in one spot, we could have been in trouble. Daniel pushed us behind a dumpster and crouched low.

"This doesn't feel right," I whispered into his ear.

He nodded but put up a finger—our sign for *I want to check it out*. I nodded but swallowed back the fear in my throat. I slipped my hand in my pocket, my fingers grazing my phone. It helped my nerves.

Daniel tapped at his ear and did a V-sign to his eyes. Listen and watch. We peeked around the bin. I instantly recognized the two fae from earlier. The scary Viking and the model stood opposite a smaller but toned red-headed man. Actually, anyone seemed small next to the Viking. The redhead had a matching beard covering his features. He appeared to be the leader. He had a dozen men, splitting their count on either side of him. As with most fae, they were all beautiful. They were unique and different from humans but not enough you could pinpoint.

"Give it to us, Ryker. You have done your job. Now hand over what the boss paid for," the man with the red hair said, his Irish accent so heavy I almost needed a translator.

The Viking's name was Ryker. Of course it was.

"Why won't he meet me in person?" Ryker shot back.

"You know he doesn't do business like that," Red said, patience thin in his voice. "Stop playing games and give us what is rightfully ours."

"Rightfully yours?" Ryker exclaimed. "I'm not stupid. I know what it is. It is something no one owns."

"Your intelligence is certainly in question if you think you can renege on our deal."

"Listen to yourself, Garrett," Ryker scoffed. "You are his trained lapdog, not his partner."

Garrett clasped his hands. "My patience is thinning, Ryker. Give us the stone."

*Stone? Like a jewel?*

Ryker's shoulders shifted back; fists clenched. In one movement, in a blink of an eye, everything shifted. Ryker shoved the woman back, drawing his broad axe from his back. At the same time Garrett screamed, "Cadoc, grab her!"

The brown-haired man farthest from Garrett and closest to the girl leaped out, a sword already drawn. The rest of the men jumped for Ryker.

The Viking swung, his huge arms flexing as he tried to control the blade's angle. It veered toward the group of men coming for him. All managed to escape the fierce blade heading their way. With a roar Ryker swung again, connecting with one of the men. Blood sprayed. A hoarse scream curdled the night, and a body fell to the ground.

"Stop!" Garrett yelled. "You have already lost, Ryker." Garrett snapped his fingers, and the man named Cadoc moved from behind Ryker. Another form came with him as he held a knife to the girl's throat. Cadoc drew the two of them out of Ryker's reach. "Are you willing to sacrifice Amara's life for your stubbornness?"

Ryker froze, except for his arm. His axe went to his side. "Garrett, she has nothing to do with this."

A slow smile etched up Red's features. Then he looked at the wounded guy on the ground. "Get him up." Two of his men helped the groaning man. When they lifted him, half of his arm stayed where it was. My stomach constricted at seeing the detached body part. They dragged him back, surrounding him as they turned and faced the Viking.

"What's it going to be?" Garrett widened his arms in question.

Ryker shifted, looking at Garrett, then at Amara.

"Ryker, don't," she cried.

The Mohawked man's gaze was glued on the girl. "Amara." He stepped toward her. Her purple hair tangled around her arms as she reached for him. Cadoc tipped the edge of his knife deeper into her neck. Blood trickled off the blade. She grunted, forcing Ryker to stop in his tracks.

"This knife is goblin welded. If you want her to live, Ryker, you'll give us what we want." Cadoc gripped her tighter to him. "The stone is ours." He grinned and sniffed Amara's hair. "Right, sweetheart?"

Hatred narrowed her eyes, but she kept silent.

A rumble rolled over the increasing clouds. Lightning tore across the sky. A boom sounded where the light contacted with the earth. I couldn't see where it hit, but it was close enough to rattle the ground.

*What the hell?*

"We got to get out of here," Daniel whispered in my ear, his gaze studying the sky.

I agreed wholeheartedly. This entire mission felt wrong from the start. Daniel's warm body stepped away from mine. The current stirring between our two forms when we were pressed together did not diminish when he moved away. The hair on my arms sang with the electricity in the air. Magic was growing denser.

Daniel touched his halter and held up two fingers, flipping them. *Switch*. I shoved my dart gun back in my belt and drew my fae gun.

"Leaving so soon?" a voice spoke above us, causing me to jump. "Look what we have here. Human spies." One of Garrett's men stood on top of the dumpster we were hiding behind, peering down at us. He had shoulder-length wavy blond hair and soft brown eyes filled with mischief. But not the fun kind. He was tall and lean and like most fae, very good looking. "You can't go. The party just got started."

Daniel whipped around and withdrew his real gun in one fluid movement.

The light-haired fae laughed. "That is so adorable."

Irritation spurred in my chest. Daniel and I had captured hundreds of fae during the last couple of years. This one was acting like we were no threat at all. My gun was out and pointed at the man. "Back off."

The man held up his hands and jumped down from

the bin, landing silently. A smirk danced on his face. Daniel shifted around the guy, pressing the barrel to his back.

"We don't want trouble. I only want to get her out of here. Safe," Daniel said.

"No trouble?" The fae scoffed, his arms still up. But it didn't feel like he meant his surrender. "I know what you are. You create trouble."

"Maxen, we don't have time for you to play with them." Garrett sighed.

Maxen winked at me, then with speed hard to track he twisted and snatched the gun from Daniel. With one hand he claimed his prize and with the other he punched Daniel. Hard. Daniel stumbled back but did not fall. His training had him jumping forward to fight the fae. We had gotten into plenty of fights with fae. We always won.

I kicked, connecting with Maxen's stomach. He folded over as Daniel's elbow crunched down on his back, hitting his kidney. Daniel's gun fell from Maxen's hand, clattering to the ground. Daniel swiped it up, smashing it into the back of the fae's head. The man fell, unconscious. Daniel was impressive in a fight. He was clean, controlled, and swift. Daniel pointed his gun at the rest of the fae and moved us back toward exit.

"I'm impressed. That never happens." Garrett clapped his hands slowly. His form now fully faced our way. We had captured his complete attention.

The sky flashed again, and lightning zigzagged across the dark, furious sky. Lightning storms were nothing new to Seattle, but everything about this one tickled at my seer senses. Its energy prickled the back of my neck, triggering my intuition.

"Not here for your amusement." Daniel's voice broke through my fixed scrutiny of the storm. "Let's all leave here unharmed." My neck craned to look at him. He was motioning with his head for me to move toward the exit.

Garrett laughed and took a step toward us. My mind tried to evaluate the scene and figure out how we could escape. Running seemed to be our only option. It was a feeble plan, as we would have to run like hell and hope they stayed behind with Ryker and his girlfriend.

My hand quaked only slightly as I held my handgun on Garrett. "Don't get any closer." Sometimes I sounded like a cop drama. "The bullets are fae-made. I will shoot to kill."

His eyebrow curved up. "The human has come to play, huh?" His accent again was so thick it was like walking through mud trying to make out what he was saying.

Daniel pushed his gun forward, the muzzle never wavering. "If you move one more step, I will show you how much we like to play."

The Irishman's smile curled the side of his mouth. "I love when your kind thinks they are on the same level as us." He winked at me.

It was my fault. I should have noticed Garrett was trying to distract me. If I had been doing my job, watching Daniel's back, I would have seen Maxen was not actually unconscious.

The body lying on the ground lurched up, his outline hazy with speed, and moved behind Daniel. It was a split second, but it felt more like years passed, because my brain suddenly understood what was happening.

"Daniel!" I took a step toward him. "Noooooo..."

The man's hands snatched Daniel's neck and twisted. The sound of a spine snapping echoed in my ears, each vertebra popping like bubble wrap. Daniel's eyes widened with realization before his life fled from him. His body fell in a heap.

A blood-curling scream rang in the air—the sound of my heart being sliced in half. As if the storm felt my pain, a bolt of lightning hit the building next to us. The roof ignited with fire. Heat swept down on our group, but none of them seemed to notice.

My body was paralyzed; my eyes locked on Daniel. My mentor, the man I loved, my partner. Dead.

Chaos broke out around me in an indistinct blur. Yelling and movement circled me, but nothing mattered. I found myself on my knees beside Daniel, screaming at him to wake up. Irrationality took over. He'd be mad at me for letting my guard down. For not taking my chance and running. I was going to die. These men would kill me. But without him, I no longer cared. He had been my whole world.

*Lexie. You have Lexie.* I could hear him respond. The dream of him and me taking Lexie away and starting our family far away from this life had been the reason I kept getting up in the morning. Now the dream was gone.

A body landed next to me as the Viking tried to get to his girlfriend. "Ryker, get out of here," the girl repeated over and over. His answer was to growl and dive deeper into the throng of men. There were more of them than him. He was fighting a losing battle. The dozen men finally halted him with guns and knives pointed at his head and chest.

"Ryker, give us what we want, and you can go." Garrett strode to him, ignoring me. I was clearly little threat to Garrett, but I also knew he would not let me walk away from here. My gaze darted around the alley. My only escape was behind me, and I was sure I wouldn't get far. "You have my word."

"Your word is what I wipe my ass with each morning, Garrett." Ryker's lip hitched up in a snarl.

Garrett's eyes glinted in amusement. "You don't trust me? I am so hurt." He took a methodical step closer to Ryker. "Where is the stone?"

Ryker's expression gave nothing away. He kept staring back like Garrett was a brick wall.

The reality of Daniel's death and my situation was sinking in. My fingers shook as I touched his face, lowering his lids. "I love you," I whispered. I never told him in words. I knew he knew, but the regret of never actually telling him sat heavy on my heart.

As the fae continued to argue, I assessed my escape options. I had been trained for situations like this, but if Garrett wanted me, I had no chance. If I must join Daniel, I would go down fighting. I gripped the butt of my gun tighter. I was a collector, not a killer, but if I had to shoot every person in this alley to get Daniel's body out. I would do it.

My legs straightened to bring me to full height. I drew and aimed at Garrett's heart, using the huge Viking as a shield, my finger ready to pull the trigger.

The special bullets were designed to kill fae. Eventually. Going straight into their blood stream, ultimately poisoning them.

Lightning continued to flare across the sky. Sirens blazed over the wind, the air crackling with energy. The top of the Space Needle peeked over the roofs of the alley we were in. The air was suffocating with a force and power I'd never felt. As I looked up, a rod burning with flames of blue and green ripped across the sky, slamming into the iconic monument.

A roar deafened me as the electricity hit the metal and reflected off the tower, directly for us. The bolt fixated on Ryker, slamming into the middle of his chest and throwing him back. It burrowed through him, exiting his back, and found its new target. Me.

My body was thrown in the air. Screams of agony wiggled in my throat, but never made it out. Pain so unreal shredded every nerve, every fiber of my being. White blinding light took over my eyesight. Something slammed into me and flung me to the ground. The sensation felt far off. Everything did.

I could not see or feel, but my hearing recovered enough to catch the shrill sound of metal tearing, bending, and twisting against itself. The whining torment of the structure went silent for a brief second before screams and frantic footsteps vibrated my eardrums.

"The Needle is coming down!"

"Run."

These were the only things I could hear before my body felt the ground move underneath. In the distance, I could make out a hazy outline of Seattle's Space

Needle crashing in large chunks, heading for the earth below.

There were no words to explain the sound or the violence as the world shook and Seattle's icon made contact with the ground. The only thing I knew with certainty was I was going to die here.

I closed my eyes and waited for the end.

# FIVE

A faraway flap of consciousness tickled at my brain. Gradually it sharpened as pain rippled through my sleep, searing and throbbing. Every muscle burned and ached. My stomach felt as if I had been shot with a machine gun, like rounds and rounds had been torn into my lining, leaving my guts on the ground next to me. My entire body was locked with trauma, unable to move.

My lids slowly blinked, taking several times to commit to staying open. It was pitch black. I could not see anything except for a vague outline.

*Shit!* I was blind.

Then I noticed warm breath fluttering over my cheek. My brain started to understand the object obscuring my vision was a body. I squinted at the form on me. I was not blind or paralyzed but had a six-three solid man with a Mohawk on top of me. I tried to shift, but he didn't budge, still out cold. His torso curled protectively over mine. Wreckage laid in heavy clumps around us and on his back. I was sure he had crashed into me facing the other way. When had he turned around? Sheltering my body with his?

"Hey. Wake up." My voice came out weak and cracked. I choked and coughed on the dirty debris thick in the air. With all my might, I rolled him off me. He groaned when his back met with a pile of rubble. Air ballooned in my lungs as I took greedy gulps, but I cringed instantly, pain erupting through my chest and stomach. I lay locked in agony, staring at the brightly lit sky. Red and orange reflected off the clouds, declaring fire was burning hot in the city.

The man, Ryker, stirred beside me. His lids fluttered open, and he stared silently above. His expression was severe, etched with an underlying fury. We lay next to each other in silence, edging back into reality. Distant sirens, cries for help, and the steady roar of flames consuming its prey reached us.

Ryker sat up, an animal-like cry launching from his throat. He clutched at his chest, feeling around frantically. Rising hysteria showed in his movements, and he vaulted to his feet. Blood dripped from his back where pieces of metal, rock, and cement had landed. The axe hanging across his back protected him a little, but from his head to his ankles he was cut and bloody. Given the circumstances he could have been worse. And fae healed quickly.

"No," his deep voice muttered. His unsettling white eyes moved around with desperation, which sent a lump of ice to form in my lungs. He had been terrifying before, and now he was even more so. He looked like a cornered animal, ready to strike.

I sat up. Fear wrapped my gut, prompting me to find a way to escape. My instincts channeled all thoughts to nothing else than getting away from him.

"What happened? Where did they go?" The Viking's

actions were more and more agitated.

Night consumed the demolished passage and rendered it nearly impossible to grasp a way out. Clouds of dirt billowed in the air, settling on us. I squinted and searched for an exit. Climbing to my feet, I noticed the entire alleyway was filled with at least two feet of wreckage, except for where we had been. It was as if a force field encased us, defending us from most of the falling fragments. Another thing I noticed was we were alone in the alley. All the other fae either ran or were buried.

My heart stopped beating.

"Daniel!" I screamed, forgetting about everything else, including my self-preservation. I tripped and fell on my knees as I climbed over the piles of rubble, trying to get to the spot where Daniel's body had fallen. I felt no pain as my fingers dug into the rubble, the skin tearing from the tips of my fingers.

"Daniel." A choked sob clogged my throat. Fragments rolled down the mound. Like a dog searching for bone, I dug at the pile. I knew he was dead, but it didn't stop me. The desperate desire to see him, to touch him, to not leave him buried under the debris by himself pushed me through my pain. My eyes blurred with smoke and tears. Even against all logic, I still held hope I was wrong, and if I reached him, he would be alive.

Hope could be an unforgivable bitch.

I pulled a block away and gasped. A hand. His hand. My bloody fingers stretched to touch his cold, dead ones. My heart seized in my chest and a lump crawled into my throat.

Then I was off the ground and being pulled back. One muscular arm clamped around my waist, the other slithered up to my throat, locking at the base of my jaw. "How did this happen? How do you have them?" Ryker growled into my ear. My shock kept me mute. He shook me, compressing down harder on my vocals. "Tell me, human!"

"I-I... don't... know... what... you're... talking... about." It burned as I forced out each word.

He dropped me, and I landed hard on my kneecaps. I scrambled up and faced him.

His pale eyes drove angrily into me, his nostrils flaring, his muscles twitching and flexing with wrath. "I am no fool. Now give them back before I crush your windpipe into dust and stuff your body in with your boyfriend's."

There was not one ounce of falseness in his voice. He would kill me without a thought. Actually, he'd probably enjoy it. My hand inched up to my stomach. My pistol was long gone in a grave of rubble, but my dart gun was still hooked to my waist. I swallowed. "I don't have anything of yours."

His arm jetted straight, his hand going for my throat. With my reflexes ready for his attack, I yanked the dart gun and aimed at his neck. And shot. The dart burrowed under his jaw. He didn't even flinch, but his arm stopped its progression to me. He blinked once, and I saw ire growing in his eyes. His rage seemed so palpable my skin could almost feel it coming off him.

It was now or never.

He lunged for me. I scrambled back, managing to keep my feet underneath me. I turned and ran. The feel of his hand through my hair sent my muscles into full throttle. Like water through fingers, I slipped from his grasp. Adrenaline pushed me over the uneven mounds, my gaze locked on my goal: the ladder on the side of the wall leading to the roof. It was my only way out of here.

The sound of tumbling debris came from behind me. The Viking roared a frustrated, crazed cry. My head swiveled over my shoulder to see him collapse in a heap. He struggled to get back up, but the drug was rendering his limbs useless. His lids lowered halfway, but he kept his eyes on me. Revenge echoed deep in them. If he ever found me—I looked away, continuing with my escape. I could not think about it right now. I pulled myself up the rungs of the ladder and onto the roof. I gave one last look at the one who wanted me dead and to the man who was. I clenched my teeth together, turned, and ran for my life.

# SIX

From the rooftop, I could see the destruction of the city was greater than I imagined. My brain could not take in what stretched in front of me. Half the Space Needle was gone. The iconic structure lay in heaps all the way through downtown, cremating whatever was in its wake. Jagged ends of metal from the bottom half of the structure stuck up at different levels like a mountain range, as if someone came along and broke it off like a toffee bar, crumbling it in their hands and spreading bits around the base.

Fires dotted the city landscape like cluster of stars, igniting the sky and billowing into clouds of smoke. Seattle was gone. Most of the new apartment buildings which had sprung up daily in lower Queen Anne and Belltown were no more than kindling.

I searched for the landmark that should be near my house. All I saw was smoke mushrooming up into the atmosphere, creating a wall.

I grabbed for my phone. The screen was cracked, but it lit when I pushed the button. It was the only thing I had. Everything else was in my bag in the car, the car which was now under an office building. There was probably no cell service, but I desperately needed to know if Lexie was all right. I was about to punch in her number when a blast sprouted from the area I was watching. My gut twisted and my feet took me off the roof into the street, fear pumping my legs.

*Lexie!*

She was my only thought as I ran for the house. Seattle was on fire, buildings and bodies were scattered as far as I could see. It looked like someone had bombed us—ground zero in a war. My stomach heaved as I ran around bodies lying in the streets, chunks of building crushing the fragile bones to dust. Broken lines shot water into the sky, raining down on us. Flames lapped the buildings, consuming them with ferocity.

My determination to get to my sister was the only thing keeping my legs moving. The wails of people and sirens looped in my brain, settling in as white noise. *Lexie.* I had to make sure she was all right.

My leg muscles strained, but I pushed harder, curving down the road that took me home. A whimper splintered from my lips. The street was ablaze with rows of houses of neighbors I had known for years. Homes burned—from residences of drug dealers to a granny who struggled to live on her retirement. Even when I saw our house at the end of the court, I didn't stop. My mind wouldn't accept what was in front of me. Jo's beat-up Camaro was parked in the driveway where flames soared high in the sky. *Crackle. Pop.* My house was the tinder for the larger campfire. A few neighbors stood outside, watching their homes glow.

My gaze searched the people. "Lexie?" I screamed, wedging through the people. "Jo?"

No one answered.

"Lexie!" I wailed.

"Zoey." A hand came down on my arm. "We tried to get to them." My next-door neighbor, George, spoke softly. His eyes were full of sorrow and apologies. "I am so sorry."

"No." I shook my head, turning back to the burning remains of our house.

"I could see Jo passed out in her chair, but I couldn't get to her. The flames were already too high. I called to her, but she wouldn't wake up." George choked, shaking the memories from his mind. He had worked fifteen years for a road repair company. When he had gotten hurt, they found a way to "let him go" so they wouldn't have to pay for workers' comp. His knee and back would never let him work a physical job again. His wife barely made enough to get them by. He hobbled closer to me. "I'm very sorry, Zoey."

"Lexie?"

He shook his head, his neck bobbing lower in grief. He didn't need to say anything. I understood.

A strangled cry tore from my throat. I ripped my arm away from his and moved closer to the house. The heat of the fire singed my face. An outline of a wheelchair could be seen through the flames in the kitchen.

I cried as I sank to my knees. I was supposed to protect her. Keep her safe. I failed. Tears, which had yet to surface for Daniel, broke through. Everything I had fought for. Everyone I had loved. Gone.

I curled my legs, my wails growing fiercer—a possessed madwoman in the streets. Sadly, I knew I was seeing only a hint of the destruction this electrical storm caused. I wasn't the only one to lose everything.

I sobbed, and my body shook with grief. My sister had needed me. The thought of her screaming my name, trying to get her wheelchair out of the house in time, and other horrific images filled my head. And the person I needed most, the arms I craved to hold me, would never be again. After Daniel, she was the only reason I would have carried on. Now there was nothing.

*Daniel.*

*Lexie.*

I should have let the fae kill me when I had the chance.

I didn't know how long I sat, but when the flames scorched my skin, hands wrapped underneath my arms, pulling me up and away from the encroaching fire.

"You want to get burned as well?" A deep voice spoke into my ear. "Do it after I get my abilities back."

My stomach dropped. I whirled to face the looming figure. The refection of the flames flickered off Ryker's harsh features. Dread dropped over me. "Get away from me." I took a step back from the creature, wiping harshly at the dried tears lining my face. "Leave me alone. I don't have anything of yours."

"Whether you want to admit it or not, you know you do. You somehow took them," he sneered. His heavy boots hit the road as he stepped closer to me. My neck had to tilt my head to look at him. Man, he was big. "Believe me. I would love to leave you alone." He paused, his face moving closer to mine. "Actually, I would like to kill you... revenge for all the fae you captured and murdered. Or for shooting me earlier."

"I haven't killed anyone."

"Stop lying to me. I know damn well what you are and what you do."

Air blew out my nose as I forced my head to stay up. *Lie?* Our organization did not murder fae. We might collect them to test, and some may die in the process, but far fewer than how many humans they killed. I had seen firsthand a fae murder one of us. Not counting Daniel. It was our last group hunt, the fae ripped out a collector's throat in front of me before going for his partner. They didn't care for human life; they thought of us as insects. Beneath them.

"I've heard of your group. You are a bunch of sick fucks, but unfortunately I can't kill you... yet." His white blue eyes looked me up and down with disgust. "When I get my powers back, human, that will change."

I swallowed back the lump of fear clogging my throat. *Think this out, Zoey. He thinks you have something of his. You live as long as he believes you have what he wants.* "Not a very good incentive. If I give you back this *object*, I die."

His intense eyes wandered over my face. "You have no idea what you are holding, do you?" This realization seemed to surprise him. "You think it's something you can simply hand over to me?"

"I don't care what it is," I screamed. "And I love how you call me a sick fuck and a killer when you are the ones who slaughter us. You murdered Daniel."

"I didn't touch your boyfriend."

"Your kind did."

"Oh, I see. We are all alike, huh?"

"Aren't we to you?" My voice stabbed into him. He blinked, not responding. *Exactly.* I had tripped him up in his own game. Any patience I struggled to find was gone. I had enough of this guy. My heart had curled in on itself and was slowly dying, and it felt like he was poking a stick into the dying carcass. "I don't have this stone or whatever you were talking about, so go away."

"You think it's the stone I'm aft—"

I cut him off. "Look around. The world has fallen around our ankles."

"It's not my world," he mumbled, but I ignored him.

"I just lost my partner, my sister, and the woman who has raised me since I was thirteen." I shoved at his chest with no result. "Stay away from me." Before he could grab for me, I swung and tore off at a run.

There was only one place I could go. Only one place I was safe. The business building we used to enter the DMG was probably gone, but the structure below the earth was built to withstand attacks of all kinds, from humans or from "aliens."

Two alternative routes led into the headquarters. The closest one was more than two miles from here and ran alongside the underground sewer system. It was my best chance.

My feet slapped against the pavement as I sprinted away from the only house I ever considered home. Not because of the bricks and mortar or even Joanna. Lexie had made it a home.

My home was burning into embers and ash.

Along with my heart.

Adrenaline only rallied my system briefly before sorrow took over, almost crippling my muscles. My beautiful, brash-mouthed little sister, whom I adored more than life, was dead. Wasn't it enough she was born crippled and unloved by her mother, but to die so brutally at the age of twelve?

Stumbling to a stop, I leaned over, throwing up in the street. Daniel and Lexie were both taken from me in a blink of an eye. All my dreams vanished with them. Bile came up again, emptying my stomach. It was so hard not to curl up in the middle of the road, but the idea of the enormous fae finding me kept me moving.

People were in the streets, crying and screaming for help. The devastation was so great the fire departments, police, and ambulances couldn't help with all the damage. From what I had seen, most roads near the center had been destroyed. And even if a fire station or hospital survived, there wasn't enough electricity to get to all the places needing aid. The strange storm had blown out all power, creating an eerie isolation in the outskirts of town. The closer I got to the city, the more the sky glowed but not with city lights. Fire raged, keeping the downtown area bright.

I reached the tunnel with no Viking attack and heaved a sigh of relief when I got to the entrance of DMG. Electricity was still working here. The DMG worked off the grid, on its own power supply, and never had to worry about outages affecting them from above. I punched in my code, and the doors slid open, allowing me entrance.

Visually, every inch of HQ seemed unchanged. But to me nothing was the same. My shoes shuffled down the hallway leading to Dr. Rapava's office.

"Zoey!" Kate's voice came down the hall, her head poking from the conference room. "Oh my god. I am so happy to see you. You look awful. Are you all right?" She didn't give me a chance to respond. "I'm so glad you are safe. We were worried about you." Kate gave me a quick hug before shepherding me through the door. "Come, we're all in here."

*No*, I thought. *We're not all in here.*

I stepped into the conference room filled with collectors and scientists. Every head swung in my direction. Dr. Rapava's eyes widened as if I were an illusion.

Bloody, dirty, my hair and clothes singed, cuts and bruises all over—I must have looked a sight.

"Ms. Daniels, you are alive." He seemed very surprised I was standing in front of him. "But your monitor..." He stopped, then mumbled to himself.

Kate put her arm around me. "What he means to say is we were very worried about you. We thought something happened to you. Both you and Daniel..." She glanced behind me, suddenly realizing I was alone. "Where is he?"

Pain grabbed my lungs and squeezed them with force. Only a cracked gasp made it out. Being alone, I did what I needed to do to get here. Now I was safe. I felt my walls, which had kept me functioning, come down. My body bowed forward as a guttural wheeze broke through.

"Oh no," Kate whispered before pulling me back into her arms. My pain went past tears. I grappled for air, and my heart ripped into pieces.

Not counting an hour ago, the last time I cried in front of people was when I was ten. A girl had punched me to get the bike I was riding. It was a hand-me-down, but it had rainbow tassels hanging off the bars, and it was mine. I loved it. It came from one of the nicer foster mothers. When the older girl took the bike, I cried because I didn't want to lose the precious item. Then I cried because I was afraid the foster mother would get mad at me for losing it and send me away. My tears turned to anger. I tore after the girl and pushed her off the bike. I punched, kicked, and bit until someone pulled me off. The girl was taken to the emergency room. The ironic thing was the foster mother did get rid of me... because she feared my temper and violent outburst. I had only been with for her a month before being carted off to another house. The very thing I was afraid of happened. I learned people didn't really want me to be myself, and I learned to adapt and play whatever role I needed to survive. Still, there were times when the violent nature, the dark side of me, would boil to the surface. It was a side I even tried to hide from Daniel.

Not a tear fell now, but a surging, choking sound heaved deep from my gut and up my throat. I planted my hands on the cool tiles, keeping myself from toppling over. I didn't remember when I actually collapsed to the floor, but I found myself curled over my knees. Kate sat next to me, her arms wrapped around my shoulder, rocking me. "Shhh..." She stroked my hair. "I'm so sorry."

I blinked, soot from the fires outside still blurring my vision. I caught the group staring at me with sadness, shock, and unease. Losing Daniel along with

Seattle getting destroyed by some freak storm was a lot for them to absorb.

"How?" Peter choked out. He had been an old military comrade of Daniel's. They had been through a lot together. His face showed the agony of another fallen soldier.

"Fae. A fae named Maxen killed him. A lackey of someone called Garrett." I was surprised they could hear me. My voice sounded weak and wobbly.

Dr. Rapava jerked at my declaration. "Garrett?"

"Yes." I wiped my face and stood. "Why?" Kate used my arm to pull herself from the floor with a grunt. Her bones cracked as she straightened.

The doctor looked down, shaking his head. "I have heard the name come up quite a bit when talking to our test subjects. He seems to be a front-runner in the underground fae community."

"I'm going to kill him and his whole group." Rage tore up my esophagus. Daniel would be avenged.

"Zoey, you need to stay focused." The doctor took off his glasses and cleaned them on his lab coat before replacing them on his nose. "This has been a very long emotional night for all of us. Unfortunately, things are only going to get worse. This storm was not natural. The fae magic responsible was unfathomable. It almost broke our equipment."

I wasn't crazy. I knew I felt something odd about the storm.

"It is starting. The fae are declaring war on us. This weather attack was their way of broadcasting how easily they can bring us to our knees," Boris stated. "If they can do this, who knows what else they can do?"

"Do what?" A woman's voice spoke from the far side of the room. I turned to see Sera and Liam coming through the doorway.

"Good. You two are safe." Dr. Rapava gave a swift nod to them.

"We tried to call, but all cell service is down," Sera replied.

"What's going on? This city's leveled." Liam strode by me, heading for the oval meeting table.

Sera followed, but her gaze never left me. Her foot stumbled, and she stopped short. "What the...?" Her voice tapered off, and her eyes grew wide, zooming all over my face and body.

"What?" My lids dropped into a defensive glare.

"How is it possible?" The timbre of her voice went up.

Kate glanced between the two of us. "What is it, Sera? What's wrong?"

Sera looked at her then around the room. "You don't see it?" All sets of eyes landed on me, then to Sera in confusion.

"See what, Sera?" Rapava came around the table.

Sera licked her lips, her attention coming back on me with even more intensity. It was as if she were reassuring herself that what she saw was real. Something in my gut cramped with warning.

"Her aura." She pointed around me. "It has magic in it. It's thick and swirling with colors. She has a fae's aura."

"What?" I froze in place.

"It's not strong, but it's there." She turned to our fellow seers. "You see it, too, right?"

Marv and Matt leaned closer, their intense gazes centering on me.

Matt bolted up first. "Holy shit."

Marv squinted harder, then a gasp came from him. His chair slammed back into the wall, toppling. He stumbled away from me and fell over it.

Spikes of alarm shot up through my veins. *Run. Get out,* they screamed at me. My legs tensed, taking a step in retreat from Sera and the others. *Why did I want to run? There was nothing to be afraid of. Not from them.* But my intuition was telling me the opposite.

"H-how is this possible?" Marv's panicked voice and fear filling the room only tapped deeper into my reflex to bolt.

"Everyone calm down," Dr. Rapava coolly addressed the group, walking to me. "I am sure there is a perfectly reasonable explanation for it."

Neither he nor Kate had the sight, so they had to trust what my fellow seers observed.

"There is no reasonable explanation for a human to have a fae aura." Sera's words were clipped, accusatory. "What did you do?"

Rapava gave Kate a look, and she immediately took Sera by the shoulders and led her to the table, away from me.

The doctor loomed over me; his reserved nature suddenly felt threatening. *Run!* My muscles twitched at the command. He took out his tiny flashlight, shining it into my eyes. "Look up."

"I can't believe this," Matt mumbled from across the room.

"How did you miss it?" Sera fired at him.

"It's so slight I'm surprised you saw it."

"What are you talking about? She is glowing like the Fourth of July." Sera waved her arms toward me.

"No, she's not. I can barely see it," Matt snapped back. He always hated the fact Sera and I were more powerful seers. "Plus, we just found out Daniel is dead. I wasn't really looking at her aura."

"What?" Sera and Liam said at once.

"Daniel was killed tonight," Kate replied somberly.

"Look down," Rapava ordered me.

I was restless. I needed to get out of this windowless room and escape all the stares, brimming fear, and condemnation.

"What happened tonight, Zoey?" Rapava stepped back, done with his eye exam. There was something in his tone that struck my nerves.

My heart thumped in my chest. The room was silent, everyone waiting for a word to leave my lips. I tried to go through the events the best I could, but something stopped me from disclosing the truth.

"Did a fae touch you?" the doctor questioned unemotionally. He was never one for showing feelings, but this voice was different. I had heard the tone when he was talking to the fae. His science experiments. His subjects. "Any body fluids exchanged?"

My neck snapped up. "What?"

"Like blood or semen."

"Semen?" I screeched. "How would I have fae semen in me?" Silence and stares from everyone in the room caused a light bulb to ping in my head. "You think I'm having sex with a fae?"

Rapava frowned. "I did not say it was consensual. I actually hope not. But the only explanation I can think of for your emanation is if you were impregnated by a fae."

My jaw fell open. Shock silenced me for a moment. It took a while to get over the fact he would prefer I'd been raped in order to comprehend the rest of his sentence. "You think I'm pregnant?"

*What the hell is going on?*

"It would explain your aura." Rapava appeared to already believe his theory.

"You are disgusting," Sera sneered, her expression filled with loathing. "It's no better than screwing an animal. Worse actually."

Flabbergasted, words would not come to my mouth fast enough.

"Did Daniel know about this?" Peter vaulted from his chair. "How could you do this to him?"

"What? No... I-I am not pregnant," I proclaimed. No one seemed to be listening to me. The room was full of people talking and shouting over each other about the new revelation. My head spun. Tonight had been one traumatic event after another, and my nerves bent under the weight.

"Zoey, I would like you to come with me." Rapava grabbed my arm.

His harsh touch stirred more anxiety. *Get out! Get out!* "Wait! Why? What's going on?" I tried to tug out of his viselike grip, but the older man was stronger than he looked. Or I was extremely weak after my night.

"I only want to check you. Make sure everything is all right." He hauled me toward the door.

"What? No!" Panic took over. My street-survival instincts kicked in. I jerked and wrenched against his hold. His hand lost its grasp, and I heard him yell. Liam bounded to us, his hands grappling for me.

"Don't hurt her. If there is a baby, I want to test them both."

"There is no baby," I shouted, but my words were swallowed by the commotion in the room. I elbowed the body behind me, but Liam's long arms wrapped around me, pinning my arms to my sides. I slammed my head back, cracking into his face. He swore as his grip loosened. I kicked back, pushing him away from me. Free. I ran for the exit, pulling the door open. A small fist came out of nowhere and slammed into my cheek. Fire burned up the side of my face. My body tumbled awkwardly to the floor. It felt like a thousand hands descended at once, holding me down. Liam, Peter, and Hugo surrounded and restrained me.

Sera stood, shaking out her hand, looking down at me with disgust. "Never thought you were capable of this."

"I didn't," I tried to say, but stopped when I saw Dr. Rapava squat next to me, a syringe in his hand.

"I am sorry we have to do this, Zoey, but you should have known the consequences of your actions." The needle broke through the skin, burrowing deep in my arm. Heat rushed into my vein as he pumped the liquid in my body.

"But... I... did..." My mouth stumbled over the words I desperately wanted to say. Their faces swam in my vision. "Wrong."

*No, that's not what I meant.*

Everything dimmed until unconsciousness lapped over my body, taking me into the depths of sleep.

# SEVEN

The blurry radiance of light showered down on me like the sun. My lashes flickered a few times, trying to clear my vision. The indistinct luminous blaze collapsed into one single bulb hanging above me. My body stretched lengthwise on a hospital bed; the glint of the metal roller bars drifted through my sight. I twisted my head. The pain in my face and the heaviness under my scalp caused a groan to escape my lips. The room swam in my drug-induced vision, taking its time to sharpen enough for me to make it out. The place wasn't familiar, but the style was—white walls, linoleum flooring, and no windows. Lots of rooms and labs I'd been in looked similar to this one. I was somewhere in the DMG. I had explored the first level of the bureau thoroughly, and I knew there existed lower levels where Dr. Rapava's labs were. But I wasn't allowed to go down there, not having the necessary level of clearance.

The fact I was below now sat wrong with me. We had a room upstairs where we got examined and mended by the doctors. Why didn't they simply take me there? I tried to push myself up, but my arms and legs didn't comply. *What the hell?* The pressure around my limbs took precedence. Thick leather straps circled my wrists and ankles, latching me to the bed.

Panic shot up my chest like an arrow, and I fought against the restraints. My hands banged against the side rails as I tugged against the cuffs. The longer I struggled, the higher my anxiety mounted, sending me into a frenzy. Adrenaline spiked my blood stream, and with a hard wrench, the bounds around my wrists ripped from the bed. My fingers immediately went for my ankles, releasing myself.

When I was free, I sat, my breath labored. They'd used medical restraints. They considered me a danger?

"Damn impressive," a small, high voice spoke.

My body reacted first, jumping from the bed onto the floor. My gaze searched the room for the voice.

"Especially for a human. The snarled grunt at the end was a very nice touch."

My head jerked around, still trying to locate who was talking. "Who are you?"

"My name is Spriggan-Galchobhar," the childlike voice replied. "My friends call me Sprig. Oh, right. I don't have any of those anymore. We'll, except Sussanna." This time I could tell it was male.

"Okay, Sprig whatever-the-hell-the-rest-of-your-name-is, where are you?"

"Here," he replied. I straightened, spinning to hone in on the sound. There was nothing but a few empty hospital beds, two examining tables, and a long lab table dressed with tubes, metal boxes, and beakers.

"Where?" Irritation edged into my words. *Why was this guy messing with me?*

I heard it sigh. "Okay. Let's play a little game. You

walk to the table until you hit it. Stop. Then look down. Game over. Now doesn't it sound like fun?"

My lips curled into a frown. I didn't respond but walked to the counter. I scanned the room for anything which might suddenly jump at me. My fingers automatically reached for my gun. Gone. Of course. Even if I hadn't left my gun back in the rubble, I was a threat, and they would take it away. My dart gun was empty anyway, having already used it on Ryker, but I longed for the security of it. My phone was still lodged deep in my pocket, but it was useless.

My ribs tapped at the edge of the table as I came to a stop. Nothing sat directly in front of me. There were tubes to my left and a metal box to my right. "All right..." I was about to continue when I felt tiny hands grab my T-shirt, nails sinking into the fabric.

"Holy hell!" I screamed, jumping back away from whatever had touched me. My stunned gaze followed the line of the fabric sticking straight out and fixed on the miniature claws poking out of the metal box. I hadn't noticed the holes in the top. With another jerk, my shirt pulled free.

Two brown, furry arms squeezed out of the holes. The shape, size, and color looked like they belonged to a small monkey. Then they did something I wasn't expecting. They waved at me. "Hi, yeah, hello." The little fingers wiggled around.

My lids continued to blink, and I stared at the cage. I had seen a lot of crazy shit in my time. A lot of fae took on shapes of animals or people, but they had a glow around them, which told me it was glamour. There wasn't any aura surrounding these arms. Also, when fae shifted into their alternate form, they took on the qualities of that animal. They could no longer talk, not with words anyway.

Suddenly the hands disappeared, and a large eyeball popped into view. "Look at that. You're much taller standing up."

A monkey was talking to me. Was I dreaming? Was I actually unconscious someplace, imagining all this? My hand went to my face, tapping at my puffy cheek. I hissed in pain. Nope, I was awake. I took a tentative step to the creature. "Y-you're a monkey. How are you talking?"

A small huff came from the box. "I am not a monkey. I'm a sprite!"

I hadn't seen a sprite in person. Most stayed in the Otherworld. But I knew what they looked like from the records DMG had us study. They were tiny, no more than four or five inches. They were long-eared, round-faced, adorable little things with wings. They were exceptional because they had the consistency of a ghost. *Sprite* is derived from the Latin word *spirit*, and they do appear more ghostly than a real being, but you could hold them and catch them like a solid organism.

He didn't appear to be a sprite. "You look kind of like a monkey to me." There was silence from the crate. "Hello?" I bent over, closing one eye to see in.

"I am *not* talking to you anymore."

Oops! I hurt little monkey-man's feelings.

I reached for the cage latch. This was probably a dumb move, but my curiosity to see this creature shattered my common sense. Slowly, I lifted the lid. Light streamed into the box, exposing the creature. Soft brown fur covered his entire body except for his face, ears, and the pads of his hands and feet. His little white face was in a heart shape, leaving his huge brown eyes even more endearing. He looked like a baby capuchin monkey, but even smaller than I remembered the breed. He was only as big as a sprite—four or five inches max. I immediately wanted to put him in my pocket and protect him.

A water dish and a tiny stuffed toy sat in the far corner; Sprig sat opposite them. His arms crossed and his dark eyes glared into mine before he turned his back to me.

"I'm sorry... Sprig was it?" Did I just apologize to a fae creature? "But you're a monkey."

He swiveled around on his butt, facing me. "On the outside, but the inside is pure sprite."

"How is it possible?"

"I was use—"

He was cut off by the doorknob rattling. I whipped around to see Dr. Rapava enter the room. His eyes widened at the sight of me. "How are you awake?"

The notion of me being awake hadn't crossed my mind. I figured it had been hours since they sedated me.

"There is no way you should be awake and standing." His confusion trickled trepidation through me. "It's only been twenty minutes. You should have been out for at least an hour." He stepped farther into the room, his head turning toward the bed. The thick leather cuffs hung limply against the side. "How did you get free?"

Deep warning bells went off again, but my legs stayed melded to the floor.

"You are taking on its qualities." He nodded, as if confirming whatever theory he had in mind.

"I am not pregnant," I finally whispered.

Rapava glanced down at the files in his hand. "These tell me different, Zoey."

"What?" My back strummed as I over-straightened. "They say I'm pregnant?"

The doctor stepped into the room, shutting the door behind him. His restriction of my exit pumped more anxiety into me. "The pregnancy test came back inconclusive. Your general makeup is the same, except for a section in you, which has come back positive for fae DNA. I may not be able to hear a heartbeat, but I have no doubt you are carrying a fae offspring."

My whole world seemed to turn upside down. As sure as he was I was carrying fae spawn, I knew I wasn't. I would never even touch a fae if I didn't have to. The thought of having sex with one made me retch. The last time I had sex was more than a month ago after a very intense training session with Daniel. It ended with him driving me home and a platonic nod goodbye. Chaste and by the rules. He had me really riled up, and I didn't want to be a good girl. After he dropped me off, I took out my frustration on some guy I picked up at the bar. A human man. We had been safe, and my monthly visitor four days later confirmed it.

He looked down at his clipboard and became even more formal than he usually was. "When were you assaulted, Zoey?"

"I-I wasn't assaulted." My mind spun, not able to grasp anything substantial.

"I see." Displeasure coated his words as he checked

something on the form. "When was your last sexual encounter with a fae, then?"

My head slowly shook back and forth. "No! You don't understand."

Rapava's hand came up, pen twined between his fingers. "I will not lie. I am greatly disappointed in you, Zoey, but in order to deal with this, I need you to be completely honest with me. We need to know all the facts, so I know how to handle it." He cleared his throat. "Now, tell me when you last had intercourse with a fae. When were you penetrated?"

I cringed at his words, feeling dirty and disgusted, but they did trigger a memory of the night. My hand grazed my stomach. It was still tender from where the lightning bolt went through. Penetrated. *Duh, Zoey.* "It was the lightning bolt!" I motioned frantically at my stomach. "The lightning did it." Okay, now looking back, I can see how crazy it sounded.

Dr. Rapava stared at me before his robotic voice filled with an emotion I had never heard from him. Disappointment and shame. "I think you should lie down."

"No! You don't understand. The storm wa—"

Rapava's legs moved in the direction of the wall, stopping my words. He punched his finger into the intercom button. "Liam, can you and Sera get down here? She is awake."

Terror constricted my lungs. *Threat. Enemy.* The words pumped through my blood into my thoughts. My reaction was immediate. Like a trapped animal, I squatted lower, preparing myself to attack. I had been in a lot of predicaments in the past, and I had always gotten out. Whatever it took, my self-preservation dominated.

Swiping up the closest thing, my fingers curled into the holes of Sprig's cage. A squeak came from him as I dumped him out and tossed the metal box at Rapava. Adrenaline allowed me to heave the container with precision and speed, nailing Rapava's head. He crashed to the floor under the force. He groaned and rolled to his side. I only had seconds before he would be back up, or Liam and Sera would enter the room. If they did—game over.

"Take me with you," Sprig chirped from the counter. It was a natural reflex to shake my head. I collected fae; I didn't set them free. He leaped off the table, following me as I dashed for the exit. "Please, don't leave me here with them. I can help you."

I swung the door open, and it crashed against the wall close to Rapava. I sprinted down the hallway.

"You can't go out this way. All exits are equipped with a fae alarm," the monkey screeched as he scampered next to me.

"Good thing I'm not fae, then."

Sprig's tiny form silently kept up with surprising ease as the smooth floor squeaked under my boots. Muscles in my legs tightened as I veered around a corner, leading me to the exit. Instinct was all I had to go on because I had never been this deep in the DMG building. Natural deduction skills had me following a route as if I were on the floor I knew. Most likely, they had been set up similarly.

My lungs throbbed under my ribs, more from panic than exertion. My eyes were set ahead, but I was aware of every door I passed, afraid something would leap out. I skidded, rounding another corner. Stairs. My exit leading up was in sight. A machine similar to the ones for airport security bordered the end of the corridor before reaching the stairs. The moment my toes crossed it, the buzzer sounded, belting a loud signal off the walls. *What the hell?*

"Not fae, huh?" Sprig skidded into the back of my boot. "I told you the doorways are lined with anti-fae material. If we step over, it sets off a warning bell," Sprig spouted nervously.

But I wasn't fae. Had he crossed it the same time I did? I had no time to wonder as shouts and the vibration of feet plummeting down the stairs whirled me around to head back across the scanner and into the depths of DMG.

"Hurry, Liam." Sera's voice rang through the corridor.

Sprig squeaked with fear, his body stiffened and toppled in a heap.

"What the hell?" I bent over his little body. "Sprig?" His tiny chest moved up and down. He was still alive. I swept him up in my arms and took off in the opposite direction from Sera and Liam.

I turned toward the closest door, twisting the knob. Locked. I tried a few more. All bolted. Sprig stirred in my arms. I searched behind me, then back at the stairs. *Shit!* I had nowhere to go. Liam and Sera were getting closer—only seconds from hitting the bottom of the steps. Soon they would see me.

The last door opened for me, and I raced through, closing and locking it behind me. Liam's and Sera's shouts drilled through the wood.

"She went in there," Liam bellowed.

Dread wrapped so tightly around my lungs it broke off my air supply. I only had a second to examine the room before Liam's fist cracked into the panel. The space was another lab. There were different types of equipment and devices. Attached was a smaller room with windows, a room within a room. An operating table with chains hanging off the side was located in the side space. Whatever they put on the bed, they restrained and observed from this outer room. My insides constricted at the thought. But right then I didn't have time to dwell on anything.

*Bam!*

The door shook again under Liam's strength.

Sprig perked his head up. "How did we get here?" He looked up at me studying me. "You saved me?"

"I-uh." I didn't have a response to his question. Why did I save him?

"I am indebted to you." He jumped from my arms onto the counter.

"What happened?"

"I tend to fall asleep at the most inopportune moments."

"You're a narcoleptic?"

"In so many words."

"What words would you use?"

His brown eyes stared blankly. "Those I guess."

A narcoleptic monkey-sprite. This was a new one for me.

There were no windows since it was far below the surface, the only door being the one we came in. What the hell was I going to do? How would I escape? *Think, Zoey. Think!* The fan kicked on, pushing air down on me. My gaze went up, searching the air vent. "That's it."

"What's it?" Sprig replied.

The air had to be pumped down here. My hope locked on the idea if the vent moved the air to all the rooms below, it would lead to the surface.

"This way," I shouted and leaped on the counter and pointed at the ceiling panels.

"Ah, got it, *bhean!*" He clambered up the cupboard to the ceiling.

I scaled after him. Slipping into people's houses from an open top-floor window had once been my specialty. My tiny, limber nine-year-old frame could get into any snug or high place with no problem. My body had developed since then. My ass was a lot more rounded, my boobs more defined. I loved them, but it did make it a little harder to crawl into small spaces.

"Zoey, come out now. You have nowhere to run," Sera screamed.

The door shuddered again as an impact hit lower. *Sera's foot.* I had been on the receiving end of her kicks many times. Her legs were tiny but powerful. She bruised my ribs a lot during training. Don't get me wrong—I had gotten her back—but deep down I knew I held back. When I would feel the blissful level of excitement pumping into my veins, when I wanted to tear her apart, I would walk away. This type of fighting was never allowed on DMG's mats. Daniel would never have condoned it. And I had never wanted him to see the dark version of me.

I pushed my foot off the last shelf of the cabinet and hit at a ceiling panel, exposing the open rafters. Sprig jumped up, gripping one of the metal braces. I crawled behind him, lifting myself to the supports. Wiring, metal beams, and insulation filled the space like an obstacle course. I had barely put the panel back in place when I heard the door splinter. *Please, door, hold a little longer.* I needed a bit more time to get out of this space before they figured where I went.

Sprig bounced from beam to beam, chirping and chattering like I had seen monkeys do on the Discovery Channel when they got riled up. "Shut it," I whispered hoarsely, following his lead toward the far wall.

An opening cut into the wall went up to the surface, bringing fresh air to the underground sections. My trail to freedom. The metal vent stuck out of the wall enough so I didn't have to go in where the fan circled around like blades of death. I unhooked a panel on the side, letting it fall open.

Sprig's nails dug into my jeans as he climbed to my shoulder and then leaped to the outlet. Fae of any kind had always been the "enemy," but in a matter of minutes, I had come to feel an alliance with the monkey. It was nowhere near fondness or even compassion but more a convenience—*we're in this together* kind of feeling. I assumed the moment we got through this predicament, things would change. We would go our separate ways, and he would deal with finding safety on his own.

It took me a couple of tries before I jumped high enough to get the majority of my upper torso into the opening. The sharp metal stabbed into my abdomen. My fingers scratched for any kind of traction, and my legs swung violently underneath me. A trickle of sweat trailed down my forehead into my eye.

"Come on. Hurry!" Sprig bobbed around me anxiously.

I grunted and pulled myself up into the space. My legs slipped, and I crashed to the floor near the vent. All I wanted to do was lie there and pant like a dog, but I had no time. Sera and Liam were far from dumb. If they got into the room and figured out where I went, they would know where I was going. Even with all the work to get out, there was a good possibility in the end they would be standing by the ground flue and lead me right back to where I started.

Rolling over, I got on all fours and crawled. It was pitch black, and my hands felt their way through the space, colliding with cobwebs and rats. I reached forward, my fingers sliding over something soft.

"Hey," Sprig yelped. "Stop grabbing my ass."

I jerked my hand back.

"I mean, I don't think we know each other well enough yet. At least you could buy me a few drinks or something first."

I snorted.

"I am all for the incentive. I like a woman who goes for what she wants."

"Please, shut up now," I groaned. Great. I had a chatty, frisky monkey-sprite on my hands.

"You're the one who grabbed my ass."

"I didn't mean to." I skidded forward on my knees.

"Still your fault."

Maybe the toy in his cage was more than something he curled up with at night. "Am I going to have to get you a stuffed animal to be alone with?" I sighed, feeling the tunnel take a sharp curve upward. "Hell. It's straight up from here."

Sprig stayed silent.

"Sprig?"

"Not. Talking. To. You."

"Again?" I shook my head. Standing in the vertical tube, my eyes tried hard to adjust to the pure darkness. All they could distinguish were strange shapes, which I knew weren't actually there.

"You insulted Sussanna at a time when I had to leave her behind. She will be so upset with me."

"Who is Sussanna?"

"She was my companion for the time I have been here and always there to comfort me. Such a good listener."

I gripped the sides of the slick walls, found small edges to put my boots on, and pulled myself higher, making my way up the tube.

"She has such big black eyes," he continued. A memory made me think back to the toy in his cage. A bear.

"Would Sussanna be considered alive?"

Sprig climbed my back, settling on my shoulder, his tail wrapping my neck. "Alive is such a technical term."

I bit my lip, laughter bubbling up. "So... she's a stuffed animal?"

He sighed deeply in my ear. "In the most basic meaning, I suppose it's what she is. But she has been my friend for more than five years."

That was actually sad and sweet—mostly sad. I was about to respond when I saw light gleaming down on me. Freedom. It was so close I could taste it. Trails of sweat etched my face as I forced myself forward. The vision of hope giving me newfound energy. My legs shook as I pushed myself higher, and my hands reached for the gap. Smoke and ash blocked out the sky, but raging fires from all around illuminated the billowing clouds.

Sprig climbed along my arm toward the latches on the edges of the vent. That's when I noticed it was bolted down.

"Shit! No..." I felt tears pricking at my eyes. Of course they would bolt it. They wouldn't want anyone to be able to get in. Or out. Once again, I was trapped. I couldn't go forward and couldn't go back.

"Watch and learn." Sprig's little fingers touched the bolts. One by one they popped out of their holes, falling below.

"How the hell did you do that?"

"Magic." Sprig touched the last one. "We sprites are very talented." His little brown eyebrows went up and down.

Right then I was extremely thankful for Sprig and his fae magic.

*Another first for me.*

I lifted the cover off and let it tumble to the side. Sprig jumped out, going beyond where I could see him. With a grunt, I gripped the sides and pulled myself over the rim. My arms trembled underneath me. They were giving way when a hand grabbed the back of my neck, gripped my hood, and yanked me out of the hole.

"You're not getting away from me again," a man's voice growled into my ear from behind and slammed me back on my feet. A slipknot captured my wrist before he wrapped the other end around his own. Normally, this would have been my first concern, but what was in front of me moved this problem behind.

Lying on the ground at my feet was Sprig's body, curled in a ball. This time I was sure he was dead. "What did you do?" I demanded. "Did you kill him?"

Ryker snarled at the lump on the ground. "What do you care? It's a fae. I can sense it."

"It doesn't mean I want him dead. He helped me."

The Viking gripped me tighter and shoved me forward. "I didn't touch it. It collapsed when it saw me."

A breath of relief came from me. I felt strangely happy the little monkey-fae wasn't dead but sleeping. I hadn't believed him about being narcoleptic. "He saw you and passed out." I laughed, but there was no humor in my voice. Distance grew between us and Sprig. Ryker forced me to move quickly down the street.

"It happens." Ryker dragged me into an alleyway. "Now, shut up."

"We can't leave him. He'll be captured again."

"Not my problem."

My determination to struggle against him was nil. There was no point unless I wanted to gnaw my arm off, which I didn't. Not yet anyway.

The Capitol neighborhood of Seattle, above where DMG headquarters was stationed, survived only marginally better than downtown. Buildings still burned, and many were collapsed into piles but more sporadically here. Clusters of people roamed the streets, looking lost and terrified. A pregnant silence held an eerie absence of voices—the dead filling the vacancy with their silent screams.

The sound of helicopters came from above, their spotlights the only thing signaling their location, like the Bat-Signal. The smoke and debris clotted in a dome over Seattle.

My arms were jerked forward, tearing the skin at my wrist. "Hurry up, human," Ryker growled, glaring over his shoulder at me with glowing white judgments of hate. "You are testing my patience."

"You have patience?" I countered.

I tried to escape him when we came across others, but quickly I gave up screaming and fighting him. No one looked. No one cared. My energy was being wasted. There was so much yelling and commotion going on in the streets mine got lost in the sea of turmoil filling Seattle.

His scowl only intensified before he yanked harder on the rope, dragging me forward. A couple of choice words were mumbled under my breath, while my feet tried to speed up enough to keep up with his pace.

# EIGHT

Time wore on, and Ryker kept up his punishing speed. My feet and body ached. The tiny bit of energy I had left kept one foot moving in front of the other but didn't stop me from stumbling and falling.

"Get up," Ryker barked, tugging on the cord linking us. "Or I swear I will kill you, human."

I swallowed, my throat dry and coated with the grime of the burning city. "Then do it." I crawled to my feet and peered up at him, with no fear or doubt. "I beg you. Do it. I have nothing left."

His lips pinched. His eyes searched mine, seeing the resolve behind my words. He breathed out methodically and looked up at the sky. He shifted his feet and turned and yanked me forward. "Keep moving."

"No." I stood my ground and almost went into the pavement when the line pulled up short. "I have to stop."

"Not yet." He faced me.

"Yes, now." I gritted my teeth, trying not to feel the intimidating way he loomed over me. He could snap me in pieces.

His chest puffed out as he drew in a huge gulp of air. Heat radiated off him, directed at me. We stared at each other for a good minute before he finally spoke. "We'll find a place to stay for the night, but you're gonna have to keep going until I find one."

I nodded.

We were far from the heart of the city in the north suburbs when Ryker finally found us a sketchy motel. Not as much was destroyed this far, but all electricity was off. I wondered how far the effects of the storm actually went.

There was no one at the desk, although I doubted it would make a difference to Ryker. He didn't seem like the *pay for a room* type. He carted me off to a room farthest from the street and office. He only nudged the door with his shoulder, and it cracked open.

*Damn!* He was either extremely strong or the quality of the building materials was poor. I voted for both. He towed me into the small, dingy bathroom. No lights made the room even more horror-movie ready.

He unwound his arm from the rope and marched me to the bathtub. "Get in."

I was beyond tired and only wanted to stop walking and sit. So I did. He tied my wrists together, then took another rope from the handle of his axe and tied my wrists to the metal spout. He tugged on it a few times, making sure it was secure before he walked to the bedroom. There was a sliding sound, like he was dragging a piece of furniture across the room. A bang on the door confirmed my theory as the dresser blocked the broken door—trapping us in.

Heavy boots stomped back to me. "Now, go to sleep.

If you try and escape, I will tie the rope around your neck tomorrow and drag you."

"Like a slave." I frowned.

"No." He grabbed the knob of the door. "Like livestock." He slammed the door, encasing me in darkness.

I called him a few names but very halfheartedly. My lids no longer wanted to cooperate nor listen to me. Most of my body was rejecting my orders. It demanded sleep and food. Food seemed out of the question for now. Leaning my head against the tile, I surrendered to the other demand before my body went on strike. It needed to shut down, to leave the trauma of the day behind for at least a moment.

Helicopter beams flashed through the bathroom window, forcing my lashes to rise. It felt as if I only closed my eyes an instant before. They burned with the need to shut and continue sleeping.

Another flash of light reflected through the frosted window. The low vibrating pattern of the rotors advanced close above the one-story rat-infested lodging. I figured they were out in response to the storm, but my paranoia fused a tiny flame in my brain. *What if it was for me?* The probability of someone or something out there hunting for one of us was high. I couldn't fathom I'd be worth enough for the DMG to get a search party so advanced looking for me, although the little voice in the back of my head still nibbled at the idea.

Sounds from the other room revealed the Viking was awake. The bathroom door squeaked open. His outline encompassed most of the doorway. I could not make out his face in the shadows, but his eyes glowed in the darkness. It seemed to be a fae trait—very bright, unnaturally colored eyes. I stayed silent as he continued farther into the room, fear spiking my adrenaline.

No fae would go out of his way to save humans if he were only going to kill them. Right? I really hoped so. At the moment, logic told me I would be all right— until he found out I didn't have what he was seeking. A part of me wished he would end the pain that strangled my heart and soul and stop the image of Daniel's dead body at my feet, his eyes staring blankly at me.

He had almost kissed me for the first time barely a few hours ago. So much should have been ahead of us. He wasn't supposed to die. He was the man I was meant to grow old with. My heart crushed under the weight of the knowledge we would never be. Then my mind tormented me more, creating Lexie's voice, calling my name as the flames overtook her.

"Stop," he said, his tone angry. I hadn't made a peep. "They'll be able to sense you a state away."

"Who?" I spit out. "I didn't say anything!" Sirens and helicopters howling through the streets muted my cries to nonexistent.

"I didn't say *hear*. I said *feel*. You humans broadcast your emotions like radio." He paused, his jaw clenching. He really hated humans, which was amusing since the feeling was mutual. He paced the tight box, his figure stiff and anxious.

"Are those guys still after you? The ones who took your girlfriend?" I asked. "Garrett, right?" A muscle twitched at his temple. His white eyes appeared turbulent with guarded rage. Tattoos down his neck flickered with sparks. Instinctively, I leaned back. He was a terrifying sight. "What the hell? Your tattoos..."

Ryker gripped his fists tighter. "They are my birthmarks. I was born with them. They're attached to my fae magic. Or they used to be."

"Do they flicker when you use your powers?" My geek brain kicked in, fascinated by this new species of fae. Nothing like him was in our training books.

He moved to the window, ignoring my question. Finally, a deep grumble came from his throat. "You do not speak of Amara. Am I clear, human?"

"I have a name, you know."

"I don't care what your name is. All you humans are no more than a group of imps to me."

"A fae way of saying I'm scum?" Ire spewed from my lips.

He snapped his head to stare down at me. "Are fae anything more to you? You experiment and run tests on us. How many of my kin have died for your research?"

"At least we act for the greater good. What do you do it for?"

"Good for who?" he snapped at me with condescension.

"We are trying to define the DNA of fae and clone them. We are saving lives, fighting against diseases and disabilities. Children with cancer, people with severe disabilities. What we do is beneficial. If some fae die in the process, I am sorry."

"You're sorry?" He gripped the tub, leaning into my face. "How many of us died so *one* of you could live?" He took a long drag of air through his nose. "Don't get high and mighty with me, human. You think of fae no better than I think of humans."

A chill filled my belly. There was truth in his statement. As much as I didn't want to admit it, I did consider fae inferior. Testing on another species to help my own, even if it caused pain to one, benefited mine. Human life, especially with having a disabled sister, was worth more to me than a species I had been trained to despise. But we tested; we did not seek to kill. When we went on hunts, we packed stun guns. We only had guns loaded with fae bullets for backup. I used them several times but had never killed a fae. Daniel killed one, but it had been about to tear into my neck. The memory of Daniel clogged my throat. I pushed the incapacitating thought of never seeing him again deep inside.

My street reflexes wanted me to fight this jerk, but what I learned in my psychology classes told me to familiarize myself with my kidnapper. Become more than a faceless target. Wasn't sure if this theory worked on fae, but I was willing to give it a try. "My name is Zoey. Zoey Daniels."

He pushed away from me, going to the sink area. "I don't give a fuck."

"You kidnapped me and say I have something of yours. It seems we're together in this. I'm a target now, too," I said. "It will help if I know what is after you. Why did they take Amara? What is it you have they want so badly?"

"Let's say I have something *many* people want. Desperately."

I shifted to face him, needles of numbness prickling

at my rear. Bits of conversation from my earlier encounter with him came back. "This stone... it's what you think I have, right?" He tilted his head as if I were the stupidest person on the planet. "So what is it you think I have if it's not the stone?"

A frustrated growl gurgled up from his throat. He squatted next to the bathtub. "I never said you had it." He rubbed at the loose hair on top of his head. "Let's see if you can keep up..."

My lashes lowered as I glowered at him.

"You understand I am fae, right?" he mocked.

My glare narrowed with more contempt.

"All right. We're together so far." His condescending tone made me want to slap him. Hard. "I am what you call a Wanderer. I have certain powers. Or at least I did till you took them."

"What? I—"

He held up his hand, interrupting me. "You recall lightning hitting me?"

A patronizing smile grew on my mouth. "Yeah. Best part of my day so far."

He did not find me amusing. "This." He tapped at the ropes holding me prisoner. "Is the best part of mine."

The raw hatred and disgust I felt for him shook me to my core.

A glint flickered in his eyes as my shoulders hunched tighter. "The lightning went through me and went into you, taking my powers with it." He nodded to where I was struck. "You carry them now."

"Excuse me?" This guy had lost his mind. "You're saying they were transferred into me?"

"Yes." He nodded, using the side of the tub to push himself up.

"You're crazy." A strange laugh erupted from my mouth. "I'm talking padded-walls loony."

"I can sense them. How do you think I was able to find you both times? I know my own magic. It calls to me."

My mouth opened and then shut. Was this even possible? Was it what Sera saw? Why Dr. Rapava claimed I was "carrying" a fae baby? And what about the fact I couldn't go through the fae-blocking door without the alarm going off? If I were human, I should have been able to walk through without a problem.

"I don't know how it's possible. I've never heard of anything like this happening. But it has. I first thought it was something your group did, but now I realized you humans aren't smart or skilled enough to pull something like this off." He began to walk in circles, his hands on his hips. "The storm was carried out by a fae. I have been around for a long time and never felt anything like the magic in that lightning."

I kept silent, wanting to hear what he thought about the storm, and if he knew more than the DMG did.

"It was not a storm from the Otherworld, but it *was* fae-made. Whatever or whoever created it possesses capabilities unheard of in our world. No fae should have the amount of magic it took to transfer powers to another, especially a human. It shouldn't be possible."

"Well, I've learned with fae never to doubt what they are capable of."

He pinched the bridge of his nose.

"What are these abilities I'm holding?" Not that I believed the insane man, but it was good to humor crazy people.

He pressed his mouth together. He didn't want to tell me.

"Look, if I have these *powers*, then I need to be aware of what they are and what I can do."

"Believe me. You would have used them already if you could."

"How do you know?"

"Fae's powers are instinctual. They are not always something you can control when you first start learning them. They tend to come out in extreme emotions. If you were able to use them, they would have gotten you out of the building... or out of here."

I glanced down at the rope binding me to the tub. Closing my eyes, I willed these powers to do something. Nothing happened. "Tell me what you... they can do."

He stared out the window for so long I thought he was ignoring my plea. "A Wanderer is a jumper. We can blink in and out of time and space. Travel anywhere we want in the world in an instant."

*Wow! Cool!* "That would be handy about now." I tugged at my restraints. "So you think of somewhere, and it takes you there?"

Getting him to confirm or deny this was like pulling teeth. He didn't like talking about himself. "It works in many different ways." He rubbed at his chest. "It's all I'm telling you."

"But if I'm carrying these powers, I should know what they're capable of."

"Exactly the reason I don't want you to know."

"It's clear I can't use them, and I'm not foolish enough to think I can get away from you, especially if you can sense them. Untie me. I won't run." A notion came into my head, my shoulders drooping. "I have no place to go anyway."

He snorted. "I'm not stupid, human. You are staying tied until I find a way to get them back." He walked into the other room and came back with a pillow, tossing it in the tub next to me. "Sleep tight." He nodded down at my ropes, then closed the door and shut it firmly behind him, leaving me alone in the bathroom.

"You son of a bitch!" I screamed, thrashing against the sides of the tub. "You fae are all alike... narcissistic, cruel, deceitful assholes."

"Funny. Sounds like humans," he yelled through the door. I could hear the springs of the bed respond to his weight. Bastard. He had a nice soft bed. I got a cold, hard tub too small to even lie in.

"I have to pee," I hollered.

"Good thing you're in the shower."

My life mostly consisted of rough circumstances, places where I needed to be on guard. This situation kicked in my defenses. My past was not clean, and I had my fair share of red marks on my record. I'd been in a knife fight with a gang of girls and shot one of my foster fathers in the thigh. I had been aiming for his balls, but he'd moved. That was one of those homes I tried to block out, although it did remind me every day why I fought so hard to keep Lexie protected. Why I gushed about Joanne when a service agent would stop by to review our living situation. I never wanted Lexie to go through something like I had. Now she never would.

The moment I was loose, I was going to find the sharpest object and stab it into Ryker's throat. I would never be a victim again.

# NINE

The tormented sounds of the war zone outside bled more and more into the background as the events of the day overtook my thoughts. Exhaustion, heartache, and being hit by a fae-induced storm curled my body against the side of the tub. My arms and butt lost feeling hours ago. Horrific dreams layered the surface of my sleep, keeping me from truly falling under. Moments of bliss would seep into my mind, then a picture of Daniel or Lexie slammed into my head, popping my eyes open. A sharp sob would tear into my chest, bringing me back to reality.

The darkness hung around, suffocating, brewing an edgy and frightening chill into my bones. I hated the dark. Too many evils hid in the corners. The only light coming in was from the top bathroom window. We were away from downtown fires, and the spotlights from the helicopters were becoming less frequent.

I hunched my neck tighter against my shoulder.

"There you are," a squeaky voice muttered.

It jolted me; my wrists burned against the tug. "What the hell?" I glanced around the dark, my heart skipping.

Through the shadows I saw movement through the air/heater vent on the wall.

"I have been searching for you for hours," the thing grunted as it wiggled its body through the metal gaps.

My eyes narrowed. "Sprig?"

"How many monkey-sprites do you know?"

I cautiously glanced toward the closed bathroom door, straining to hear any movement from the next room. "What are you doing here?"

"Sprites take obligations very seriously. I cannot leave your side till my debt has been repaid." The creature jumped down from the duct and trotted on all fours across the linoleum flooring. The tiny body leaped on the side of the tub. His little primate toes curled tightly to keep from slipping. "Oh, did I interrupt something?" He tilted his head, looking down at the rope around my arms.

"Funny."

"Hey, no judgment here."

My brain was still having a hard time wrapping around a monkey-sprite talking to me.

"Actually, your debt could be repaid faster than you think." I kept my voice low, my attention constantly darting to the door. "Get me loose, and we'll call it even."

"You have no say in when the debt is repaid. It's the only one who knows." Sprig crept around to the faucet, his small but nimble fingers getting into the gaps of the intricate knot. I tried to keep still as he worked out the binding.

This was not my first time being tied up. One time was when I turned twelve. It was the house before Jo's.

It was my foster parents' way of dealing with me. They left me in the closet all night to "contemplate" my actions. I ran away the next day. Three months later, they placed me with Jo. It was when my true fear of the dark set in. When it was pitch black, my mind took me back to being tied and locked in the closet. I couldn't say all my foster parents were awful, but those were the ones who stuck in your mind.

"Monkey's uncle. Who tied this knot? A pirate?"

I smirked. "He could be. He looks like one... a Viking pirate."

The creature froze. "This Viking pirate doesn't happen to have markings all over, white eyes, and goes by the name of Ryker?"

"Yeah. Why?"

Sprig jumped back from the rope. "Oh, you didn't tell me. Sorry, I can't help you."

"What?" I wailed a little too loud before continuing in a low, harsh whisper. "Why?"

"Ryker the Wanderer. Do you not know who he is?"

"Yeah. Ryker the Wanderer," I said with derision.

Sprig crossed his arms, the human gesture looking odd on a primate. "You have no idea who you are dealing with, do you? How did you get hooked up with him?"

"It wasn't by choice, as you can clearly see." I flapped my pinned hands. "And I would like to get away from him. Help me, please?"

Sprig shook his head.

"You don't remember seeing him pull me out of the other air vent?"

"I don't recall anything of the sort. And I think I would remember seeing the Wanderer." He clicked his tongue at me.

"What do you mean you don't recall?"

"When I fall asleep, I don't remember things." He shifted nervously. "In stressful situations, I go to sleep. That's a lie. I fall asleep in non-stressful situations, too." He continued to rattle on. "Actually, it's really whenever. But I lose memory around those times."

The door swung open and ricocheted off the wall. "If you touch those ropes, you'll find your intestines being used for rope." Ryker's face contorted with anger, his words meant for Sprig, but his scowl was on me.

Sprig squeaked and scrambled out of the tub, hopping onto the counter.

"How did you find us?" Ryker uttered through clenched teeth. I stared at him, waiting for his wrath. I could feel it bubbling under the surface, ready to boil over.

"I'm in her debt." Sprig folded his arms. A tiny light flickered on his wrist. "I'm connected to her until the obligation is repaid."

"What is this?" Ryker moved swiftly into the bathroom, pointing at the blinking bracelet wrapped around Sprig's little wrist.

Sprig looked down, confusion crossing his face. "I don't know. It's never flashed before."

"You stupid idiot!" Ryker's voice hollered. "It's a tracker! You are leading them right to us." Barely had Ryker uttered those words when a loud boom echoed through the bathroom.

The outside entry of the hotel room shuddered under

a blow. I yelped in surprise as another bang vibrated the door, causing it to hit against the dresser.

Ryker's reaction was instant. He slammed the bathroom door, locking it. He quickly searched the space for anything he could use to block it.

Another thwack sounded against the main entry.

"Dammit!" He sailed toward me. With one tug, he broke the faucet from the wall and then picked me up, throwing me over his back. "We have to get out of here."

"How?" I looked around wildly. "There's no way to escape."

The sounds of wood splintering crackled through the air, followed by sharp shouts from men.

Another guttural growl came from Ryker's chest, his markings sparking with tiny fuses. "Of course, when I need my powers the most..." He moved me onto the counter as another loud crash came through. The dresser toppled. They were in. The bathroom door was like paper. It wouldn't take them long to break this one.

"What do we do?" My heart pounded in my chest.

His focus skimmed the bathroom. "The window is the only way."

I looked up at the tiny opening and back at him. "And how are we going to do that? My ass can't fit through there."

The door shuddered, and a hole was torn through the wood. "Come out. You have nowhere to go."

Ryker's frustration went from the men to me. "This would be a good time for those powers to kick in." He leaped onto the tub rim. Using the handle of his blade, he smashed out the window. There was no way I could fit through it, and I wasn't sure how he thought he could.

"Um? Maybe I can suggest another way out?" Four screws fell to the floor before the metal covering off the heater/air outlet tipped forward, crashing onto the linoleum. As soon as Sprig dropped the cover, the sound of gunshots echoed in the room. The men on the other side were shooting at the handle. It was only a matter of seconds now.

Ryker needed even less time. It wouldn't be long before the men would know what we were up to—if they didn't already. I was in his arms as he sprang for the opening. He shoved me into the space before he joined me. The space didn't hold his frame, so the metal and wall fractured under his weight. One perk about this cheap one-level motel was the air vents went straight outside. The passage needed a little encouragement. Ryker's fist and leg smashed against the metal while I also kicked at it. The screen popped off under Ryker's strength like a Tupperware top. For as large as he was, he was nimble and swift. He scrambled out, grabbing the restraints that still bounded my hands, and tugged me to my feet. Tiny nails dug into my skin as Sprig vaulted onto my shoulder. His tail wrapped firmly around my neck, and his hands clung to my hair.

"No!" Ryker picked Sprig off my shoulder and flung him to the ground. "Your tracker put us in this danger."

Sprig looked down at the bracelet with a panicked expression. "You can't leave me here. You can't..." He tilted over, his body rolling into a ball on the concrete.

"Damn, that's weird." I gazed down at the snoring creature.

Ryker grabbed my rope and yanked me forward.

"We can't leave him."

"Then your humans will keep finding us," he spit out as we ran.

The Wanderer was right. Until Sprig got rid of the tracking device, he was a threat to us.

Ryker picked up his pace, dragging me while the water nozzle smacked against my elbows. Shouts and gunfire wailed behind us. The whizz of a bullet zipped by my ear and thudded into the tree beside me. The protruding cartridge stuck out from the trunk. It was a dart, a nerve paralyzing tranquilizer. We used them in collecting fae. We didn't want to hurt the specimen, so we'd knock it out to take it back to the lab. My head craned to take a quick view behind me. Eight men wearing tactical gear, guns, and bulletproof vests bearing the FBI insignia ran around the building toward us.

In one moment, my world shifted. They didn't want to kill me. This feeling had been stirring in me the instant I stepped back into HQ, but now I fully understood. I was no longer the collector. I was the collected, the hunted—a specimen to test.

Ryker did not slow, and eventually the constant tugging on my wrists annoyed him. He finally cut off the faucet dangling from my arms, but he didn't seem ready to free my wrists. "For the gods, human, hurry up."

My lungs ached as they tried to capture breath. The early morning air was saturated with soot and ash, aggravating my airway. The rise of the sun brought the harsh reality of the storm into full color. Throngs of deep gray smoke-filled clouds curled up from the ground like twisters in the sky, filtering the sun. Several times I had to stop in shock at the sight of the city. Most of the main downtown and the areas near the Space Needle were obliterated. Overnight fires had eaten their way through the collapsed buildings and started on the surrounding areas of Capitol Hill and Queen Anne.

Hundreds of people wandered in the streets, coated in blood and soot, not knowing where to go or what to do. Tears flowed more steadily than the broken water mains. Helplessness, fear, and devastation hung heavy in the atmosphere. Most survivors dug through the wreckage, hunting for people and lost items. Buildings that used to stand proudly in the sky were crumpled messes of rubble under their feet.

My mind had trouble wrapping around the picture in front of me. Less than twenty-four hours ago, I had been in a car with Daniel, where we almost kissed. Our future had been unsure, but it was moving forward. I felt so certain my life was proceeding in the right direction, and Daniel was a huge part of it. Only two hours before that I had gotten Lexie from school, lecturing her to start on her homework before I had to set out on another "emergency meeting."

Blood and tears soaked the streets. So many lives had been lost and destroyed. In one strike of lightning—by one action from a fae—our world had been shattered.

The unbearable pain faltered my step, but I stuffed it back, pushing it under my thick facade. From a very young age, I had hidden my emotions. In my world, you could not show weakness. This was even truer for me because my face didn't fit the image of a street kid.

My fight had been an uphill battle, trying to prove myself. So many girls didn't think I belonged, and so many guys thought they could take advantage of me. More times than not I had to prove I was capable of handling myself. The other times—let's say I had spent many nights in the ICU.

"Where are we going?" I asked for the umpteenth time.

"Between what is hunting you and what is hunting me, we are safer getting lost in the chaos and smells where there are more people." He didn't bother looking back at me.

I halted my feet, pressing them into the pavement, causing him to stumble back.

"What the fuck, human?" His unsettling eyes swung back at me with exasperation.

"Untie me." My body stiffened. "Now."

His lip curled and he stepped closer, his face only centimeters from mine. "No."

I wanted to retreat; the intensity of his nearness was disturbing. My education of fae schooled me to fear him, to hate his kind, but I was not the type of person to back down. I usually challenged. Daniel had loved this about me, even when my will overshot my skills by miles.

"I am not going to run. I've learned if you aren't the biggest or most feared kid on the playground, you befriend the person who is." My voice clipped every word harshly. "Plus, you dragging me through the streets with my arms tied is only going to cause unwanted attention."

"You think these people see beyond their own suffering right now?" He stepped back, opening his arms, motioning to the grief-ridden citizens.

True, they did not seem to be aware of us or anything else around them. But others might be. "Different groups are out watching for us. Don't you think someone who is on the lookout for a Viking doppelganger and brown-haired human with her arms shackled is going to notice we happen to fit the description?"

His lips pressed together. He stood for a long time looking around before he drew his knife. "If you even think about escaping..." He let the threat go unvoiced.

"You'll what? Kill me?" A smug grin drew up my mouth. "Won't your powers die?"

He watched me, then slowly sidled up to me, spreading his legs so wide we were around the same height. A garish smile adorned his mouth as his fingers came up, tucking a piece of my hair behind my ear. "I won't kill you." Cold air caught in my lungs at his touch. His voice went low and harsh. "But the torture will be so horrific, so acute, you'll beg me to end your life."

He drew the knife between my wrists, and with one tug, the blade sliced through the rope like it was floss. The relief to my raw arms was instant.

My life had been threatened many times before. Men and women had waved their guns and knives in my face. Most of the time, it had been a front. Their own fears and insecurities were masked by the weapon in their hand. But nothing came close to this; he was different. An internal warning told me he would enjoy inflicting pain on me. Measured shallow breaths did little to hide the jolt of fear racing in my body.

He smirked and moved away from me. "We need to find supplies and a place to hole up for the night."

I rubbed the red, tender flesh on my wrists as I quickly followed him. He bounded across the obstacles while I stumbled and tripped over a refrigerator, an office desk, and other broken furniture. The knowledge there were dead bodies under my feet was not lost on me. It made me more appreciative I was alive. Although there were moments when my mind would wander to Daniel and Lexie, and I wanted to join them—to never feel again.

My foot slipped on a baby's stuffed animal, stabbing at my heart. Bending down, I gripped the plush toy. It was covered with ash. Did the child who owned this plaything make it out? I squeezed my lids together. I wanted to believe the family had been on vacation, visiting family somewhere, anywhere else but here. *This baby is all right.* It was a lie I needed to believe.

This city had lost so much. I had no clue who caused it or why. Did they know the level of damage they had done here? How many people they killed? Was this what they wanted? Why would anyone do this? What purpose did it serve?

My gaze landed on the set of wide shoulders moving ahead. Both the DMG and Ryker said the storm was caused by a fae. Fae hated humans. Was Rapava right? Was this their way of eliminating us? Was Seattle only the first city? Kate told Daniel and me something was happening. Was this it? Was war being declared on Earth? Instead of aliens in spaceships coming to annihilate our planet, it was going to be fae with wings and swords enhanced with magic that could level this world.

Impulse stopped my feet from shadowing Ryker. He was the enemy, too. All he wanted was to get his powers and girlfriend back. He would kill me after I was no longer needed.

Awareness of my surroundings had me scouting for an escape plan. The little voice in my head said I was connected to him because of the powers I held, and I could not really get away. This opinion was lost in my itch to flee. Self-preservation was a hard thing to overrule. Even the notion of possible torture if I tried to run didn't break my determination. My attention landed on an alleyway only partially destroyed. A small hole between the blended buildings appeared to be enough room for me to get through. Not him.

With a fire lit under my ass, I darted for the gap. A voice boomed behind me when I got to the opening. I scrambled in, the knees of my jeans shredding across the rough bricks. The tiny opening widened into a large alley, and I tore down the uneven pavement, dodging chunks of stone, crushed dumpsters, and squashed cars. Another backstreet cut off from the main one, and I curved my direction down the passageway.

Then it hit me. I had no idea where I was going or any plan past getting away from Ryker. I was not impulsive, although I was not a thorough planner, either. I usually sat in the middle. My past was full of times I acted instantly and other times when I assessed a situation to see the best way out of it. It was the reason a lot of girls lost in fights to me. I wasn't the biggest or toughest fighter, or even the most skilled. But they usually acted out of passion and didn't take a minute to learn my weaknesses. Combat training with Daniel instilled these natural instincts in me. With fae, you had to be on guard, ready to act at a moment's notice and alter your plan but also remain aware of your surroundings and opponents.

This time I reacted purely on fear. *Okay, Zoey. Think.*

Buildings blurred as I ran by, my energy draining. I couldn't stop, not till I was in a safe place. I couldn't go back to HQ; they were after me. But was it such a bad thing? They wouldn't hurt me. They were only curious. What if Ryker's powers could help people? Heal the wounded or end cancer? Wasn't that what I wanted? So why was it different now that they were trying to collect and test me?

The insight stopped my legs. Why *was* it different? I should be stabbing those needles into my own veins, hitting the button to scan my brain and insides. I needed to assist in taking samples from my tissues. I was still on their side. So why did I run from them? Because it was me.

The collecting and testing of fae never registered on my sympathy radar. They were beasts. Creatures who fed on humans and wanted to destroy us. But when the dart came for me, something altered. To them, I was no more than one of those beings, to be hunted down like an animal. Fury spiked up the back of my neck. I was *not* one of them.

Part of me wanted to head toward the entrance of DMG to let them test me till they found cures. The other part wanted me to run in the opposite direction, telling me I wasn't safe with them. I was truly screwed—nowhere to go and no one to trust.

*You need to get out of town. Get away from all this.* It was the first and only idea I had. Following my own proposal, I picked up my pace, proceeding to the street leading out of Seattle. Eventually, I might run into someone with a car willing to take me to the next city or maybe the next state.

The only thing hindering my plan was the need for something to eat. The last time I ate was the snack of carrots and ranch dip I shared with Lexie after school. Jo was not a shopper, and when she did, it was crap like chips and TV dinners. With my own money, I tried to get Lexie and me real food. I was no cook, but I tried to balance Lexie's diet. Because of her condition, staying healthy and strong was essential.

I had no money. My bag was back in Daniel's car, which was crushed under millions of pounds of concrete. From a distance, I spotted a gas station. It didn't appear to be touched by the storm or fire. Food was a necessity, and stealing was my only option.

The closer I got, the more surprised I became to see the building intact. Humans in a full-blown crisis were predictable. They freaked out, letting reasoning and thought go to the wayside. A lot would use it as an excuse to rob and ransack their own people. Now I was only going to do one of those.

As I made my way down the street, people milled around; most ignored me. The shock was still too deep for them to register what had happened. I snuck around the back. I was exceptional at picking locks, but I didn't have any bobby pins on me. I had to do it the old-fashioned, crude way. I picked up a rock and smashed the handle till it clattered to the ground.

Guilt streaked across my chest. *Sorry*, I mentally expressed to the unknown person who owned the place.

Funny. I never used to feel remorse. I didn't realize how much Daniel and Lexie had transformed me over the years. I used to be the kid full of attitude and problems: breaking into people's houses and cars, stealing, getting into fights, giving every teacher and foster parent hell. Some deserved.

It all began to change with Lexie. I wanted her to have a good role model. Since I knew Jo wasn't capable, it went to me. Lexie looked up to me anyway and followed my every move. I couldn't tell her to do well in school if I didn't. How could I convince her she was worth more, if I didn't believe it about myself?

I barely graduated high school, entering community college only in hopes there was more out there. Then I joined DMG, and under Daniel's strict guidance and rules, I actually started to get good grades and to believe there was more, taking action to change my life. They both gave me dreams and aspirations to get out of the cycle I had been condemned to as an infant, to turn around and help others like me get out of what felt like a helpless situation.

There was only one thing I hadn't given up till the last possible moment. It brought in money for Lexie and helped curb my temper. I stopped soon after I became a member of the DMG and my feelings for Daniel grew. Daniel would never want to be with a girl who fought. Not the way I did. He deserved a woman.

The unlit store was eerily quiet as I snuck in. The only light coming in the hazy windows was on the far side near the cash register.

Even though it was well into morning, the sky grew darker under the ash and embers rolling over Seattle.

I immediately snatched a candy bar and shoved half into my mouth. Munching hungrily, I grabbed a messenger bag off the display rack and hurried to the cashbox, taking a set of bobby pins from the shelf as I went. I hated to steal the money, but hopefully the owner was insured. In desperation, right and wrong were not so definite. At least now I felt bad about it. That was something. The drawer popped open with a few twists of my pins, but there was only a few hundred in cash and change. The bills went into the pocket of my new bag, along with my cell. I wanted nothing in my pockets. Too easy to fall out or for others to steal. Water was next on my list. Then, I moved to a row of canned food, the ones with pull-off tops. I would need more than candy bars for food, even though they weren't light to carry.

As I filled my bag, I heard a car door bang. Peering around the aisle, I saw a truck parked next to the closest gas hose. Two men piled out of the vehicle. What were they thinking? There was no electricity and no one here. Did they think they could fill up like every other day?

One man fumbled with the pump, swearing at his friend when nothing happened.

"I told you, man. You can't get gas with no electricity," the passenger said back.

"Fuck you," the short, squatty driver replied. "I'm on empty. We can't get out of here if we don't find a way of filling up."

"You won't be able to get it that way, but I know they have tanks under here we can siphon from."

"Such a bad idea," I mumbled to myself, continuing my own quest.

Wheels screeched to a stop outside the window. I popped my head around the corner again. Another car pulled into the gas station, thumping with music. My adrenaline picked up when three men exited the car, all carrying bats. They reminded me of guys from my neighborhood, trouble written in the way they carried themselves. I needed to get my stuff and get out. Now.

Voices drew closer. "Get the cash, and let's get out of here." Glass cracked as two men took their bats to the window. *Where was the third man?* No time to dwell on his whereabouts, as they were after the cash. The very same money tucked in my bag.

I rushed for the back door and swung it open. The third man's foot was still in the air, and he looked a little stunned at how easy it was to open. His eyes shifted over me, immediately taking in my overfed carrier. "Well, well... looky here." His teeth were large and dominant as he grinned at me. The other guys who tried to break through the window gave up their endeavors and came around the back.

"Look, boys. We have a little kitty burglar." His friends looked me up and down, their eyes glinting. I recognized the intent.

*Dammit.*

"I like pussy... cats," one of the men said. He wore a Mariners baseball hat. The last one had on a Seahawks T-shirt. My mind already named them: Teeth, Mariner, and Seahawk.

Teeth took a step in. I backpedaled farther into the store away from him. "Don't be afraid of us, girl. We promise to all be gentle." Teeth laughed.

"I don't." Seahawk shook his head.

My attention went quickly to the two men out in the truck trying to unlatch the covers to the gas tanks. Would screaming for help work?

Teeth sensed my debate, leaped forward, and grabbed me, his hand covering my mouth. I tried to scream, but he pulled a gun from the back of his pants and shoved it into my temple. "Get the cash, and let's go. We can take her for enjoyment later."

Rape happens a lot more in bad neighborhoods or in foster care than most will admit. People are so angry about life, and they need to feel in control. This somehow makes them feel powerful and in charge. It's disgusting the way people can rationalize violence like this—an extreme version of bullying and getting off by making someone feel weak and helpless. I would not go back to being a victim.

Mariner rifled the register. "It's gone."

"What?" Teeth gripped me tighter.

"The money is gone."

*Oh hell.*

There was a moment of silence while his brain figured out why the money was missing. Then he turned me to face him; burning rage filled his eyes. "Did you take the money, you fucking bitch?" The gun barrel tapped against my temple.

No response came from my lips.

"Give it to me. Now, skank." He cocked the hammer.

*BOOM!*

An explosion hit the glass from the outside, splintering the window into such small pieces it turned to dust. Racks and shelves flew along with the four of us as the pressure pounded into the small store. Time slowed as I soared into the air, my brain noticing bits of the gas pumps and two cars on fire were tossed high. I did not see the other two men, but there was little doubt they did not survive. *Idiots.*

When I did hit the floor, my lower back collided with a magazine rack, then slammed into a counter, causing a hot dog roaster to topple, crashing next to me. The pain was ruthless; my body immediately going numb. I lay in a daze. Everything stilled around me, except the crackle of the blazing gas pump. The three men sprawled unmoving in different parts of the store. One faced me; eyes open. Dead.

Nothing registered, especially the passage of time.

A muffled voice drifted to me. There was a person next to me, speaking. My ears rang so loud I couldn't make out words. With all my might, I willed my head to turn.

I recognized the man, but the identification didn't go any further. His hands were drenched in red. He fumbled with something behind him, a loud snapping of metal, then I was in the air. I couldn't feel his hands or my body as he lifted me. He pressed me close to his chest, extracting us out of the shambles.

Consciousness weaved in and out. Every time sleep claimed me, I was shaken awake by a shirtless guy. His muscular torso labored in breath as he ran. *Why was he topless?*

Sensations gradually came back. Pain in my side was the first throbbing I experienced, but it was a dull ache.

"Stay alive, human," Ryker's gruff voice snarled in my ear. The shrill ringing in my ears had dampened to a low hum.

"Hospital," I managed to mumble.

Ryker shook his head. "No. They're searching for you. They will have people staking out places like that. We can't take the chance. The medical centers will be overrun right now with people hurt last night. You will die before they're able to help you."

My head fell back against his arm to look up at him. He seemed to understand the question in my eyes.

"I know a healer." Ryker's lips pressed together. "I hope she's there." As we zipped through back alleys, my lids slowly closed. "No." He roughly shook me. "If you die, my powers will be trapped inside you. I will never be able to get them back," he growled. "Fucking stay awake, human!"

"Kiss my ass, Wanderer." My tone didn't come out nearly as strong as I would have liked.

He sighed.

I forced my lips into a smile. It took more energy out of me than I planned. My head bobbed and rolled to the side. The throbbing in my side had been growing steadily worse, but until my gaze landed on it, I didn't think it was more than a bad bruise. In Ryker's large hand was a balled-up shirt, his T-shirt, which was soaked with blood. Protruding from the shirt was a chunk of metal embedded in my side. It was a piece of the magazine rack I had slammed against.

Panic circled around my throat like a dust cloud, choking me. The natural instinct was to pull it out, to get the foreign object out of my body, but I knew Ryker did the right thing leaving it in. I would have bled to death in a matter of minutes if he withdrew it. The body and brain were amazing things. They were protecting me from unmanageable pain.

"Don't look at it."

My gaze turned to the ash dropping on us like dark snow. Small charged flakes gracefully fell from the burning sky—the tears of the buildings and people who were no longer here.

The remains of people's lives settled on my face and lashes. The heavy sadness and memories in each fragment pushed on my lids till they could no longer stay open. Pain, stress, and shock shut my body down, protecting it from the harsh world and memories of the people I lost.

# TEN

"Hey, girl. Time to wake up." A hand tapped roughly on my cheek. My lids lifted, wide and confused. Bright hazel eyes contemplated me. A woman with long, thin beach-blonde dreads leaned over me. "Finally decided to join us again, huh?"

I touched my cheek. *What the hell is going on?*

The room was doused in candlelight and the glow from a fire. In the soft light, she appeared to be in her mid-thirties. She was naturally beautiful, but there was something unique about her beauty, a confidence in her own skin that shined through.

That and she was fae.

"Where am I?" My voice cracked with dehydration. She helped me sit up. One arm was covered in a tattoo, the other had a band wrapped around her bicep, and a handful of bracelets dangled from her wrist. The cot underneath me creaked and moaned as I wormed up. The ache in my side struck so fast and quick it ripped the breath from my lungs. Pain filled me as I snorted and grunted in agony.

"Take these." She dropped two white pills in my palm and handed me a cup of water.

"What are they?"

"Painkillers," she snapped. "Now take them and shut up."

"Who are you?" I glanced around. The tiny, dark, cluttered room smelled of fire, herbs, and rubbing alcohol. It was a windowless space with tons of plants lining the shelves and filling pots on the floor. A small clay fireplace burned in the corner with an overstuffed loveseat and a side chair facing it. Books were stacked in every corner and were being used as a side table for the sitting area. It was bohemian chic without the chic part.

"My name is Elthia, but having my name does not answer the question you seek."

"What do you mean?"

"My name is only something you call me. It is not who I am." She brushed her dreads off her shoulder.

"O-kay. Then, what are you?"

"I am a healer. I mended your outer injuries. Your inner wounds are too deep. They are tearing you apart.

I rubbed at my head. Let's try another approach. "How long have I been out? How did I get here?"

"You have been out for three Earth days. And you came here by way of a god." A glint stroked a secretive smile across her lips.

I groaned and looked down at my palm and tossed the pills into my mouth without hesitation, hoping they were poison. The New Age—or maybe in her case, Old Age—spiritual crap was too much for me. My brain could barely hold a thought.

*Pain. Too much pain.*

The water was cool and soothing as it slid down my throat. Discomfort kept me from caring I was only in my bra and panties. She didn't strike me as someone who cared much for clothing. Tape wrapped my waist, holding a huge piece of gauze in place, which was dyed a soft pale red.

Right. I had been impaled on a magazine rack because two stupid idiots tried to siphon gas from the tanks the wrong way. But how mad could I be when their actions had stopped me from getting kidnapped, raped, and murdered?

My memory gave me glimpses of a shirtless man carrying me. Bringing me to this place.

*Ryker.*

"Where's Ryker?" My voice sounded hoarse. Talking took a lot of effort. Tired. I was very tired. My lids lowered under the heaviness. My head dropped farther into my pillow. Pain dissolved away from my side, and a sensation of floating took hold. Light from the fireplace swayed in my vision, turning into a version of animated characters dancing a waltz.

"What's in those?" I held up my hand where the pills once were, watching it make impressions in the air in different colors.

"It's a home remedy." She smiled.

"I feel... a-mazing..." It was all I could get out before I heard her shush me.

"Sleep, girl."

"Okay." I nodded and drifted off, the drugs taking me to faraway lands, which seemed very similar to *Fantasia.*

When I woke again, I felt much better. The pain in my side was still there but was a dull throb instead of razor sharp. My head rolled to the side, hearing a steady rhythm of breathing. Ryker sat in the chair; his head fallen back in sleep. The fire shimmered across his chiseled face. Even sleeping, he was intimidating.

Sensing my gaze, he lifted his lashes, and his eyes locked on mine. I could not decipher any feelings underneath his stoic shell. He did not move an inch or utter a word. His glower only grew more intense, capturing the air in my lungs.

I turned my face to the ceiling. "If you're going to torture me for running, then this is the perfect time. I'm defenseless and vulnerable."

The chair creaked as he got up, his boots hitting the old wooden floors.

"Seriously, do it now." I probably shouldn't have been encouraging him to hurt me, but if he were going to do it, I wanted it over with. Then, maybe Elthia would give me a few more of those White Rabbit pills. They were amazing.

Ryker reached the side of my bed. He still did not speak, which irritated me more than the idea of him torturing me.

Narrowing with annoyance, my eyes flickered to his face. "Oh my god. Talk. Say something." I tried to sit. It hurt like hell, but I was not going to show him I was in pain. I wiggled up enough to lean against the wall.

"You've been unconscious for a week now. I had many opportunities to hurt you."

A week? Last time I was conscious, it had only been three days.

His eyes darted to my waist and slowly came back up to my face, stalling for a bit around my boobs. His lids narrowed, his eyes flashing with disgust. Even though I hated his guts, his revulsion of me, of my body, hurt. No, I wasn't stick thin like his model girlfriend, nor was I fae. Instead, I was two things he obviously didn't like—human and curvy. I snatched the blanket and pulled it higher.

"Don't flatter yourself." One of his eyebrows twitched.

"Go fuck yourself." Wow. He seemed to bring out the best in me.

He clamped his jaw together and leaned over, placing his palms on either side of my pillow, barricading me.

"Do not piss me off, human. I can rip you in half without even trying," he hissed through his teeth.

I pressed my head back onto the wall, trying to put distance between us.

He only moved closer; anger heated his eyes. "I have to keep you alive, but there is such a varying range in that. You only need to be breathing. Somewhat."

I forced my chin to stay up; my fists clenched. I would not give him the satisfaction of seeing me flinch. I held my ground. It's what I did. Actually, with an ordinary guy, I would use this situation to my advantage, but Ryker was not a normal male. He did not find my curves a distraction but more an aggravation.

"Do what you need to do," I growled back. He did

not move. Our eyes locked in a standoff. My chest rose, air skimming in and out.

"I got the girl some clothes. I hope they fit." Elthia's voice traveled to us from above, her feet clomping down the groaning wooden steps.

Ryker twisted and sprang away from me, putting space between us. By the time Elthia reached the bottom, Ryker stood by the sofa, his hands clasped on his hips. She looked at him, then at me. Her brows inched down, creasing the bridge of her nose. She cleared her throat, quickly shooting Ryker another look, before turning her attention back to me.

She held up the garments. "Jeans, tank top, sweater, and a jacket someone left at a laundromat. I doubt they'll be coming back for them." She tossed the clothes at the foot of my bed. Her own outfit was made of white linen pants, layers of tanks, and a brightly colored scarf wrapped around her hair, keeping it off her face.

"Thank you." I shifted the blanket, holding it firmly to me as I reached for the clothes. The stretch pulled at my stomach wound. I flinched, pain flooding me.

"Sorry. You need to heal, but I can't have you here. I think someone is already watching my place." She turned to Ryker. "Garrett has spies everywhere. You have a bounty on your head, and if they even suspect you are here... I've already risked too much by having you this long. He will eventually come here looking for you."

It wasn't what she said, but how she said it, and the meaningful glance she gave Ryker revealed they had history. My intuition told me they had been lovers.

I studied her closer. She was bohemian, carefree, and pretty. She was taller than me, but her figure was actually very similar to mine. Much curvier than Amara's. But where I was toned from training, she was softer and more womanly. She was warm to his aloofness. Unlike Amara, she probably loosened his tightly wound ass.

Ryker nodded. "I understand, El. I appreciate what you have done for us. As soon as she's ready, we will get out of here."

She shifted her stance. A longing spread over her face, and she nodded. "Be careful, Ryker. Garrett is dangerous, and he wants nothing more than to find you." The yearning vanished from her expression. She turned and jogged up the stairs.

He watched her disappear, then whirled on me. "Get dressed."

"Ex-girlfriend, huh?" I swung my feet over the side, placing my toes on the smooth wood.

"Dress. Now." He crossed his arms.

"Touchy, aren't we?" If he was going to harass me, I would do the same in return. "Bad breakup?" I tilted my head in false pity. "She dump you?"

A rumble echoed in his chest, which only made me smile wider.

"Doesn't seem your type. She's cool. I thought you liked the skinny, bitchy ones. Amara know you dated such a free spirit?" The moment her name crossed my lips, I knew I stepped over the line.

He bolted for me, his arms latched on to mine, and he heaved me onto my feet. The abrasive moment wrenched at my stitches. Deep red colored the gauze.

"I told you to never speak her name."

The tattoo up his neck sparked before he took a deep breath and pushed me away from him. "Now get dressed before I do it for you."

"Oh, I think *El* will get a little jealous if you do." I put special emphasis on the pet name he called her.

His chest went in and out in a fast, repetitive motion, his fists clenching at his sides.

This girl hadn't shown herself in a while—the girl I was before I met Daniel—angry, argumentative, and aggressive. Taunting was a favorite pastime on the streets, and I was good at it. Three years of Daniel mellowing me was tossed aside in only one week with this guy.

Ryker took a step to me. He swiped the tank off the bed and pulled it over my head. "Arms up."

"I am not a child."

"Stop acting like one." He grabbed my arm and threaded the top through.

I stepped away from him. "I can dress myself."

"Then do it." He crossed his arms and waited for me to continue.

"You can go. I've been dressing myself since I was three."

"Then you should be better at it by now." It was clear he wasn't leaving.

I sighed and pushed my other arm through the hole. It was my bad side, and I balked as anguish ran up my torso, freezing my arm. I pinched my lids together, breathing through the pain.

When the stabbing ache subsided a little, I tried to go on. The tank top was the easy one. I pulled the sweater up my arms but couldn't get it on.

Ryker stood there, watching me. "Do you need help?"

I glared at him, my upper lip rising in a snarl. I tried again, the sweater neck getting caught on my head. Dizziness had me bending over. Either I was going to throw up or pass out. Both sounded awesome. "Yes. Fine. Help." I gave in.

The sweater covered my face, but I could feel the heat of his body step up to mine. He got my head through the sweater's neck and tugged it down more gently than I imagined. It fit but was a bit snug. Where I was raised, most girls went out of their way to emphasize certain parts of their figures. On the other hand, I didn't want to be noticed any more than I was. I preferred loose clothing rather than tight.

My pride took a hit when I tried to get the skinny jeans on. Getting them over my thighs and hips without dancing like a hyper Chihuahua was impossible. Sweat beaded my forehead. I was in pain and exhausted and only wanted to lie back down and go to sleep.

"This is taking forever." He bent and grabbed the waist of the pants. The hair on top of his head brushed my legs, tickling my thighs as he straightened. His knuckles ran along my legs as he yanked the jeans up to my waist. He quickly zipped and buttoned them before kicking my boots to me. "I think you can do those yourself."

I swallowed, my throat dotted with dry patches. Sitting on the bed, I slipped my feet into the boots, zipping them up. I just had a fae touch me, really touch me. It wasn't desired on either side, and it left me uncomfortable and flustered. Not in a million years did I imagine a fae would be dressing me. There were many things in the last couple days I never thought possible, but this one might top them all.

"Here." He tossed the messenger bag I stole from the convenience store on top of my newly inherited jacket. "Let's go." He started up the stairs.

My legs trembled as I stood. I grabbed the coat and looped the bag over my head, placing it on my good side. My hand felt my phone inside. It was a strange comfort, even if it couldn't call anyone. It was the last thing I had of my old world and life. Before Ryker. For better or worse, I was stuck with him. Disasters sure did make for interesting bedfellows, even if it was only temporary.

Yeah, I didn't really like that saying. The thought of him in bed—I shook my head and followed him upstairs.

Elthia was sitting at the kitchen table and drinking something that smelled like rosemary and wet dirt. Ryker dropped the fake door back onto the floor, covering the entrance to the basement with a rug where she hid us—a secret room for stowaways.

She gripped her cup; her legs folded underneath her.

"El, I owe you." Ryker pushed me toward the back window. Rain pelted the glass, the evening light giving the room a dim glow.

A tortured smile worked up to her eyes. "Yeah." I had teased Ryker about her dumping him, but it was clear it was the other way around. Even if she let him go, she was still in love with him. She pushed her shoulders back and stood, a forced smile on her face. "Don't be a stranger, Ryker." She planted herself in front of him, her body leaning into his. She reached up and touched his face. "I can feel you. Your heart is still seeking," she whispered to him.

I turned my head, staring out at the rain. Their reflection animated the glass. I felt I was intruding on a private moment.

"If you ever need me... for anything..."

He cleared his throat. "I know."

"If I hear about anyone who can help you get your powers back, I'll send word. Watch our spots."

In the window reflection, I saw him kiss her head gently. He pivoted on his heels, his eyes catching mine watching them. His expression went from soft to stone. Raging hate pummeled through the window at me, as if it were my fault he was leaving. His anger only pissed me off. I was injured, tired, hungry, and about to be drenched. I didn't want to go either. Ryker opened the window. Her cottage backed up to an alleyway, the rear of other houses sharing the lane.

"You have enough food?" she asked.

"Yes, Elthia. You have done more than enough."

*Food?* My stomach rumbled on cue. Loudly.

Ryker tilted his head, glaring at my rumbling tummy. I rubbed at it, telling it to be quiet. He crawled through the window and jumped to the ground.

"Thank you, Elthia."

I sat on the sill. I didn't know what else to say. How did you thank someone for saving your life, when most likely she only did it because Ryker asked her?

She bit at her bottom lip. "If you get him killed, I will hunt you down." Her tone was not spiteful, merely matter of fact.

I paused. "All righty." Giving her a nod, I turned to go through the window. Information like her threat was always good to know.

"Take the green pills until you run out and the white only when you need them," she said before she closed the window, shutting us off from the warmth and safety of her home.

Rain tapped on my head. I slipped on the jacket, tugged up the hood, and trailed Ryker through the dark alley, back into the cold world where everything was out to get us, and nowhere was safe.

# ELEVEN

Rain always looked romantic in movies. Almost sexy. Let me tell you, there was nothing remotely sexy about being so chilled to the bone your body was vibrating with tremors. My teeth chattered so loudly that Ryker yelled at me a few times to "keep it down." Between my teeth and my growling stomach, I was like a one-man band.

"As if I can help it." *Bastard.* For some reason, it felt more meaningful to call him names in my head. He didn't seem to care when I said them to his face. And, well, that took all the fun out of it.

Ryker skirted the water, following the piers along the harbor. Night had crept in, sneaking over us and deadening the gray sky till it was black. We turned up a street, and lights from a distance blurred my eyes. "What is that?" I pointed. "Does the city have electricity again?" I'd been unconscious for a week. A lot could happen in that time.

"Red Cross," Ryker stated. "They're running off government-issued generators. When you were unconscious, they erected shelters here and on the north and west sides. Your president has declared Seattle a natural disaster zone."

Hope lit my numb muscles. "They'll have food and blankets." My feet moved before I even asked them to.

"Wait." I heard him call, but I kept moving. A block away, my feet stopped short.

"Dammit. I told you to wait," Ryker growled, stopping beside me. His attention quickly turned to what I was staring at.

A news crew stood in front of the shelter...their equipment plugged into their own portable generators. A petite brunette stood in front of the camera, wearing a wrinkled beige skirt and jacket, surrounded by handfuls of people with signs. Some conveyed destruction was a result of global warming; other posters suggested aliens had attacked us. But one demonstrator stood out. Glowing with fae glamour, his sign stated the end of the world was upon us. The back of his board had a fairy on it.

"Why would he do this? He's fae." I pointed at the man.

"Because some fae don't want to hide what they are anymore. They want humans to know about us. To take back what they feel was once theirs." Ryker brushed the rain off his forehead with the back of his hand. "They are provoking the Seelie Queen to act."

I had heard about the Seelie Queen. Most fae we captured had nothing nice to say about her. Ruthless and cruel seemed to be the most common descriptions. I didn't need to know anything else about her. She was fae and despised humans. She was an enemy, plain and simple.

The camera lights came on, and the woman anchor began to speak into the mic. "Today we are at the Red Cross center located in downtown Seattle." Soft rain dampened her fluffy-styled hair. "Thousands have come to seek shelter here. Already, it has reached its max, and hundreds are still outside, homeless and starving." She pressed at something in her ear. "Yes, Dan, the electric storm, ES as the locals are calling it, has affected the area more than a hundred miles in all directions of Seattle. Scientists and experts have no idea what caused a storm of this magnitude to hit such a narrow area, then spread so far. The lack of knowledge of what could create such a disaster has left people to formulate their own ideas." She took a pause, motioning to the signs around her. "No matter the cause, the fact remains as of now 2,059 are confirmed dead and at least 3,000 are still missing. With each passing day, we know the death toll will only rise."

"We need to get away from here." Ryker grabbed my arm. "We can't risk it with cameras and fae around."

"What? Why?" All I could think about was being warm and fed. Rain slid in rivers down my face, too fast for me to bother wiping it away. It pooled at the base of my neck.

He studied me, his expression considering if I could really be so stupid.

"Right." Disappointment clamped on my gut and hunched my shoulders. We were both being hunted, which meant we had to stay away from public or government-run facilities. If we were caught on camera, it would not be good. Most likely the DMG and Garrett had these places staked, ready for us to pass through.

"We have food for tonight. Tomorrow morning I'll investigate the area first." His attention went from the glow of the tents to the dark coldness behind us, his hand still clutching my arm. "If we do go in tomorrow, we will need to be extra cautious, and it is only to eat and get supplies, then we get out." He tugged me down an alley, away from the warmth I wanted badly.

I stepped from his grasp. "You might not need food, but I do." I poked at my torso. "Human needs nutrients."

He put his hands on his hips and looked to the side. "Fine. We'll take cover in one of those buildings." He nodded toward the warehouse buildings near the ferries.

"They look warm and cozy." I wrapped my arms around myself.

"Stop pouting, human." He swiveled and started for the building. "Or I'll—"

"Most likely kill me in the morning?" I derided, cutting him off with one of my favorite movie quotes.

He looked over his shoulder, his lids narrowed. "I wish."

He really was a killjoy.

"Be careful, human. One day I might decide my magic isn't worth keeping you alive for."

Nothing like a good old-fashioned death threat to get your blood boiling again.

We walked in silence to the warehouse. He climbed the fence. The *Do Not Enter, Private Property, Trespassers Will Be Prosecuted* sign taunted us in big red letters. "Come on."

I laced my fingers through the gate and pulled myself up. Every move was torture to my wound and tugged at the stitches Elthia sewed into my side. My limbs shook with cold, and it took me a couple tries before I got over the fence.

Ryker snapped the padlock and chain off the door. "I haven't had to break a lock since I was a child," he mumbled to himself. I was aware he could jump in and out of places, but it was time I really understood his powers and what I was holding.

As he slid the door closed, the relentless rain finally halted its assault. The space was dry, but the metal siding and cement floor produced an even colder chill in the room.

"We need to be careful, but I'll make us a fire in one of those metal drums."

He found some newspaper and old rags still saturated in oil from the boat engines. He pulled a lighter from his pocket and flames engulfed the material at the bottom of the barrel. I hovered so far into the container I almost fell in. My bones creaked as they thawed, muscles throbbing, unwinding their tight grasp on each other.

Ryker made his way around the building, checking for any threats. "People are definitely staying here. There's food and bedding upstairs."

"Really?" The thought of leaving the warmth of the fire to go back in the rain almost incited me to chain myself to the drum in protest. Whatever expression was on my face must have conveyed my reluctance.

"As soon as you are warm and have eaten, we take off. I do not feel like dealing with whomever is staying here."

I frowned but nodded.

Instead of using the food he was carrying, Ryker stole cans of raviolis and fruit from the current guests and passed them to me. He dragged two crates from against the wall and set them close to the fire. I plopped down and popped the tops of the rations and dug in, not bothering with heating them. All the work of getting the food from the gas station, and most of it didn't make it. Only a few granola bars survived the explosion and journey to Elthia's. I got impaled for nothing.

"How long were you and Elthia together?" I popped the top of a can of peaches, struggling to picture them together.

Ryker stared at me from under his lashes. His jaw gnashed in warning.

"We are going to be stuck together for who knows how long. Tell me something about yourself."

Ryker finished his pasta and set the can to the side. Silence.

"Come on. I'm not going to relent till you tell me something. Tell me more about these powers I'm carrying... or why Garrett is after you?"

Ryker ripped off the top of his peaches, drinking the sugary juice before he started on the fruit.

"I think I have the right to know what is going on since I am holding these powers of yours."

He tensed. "You have no rights to anything."

"Because I'm human?"

"And annoying as hell." He ran his hands over his hair. It made me curious what he would look like with the braids undone and his hair down. Would it give a softer illusion to him? Although that was all it would be—an illusion. "I get it. You're the stoic, silent type."

"And you're the obnoxious, gabby type."

A rankle of irritation bumped along my spine. I took a deep breath, turning back to my meal. A few minutes of us eating in a strained muteness passed before Ryker set his second tin down. "All you need to know is Garrett is after me, and he will not stop until he finds me. He has taken Amara, and he will go after you next if he can't get to me. He has no idea I no longer have my powers, and I plan on keeping this information from him."

"What is this stone he wants? Is it worth a lot?"

"It's not a stone like you think. It's not a diamond or any kind of gem. It's what this stone can do which makes it desired." Ryker leaned his elbows on his legs. "Garrett is not the one I'm running from. It is the man he works for. No one has met him in person; Garrett is his face and hired muscle. They call this man Vadik, and he is wealthy, extremely dangerous, and powerful. He hired me for a job. It wasn't till I had the object in my hands I realized what he was having me steal, and I ran. Let's say this man is not too happy I reneged on our deal. He will do everything in his ability to get it back, and I will do everything in mine to keep it from him."

"Even let him have Amara?"

Ryker clenched his fists. "The stone cannot get into this man's hands, no matter what. Amara understands."

"So you sacrificed her? You can simply let someone you love be thrown to the wolves?"

"You know nothing about the situation or her, human." Ryker's tattoo kindled with energy. "I will get her back."

"I know nothing because you won't tell me anything," I challenged. "What does this stone do? Why is it dangerous for Vadik to possess it?"

Ryker rubbed a hand across his mouth, contemplating. "Have you ever heard of the Stone of Destiny?" I shook my head. "In fae mythology there are four magical artifacts: a sword, spear, cauldron, and the stone, *Lia Fáil*, Stone of Destiny. Most think because no one has seen any of these objects for centuries, they are merely legends. Legends often stem from truth. These items are so powerful they can destroy the world, if put in the wrong hands."

"You're actually being the good guy here?"

"Good and bad are only a matter of degrees. My interest in the object is not your concern."

"Really? Not my concern? You can destroy the Earth instead of this man, Vadik?"

"I do not wish to destroy Earth or take over. My interest in the stone is a lot less diabolical."

"Money."

"Partially."

"And now you have this guy by the balls while you are marketing the stone to others?" I inclined forward.

"I won't let it fall into anyone's hands. It's far too powerful. But my ultimate goal is money." He shifted on the crate. "No matter the amount of money, I will not give it to Vadik. It has to be the right person, for the right price."

"Your version of ethics?" I snorted. "Glad you are choosey about who gets to destroy us."

"Believe what you want about me." He slipped off the box and rested against it. "The stone is capable of destroying, but it is also able to create. It depends on the holder's intentions. And I didn't say it was Earth it would destroy. You assumed I was speaking of Earth. It can cripple the Otherworld as well." His lids drifted close.

"Would you let your world be destroyed?"

He grunted. "Like you care what happens to the Otherworld."

My mouth opened, then closed. He was right. I was being a hypocrite. The fae world felt like this faraway dreamland that didn't actually exist. If something happened to it, would I be upset? Most likely not, because it didn't seem real to me or hold people I cared about. It held creatures I considered cruel and soulless.

"But don't worry. Most fae would not want to destroy Earth. It's like a buffet of sin, debauchery, and hate. All the things dark fae live off. They need humans."

My nose wrinkled in disgust. "And you don't? You're dark fae."

"I am special."

"You're a pig."

"Oink."

It was best I moved away before I punched him. It was colder the farther I moved from the fire, but I figured it was better than breaking my hand hitting his face. I found a pile of blankets by the stairs and curled into them. With my belly full and the pills Elthia gave me to lessen my pain, I quickly drifted to sleep.

A hand slipped over my mouth, jolting me from my

slumber. A scream quaked in my chest as arms pulled me back into its form. Heat radiated off the body, pushing through my clothes into my back.

"Shhh..." Ryker whispered close to my ear, keeping his hand locked on my mouth.

My brain was trying to grasp what was going on when I heard the voices. The door rolled back before a clatter of feet moved across the stone.

"What the fuck? Someone broke the lock," a male voice echoed off the walls. "Dart. Check every inch. If the asshole is still here, I want him found."

*Hell.* We didn't plan on falling asleep. Not for this long, anyway. Now we were going to get caught by the prior inhabitants.

"Yes, boss." The small man hightailed it up the stairs, his feet inches from our faces. I sucked in a breath, pressing back into Ryker. The guy's speed gave me no doubt as to why he was called Dart.

In the darkness I could make out the forms by the door, more than a dozen of them. Ryker pulled us into the darkest shadows under the stairs, but it wouldn't be long till they found us.

"Do you think it's the Scorpions?" another male voice asked.

"I'm in charge of this city now. If they don't bow to me, they will fall. The government has no control here anymore. And I plan to keep it this way."

A burly man walked in, his automatic weapon at his side. "All clear outside, Marcello."

The leader, Marcello, folded his arms across his chest. Tension filled the air. He appeared to be in his thirties. Dark, wavy hair curled around his ears and neck accenting his olive skin. He wasn't especially tall or good looking, but he held a power that drew you in, almost fooling you into thinking he was.

"Sorry, I meant Boss." The man looked at the floor.

"I know the loss of my brother is an adjustment, but if you disrespect me again, you will be joining him. Six feet under. This goes for any of you," Marcello threatened. "I have been lenient. But no more. The next person who disrespects me will be taken care of. Got it?"

He wasn't the normal gang leader I pictured. He was dressed nicely, and he spoke like he had been educated. It wouldn't be the run-of-the-mill gangbangers who would take over the city. It would be the smart, crafty ones—more like the mafia. Everything would be thought through and planned. It would not be based on random violence as much as who had the most power. Not to say there wouldn't be a lot of carnage as he achieved it, but the leader would be methodical and smart about his decisions. He'd treat it like a business and not because he was an angry young punk looking for a fight. This made me fear them more.

"Marcello..." Another man entered from outside. "All the supplies we looted from the Red Cross are secure in the storage units."

Marcello drew his pistol from his waistband and shot the guy between the eyes. Ryker's hand pushed against my mouth tighter, keeping in the scream. Blood spilled from the hole in the man's forehead, his body hitting the concrete.

I curled farther into Ryker's strong torso and tried to swallow back the automatic panic. I had seen a lot of men die in my time, but you never got used to it and just got better at hiding your shock. It had been a while since I'd seen this kind of point-blank kill.

"This," Marcello gestured with his arm as he continued, "is a warning to all of you. I am true to my word. The same fate will come to the next person who insults me. Let's not forget it again."

All the men bowed their heads in recognition of Marcello, doing a good job of not reacting to their comrade's death. Using fear to control people was an excellent tool if you wanted to stay in charge.

Metal through the brain did not seem like a fun way to go. I frantically looked around for an escape.

"We're trapped." Ryker spoke softly. "I am going to have to do this the fae way."

What did he mean by *the fae way*?

He gave me no time to ask before he spoke again. "Stay here." Ryker's lips grazed my earlobe as he talked. "Do. Not. Move." The heat from him evaporated as he slipped from under the stairs, his arm reaching for his axe.

I hated sitting back. It was not something I was good at, but I also knew these men were armed with guns and probably knives. I was in trouble without a weapon. If I tried to take them on, the outlook for me was neither a bright one nor my life a long one.

Through the gap in the stairs, I saw Ryker silently slink behind one of the men, knocking him out. He lowered the torso without a sound. I was glad I never ran into him when I had been collecting. His movement and stealth for such a muscular guy was something I had never seen. Daniel trained me thoroughly, but we would have been no match for Ryker.

"Boss," a voice rang from the second-story catwalk. The man called Dart was pointing at Ryker. In a blink of an eye, Ryker pulled out another dagger and flung it at Dart. The knife pierced the middle of his chest. Dart stilled before his body tipped forward and fell over the railing. His head hit first, exploding like a pumpkin. Blood and brain matter splashed on the floor.

I turned away, a retch gagging my throat.

Marcello's men reacted instantly, drawing guns. Ryker leaped for them, his axe swinging. Gunshots boomed through the space, bouncing off walls and the sound assaulting my eardrums. I capped my ears and hunched, trying to make myself less of a target. Ryker sliced through one man and swung the end of the stick back, the wood handle meeting the middle of another man's forehead. Two. Three. Four. Five. In a matter of seconds, half the men hit the floor, bleeding or out cold. The other gang members would not relent till all were down. Marcello raised his pistol and shot at Ryker, the bullets tearing through his clothes and boring deep into his body. It slowed him only a bit, but he kept a steady pace till he reached the leader. Marcello emptied the magazine, the ting of the casings hitting the floor. Ryker's hand wrapped around the gang leader's neck and lifted him off the cement.

"You humans never learn," Ryker seethed and then tossed Marcello across the room. He collided with the cement wall and tumbled to the ground, motionless. Silence took hold of the large warehouse, except for Ryker's deep breaths and the ringing in my ears. He bent, his hands on his knees, and grunted in pain.

I crept from under the stairs. "Are you okay?" I moved next to him. "That was insane. Seriously. I don't want to admit it, but I'm impressed." He grunted again in response. A tapping sound on the ground drew my attention to the blood leaking from him. "Oh my god, Ryker."

"I'll be fine," he gritted through his teeth.

"Yeah, I know." I shrugged. "But it still has to hurt like a bitch."

He snorted, shaking his head. A slight smile hitched the side of his mouth. "Yes, it does but still less aggravating than you."

"Sorry. If you were looking for sympathy from me, you're not getting any. I know you can't be killed by normal bullets."

He struggled to straighten up. "I won't die, but it doesn't mean getting shot twenty times doesn't do some damage. And hurt like hell." He looked around at the scattered bodies on the floor. Most were living except the guy Marcello killed, one Ryker sliced into, and Dart who fell from above.

"We need to get out of here before they wake." Ryker hobbled for the door. "I need to find a place to rest for the night."

"Let me help." I went to his side, pulling his arm across my shoulder.

He shuddered. "I don't need your assistance, human."

"Fine." I stepped away. "Crawl for all I care."

"I would rather," he snarled.

"I'd prefer you did, too." I stomped through the door, letting it slam in his face.

# TWELVE

The one thing I learned from the night, besides seeing Ryker's ninja talents in person, was Seattle was being taken over. And more than one gang was vying for control. Their fights never worked well for the rest of us.

Now Ryker and I had another worry. Not only were DMG and Garrett after us, but once Marcello woke up, he and his men would be pissed. They would not rest till they found us. Retaliation on someone who made you look like a weak fool would be dealt with.

We bedded for the night in an already ransacked café. All food and bottle liquids were gone, but there was one thing left which made me happy. I sucked contently on chocolate-covered espresso beans, trying to stay awake as I kept watch. Ryker fell asleep the moment his head hit the upholstered bench. He tried to stretch, but he could barely fit on it. He warily gave me an extra dagger he had strapped to his leg to defend myself. I was curious how many "extra" daggers the man had on him. Visually, I could count five. Who knew how many I couldn't see?

The axe, against my pleas, was off limits. It was non-negotiable, no matter how many life-and-death situations I gave him. I think he was too worried I would use it on him.

*Very tempting.*

In an employee locker, I found some Advil and swallowed them along with the medication Elthia gave me. The stitches in my side weren't bleeding but pulsed with forceful pain. I snuggled into the corner booth and held vigil, sucking away at my source of caffeine.

A clank of metal falling in the back room stilled me. My muscles and lungs froze mid-movement. My head tilted, listening, hoping it wouldn't tell me it was something more than a rat trying to scavenge for food. Another knock and scuffle stirred on the other side of the door where the kitchen was.

"Ryker?" I whispered hoarsely at him. "Ryker!" I threw a spoon at his head. Nothing. Not even a twitch. He was dead to the world as he tried to heal. I hated thinking because he was out of commission, we were helpless. I could fight. Hell, I used to be very dangerous. Some even feared me. But I hadn't been that person in a long time.

I scooted to the end of the bench. A loud crash of dishes falling to the tile floor had me jumping out of the seat. I gripped the knife and tiptoed to the kitchen, peeping through the circular window in the swinging door.

Neither the DMG nor Marcello's gang would bother sneaking from behind. They would crash through the front door and take us. Fae were more devious. I would not put it past Garrett to play with us.

My shoulder pushed into the door, opening it as quietly as I could. It took a while for my eyes to adjust to the shadows. Broken dishes cluttered the tile, but the place had already been destroyed by looters, so it didn't make much of a difference. I snuck farther into the room, the dagger ready to attack.

An object jumped on my shoulder, latching onto my neck. A furry substance brushed across my face, and I let out a piercing scream.

"It's you! I found you," a voice squeaked into my ear, and little hands touched both sides of my face.

"Sprig?" I took in a gulp of air.

"Of course." He patted my cheek. "Seriously, tell me, do you know other sprite-monkeys? Is it why you get confused so easily?"

I put a hand to my chest, trying to calm my nerves. "No. Only you."

"Then you shouldn't be perplexed each time."

"Sorry. Still getting used to the idea of a talking monkey," I said in a shaky breath, my shoulders finally relaxing. "How did you find me?" Then my eyes darted to his wrist. The bracelet was no longer there. "How did you get away?"

Sprig jumped off my shoulder onto the counter. "Yeah, thanks for leaving me, by the way."

"Sorry. I didn't really have a choice at the time."

Sprig sat on his hind legs, crossing his arms. "Yeah, you're still with the psycho prick. I can smell his blood all through the place. Did you finally shoot him?"

"Not on this occasion, but it's only a matter of time." I smirked. "And again, I'm not staying with him by choice. It's complicated."

"Yeah, I'll bet." Sprig winked. "I've seen the size of his hands and feet."

"Ugh. Don't gross me out." I flinched at the imagery. "How did you find me?"

"I told you. I have a debt to repay. I can always find you. It took me a while to get away from those trackers and to get some gullible knobhead to take the bracelet off without me having to open my mouth. Not an easy feat, may I say. I'm hungry." Sprig's attention went off on another tangent. I was thinking my little narcoleptic had an ADD problem as well. He jumped from shelf to shelf searching for food. He took something from a Tupperware box. "What is this?" He sniffed it.

"A bay leaf. Don't," Sprig shoved it in his mouth, "... eat it," I finished.

He munched on the leaf and shrugged, stuffing more into his mouth.

"If you get sick, don't blame me."

"I never get sick," he huffed. "Except the time they gave me Cheetos. I ate the whole bag, then threw up."

"Sounds about right."

"What's the plan?" He hopped to another shelf and sprinkled paprika in his mouth. "Ahhh!" He batted at his tongue. "I thought it was cinnamon."

"Follow me." I motioned to the dining room area. He tailed after me and hopped onto the table. I grabbed my bag and retrieved a granola bar. "We'll share."

Sprig's eyes widened in awe. "Is it one of those honey-filled delights?"

"Uh?" I read the description. "It has honey in it."

He licked his thin, little lips, prancing in place. "Honey, honey, honey," he chanted.

I split the bar and gave him half. He pinched it from my finger and sniffed it. "Oh yeah." He took a bite and fell back on the table, wiggling in utter bliss, like it was catnip for monkeys.

Honey. Right. I had forgotten. When I first started at DMG, I had read the best way to collect a sprite was by laying a trap of honey, any variety. It was their Achilles' heel. All fae liked sweet items, but honey was a sprite's first love.

"I'm gonna take a guess here... you like honey."

"Sent by the gods," he mumbled between bites. His lids closed, and in an instant a soft snore came from him. He was sound asleep with a piece of the bar still in his clutch and in mid-chew.

I snickered and shoved the other half in my mouth. I settled back into the corner, eyeing both my companions. How much my life changed in a week. How much I had lost. Loneliness took hold, cracking at my heart. I dug back into my bag, grasping my beat-up cell phone. The screen was cracked and the battery was dying. Soon it would be useless, but I needed to see them again.

I clenched my teeth, the ache in my heart unbearable. Still I had to look. My need to not feel utterly alone eclipsed the pain I knew I would experience.

The first picture was of Lexie. It was after her doctor's appointment, the one where they told me her blood work wasn't looking good. I decided to take her to her favorite doughnut place as a treat. She was stuffing a doughnut in her face and flipping me off. The next one was the same morning, but it was simply a picture of her giggling. I didn't remember what made her laugh. It didn't matter. I was now glad I never told her what the doctors feared—she would be completely paralyzed.

The next one was of Daniel and me. It was of the two of us at Kate's birthday. Teeth sawed into my bottom lip as I held the picture to my heart before looking at it. Daniel's face smiled at me. This was the night I remembered feeling something change between us. All the hope I had for us when I took this picture. The innocence of thinking we had forever ahead of us. You always think there will be a tomorrow. More time. Then the tomorrow is taken from you, ripping hope and your future from you. I placed the cell on the table, my head falling back against the booth. I had eaten a dozen espresso beans, but nothing could stop the ache from dragging me into a sleep. I needed an escape from the unrelenting loss.

"I know him." My lids opened to the picture of Daniel shoved in my face. Sprig's fingers wrapped around the edges of my phone, bringing it so close my eyes crossed.

I pushed it away from my face. "What?"

"I know him." Sprig brought the snapshot near again.

I snatched it from his hands and placed it on the table. Dawn light filtered through the blinds of the café. "What do you mean you know him?"

"He came to the lab a few times."

I straightened. "Daniel worked at DMG, but I doubt you'd know him. He was a hunter. He didn't go in the labs. None of us did."

Sprig shook his head, his finger tapping on the

screen. The battery blinked red. "No. He came a few times. He talked to me."

"Talked to you?" My eyebrows lowered in a crease. "I think you are confusing him with a scientist. Daniel never went down there. We weren't allowed." I hadn't even known the level Sprig was on existed. Daniel made it clear he knew nothing about the lower levels. *"I don't know what they do there. I don't want to know."* I remembered thinking his statement was strange. It almost sounded anti-DMG. But if he did know about the lower levels, why would he lie to me?

"Are you sure?" I held up the picture of Daniel and me. "He was the one you saw?" It held for another moment before the battery died, the screen going black.

He nodded. "Yeah, he was wearing the same sweater. And he said his name was Holt."

A small gasp came up. Why would Daniel be going there? Why wouldn't he tell me? When I met Sprig, I realized the DMG scientists were going much further than testing and taking samples. They were taking parts of animals and fae and joining them to make a Frankenstein-like monster to experiment with and torture. If I were honest with myself, would I have found it ghastly even a week ago? I would have been against it, but more for the animals' sake, not the fae's.

"He asked me all these questions about what was being done to me." Sprig's attentiveness was drifting as he dug in my bag, finding another candy bar. "Can I have this?"

"Sprig, what did Daniel ask you? What did he want?" Sprig wrinkled the wrapper till I took it away from him. "Sprig?"

"Uh, I don't remember. About the experiments. If I knew of others..." Sprig tried to grab the candy back. "I don't remember anything more. He wrote it all down, so why don't you go bother him?" He jumped for the package I kept out of his reach.

"He's dead."

"Oh. Sorry." Sprig paused.

"You said he wrote everything down."

"Yeah, he had a folder full of notes. And he told me not to tell anyone he'd been there."

I lowered the bar and let Sprig take it. I knew I wouldn't get much more from him, but something told me not to forget this information. Daniel knew something and had kept it from me. He was also hiding it from the DMG. Why? I needed to discover what was going on, and Daniel was the only one who could provide the information. Well, Daniel's apartment hopefully would.

By the time Ryker woke up, I was climbing the walls. It might have been the burning need to go to Daniel's or the twenty-seven chocolate-covered espresso beans I had while waiting for Ryker. Who knew? Guess it would remain a mystery.

He scarcely sat before I bounced to him. "We're going to Daniel's. Okay? Okay. Let's go!" I clapped my hands.

Ryker's gaze narrowed on me.

"Come on, get up." I bobbed on one leg, then shifted to the other.

His head moved around the room, taking in his surroundings.

"Ryker, we have to go." I continued to bobble.

His hand came up and covered my mouth. "Shut up."

I blinked rapidly. Then I licked his hand.

"Ugh." He drew it away, drying his palm on his pants. "What the hell are you on right now?" he grumbled, swinging his legs to the floor. He rubbed at the top of his head.

"Someone's grumpy."

"Maybe because I got shot more than twenty times, and I'm confronted by a strung-out cheerleader."

"I'm not strung out," I babbled quickly, which caused an eyebrow to quirk. "I'm not."

"If she is, she didn't share." Sprig hopped from the table where he had been sleeping. "All I saw her eat was a ton of these things." Sprig held up an espresso bean.

"Fuck." Ryker put his arms on the table and sat back with annoyance. "How the hell did you find us?"

"I told you. I owe her." Sprig looked at Ryker then at me. "Both of you really have crappy memories." Funny coming from Sprig.

"He doesn't have the tracker on him anymore. I checked." My sentence coming faster than my lips could form the words.

"You are cut off." Ryker pointed at me, making my relentless bounce deflate a bit.

"No! Why?" Caffeine. He couldn't take my caffeine away from me.

Ryker motioned to me. "How many did you eat?"

"Twenty... or maybe it was closer to thirty."

Ryker laid his head back on the seat.

"Maybe he should have some?" Sprig fake whispered to me, and I nodded.

"So what is this about going to your boyfriend's house?"

In one sentence, my buzz fizzled.

Boyfriend. Daniel.

As Ryker ate one of the breakfast bars, I filled him in on the conversation Sprig and I had. How he knew Daniel.

"Why would I care?" He tossed the last chunk in his mouth. His shirt was filled with bullet holes and caked with dried blood. Through the tears in his shirt, I saw his skin was red and angry, but the fissures were healing. Fae were incredible at mending quickly.

I sat with one leg folded in front of me on the bench, facing him. Sunlight came through the window and warmed the spot where I rested. "I know you hate me. Believe me, the feeling is mutual, but we are stuck together." I waited for him to respond in some way. He was staring at the ceiling, then looked at me, like telling me to continue. "We're both going to have to do things we don't want. I have to deal with this Garrett thing, and you have to deal with the Daniel thing. There is something going on. It's important. I can feel it in my gut."

He was about to respond when I held up my hand.

"I don't care if you have no interest in my life. I don't need you to, but I'm going. You can either stay here or go with me and protect your resources." I touched my stomach, where I sensed his powers occupied. I knew there was no chance in hell he would let me out of his sight, so I figured it was better to coerce him with something he did care about. During the years I became very good at finding a person's weakness and using it against them.

Ryker's lips thinned, his jaw locking. He knew what I was doing, but it didn't make it any less true.

"What else are we going to do today? It's not like we had plans."

It took him a while before he let his shoulders fall. "Fine. But only because you will go no matter what I say and probably get killed, tripping over your feet or something."

"Yay," I responded with a sarcastic cheer and glanced at Sprig, who was emptying all the salt shakers and making piles with them.

"Yay," Sprig mimicked, then paused. "What are we excited about again?" ADD at its finest.

"Oh, and I was never a fucking cheerleader."

# THIRTEEN

I had only been in Daniel's apartment a handful of times. He took me there for the first time after a year of knowing each other. It followed a collecting mission that didn't go our way. The goblin had several buddies we hadn't expected. They were usually solitary creatures, but this one had comrades who attacked us from behind. One bit my arm, forcing me drop my weapon. After three more showed up, Daniel knew it was time to escape and cut our losses. When hurt, we usually went back to the DMG. Rule three in our handbook: If injured by a fae, you cannot go to the hospital. We were to go back to HQ and get fixed by their medical team.

The rule never bothered me. I hated the idea of going to a hospital of any sort. But I wasn't stupid. I understood the government secrecy in what we were doing. Questions would be raised, especially about what caused our wounds. Too many inquiries. The section of the government I worked for was unknown to even some of the highest officials. We were so secret the President of the United States didn't even know of our existence, like an *X-Files* group. Imagine the mass hysteria that would happen if the public learned about us or about the fae living among us, the ones they believed were only in fairytales. Except, I had yet to meet one fae who came from one of those fables. They were frightening, cruel, narcissistic beings. Most, like my forced partner in crime right now, hated humans. They either wanted to rid Earth of us or use us as slaves and energy.

My gaze fell on Ryker. His chiseled face, hidden under the beard and patronizing expression, articulated this sentiment through his unsettling white-blue eyes. His tolerance of me was only because his magic was stored deep inside me. My tolerance of him was because I had no one else, and I couldn't get away from him.

Ryker and I rounded the last stretch of stairs. My breath labored heavily in my chest, whereas he seemed barely affected by the twenty-four floors we climbed. My legs quivered, wanting to collapse. I sucked in more air, trying to slow the fluttering of my lungs. Ryker only smirked at me and went through the door into the hallway.

The corridor was dark and quiet. The only light came from the window along the hall. The plush carpet deadened any noise our shoes caused walking.

"Which one?" Ryker kept his voice low, his bright eyes glowing in the dark. Disturbing.

"There." I pointed to the farthest. "Apartment 2404." We crept to the door, and Ryker reached for the knob. My heart suddenly gave a jolt, and I stepped back.

"What?" Ryker looked around in alarm.

My eyes filled with tears looking at the door Daniel

used every day—the place he called home—where I had dreamed of moving in with him. This desire would never have come true because of Lexie, but it still hadn't stopped me fantasizing about it. Visions of my future with Daniel had filled a lot of my thoughts when the world got too intense and I wanted to flee all my pain and responsibility.

"Are you crying?" Ryker snapped.

"No," I choked. It was true, not a tear had fallen from my eyes, but inside I wanted to curl in a ball and cry till all my agony was washed away.

"Whatever you are doing, stop." His lids narrowed. "You wanted to come here. I couldn't give a shit about this or what he knew about this fucked-up, twisted group of yours."

Fury surged through my chest. My foot took the step before I even thought, closing the gap between us. His back hit the door at my sudden proximity. His nose flared, his focus hard on me. Ignoring his icy I-will-kill-you stare, I pressed my finger in his chest. "I understand that you are a selfish asshole. Not a shocker coming from a fae, but..." I leaned in, pressing him farther back. "If you insult Daniel or disrespect him in front of me again, I will kill you. And don't think I haven't done it to a fae bigger and tougher than you." This was a lie. He was probably one of the biggest and toughest fae I had run across yet. I had encountered things with wings, large daggered teeth, nails like knives, but there was something about him that made me feel even those monsters would fear him. There was something volatile and charged within him, like if he let himself off the leash, he would obliterate everything around him.

My five-five frame only reached the middle of his chest; I felt dwarfed compared to him. I still thumped my finger on his chest like he should fear me. It was how you dealt with things where I came from. Size had little to do with power or control.

He didn't look like he followed the same rules. He flexed the muscles of his jaw. His hand snatched the top of my jacket and swung me around, slamming me back into the door. His face was so close to mine I could feel his breath on my neck.

"You threaten me again, human, and you will see exactly what this selfish asshole is capable of." He pressed me so hard against the door it whined under the abuse.

We both stayed there, our breaths laboring under anger and hatred. Deep down, mine was also laced with fear. He would keep me alive, but I had learned in my short life things could be a lot worse than death. Dying was often the easy way out.

"Get. Off. Me," I snarled, slamming my palms into his chest, the heel of my boot kicking out for contact. His eyes glowed brighter in the dark hallway as he gripped me tighter, picking me up and re-slamming me into the wood door. Air tunneled from my windpipe, freeing itself back into the world. My lungs snatched greedily back for the escapees. I reacted to the threat. His hand wrapped around my throat, but my teeth bit his arm and burrowed deep into his skin. My feet hit the floor. My throat felt the cool silk of air trail back into my lungs.

"Fuck!" He jerked his hand away. His blood dripped from my lip.

Daniel had spent three years weaning me from my gutter habits, sculpting me from street rat to a woman. Granted, a woman who could throw a guy on his back or kill someone with a butter knife. Still, I had changed, or so I thought. A week with Ryker and all those habits I thought I broke were resurfacing, meshing with my new behaviors.

The taste of his blood sang through my veins, reminding me of another time in my life—another Zoey. Fighting always made me feel alive, especially dirty fighting. It was one of those fetishes I kept from Daniel. He liked clean combat. He played by the rules and took it seriously. Not only did I not like playing by the rules, but I enjoyed the fire breaking them put in my belly. Many times I would let him throw me on the mat only to feel him on me, but he never let that line get crossed. Ever. He kept it very clear. He was my teacher, and we were training. I felt embarrassed at how many times I imagined us tearing off each other's clothes and doing it right there on the mats. He was rigid when it came to training or anything he considered not appropriate for a situation. If he had only known most of me was inappropriate, especially when it came to him.

"And you call me a beast." Ryker shook his hand, looking at me in disgust.

My eyes stayed on him, observing his every move.

He watched me in return.

"Lady, unless it's an herb I can smoke, get it away from me." A familiar voice came from my bag, and a head poked out. "Wait... what?" Sprig's head twisted around. "This doesn't look like a diner." Sprig wrinkled his nose. He had fallen asleep before we even left the café, and I placed him carefully in the bottom of my carrier. "Where are we? And why does this bag smell like a hippie's van?" The pills Elthia gave me did stink.

Sprig's appearance broke the heated stare of hate between Ryker and me.

"Daniel's." I peered at the monkey.

"Oh, right." He nodded then paused. "Why again?"

"Because you said you knew him, and he was involved with whatever was going on."

"Yeah, of course." He looked at Ryker and shook his head.

I sighed, then turned to the door. It was probably locked, but I still twisted the knob. It rolled in my hand, the door creaking open. Alarms went off in my gut. My head swung back to Ryker. He seemed to have the same reaction. He drew his blade. I pulled up my pant leg and yanked the knife Ryker gave me the night before. The Wanderer shoved me behind him as he softly pushed the door wider, his blade ready to strike.

Chairs were toppled every which way, and everything in Daniel's cupboards was spread across the floor.

"Don't think we are the first here." Ryker kicked a chair from his path.

No. We definitely weren't.

"Not to be rude, but your friend is messy." Sprig hopped off my shoulder to a leg of a fallen chair and bounded to the sofa.

"Someone broke in, Sprig."

"Good thing he was untidy. The robbers wouldn't be able to find a damn thing in this mess." I was about to respond, then decided against it. No point.

"This was not simply a robbery. Whoever did this had been looking for something. Thieves aren't this wasteful of their time. They go for the valued objects and get out." Ryker spoke from experience, and I nodded in confirmation. "This was done to look like he had been robbed. How long did this guy work for DMG?" Ryker made his way deeper in the room.

"Twelve years." I followed him through the living room. "He was their top hunter and trainer."

"They still didn't trust him. Why ransack his place if they thought he had nothing to hide?"

I had little doubt DMG had done this. The coincidence he had merely been robbed was far too remote on the twenty-fourth floor. DMG had been looking for something. But what? What did Daniel have they wanted? They waited till he was dead to search for it. What would make them destroy a residence to get it back? A dead man couldn't spill secrets, but something he had could.

"Sprig, will you stay here and keep watch? Let us know if anyone is coming." I spun in a circle searching for the monkey. "Sprig?"

"Yes?" His little head popped out of the cupboard where Daniel stored chips and crackers. "I was thinking. Why don't I stay here and keep watch?"

"Excellent idea, Sprig," I said and proceeded along the hallway.

The destruction continued throughout Daniel's office. The group had ripped the backs off every chair, flipped through every book, tossing them on the ground haphazardly. The room was a mess.

My shoe stepped on something soft, and I withdrew my foot to see a tiny stuffed goat on the floor. Plucking it off the carpet, I cuddled it to my chest. I gave the figure to Daniel for his birthday. He was a Capricorn and true to their traits, like self-discipline and responsibility. I teased him relentlessly about being stubborn, methodical, and bossy but unbelievably kind, loyal, and patient. The stuffed animal had been a joke, something he could toss in a drawer and forget. The fact he had held on to it—

I took in a shaky breath and jammed the goat into my bag, returning my notice to the room. Normally, his bookcase was alphabetically lined with chunky hardbacks and pristine volumes of history through the ages. He also had medical dictionaries and fiction publications of military stories and leaders. Very Daniel. Only three picture frames had broken the repetition of books but were now lying discarded on the floor, shattered.

I squatted, reaching for the first photo. It was of Daniel, his father, mother, and younger brother. The two sons looked proud and dashing in their military uniforms. The strong jawline and bright blue eyes connected all three men. The obvious family gene ran strong in the men of the family. His brother, David, had been killed in combat when he was only nineteen. Daniel didn't talk about him much. The pain even twelve years later had been very raw for him. It was the main reason he left the military and came to work for DMG. He had lost his mother five years ago to lung cancer. Daniel mentioned his father, Daniel Senior, was in north Seattle in a residential care facility, slowly dying of Alzheimer's. All I knew of his father was he had been an exceptionally high-ranking medical doctor in the military before he got sick. Daniel was silent about his family. He was never close to them. It was sad to think his father would never know or remember his only living son had joined his other boy and wife.

The next picture was a group shot of the collectors, hunters, and a few doctors at Kate's last birthday party. It was a quick gathering in the meeting room. We could never go in public together for security reasons, so we had gatherings at the DMG.

Daniel and I had finished a training session and popped over to celebrate. It was a photo I had never seen. I had a version of this one on my phone, but in this one, his arms were tight around me as we all huddled around Kate. The happiness on my face was obvious. His eyes were not on the camera but on me. In the print I had, his one arm was around my shoulders, and he was looking forward. I had been to his place several times since this picture was taken, and I had never really looked at it, thinking it was the one I had. How did I not notice this? Why would he have this picture instead of the other Kate had sent?

The truth, or my conclusion, ripped at the feeble bandages crossing my heart. My face wrinkled in agony. I looked away, grabbing for the third frame. My fingers trailed over his face. The photograph showed him with six other military guys geared for a mission. One of them was Peter. A huge smile creased and wrinkled the corners of Daniel's eyes and mouth. I bit my bottom lip, swallowing back the lump in my throat. God, I loved him. So much. The ache in my chest swallowed me whole. A drop of liquid splashed on the glass, and my hand instantly brushed away the subsequent tears. It was like inhaling knives as I sucked in a huge breath, my hands shaking.

"There is nothing in here. Not useful anyway." Ryker slammed the bottom desk drawer, turning his search to the files poured on the floor. "There is a good chance they already got what they were looking for." He flipped through papers and then threw them over his shoulder.

My gaze flitted across the room as I straightened my legs, standing. My head automatically negated his sentiment. "No, Daniel would not make it easy. He was black ops. He was trained to keep secrets."

"Sounds like the DMG does as well."

"Daniel was better." Why I felt so sure, I didn't know, but I was certain if Daniel were hiding something, he would make it almost impossible to find. You could only locate it if you truly knew him and how his mind worked.

Absently, I rubbed at my temples. I probably understood Daniel best. He had let me in the furthest, but I still was at a loss. I closed my eyes and let the room sink in. *Where would Daniel hide his secrets?* He could have concealed them so well not even the best trained eye would find it. If so, there was no way I would be able to. In the movies there would be an obvious clue, which somehow the guys who broke in missed. Real life wasn't like the movies. I had no idea where to start—or even if there was anything to find.

My legs bent under the weight of my despair, and I plunked heavily onto the floor. I placed my head in my hands and rubbed my face. The knot in my throat swelled, packing the airway till it hurt to swallow.

*Come back to me, Daniel.* My heart screamed. Smelling him and seeing his things burned at the raw ends of my torn soul. *Please!*

"Why are you sitting there?" Ryker's unhappy tone shot into my back. "This is your thing, not mine."

My head snapped around fast. I had to reach for the floor so I wouldn't fall. "Could you back off for a second? I know fae have the sensitivity of a rock, but I lost the man I love and my sister in the same day. I'm sorry I'm not dealing with it as well as you'd like."

Ryker's white eyes flared with an inner glow. "You think you're the only one who lost people? Try everyone in your family in a matter of minutes," he growled. Standing, he stomped to the door. "There is nothing here. I'll give you two minutes." He turned and left, his boots scuffing the wood as he moved down the hallway.

Most fae were awful, but dammit I had to be stuck with the biggest horse's ass of them all. A deep sigh fell from my lips. I knew I would never return here. It was no longer where the man I loved resided; it was not my future home.

My hand drifted back to the picture of the two of us in the group shot. The backing fell as I tore the photo from its frame. The fact he had this picture on his shelf meant it was important to him. It now meant even more to me.

With the image clenched in my palm, I rose. "Goodbye, Daniel." My voice was low and thick. I turned to leave, my foot kicking an object from under the clutter. A book skidded across the space and knocked into an overturned chair. *The Art of War.* The title stretched across the small handbook in gold letters. My stomach dipped. It was Daniel's favorite. He tried to get me to read it, but I fell asleep after the first page. Instead, he instilled the lessons in the book by making me recite them as we practiced our drills.

I remembered when he first gave it to me. It was only a month after I started DMG. I had yet to go in the field and truly understand the threats. I didn't take Daniel's lectures or training as seriously as I should have.

*I laid on the mat, sprawled out, the wind knocked from me.*

*Daniel came into view, leaning over me. "What was the lesson in Chapter Three?"*

*"Uh. Don't let your ass get handed to you?"*

*Furrowed lines dented Daniel's forehead, his mouth pursed. "Did you read any of the book I gave you yesterday?"*

*"The art of falling asleep?" I sat, letting him help me stand. I wiped at the sweat pouring down my face.*

*"Zoey, this is serious."*

*"I tried, Daniel. I tried four times." A complete lie. I tried once, then decided to put my earphones on and listen to music. Even my need to please Daniel couldn't compel me to read the dry, dull literature.*

*"You will try again. You'll read the entire book by this weekend, or you'll run drills until you do. I will quiz you every day."*

*Daniel's drills were not something you wanted to do. Ever. He was trained in special ops in the military and had learned torture by running till you threw up and obstacle training till your body gave up. I had done them twice and quit every time. They made me whimper merely thinking about them.*

*I strained not to let my sigh become audible. "Why is this book important?"*

*"The lesson you missed today was to not let yourself become sidetracked by things going on around you. You need to be fully aware and not become distracted. Keep your focus. Otherwise, you will get killed. You let your guard slip for a moment, and your enemy won't hesitate to use the opportunity to strike." He stepped closer, his shirt clinging to him from the morning exercise. His cologne caused me to be utterly defenseless. "And why is it important?" He looked at me, his voice low but steady. "Because we are at war. The day will come when the human race will have to fight. And I want you ready for it."*

I bent and grabbed the book and put it against my chest, holding it tightly. It was like having a piece of Daniel with me, as if he lived in between the lines. I could keep him locked safe between the pages, forever living in the typed print.

"Can I have her?" A stuffed goat popped over the lip of my bag, whirling around, as if it were possessed by a ghost.

I snapped the present I gave Daniel into my hand. "No."

"But Pam says she likes me," Sprig whined.

"Pam?"

"It's her name."

"You named the goat Pam?"

"It seemed to fit."

"Sprig, you can't have the goat."

"She doesn't like being called goat. Her name is Pam."

"You know she's not real, right? Like Sussanna."

Silence.

"You are not talking to me anymore, huh?"

"No."

"Oh, thank the gods." Ryker let his head fall back. His gaze darted to me. "Now, if only you would shut up as well, my day would be immensely better." We had been walking for a while. It felt pointless. We had nowhere to go or anything we could do. It felt like we were in purgatory—stuck between action and nothing. Ryker seemed to have run into a dead end with getting his powers and Amara back. I was latched to him with no place to go and no family. The DMG was on my ass, and the mystery of what Daniel had been doing was growing

"Making your day pleasant is not something I strive for." Sprig's head came up.

"I thought you weren't talking?" Ryker moaned.

"To her." He pointed at me. "I am going to talk to you *all* day long. I can't get enough of chatting with my favorite Viking."

Ryker rubbed at the tension between his eyes.

"So... what's your favorite color? Mine's yellow. It's such a happy color. And no, it's not because it's a color of a banana. I actually hate them. Icky fruit. Honey is yellow. I love honey. What is your favorite food?"

Ryker whipped around so quickly I almost smacked into him. He bared his teeth. "If you don't shut it up, I will do it for you. Permanently."

The mood he was in, he wasn't joking. "Here, Sprig. You can have the stuffed animal."

"Pam." He yanked her from my hands. "Her name is *Pam*." He then dragged her back into my bag.

"Something crawl up your ass today?" I returned my gaze on Ryker. He was always a jerk, but in the last hour he was being especially douchey.

"Leave it."

"No." I held his icy stare. I would not back down. "I won't. I will nag and nag till you tell me what your problem is."

He huffed and circled. His strides large and heavy.

"Ryker." I said his name in warning. I would scratch at the scab till he relented. Or actually killed me.

He stopped. His finger rubbed at his eyes and then rubbed his beard. "Elthia told me she couldn't find anyone who can help me."

"Told you? When? How?" I'd been with him every stinking moment, and not once had Elthia come.

"About five miles back. There was a code on a building."

"A code?" All the buildings, the ones standing or not, were tagged with gang symbols.

"Yeah. It was the way we used to communicate with each other when we had to."

"And it happened to be on a building we passed?"

"We had four places. She'd tag all the places with the same code. I purposely took us this way to see."

Now I understood his bad mood.

"What did it say?"

"*Tipota*. It's Greek for nothing."

"Maybe she meant nothing could be done for now."

"No." He scowled. "It means no one can help me."

His frustration grew with every step. I kept my distance and tried to stay quiet. He needed to work through it. Hearing my voice only seemed to grate on his nerves.

Our travels brought us near a Red Cross shelter. The smell of food wafted to me, and my stomach growled in response.

"You need a muzzle for that thing." He indicated my stomach.

"Sorry. I can't control my hunger," I snapped.

"We'll go there for supplies. If I feel it's safe, we'll get something to eat."

"Yes, your majesty. Simply say the word."

"Dammit," he bellowed. "Can't you obey me one time without some kind of comment or challenge?"

I dampened my lip with my tongue, trying to think through my words before speaking. Anger wanted to control my mouth, but I shoved my temper back. Keeping my voice like glass, I got close to his face.

"I am not some mindless, daft girl who will fall at your feet. I don't actually like you or trust you. I think I've been doing really well at guarding what I say. But if you demand I obey you again, then you and I will have a lot more problems than me being a good little girl."

My anger was cool and calm and far scarier than if I threw a tantrum.

Without letting him respond, I went around him and proceeded to the shelter. A little monkey hand came from my bag, high-fiving me. Sprig snickered and softly said, "You go, *bhean*."

The storage building was surrounded by a tall chain-link fence, locked with a padlock. *This was it?* I wanted to laugh. I could get over the fence or unlock the bolt in a matter of seconds. Who did they think this was keeping out?

"It's too light outside. Someone will see us if we try to climb it." Ryker evaluated our surroundings.

I was standing in front of the lock, taking a pin from my bag. "Already ahead of you." I motioned to him with my head. "Keep watch. A standard lock shouldn't take me long. "

He did a double take.

"What? I'm not as innocent as you think I am."

"I think you're anything but innocent," he sneered. His meaning obviously alluded to the DMG.

"Even before I worked with them." I yanked on the lock, popping it open.

His eyes grew wide.

"See, not helpless." I smiled haughtily and stepped inside.

He closed the gate behind us, so someone from a distance wouldn't notice anything wrong. We stayed low, progressing to the metal storage container.

"Damn." I slid to my knees, handling the lock at the

bottom. It was a heavy-duty steel padlock. "This is going to take me a little longer. You don't happen to have a Swiss army knife or something?"

His hand went to a pocket in his pants and retrieved one. "They come in handy." He shrugged. "If something I needed was in a lockbox, I had to break into it."

My shoulders fell. I thought for once I was bringing something to the table.

"You are a hell of a lot faster than me." He sensed my letdown. "I never had to rely on this particular skill too often, so I never got good at it. To be honest, most of the time I ended by hacking the box with my axe instead."

I flicked the smallest file on the knife and started to work.

A man's voice hollered close by. "No, I was going to grab more sauce for the chili."

Ryker reacted instantly. His body collided with mine, taking me to the ground. A sense of *deja vu* took hold of me as his form covered mine. He tucked his arms around my head, pulling me fully underneath him. His weight pushed on me. I couldn't move.

"Ryker, I can't breathe." I couldn't even look to see if he had squashed Sprig.

"Shhh." His eyes were closed, his mouth against my ear.

Footsteps reached the gate. We were lying only feet away from this guy. In the open. How could he not see us?

"We have no more. They took it," a woman shouted. "Shipment is coming tomorrow."

"Oh, right," he replied. The sound of his steps tapered away. Ryker took a breath and picked his head up, gazing over his shoulder at the gate.

"Okay. He's gone." He rolled off me. Taking the heat he carried with him.

"What the hell happened?"

"What do you mean?"

I sat up. "We are in the open. There was no way he wouldn't have seen us."

"Air! Air!" Sprig wheezed from my bag. "If this is how it feels to be in a threesome with you guys, I pass." He took another hearty breath. "Hate to say this, Viking man, but good work."

Ryker leaned back on his arms. "I didn't know if I could do it. I was struggling."

"Am I the only one who doesn't know what's going on?"

"He glamoured the man's mind to not see us," Sprig said.

I knew about glamour and tricks fae could do to humans. I was immune since I could see through all their magic. "And if it didn't work?" My eyebrows rose in question.

Ryker smiled tightly. "I would've had to solve it another way."

I exhaled slowly and turned back to the lock, trying to release it.

"This is taking too damn long." Sprig crawled out and went to the lock. He tapped on it, and it popped open. The memory of us crawling through the air vent in the DMG came back. He had unfastened those bolts in a blink of an eye. I was traumatized by all the events

186

before and after and completely forgot about Sprig's magic.

"Is there anything else you can do?" I tugged off the lock.

"I am really good at decoupage."

"Not really what I meant."

"We don't have time for this." Ryker pulled me to my feet, opening the door halfway. I bowed and edged in, Sprig at my feet. I flicked on my flashlight as Ryker shut the door behind us.

"Hell," I groaned deeply. The shelves sat vacant.

"I think we can assume this is where Marcello came." Ryker stepped farther in. There were only a few items left: a few packages of socks, underwear, and towels. It was probably what they rationed to every person with a bed. I grabbed a few items.

"Taking from the needy?" Ryker baited.

"We are the needy." I shoved some men's boxers into my bag, along with their version of women's underpants. "I think it's humorous you keep thinking I have morals. Believe me, I don't." Maybe with Daniel I would have had hope, but optimism for my well-being died with him.

"You worked with DMG. I never thought you had morals, but you are proving to be a lot less uptight than I thought."

"Gee, thanks."

"That was a compliment, *bhean*. Take it!" Sprig zoomed to the top of the shelving.

"Why do you keep calling me that?"

"It means *woman* in Gaelic." Ryker grabbed the last couple of granola bars and stuffed them into my bag. "Let's get out of here."

Sprig hit my shoulder and climbed down my arm. "It's all cozy in here now." He fluffed the underwear and grabbed Pam, wiggling around before finally settling in.

There went clean underwear—monkey fur splayed all over the fabric.

But with the pure bliss on his face as he purred next to Pam, I couldn't be even remotely upset.

# FOURTEEN

Rain pelted us, the murky syrup in the streets sticking to our boots.

"Are we stopping soon?" Sprig inquired. "My brain is scrambled eggs now."

"Don't talk about food." I patted my stomach. The damn thing only complained louder.

"Are you two done bitching?"

"Right, the stoic Wanderer never gets tired or hungry or sleepy." I opened my arms. "Or gets cold or has any emotions besides pissed off."

Silence.

Was I ruffling his feathers?

Ryker turned down an alley. Smoke billowed from a building oozing with the smell of food. I grabbed Ryker's arm. "We're going in there."

"No. We're not."

I rounded to face him. "Look, you can stay here in the cold. I am going to at least check it out. I am starving, freezing, and need to rest." I stood strong. Annoyance permeated his expression, but he didn't stop me.

The building was a large parking garage. Dozens of small groups sprinkled across the space. Fires were built in trash cans, barrels, crates—whatever would hold the heat. It appeared to be a scene from a dystopia movie or one after some natural disaster. The government may claim the ES was a *natural* disaster, but a lot of people knew better. There was nothing natural about it. It was fae magic, an extraordinary level of magic. I still wondered why the fae had done it. What had they gotten from destroying Seattle? Had it made it easier for them to prey on us?

Evil fucking fae.

The garage was dry and warm. We weaved through the groups, some smelling extremely foul. "Why don't they go to the shelter?"

"Shelters only have so much space. There are far more people than beds or food." Ryker kept close to me. A few men had turned to stare at me.

"Zoey? Zoey Daniels?" A smooth male voice came from beyond my shoulder. A jolt of surprise and fear wiggled along my spine, making me jump like a scared kitten.

A man in the group nearest us stood. His voice. The balding head and gray beard. I knew him well. I saw him every Monday, Wednesday, and Friday at 9 a.m. Countless mornings I would stare at the reflection of the fluorescent lights on his head while I sipped my latte.

"Mr. Kettenburg?"

"I think it's all right for you to call me Robert now." My psychology professor stood before me. His usual pants and button-down shirt and tie were replaced with khakis, a colorful sweater, and a heavy coat. He looked dirty, hollow, and broken. He was not a skinny or a tall man, which made this a feat unto itself.

"Zoey, you did not show up for the test." He spoke sternly. He was the only teacher at the college whom I liked. His sense of humor made me take to him instantly. "I'm sorry, but it's unacceptable. Unless you make it up, you are going to fail my class."

I nodded, looking at my feet. "The fact is I'm the only student who didn't fall unconscious the moment you opened your mouth and droll on for hours about our consciousness. I think you should let me slide." Three days a week we lived to give each other shit.

"You were always my favorite." A grin twitched at his mouth. "It's good to see you are all right."

I wanted to laugh. All right? I was far from okay.

He waved us over. "Come, join us. Meet my family. We were about to have some food. You look like you could use a meal."

A growl came from beside me, and I peered at Ryker. His eyes told me I'd better not accept the professor's invitation.

I swiveled back. "That would be nice. Thank you."

Ryker snarled, but I ignored him.

Kettenburg touched my shoulder. "This is... was a student of mine, Zoey Daniels. Zoey, this is my wife, Donna." He pointed at a woman in her fifties, sitting on the ground, leaning against a crate. Her styled blonde hair was streaked with dirt, along with her clothes. Her arm was injured, and a sling held it to her chest. She had a sweet round face, but it held a reserved expression. Her brown eyes glinted with pain.

"I apologize for not getting up." She motioned to her leg. "I am lucky I didn't lose it."

Kettenburg responded. "Our house was lost in the storm. Donna and my mother were the only ones home and barely escaped."

"I am so sorry."

She sniffed and blinked her lids, looking away.

"This is my sister, Marlene... her husband, Tom... my mother, Debbie... and my son, Andrew." He went around the rest of the circle. The faces all blurred together, except his son, who leaned forward to shake my hand. He appeared to be high school age and took after his father in height. He seemed the type who did very well in school but was still outgoing. His eyes lingered on my face with interest.

"Nice to meet you, Zoey," he said eagerly. I felt Ryker shift behind me.

"Marlene and Tom's home was lost as well." Robert Kettenburg motioned to the pair. They were also around their fifties, a nice average-looking couple.

My mouth pressed together, not knowing what to say about their loss. *Sorry* sounded pathetic and useless.

"Please sit. You and..." Kettenburg stared expectantly at Ryker, waiting for one of us to introduce him.

How could I introduce Ryker? *A friend* seemed like a lie, and I didn't think I could get it past my lips. *An acquaintance* sounded weird, and *partner* sounded even worse. He would hate if I told them his name, but it would draw more attention if I didn't. "Ryker." I waved to him. Ryker still stood a distance from the group, a scowl fixed on his face.

They all gave him a pleasant greeting, but you could see he made them nervous and inclined to dislike him. I heartily agreed with them.

"May I talk to you a moment?" Ryker gritted through his teeth, not even trying to appear to be polite.

With a need to compensate for his rudeness, I plastered a sweet, apologetic smile on my face. "Sorry, I'll be right back."

Ryker dragged me to a dark corner away from the family. "What are you doing?" he hissed.

"I am trying to get us a hot dinner. Can you curb the asshole tendency for at least a night?"

He tilted his head.

"Never mind."

"We need to keep away from people. It's too dangerous."

"Seriously, Ryker? He's my professor at a college. Do you think he's going to turn us over to Garrett or DMG?"

"If they come searching, he can describe us."

"Yes, he can, but I don't think he would. What does it matter? We'll be long gone by then."

"What about him?" Ryker pointed at my bag. "If he starts talking or snoring, what are you going to tell them?"

"Sprig, you'll be good, right?" I whispered into my purse.

"What's the incentive?" he replied.

"I don't take Pam away from you."

"Yes. I'll be good."

A smug smile drew across my face. Ryker shifted his weight, and his head leaned back to glance at the ceiling. Ryker's fight was waning, so I struck harder. "Right now both those groups would be looking for two people who would keep to themselves. It's actually safer if we blend in with this family. DMG and Garrett would probably bypass us, thinking we wouldn't be a part of this party." I had him; I could see it.

"But they're human." He glanced over my head, part of his lip curving in disgust, his true reason for not wanting to sit with them.

"So am I. Get over it."

He snarled but didn't add another rebuff.

"Come on." I turned toward the others. "But if you can't be nice, then don't talk."

"And you." I poked at my bag. "You stay quiet. You utter a peep, and the goat is mine." Sprig squeaked in my bag then fell silent.

We rejoined the family. I took a seat on the ground next to Robert. His son rested across the fire barrel, his eyes watching me. Ryker sat beside and slightly behind me, trying to stay as far from the other humans as possible.

Robert scooped a ration of baked beans and slopped them on top of the green beans. It was gourmet fare compared to what I had been eating the last couple of nights, and I immediately dove into the warm sustenance, happy someone was nice enough to share with us.

Kettenburg gave Ryker his portion of beans. Ryker gave a curt nod, scooting farther away from everyone. Being this close to so many humans was not compelling him to be civil. I looked back at him. He stared at his plate, a frown etching across his forehead. He tried to pull the green beans to one side, the baked beans to the other, but the dish was so mixed it was futile. He sighed and set the dish aside.

"What's wrong?" I hissed.

The flames of the fire mirrored off his white eyes when he peered back at me. "Nothing."

"Why aren't you eating?" I peeked at the rest of the group. Their attention was on the conversation between them.

"Not hungry."

I stayed quiet, but my expression pitched with irritation.

He grasped his bowl, the plastic fork in his hand dividing the contents. He stabbed at a baked bean and popped it into this mouth. "There. Are you happy?"

The way he tried to separate the items in his dish hit me. One of my foster siblings had done the same thing. "You don't like your food touching?"

His face lined with a frown.

My hand cupped my mouth, keeping back the spurt of laughter. "Seriously?" My brain could not wrap around this brute of a man being OCD about separating his food. "Haven't you eaten raw rabbits and stuff?"

"I've eaten a lot of things."

"Bloody rabbit is fine as long as it doesn't touch the raw squirrel on your plate?"

His lids narrowed as he stood, shoving the plate to me. "I'm going to patrol." His six-three frame strutted for the opening, his back rigid and tense.

"Did we upset your friend?" Robert turned my attention to him.

I waved my hand. "No, it was me."

"Is your boyfriend always this charming?" Andrew slipped nearer.

"He's not my boyfriend." I shook my head frantically. "He's not even a friend."

"Oh." Andrew's brown eyes lit with interest. Damn. Stupid move on my part. "If he's not even a friend, why are you with him?" Damn. Two dumb slip-ups.

"Uhhhhh." I poked at a green bean with my fork, shoveling it into my mouth. "He's a... cousin." The answer came out before I realized it. "You know, you can't choose your family."

Andrew shifted closer, his hip bumping mine. "Cousin, huh? Good to know." He turned and smiled, nudging my shoulder with his. "No boyfriend, then?"

"Not interested." Being back on the street seemed to bring forth my defenses. Sharp and callous.

He jerked back, air sucking through his teeth; rejection reflected on his furrowed brow.

"Sorry." I set my plate next to Ryker's disregarded one. "I recently lost someone."

"In the storm?"

*Actually, Andrew, I lost my sister to the storm and the man I loved to a fae snapping his neck.* I was certain he didn't want to know the real truth. My hair bobbed in affirmative.

"I'm sorry." He placed a hand on my back and rubbed in a circle. "We lost our dog."

I bit my lip, holding back the bitter response I felt

stirring in my throat. I never had a pet growing up, not an animal I considered a pet anyway. One house had a pit bull they trained to be a guard dog. Not people friendly. Another house had several cats that were mean as hell. They hissed and clawed at everyone. I liked animals, but I didn't have much experience with them. It seemed jarring for him to put his dog at the same sympathy level as Daniel. I understood people felt close to their pets like family, most preferring them to people. Hell, if I had one, I probably would, too.

He must have felt my haunches rising the longer he massaged my back. He pulled his arm away and let it drop. "Guess a dog isn't quite the same."

"No, but I get it."

"I grew up with him. My dad brought him home when I was five. He was a little ball of fur. He went everywhere with me." A sad longing permeated Andrew's expression. "I also lost some friends from school. No one I was close to, but still..."

Man, I was a bitch. "I am sorry." I touched his arm gently.

He twisted his head to look at me. A smile grew. Again, it hinted at flirtation and hope.

I took my hand back and shifted my look to Robert. "Thank you for the food." I got up, slinging my bag across my shoulder.

"You are more than welcome to stay here by the fire and sleep." Robert motioned to the warm flames.

My head responded in refusal. "Thank you, but no. I need to go find my... cousin."

Kettenburg looked like he wanted to say something else, but he shut his mouth and gave me a nod. I provided everyone a final goodbye nod. Andrew's eyes looked like a puppy dog's, hurt and disappointed.

Ryker was where I expected him to be—high on the roof of the garage. His back was to me, his arms folded as he stared into the murky night. The moon played peekaboo with us behind the clouds. Mist hung thick along the pier, concealing the lapping water like a magician. Ryker's head gave a little jerk, recognizing my presence, although he never turned around. I walked up, standing next to him.

"Here." I reached into my bag, my fingers grazing the soft fur of Sprig's sleeping head and grabbed a granola bar, wiggling it at Ryker.

He looked at the item bumping his chest and grumbled.

"Hey, bitch all you want. It's your only choice." I continued to hold the package impatiently. "Be happy it's plain granola. No fruit or fun goodies are touching each other."

He swiped it from my hold and removed the wrapper, stuffing it in his mouth.

"A guy like you doesn't seem like he would have issues with food. Don't you eat gruel and bats?"

"Are you trying extra hard to annoy me tonight, human?"

"It's the only thing I have left."

"You are tenacious, aren't you?"

I smirked. "Tenacious... I like it. I usually get bitch."

"You're that too."

"And you're a fucking ray of sunshine." His lips quirked with amusement.

"Holy shit. A smile?" Disbelief laced my words.

Ryker's mouth flattened. "Go get some sleep. We need to leave early tomorrow."

My legs shifted under my weight. "You don't need to sleep?" What the hell? What did I care if he slept or not?

His powerful arms fell from their fold, and he swiveled to face me. "Don't tell me you are concerned for my well-being?"

"Not at all," I said.

He watched me for a breath before he leaned above, his form overshadowing me, his forehead almost smacking mine. His eyes glinted with hate and fury. "Let's keep this clear, human. The only reason I am here is because you have something of mine. The moment it comes back to me, I am gone."

Heat rose along my neck, drifting to my cheeks.

"Yeah," I fumed. "Same here." I spun on my heels and jogged for the stairs. Anger rumbled in my stomach, burning up my spine.

"Screw him. I was only being polite," I mumbled to myself, pounding the steps on my way down.

"Are you and yourself in a fight again?" a squeaky voice came from my satchel.

I stopped at the bottom of the stairs and opened the flap. Sprig was snuggled deep in the corner with his adoptive stuffed goat wrapped in his arms. He was freaking adorable.

"No." My teeth ground together. "Man, the fae pisses me off."

"Fae are good at infuriating people, but he is exceptional at it."

"Yeah, got that." I rubbed the back of my neck, feeling the knots rolling under my palm like a ballpoint pen.

"You did give him a granola bar and were all concerned about him not sleeping."

"So? Is common courtesy frowned upon in the fae world?"

"Showing any signs of caring is saved for those in your own clan. Dark fae especially do not display feelings to other fae. It is a sign of weakness," Sprig said. "What's funny is even though you are human, I would say you really are no different."

Leaning back, I pressed against the wall, taking in this notion. He was right. Those terms did fit me. Or what I used to be. Daniel was the one who brought out the more sensitive Zoey, the one who cared about people beyond the two people in her clan. She was here now, and I wasn't sure the caring part of me would go into hiding again. Whatever Daniel did, he made me soft.

Sprig adjusted in my bag, pulling my strap harder on my shoulder. "Here." My hand slid in the front pouch and removed another candy bar. "Sorry it's not more, but I couldn't pocket the beans I had for dinner."

Sprig's eyes lit up, his hand reaching greedily for the package as I unwrapped it. "Granola shrouded in sweet honey and sugar?" He yanked it from my grip and put a chunk in his mouth. His eyes rolled back in his head, and he sank deeper into the corner. "Oh, sweet honey."

When I got back to Robert and his family, they had settled down to sleep. I could see Andrew was still awake, talking to his aunt. I felt like I was staring from the outside at a perfect family. I didn't belong here with them. I didn't belong anywhere anymore.

I veered off in the opposite direction, finding solitude in a dark corner of the warehouse. The light from several group fires reached me, but the heat did not. I tucked deeper into my coat as I snuggled on a flattened cardboard box. Sprig's soft snores echoed from my bag, already fast asleep. I moved him closer to my chest, cradling him. His heat penetrated through the bag and soaked into my shirt. Slowly my lids lowered, and I drifted off to sleep.

# FIFTEEN

Rain tapped gently on the roof. Glass bricks keeping the parking structure enclosed were tinted with a faint light, informing me it was only a little past dawn. Scattered fires still burned in the barrels throughout the garage. Only a soft murmur of voices hummed in the large area. Most were sound asleep. Robert and his family all cuddled around the fire and each other. It left a strange ache in my heart to see their family unit. They were so close and would do anything for each other. They had losses, but they still had each other, and this seemed most important to them. I felt more like an outsider. They knew family in a way I never did. No one had loved me unconditionally. Lexie was the closest, but I never had parents or grandparents, not even an uncle or aunt who loved me. The feeling was foreign to me.

The only relationship I had now was an unstable alliance with a scary-ass fae, who didn't like me, nor I him. And as soon as the need for the other ran out, the partnership would probably turn ugly fast. My chances weren't good if he wanted to kill me. With a sigh, I got to my feet and went to find my hostile associate.

"Zoey?" Mr. Kettenburg's soft call halted my advance toward the stairs.

"Yes?" I whispered. His entire family was still asleep.

He stood and came to me, a look of concern on his face. "Who is the man you're with?"

"Uh..." The response lay unanswered on my tongue.

Robert eyed me for a moment before he spoke. "Zoey, if you're into something you feel you can't get out of..." He let his sentence taper off.

*Mr. Kettenburg, if you only knew.*

I smiled. "No. It's not like that. It's complicated."

Robert didn't appear to believe me. "You can always come with us if you need to." A smile hinted at his mouth as he looked at Andrew. "Think my son has taken a shine to you."

"Thank you, but I'm fine."

He watched me, seeming to contemplate something. The silence grew into a long uncomfortable awkwardness.

I needed to change the subject from why I was with Ryker. "So are you really going to fail me, even though our school is a heap?"

"You know my rules." He crossed his arms. "Test day. No excuses for being late or absent."

I sniggered. "Yes, sir."

"But I will give you a break, if you answer me one question."

"Okay." Intrigued by what he would ask. "Shoot."

He kept his arms crossed and stared at his feet. He opened his mouth, then closed it.

Nervousness trickled into my gut. His deliberation over the question squeezed at my lungs.

"I want an honest answer." His voice turned stern. One he used a lot in class.

The hold on my chest gripped harder, and I licked my lips.

"Did you..." He stopped and took a breath. "Did you see a leopard in the picture?"

The air vanished from my lungs. I knew exactly what he was talking about. I had him three years earlier for my entry psychology class. The pictures he referred to showed if you had the "sight" or not. Most students saw a woman. I got past the glamour and perceived what she really was—a shape-shifter.

"Why... why would you ask?"

"Zoey, I know." Understanding ran deep in his eyes. "I know what you can do."

I jerked back and swallowed.

"Keep calm. I am not going to hurt you or turn you over to DMG." He patted my arm.

"How do you know about DMG?"

"I was hired by them ten years ago. They secured the job for me at the college and got me established in the psychology department. They never interceded with my teaching directly, except for the special tests."

"What? DMG hired you? Why? Are you even a real teacher?"

"I'm really a teacher," he replied. "I was working at a high school in Everett when they recruited me. I thought I was interviewing for the position. I realized the two men had nothing to do with the college but were actually with the government.

"They said the job was mine. I only had to give tests every semester, which were provided. They reasoned with my military background, I believed in duty to my country. I won't deny the shiny car, the paid medical bills, and house they provided didn't please my wife. We had been struggling with my teaching salary at the high school. My mother's doctor bills had eaten through her retirement and were now going through ours. It was tearing us apart. The new job took those problems away. And I really did believe I was doing right. I trusted my government and thought I was a part of some secret testing for educational purposes. Overall, they were harmless and didn't hurt anyone. Eventually, they had me in too deep to ever be able to leave."

Only a moment ago, the man before me had been my professor, far away from my DMG life. Everything changed.

"Why would they recruit you?"

"I asked myself the same question repeatedly. The only thing I can think of was I had a military background and was struggling for money, on the edge of divorce, and had an elderly mother moving in. I was the perfect candidate. They knew I would do it. I didn't have much of a choice. The one time I tried to refuse their order, they subtly conveyed I should be concerned about my family. Accidents happened." His Adam's apple bobbed as he swallowed. "The threat was clear."

"I am sorry." I wasn't sure why I was apologizing, but it seemed the right thing to do. "Why would you ask me if I saw a leopard?"

"They told me what to look for, what they were testing for." He shifted his weight. "I've realized for a while it was their way of trapping me in. Not too much information to be a threat, but enough. They needed me to be on the lookout for students with the sight. If you noticed, I taught every class you took in psychology, which was their doing. They told me about you, to keep an eye on you from the moment you entered my class."

He *was* the only teacher I had every semester since I began college. I thought it a funny coincidence but nothing more. Why would I? What a fool. The DMG had been controlling and watching me the whole time.

"Wait? From day one?" My brain tossed the new information around. "The test wasn't till late in the year. How did they know about me before the test?" I figured it was the test that put me on DMG's radar.

"No, Zoey. They had an entire file on you. I didn't get to read it, but they showed me your picture before you ever set foot in my classroom."

DMG had a file and a picture of me before they tested me? "That doesn't make sense."

"I wish I could tell you more, but it's all I know." He glanced around the dank, cold garage. "When things like this happen, you realize what is really important. We are going to leave Seattle." He didn't have to say it, but he was running from DMG and getting his family far away from its reach. It was pointless if DMG wanted to get to you, but I doubted Kettenburg was high on DMG's list. "When I saw you tonight, I knew I had to tell you the truth."

I didn't know what to do with this new information. All it did was confuse me more. Between Sprig telling me about Daniel and the DMG knowing about me way before they claimed to, I learned there was more going on than I'd thought. It meant something, but I just didn't know what exactly.

"Robert?" A sleepy but urgent voice called. Donna, his wife, tried to sit. "Robert?"

Kettenburg turned and moved to his wife. "Yes, honey. Are you all right?"

"I have to use the restroom."

He nodded and tried to help her stand. Her leg was wrapped with bandages. She cried when she stumbled and put weight on it.

"It's broken?" I moved to them.

"Yes, but the hospitals wouldn't help us. They have far more serious cases to deal with. They told us not to even bother waiting. They wouldn't have time to see her."

She draped an arm around his shoulder as he pulled her up.

"Here." My hand went past Sprig and grabbed the bottle at the bottom. "A heal... doctor gave me these. They're painkillers. They should at least take the worst of the aching away." I handed her the bottle full of the white tablets Elthia gave me. My happy place pills. They were amazing and ten times better than normal painkillers. I would be sad to see them go.

Water coated Robert's eyes. "Thank you, Zoey. I wish you well on your journey, wherever it takes you."

It was as if we were meant to bump into each other, but we understood we probably would never see each other again. Our life paths were taking us in different directions.

"You too."

His path was away from DMG.

My path seemed to be running straight for it.

My head buzzing with the new information, Sprig and I darted up the stairs. I crept onto the rooftop. Ryker sat with his back to me, his legs over the side of the building, the rain delicately falling on him. A deep growl erupted from the figure, discontinuing my movement toward him. I thought it was for me, a warning he didn't want me to get any closer. His fists slammed against the tar, crumbling a chunk of stone under his hand, and he snarled again. Wow, he really didn't want me near.

"Fuck, Amara..." he trailed off. Her name caused my breathing to cease. All previous thoughts about my teacher went to a file in my brain. "We had a plan." He mumbled so low I barely heard him. "You know I can't turn the stone over to him. You were the one who made me promise... no matter what happened." Frustration and aggravation strained across his back, flexing and coiling under his shirt. I felt like I was intruding on his most personal moment. I probably was, and if he turned and saw me, he'd probably throw me off the roof.

I didn't think of Ryker as having feelings, so seeing him now was disturbing. He had lost someone the night of the storm, too. Not in the way I did, but his lover was gone as well, kidnapped by Garrett. It was obvious he blamed himself, and from what he told me, he was against the wall. He couldn't get her back without trading the stone, which was not an option. I could only imagine the frustration I would feel if I were in the situation. It was like the government's policy—"we don't give in to terrorists"—because of the trend it would start if they did. But at the same time, when loved ones were being sacrificed, and it was up to you to save their lives, I couldn't imagine having to decide. If it would have been Daniel or Lexie, I would have given in; if anyone else, probably not.

Ryker stood. His arms opened to the sky, and he let out a roar, which shook the ground. His tattoo ignited. He drew his axe and began smashing into every edge and object on the roof, bashing each one into dust.

Air quaked in my chest as I watched the strength of the man before me. His shirt strained under the tension of his muscles. His light eyes glowed with rage.

He was truly the most frightening person I had ever come across. I was rigid. Too scared to run.

His blade struck the partition again. The ledge fractured in half, the top crumbling to the ground below. Echoes rang as the pieces hit cars, dumpsters, and the street. His breath pumped frantically from his lungs as he let the axe slide from his palm. Standing for a few moments, he swallowed deep gulps. The strain fell from his shoulders, causing them to droop.

It was time for me to leave. If he knew I had been watching the whole time—my foot took a step back, my boots making a soft squeak.

He froze. I froze. I think even Sprig went immobile in my bag. I was so screwed.

Ryker's head twitched to peer over his shoulder. He then turned back to the city. We stood still for what felt like centuries. I didn't want to speak, but his silence made me crazy after a while.

"I didn't mean to overhear. I came to check on you." I cleared my throat, forcing my voice to sound stronger. "I was going to leave."

"But. You. Didn't." He spoke low with zero emotion, but I could feel the spikes under it, ready to impale me at a moment's notice.

"Uhhh... well, I tried." But my legs wouldn't listen.

His profile came into view again, his jaw clenching, an eye narrowed. "What do you want, human?"

Why had I come looking for him again? After our last encounter on the roof, what made me think he would be open to me coming back?

"I don't know."

He whipped around so fast my eyes barely saw him, and like a bull, he came rushing at me. My feet backpedaled until my spine smacked into a wall. He got within an inch of my face, slamming a hand on my chest and pressing me harder into the wall. He moved in closer. "If you ever sneak up on me again..."

"You'll what?" I forced my chin to stay high, challenging him. I would not cower. He would not have that kind of power over me. "Kill me? Torture me? Do it... go ahead."

He peered down his nose at me. "Don't be so flippant about torture, little human. You won't find it such a joke when I peel back your nails or pull your teeth one by one." He tilted his head so his lips grazed my cheek. It was a tactic to keep your enemy unbalanced, giving you the upper hand. I knew all the tricks.

I swallowed. "Sounds like a kinky night." If he tried to destabilize me, I would return the favor. I leaned farther, our lips close to touching, voice low and husky, my stare livid with fury. "And keep talking, big boy. I like it rough."

"Hey! Hey!" Sprig came out of the pouch, pushing between us. "Time-out, kiddies. I am too young to see Mommy and Daddy using whips and chains on each other, especially if it's not in the fun way."

Ryker jerked back, his pupils contracting as he glared at Sprig and me. He shoved me one last time into the wall and twisted away, returning to the edge of the roof. Part of the wall, which used to reside there, was no longer—more rubble no one would notice.

Closing my eyes, I stayed for a few beats, regaining my composure. Sprig kept quiet, probably knowing it was the wisest call. When I reopened them, I watched Ryker. His arms were folded, and his head bent enough so he could rub his forehead. His shoulders sagged, like he had been defeated. I didn't know why I got the impulse to go to him, but I did. I went to his side, once again gazing at the city. This time it felt different—as if we broke through something and came out the other side, war wounded and exhausted, but still standing together. His eyes darted to me, and an odd expression oozed over his face. Without a word, I somehow knew he felt this, too. Something shifted. We both finally accepted the other as a partner. Our being together probably wasn't going to be as temporary as we hoped, and we were stuck with each other for better or worse.

Ryker smirked and rubbed at his eyes again before he emitted a half-chuckle, half-aggravated sigh.

I passed a test I didn't know I was taking. The tension he held in when I was near seemed to crumble away with the wall.

"Soooo... how are we all doing?" Sprig's head came out. "Are we going to play nice?"

"No, probably not." Ryker straightened, focusing on the beyond.

"Honesty. Good. If you want this relationship to work, you two need to keep the lines of communication open by being truthful with each other."

"Shut up." I tried to flip the top of my purse back, but he squeezed through the side and climbed the strap to my shoulder.

"Sprites don't understand secrets. We say whatever we're feeling."

"Yeah. I noticed," Ryker and I said at the same time.

"In our village, nothing stayed private for long. My mother said gossip was good for the soul. Kept you involved in each other's lives."

There was a reply on my lips when I saw three black vans pull in around the building, each on a different side. I identified the government-issued collector vans at once.

"Hell." My chest sank. "They found us."

Ryker reacted. "What?"

"DMG. They located us." I pointed to the vehicles. I had no idea how they discovered us, but deep inside I wasn't surprised. We were good at our jobs. We tracked, hunted, and collected, and we were able to locate some of the hardest fae in the world to find. The DMG was still fully functioning and had been searching for me since the day I escaped their ambush. It had been only a matter of time before they found me.

Time was up.

# SIXTEEN

The doors of the vans opened and familiar faces piled from each one, surrounding the building. Hugo and Marv moved to the backdoor, Peter and Matt to the front, which left Liam and Sera going for the ladder to the roof. The one thing about being an ex-collector was I knew how they worked and thought and the military precision they would use. It was effective and usually resulted in a capture. This time I hoped my knowledge would be their downfall. The only chance we had was we saw them before they spotted us. If I were still asleep downstairs, capture would have been done in a matter of seconds.

With the building guarded and the roof soon to be invaded, Ryker and I were left with few choices.

"There are only six of them." His chest puffed as he reached for his weapon.

"And those six come with fae-crafted bullets. They'll try to save me but might shoot you on sight." I tugged at his arm to move away from where Liam and Sera were climbing. "Even if they don't, and they use the darts? If we are even nicked by one—game over."

Ryker pondered a moment before nodding. "Come on." He ran for the far end of the roof. There was an alleyway dividing it from the building across.

"Oh, hell no." I shook my head, looking down. Vertigo distorted my vision.

"What are our other choices?"

"I can distract them." Sprig jumped off my shoulder.

"Sprig! What are you doing?" I called after him.

"Helping." He shrugged and disappeared behind the structure that held the roof door.

"Sprig!" I went to follow him when Ryker grabbed my arm.

"He'll be fine." He tucked his axe away, impatience rushing his words. "We have to jump now."

"You think he'll be fine? He'll probably keel over right at their feet."

"He made his choice. We have to go."

I bit my lip. He was right. It was our only option. My legs suddenly felt like the shortest limbs on the planet. Why couldn't I have been eight feet tall and do a split-leap across to the opposite roof?

"Don't think. Just do it," Ryker yelled. He took off, bounding for the other side. He rolled as he hit, coming back on his feet. "Jump!"

I stepped back, giving myself a running start. "Save my little, broken body."

"Freeze, Zoey!" Sera's voice shouted from behind. "If you move, I will shoot you."

Her familiar voice had me glancing over my shoulder. She stood with the dart gun pointed at me. Liam stood next to her, his fae gun also on me.

"We don't want to hurt you, Zoey, but we will if we have to." Liam said the standard scripted lines, but his words were filled with disgust. The way they stared at me showed the repulsion in their faces. I was no longer the comrade they used to train with, nor was I an ordinary fae. I was far more vile to them. Their hatred of me was personal.

Sera's focus couldn't seem to stay on me for long. Her hand trembled, and a trickle of blood seeped from her nose to her lip.

"Shit," she mumbled, then wiped her nose on her jacket, without taking the gun off me. The headache would soon follow. A creased line dented her forehead, and her jaw flexed. I knew her sight would go, replaced by snaking lines and patterns.

Deep in my brain, it triggered the fact since I'd been on the run, I hadn't gotten any nosebleeds or headaches. Well, not the seer kind. But the thought was so tiny and unimportant, I pushed it away.

"Better take your medication soon, Sera. Those headaches are debilitating. Might keep you from getting your man..." I smiled, taunting her. "Or woman in this case."

"Not me. I will shoot you, Zoey." Liam took another step, his gun ready to fire. I had no doubt he would. Maybe not to kill, but it would stop me.

"I don't think so." Sprig tossed a large chunk of brick at Liam. It crashed onto his head. Liam stumbled to the side, knocking into Sera. "Don't make me start throwing my poo at you," he yelled at Liam, then turned to me with a shrug. "I've heard monkeys do that. Now go!"

I didn't think. I ran and jumped, stretching my legs as far as they could go. The impact of the roof tore through my jeans and rocked through my bones. *Holy shit! They make this look so easy on TV*. I rolled across the rooftop, grunts tearing from my chest. Finally I came to a stop. Ryker was right there, helping me stand. Bullets tore past us, zipping so close I could feel their heat.

Ryker pulled me to my feet, and we crouched as we scurried away. Slugs continued to whizz past us, but we made sure not to run in a straight line. It was harder to hit a moving target, even harder an unpredictable one.

"Subjects are on neighboring roof. All teams respond." I heard Liam's voice in the crisp morning air.

Ryker's hand reached for the roof door of the new building, twisting till the knob broke. He shoved me inside, and we rushed down the steps. It was an apartment building. A low-income one. People lingered in the hallways, sleeping on the stairs or landings. Clothing, boxes, and junk littered the halls. I tried to step across a man but slipped.

"Hey," he yelled, then turned over and went back to sleep, a paper bag with what appeared to be a bottle of cheap liquor stood close to his head.

Far below, I heard the front door bang open.

"This way." I grabbed Ryker's arm and tugged him along one of the passages. He seemed to understand what I was thinking because when we got to the middle of the hallway, he slammed his shoulder into a closed door. It broke on his first hit, the wood around the lock shredding. Screams from a woman and several children echoed in my ears as we ran through. I didn't notice anything more than moving outlines, my focus directed on the windows. We were only two stories high. It was break-your-leg height, but not a kill-you fall.

People continued to scream and dance around us, even throwing stuff, but Ryker and I ignored them. He yanked the window open and released a small relieved huff. I followed his gaze below. The side alley was lined with old open-topped dumpsters.

Shouts coming from the hallway zipped fear along my spine. Peter was close. I heard his voice. Ryker shoved me to the windowsill, and I pushed off, letting my body fall. Only a moment after I hit, Ryker landed next to me. The smell of the rotten food, feces, and dead animals spurted up my nose, choking me. Gooey, slimy items I didn't even want to think about encircled me. I pushed through the bile and tried to get on my feet. Ryker hopped out with ease. Turning, he grabbed my waist, lugging me from the bin.

His feet were ready to run, and the second mine hit the ground, his powerful legs shot him off like a rocket. I tried to keep pace. And adrenaline did a good job—for a while. I started to lose the energy I needed to keep going.

"Come on. We are not safe yet," he chided me. We ran down Fifteenth Avenue to the Ballard Bridge. My mouth went slack when I saw the familiar forest green span. Lightning from the ES had carved a huge chunk from it, destroying one side of the passage. The watch tower, which used to stand in the middle, was gone, leaving an open angry wound. Pieces of it floated on top of the frosty channel below. No railing or even a southbound lane was left, leaving it exposed. It didn't look safe to cross, but it didn't seem to stop us. The

DMG was more of a threat than an unstable bridge. It was still attached to the other side, which was good enough.

I glanced over my shoulder to see if anyone was following us. Mistake. The movement caused me to drift to the side. My foot slipped on the fresh rainwater coating the metal. I stumbled, my head diving forward. I reached to grab for an object to stop me. Too late. The steel crossing was no longer underneath me. My stomach dropped as I plunged to the icy water below. Of all the dangerous things after me, this was *not* how I wanted to die. Taking a header off a bridge.

"Zoey!" Ryker's deep voice boomed. As gravity dragged me into the lake, all I thought was, *He said my name. He actually said it and not simply "human."* Then I hit. Frigid water slapped my exposed skin. Ice picks stabbed into me, twisting with immobilizing agony. Breath was sucked from my lungs as water wrapped me, pulling me down. This taught me not to have learned how to swim. It wasn't like I had a parent who put me in classes when I was a kid. No foster parent I had would pay for an extra like swimming lessons. As an adult, it was something I eventually wanted to do but had yet to accomplish.

Oh, the irony.

My arms and legs moved frantically but not necessarily working together or helping. Water flooded the messenger bag around my neck, towing me deeper. Panic and cold tore all common sense from my brain. My lungs twitched, screaming for air.

Sinking.

My oxygen gave out, and I gulped at the water,

filling my lungs with liquid. My mind grew hazy, my limbs no longer working.

I was going to die.

Through the murky darkness, arms reached for me, circling my waist and pulling me to the surface. We broke through, and I gasped for air, tugging it in with greedy gulps.

Coughs ripped at my throat as I hacked up some of the water I consumed. Ryker kept his form close to mine, giving me a heat source. The water had been so cold my extremities became immobile.

"Zoey, listen to me. I need you to climb on my back. Can you do it?"

My teeth rattled so hard it looked like I was nodding my head. He twisted me around and looped my arms around his neck, then swam. I floated behind him and curled my arms tighter around his neck, bringing me higher on his back. He reached the water's edge. Oil and garbage whirled around us the closer we got to the shore.

He pulled us onto a rocky patch of beach, if you could call it that. I slid off his back and rolled onto the pebbles, coughing and sputtering. My lungs rejected the water I inhaled.

He lay on his back next to me. "That was an unexpected and creative means of escape." He kept his eyes on the clouds above, water clinging to his lashes. "If you wanted to go for a swim in Lake Union, I would suggest summer next time." He took a few deep breaths. "They will be searching for us soon, backtracking when they can't find us. We need to get moving."

I didn't budge. "Hey," he called to me. "Zoey?"

Three times. He had said my name three times.

His hand came to my face, turning my head to him. "Fuck. Your lips are blue. You're blue all over." He climbed to his feet.

"I-I-I-I-m-m-m-m-f-f-f-f-i-i-n-n-e-e," I chattered.

"No, you're not. We need to get you warm before hypothermia sets in." He picked me up, the sodden pack only adding to the weight. *At least Sprig was not in there.*

"No." I shook my head. I would be damned if he was going to carry me like a baby while I was conscious. But as soon as I stood, the shock didn't let me do anything but shake like a paint mixer.

"We don't have time for your stubbornness unless you want to lose limbs." He didn't wait for my response and scooped me up unceremoniously. He moved us quickly through the streets, blending in with the darkening shadows. To me it was still torturous. Every jolt, every time he heaved me higher was like someone stabbed me with a thousand serrated knives. My lungs clenched, and the tremors through my frame grew so violent Ryker had trouble holding me.

The suburban street gave way to greenery. I recognized it immediately. I'd spent a lot of nights in Discovery Park as a teenager, getting drunk and running from park rangers. Ryker moved past the military cemetery and historic district, proceeding to the more forested, uninhabited part.

"Where are we going?" I tried to ask, but it sounded more like grunts. He seemed to understand the English between the gibberish.

"An old abandoned park ranger building. I've used it in the past. It should be safe."

My lids grew heavier, the trauma demanding me to sleep, but the pain and shivering kept me awake.

Finally, we reached the bungalow. He placed me on a tree stump while he went around, getting in through a back door. He came back and carried me inside. It was a one-room stone cabin. A fireplace, desk, chair, bathroom, and kitchenette filled the tiny space.

"I am going to start a fire. It's dangerous, but I figure there are too many clouds and smoke in this city for anyone to notice this one." He bent over the small fireplace. "You need to take off your clothes."

"W-w-w-h-a-a-t-t?"

He rolled his eyes. "You need to remove your wet clothes. They can dry and so can you... or you can sit there, get hypothermia, and lose all your limbs."

*Drama queen.*

As he struggled with his wet lighter and getting the stove lit, I grappled with my clothes. Convulsions rocked me, and my hands were not able to close properly enough to get anything off. The tank top underneath my sweater rolled up, displaying the part of my stomach where I had been impaled. In the water, the bandage fell off. There was no feeling where the tips of my fingers touched. Scaring tissue already covered the week-old wound.

*How in the hell?*

A metal rod had gone straight through me, tearing muscle, skin, and tissue. I shouldn't have been almost healed. The only thought was Elthia. Whatever she gave me must have done this. I detected the medication

221

she put in my system wasn't from this Earth—an herb from another world.

Flames flickered in the fireplace, and he stood, turning to me. He tilted his head at the little dent I made in undressing myself. My skin was still so frozen the warmth of the fire could not break through the cold exterior.

"You don't look good." He walked to me.

"S-S-Sprig?" I stuttered.

Ryker's boots tapped mine as he stepped close. He grabbed the hem of my shirt, tugging the soaked fabric over my head. "I'm sure he's okay. Don't worry about him. He'll find you soon."

Clear thoughts resisted forming in my head, but I was acutely aware of his closeness, and him tugging my jeans down.

"Lift your foot." He squatted.

I placed my hand on his shoulder, using him as a crutch as he yanked off the tight jeans. The water only glued them to me. It was like tearing off duct tape. With a harsh wrench, I went on my back.

"Sorry," he said, though he didn't sound sorry. He finished taking off my pants and straightened. His arms slipped under my legs and around my back, collecting me in his arms. My cold, bare skin burned where it touched his warm body. The numbness of most of my skin kept me from caring I was only in my bra and panties. He had seen it before as he already dressed me. In our short relationship, he had seen me in less clothing than a lot of my so-called boyfriends.

He positioned me before the fire, then placed my clothes and all the items in my bag, including Daniel's book and the goat stuffed animal, along the hearth of the fireplace to dry. Seeing Pam hit my heart. I hated not knowing where Sprig was, and if he was all right.

The picture of Daniel and me stuck out of the book, wrinkled and waterlogged, dulling the color—like we were fading away. Some of the supplies we stole and my phone were now absent. Lying at the bottom of the canal.

When he was finished, he began to take off his own clothes. My pulse spiked in my veins, sending the first round of life back into my form. He laid the axe and leather halter on the floor with care before he tore off his shirt. His bare chest demanded I look at it. The tattoo went along his neck and traveled the length of his torso in entwining lines of black. He had another one, which covered most of his back. It looked like ancient Asian symbols and etchings. I didn't know what they meant, but it was gorgeous and mysterious. He dragged his wet jeans over his hips, and they landed in a dense clump, leaving him in only fitted boxer-briefs. His tattoo continued all the way around his side to his thigh, curving over his butt.

He looked up, and I darted my eyes back to the fire. He put his clothes next to mine on the hearth. "Your wound is healing." He nodded toward my stomach.

My head trembled in choppy movements. "Y-Y-Yeaaahhh."

He sat next to me. "You can go to sleep if you need to." His voice sounded tight and uncomfortable. I'm sure being half naked next to a human created unpleasant feelings in him as it did me.

I nodded and rested on the dirty, scratchy rug. Everything in me hurt. I shook uncontrollably. It had lightened, but not enough. I curled in a ball, fighting the chill in my bones. I heard Ryker sigh deeply, the wood floor creaked as he moved in behind me.

He didn't say a word as he pulled my body into his. He curled around me, his large build engulfing me in heat. He rested his head on his bicep, snuggling mine into the curve of his arm. It was like being wrapped in an electric blanket. My muscles instantly responded, melting into him. His skin scorched mine, but this was the good kind of pain. After a while, the warmth allowed me to sleep.

I awoke to darkness. Only the smoldering embers in the fire gave a little light to the room. I stretched, spasms of pain working along my clenched tendons. The violent shivering finally eased, and my skin turned from purple-gray to a healthier white-gray. At least it was now in the neighborhood of my natural color. Heat from Ryker coated my limbs in a blissful sphere, relaxing the tension his closeness brought.

*Zoey.*

He said it. It was the first time he actually used my name. It was so jarring to have his lips curve over the letters of my name. The way my heart pounded when his deep voice called for me. Granted, I was free-falling into the sea, but strangely I almost forgot about the fact I couldn't swim. When I heard my name, there was nothing else. I rubbed at my temple, trying to push all thoughts of him saying my name or the fact I was lying practically naked next to him.

I glanced at him. He lay on his back, one hand on his axe, the other curved around me. His chest moved in steady measure, fast asleep. It was a rare time I could study him without him knowing. My eyes mapped his appearance, taking in every detail. Deep scars lined his face, shoulders, and torso. The skin grew over the wounds in a slightly lighter shade than the rest. I followed the lines of his tattoos in more detail, especially the one curving across his hip onto his ass. I would be lying to say I didn't enjoy watching him undress.

His strong chiseled face, tight braids, and Mohawk gave him a ruthless appearance. He was a guy other girls, against all better judgment, would find themselves extremely attracted to: dangerous, tough, distant, and confident. He demanded you be sexually drawn to him, without him doing a thing. He was hot; there was no denying it. Not pretty like some fae I'd seen, but masculine and intense. Like sex with him would be anything but sweet and timid. Primal and all-consuming were the descriptions which came to mind.

Daniel was the only man I ever looked at, so I never thought about being attracted to a fae. It never seemed probable. I knew too much and saw them differently than other humans did. Being this close to Ryker, I understood the lure. His physique alone would make most people get on their knees and thank his mama.

A soft moan came from Ryker, causing me to jump. I froze, waiting for him to open his eyes and catch me in the act. He mumbled, turning onto his side, facing me, still sound asleep. I released a slow breath. It would have been embarrassing and really hard to explain. *I hate you, but I watch you sleep.* Creepy.

I readjusted myself on my side and faced away from him. My head scarcely settled on the rug when a hand glided along my butt, slinking to my waist. Like an animal stuck in headlights, I went immobile. Everything went on lockdown. Rough palms traced my hip, moving softly but urgently up and down my thigh, curving toward the front of my underwear. My skin flamed where his hand slid, tingling with pleasure. Ryker's breath was suddenly in my ear as he snuggled closer behind me.

*Zoey! Move!*

I was about to clamber away, shouting at him, when his arm pulled me closer, drawing himself tighter into the back of me. Thin underwear and his boxer-briefs were the only things keeping him from finding his way in. My mouth fell open, but nothing came out. He was blistering with heat, extremely hard and huge. My heart thumped in my chest, my body responding to his touch.

"Mara," he whispered. His lips skimmed the sensitive area behind my ear.

Her name was like jumping back into the lake.

"Ryker!" I struggled from his grip. "Wake up!"

He lurched, and his head popped up. His grip on me loosened in an instant. I scrambled away. I turned to face him, clutching my knees.

His expression was clouded and confused. He looked around wildly, then bolted into a sitting position. Like a gradual tide coming in, recognition slowly washed over him, and he seemed to realize where he was and who he was with. He rubbed at his face, his lungs coming back to a normal pace. We sat in silence; neither of us seemed sure what to do or say.

His shorts still bulged.

A growling noise gurgled in his throat before he climbed to his feet. Anger pulsed off him. His fists clenched at his sides. "Go back to sleep. I'm going to go patrol the area." His voice was low and severe. He swiped his axe off the floor and pulled on his half-dry shirt and pants. Without another word, he stomped from the cabin, slamming the door behind him.

I curled my arms tighter around my legs and pulled them to my chest, trembling. I wasn't sure if it was from anger, the cold, or disgust. Maybe all three. I pressed my lashes together, trying to dispel what happened from my thoughts. There were so many things wrong with the scenario. But what made my skin itch the most was I could still feel him pressed into me. An impression of his hard-on burned into my skin, initiating dampness below.

My reaction, natural or not, appalled me.

The need to cover myself pushed me to my feet. My clothes were still damp, but I tugged them on anyway. I was restless, requiring my legs to move. Sleep was not going to welcome me back now. Instead, I headed outside for some air. There was a tree next to the cabin with a lookout plank. He could guard from below, and I would watch from above. As long as we didn't run into each other, I didn't care.

My feet and arms protested the climb, but my mind was set. I reached the top and collapsed on the wood. The moon forced its way through the dense clouds, casting an eerie glow on the sound, not too far away. The water lapped delicately. It was soothing. I reclined into the trunk of the tree and listened to the sea play and the trees talk to each other.

# SEVENTEEN

Ryker found me asleep, curled in a ball the next morning. My eyebrows furrowed when his head popped above the plank. I was about to tell him to leave me alone, when he spoke. "You'll want to see this." His voice sounded direct and unemotional. He disappeared down the ladder.

I sat for a few moments debating if I should follow. My curiosity finally got the better of me, but I moved slowly. I throbbed as if I had put myself through a spin cycle, but I kept the soreness to myself. When I reached the porch, he stood, silently offering me my bag. I snatched it from his hands, slipping the strap over my head. Peering inside, I saw he placed the contents that had survived the fall back inside. Seeing Daniel's book calmed my irate mood. It was waterlogged, but it was still with me.

"All our supplies are gone." He rolled his jaw. Tension crept over us.

"Great," I exhaled. "What did you want me to see?"

He flicked his head high, his glower still hard on me.

I glanced up. Hanging from the rain gutter was a bird feeder. The object inside caught my attention. Sprig was sprawled on his back sound asleep. His legs stuck up the side of the clear casing because his frame was too big to fit in the narrow feeder. Birdseed stuck to his lips and fur.

"Sprig!" I tapped at the case.

He lifted his head, looking around dazed. "Is not home right now. Please leave a message." He mumbled and fell back to sleep.

"Get him. We need to go," Ryker said.

"And I need food," I mumbled. "Guess we all want things we can't have, huh?" The moment the words came from my mouth, I realized they could be taken another way. I flinched and glanced away from him. I could sense his anger coiling, winding inside, ready to spring.

He whipped away from me and took off down the porch steps. "We'll head to the shelter. We need supplies anyway," he declared, like he was doing me the biggest favor in the world. His pace didn't ease as he strode into the forest, not waiting for any sort of agreement or acknowledgment from me.

"Come on, Sprig." I lifted the top of the bird feeder and pulled him out, tucking the sleepy monkey into my bag.

"Why is it damp in here? And Pam smells like seaweed," Sprig hollered.

"You don't wanna know," I muttered and followed Ryker.

Ryker and I said nothing as we traveled out of the woods and through the city to the shelter. I hoped we wouldn't have to go back to town so soon. We were trying to limit our visits to only when absolutely necessary, especially after the DMG's attack yesterday.

"This is such bullshit," Ryker grumbled. His mood was stormier than the dark clouds building above our heads. "If I had my powers, I could fuckin' steal what we need without anyone even knowing I was there. In and out. Done."

The mess and resident tents full of people were much too dangerous for us to stay in—rows and rows of cots and sleeping bags with no protection. But our self-imposed rule did allow us to get a quick breakfast and sometimes basic supplies and medicine—if Marcello and his men hadn't gotten to them first.

"Yeah, yeah. Life would be rainbows and unicorns if it weren't for me." My mood wasn't much better. We were doing everything in our power to avoid the topic of last night. To me, the faster we both forgot the better. He sent a glower my way. "Sorry. Maybe for you, instead of unicorns and rainbows, I should say pillaging villages and getting drunk off mead."

"Mead?" He shook his head. "You actually think I'm a Viking, don't you?"

"You look and act like one."

"*And* you're an asshole," a voice came from my bag. "Isn't it the main criterion for a Viking?" I swatted at my messenger bag, shushing Sprig. Anyone close by would find it rather odd my tote talked.

Ryker ignored the voice in my bag. "I lived for a very short time in the Netherlands but long after the Vikings inhabited the area."

I rolled my eyes. "Whatever. Close enough."

He could deny it all he wanted, but his genes had to

be directly linked to the Norwegians. He was the archetype of what the History Channel portrayed as a Viking. He looked like an actor ready to step onto a movie set.

"Get some food, human. Then let's get out of here."

We were back to "human" again. Fine, two could play that game.

"Yes, master fae." I bowed my head subserviently, my expression tight and full of mockery. His scowl deepened, curving between his eyebrows. He snarled but didn't say anything. For some reason, his irritation only pleased me.

I let him walk in front of me, a gratified smile curling my mouth. It quickly fell as I watched him stride to the tent. His ass was so taut and full it would drag anyone's focus to it. It looked like every time he flexed his foot to step, it was standing up waving "Hi! I'm Ryker's ass." His muscular broad shoulders and narrow waist seemed to demand attention also, but it was large hands dangling at his sides that captured my full focus, the hands that had brushed across my skin, leaving quivers in their wake. Fingers that dug into my skin, pulling me into him. Hot and ready.

A flush burned along my neck to my cheeks. *Revolting, Zoey.* I shook my head, clearing the memory. I folded my arms over my chest, looking away. My sour mood turned bitter and acrid in my gut.

"Now you stay quiet." I poked at the side of the carrier. "We don't need any mass hysteria because you can't keep your trap shut."

"Wow. Someone's cranky today. You part Viking too?"

We stepped into the tent. Hundreds of people milled around in line and at tables. The odors of eggs and oatmeal wafted to my nose, and my stomach rumbled in response. The last things I ate were some green beans and baked beans.

The wait in line was agony. Ryker remained on high alert, constantly examining everybody entering or exiting the tent. My empty stomach and the wish to be away from him turned the delay into a test of my will. Many times in my mind I had myself running for the door, escaping from my prison warden. Sprig was being so good at being silent, I was positive he had fallen asleep, which would be fine till he started snoring.

"Hey." Ryker pushed a tray into my hands, gathering my attention to him. He sighed deeply when he tried a second time for me to take the item. His patience with me was nil today. The way we were going, we needn't fear outsiders. We would take each other out.

Wanting to control portions and keep order, men and women with hairnets served us. Slops of runny eggs, soup-like oatmeal, and slices of stale toast were divided among the masses, running amuck on our trays.

My lids blinked innocently, my expression turning extra pitiable. "Ma'am, I'm with child..." It was somewhat true. Sprig acted like a baby. "I was hoping to get extra toast. You know, to calm my stomach." I gently rubbed my belly. Again, I wasn't lying. I did feel sick to my stomach. But this was entirely due to the night before.

The tall, big-boned lady peered at Ryker, then back to me and nodded. Now I truly felt ill. Her expression softened as she looked at him and leaned closer to me, dropping two more slices of toast on my plate. "Of course, dear. I remember going through the same thing with my first. I was sicker than a dog." She squeezed my hand and winked. It was coming, I saw it. The unsolicited advice others seemed almost possessed to give new mothers. "What helped me were saltine crackers, honey, and watermelon. Also acupuncture."

The smile on my lips was forced higher. "Thank you." Yeah, I'd get right on it, especially the acupuncture. I almost snorted at the thought of going to a spa right now, as if Seattle wasn't in a major catastrophe. Sure, a spa sounded nice.

Ryker grabbed the platter from my hands as I went to get our coffee. He liked his strong and black, but I missed Starbucks. There were no caramel flavoring or whipped cream options in purgatory. I grabbed several packs of powdered milk and sugar. Nothing was going to make this crappy coffee better, but it was caffeine, and I craved it.

I held the styrofoam cups and followed Ryker to a table. He picked one alongside the wall facing the entries with no one behind us. My training didn't like leaving myself vulnerable either, so we sat side by side, both ready to act if need be. It was also easier to keep the bag between us, hiding me feeding Sprig.

Ryker set the food on the table, letting me crawl in first. I kept my bag strapped across my chest in case we needed to run, but I settled the sack on the bench, freeing me of the extra weight. The table dipped when Ryker sat, bumping my side higher. He was as far from fat as you could get, but his muscle mass was solid and heavy.

He stared at his breakfast, tugging at his plastic cutlery, and his shoulders sagged an inch. A frown puckered his forehead. My gaze followed, and I knew instantly what was troubling him. His food was touching. Actually, his portions went beyond touching; they were in a full make-out session. The oatmeal swam precariously around his eggs.

Examining my plate of food, it was clear my oatmeal and eggs were a little less venturous. The extra toast the woman gave me kept the portions divided. There was some interaction, but not like his.

I breathed deeply and slid my tray to him while grabbing his. The deep indention across his forehead eased at the switching of trays. He grabbed his fork and began eating. He munched quietly on his segregated breakfast. Movements bumped my leg as Sprig stirred next to me. I snatched a piece of toast and stuffed it into the opening.

"What? No butter? What kind of establishment is this? This tastes like cardboard." The piece of bread shot from my bag and landed in my lap.

"I swear, Sprig, if you get us caught," I mumbled harshly at my bag.

"All I am asking for is a little butter and honey," he squealed back. "It's not like I am asking for nectar pancakes with boar sausage... oh, and sweet buttermilk." A dreamlike sigh came from him.

"Shut up." Ryker hit the bag, resulting in a high-pitched yelp. A few heads spun in our direction. My face burned with chagrin.

"Sorry." I patted my chest. "Indigestion." When everyone finally turned away from us, I glared at my handbag. "You better behave, or we will not get you any more honey bars." It was an empty threat, and we all knew it. Still, it was a threat, which might make him be good.

I grabbed a caddy with butter and spread it thickly over the toast. "Here."

"No honey?"

"I've seen you eat. Butter I can clean; honey I can't."

"Eat it and be grateful," Ryker commanded.

Jeez. It was like we jumped into some alternative universe. Was this what Ryker and I would be like as parents? I immediately squashed the thought and focused on my breakfast.

My fork dove into the lukewarm eggs. Food was food. And hot food—or semi hot—was even better. But damn. They did make sure no flavor made its way into the ingredients.

Whatever expression Ryker saw on my face, it compelled him to reach out, clutching a box full of salt and pepper packets and pushed them to me. *Salt. Yes.* My hands tore eagerly into the small packages and doused my food. I loved salt. Potato chips, popcorn. I liked it all. Even more than sweet, salty items were my vice.

When I finally put the coffee to my lips, I almost spat it out. I knew it would be bad, but this was disgusting. The acidic flavor gagged me. "This is awful." Still, I held the cup, about to take another drink. My body's need for caffeine dominated my taste buds.

Ryker took the coffee from my hands. He dug into the caddy, grabbing a package of honey, and poured the thick liquid into my cup. He then stirred it and handed it back to me.

"It won't be like your foo-foo coffee you're used to, but it should be more tolerable."

Taking another sip, I nodded in agreement as the sweet substance slid down my throat. "Still crappy coffee, but thank you."

His head turned to me, our eyes connecting. "You're welcome."

In that moment, the angry tension between us receded. A truce or maybe understanding took up the space instead. We would not talk about the night before or act like it ever happened, pushing it to the far reaches of our minds. Being mad at each other wouldn't help us. We needed to be somewhat cordial. We had to be a team.

"She gets honey, but I don't?" A quiet but passionate whisper came from between us.

"You are not eating honey in my bag," I said into my cup, taking another swig.

Ryker huffed and grabbed several plastic packets of honey and shoved them in with Sprig.

A gleeful monkey chirped in response.

"Ryker," I exclaimed, glaring at him with disbelief. "I told him no."

"It'll shut him up." He shrugged. "It's only honey. What's it really going to hurt?"

Again, the surrealness of the moment sank in. A smile slowly curled my mouth. "If we're not consistent with him, he's not going to learn." I used my best "mother" voice. "He needs rules, and you cannot undermine me when I tell him no."

Ryker eyes widened slightly before he got my joke. He snorted, looking back at his plate.

"Guess we know who the fun parent is."

I laughed—an actual belly laugh. It was the first time since Daniel's and Lexie's deaths. It felt good.

Ryker was on watch as I looted the storage unit. I tried to keep it to only things we needed or might be able to trade. If I was supposed to feel guilty, I didn't. Not really. I felt more shame than when I was younger, but this was survival. Times were different now. When events like this happened, you survived any way you could.

A tap on the door told me to hurry. I glared at the door, even though he couldn't see me.

"Here, you'll need these." Sprig threw a box at me.

"These are condoms," I whispered hoarsely at him.

His eyebrows wiggled. "I felt the tension earlier. I say fight it until you need those."

"Ugh, Sprig." I tossed the box back at him, nicking him in the head. A chuckle came from him as he leaped to another shelf.

"And I said candles, not condoms."

"Same difference."

"Really?"

He winked. "Both burn vigorously all night long."

"I'm seriously gonna be sick."

A double knock shook the door, quickly followed by another. "Shit." It meant someone was coming straight for us.

"What are you doing? No one is allowed back here." A man's voice came from the other side of the door.

"Really? This isn't where you can smoke?" Ryker's tone was sarcastic.

"No. You need to go." The man's voice held a note of fear. Ryker was intimidating, and this man was probably thinking he was a troublemaker. And he'd be right. Ryker emanated danger and violence. He looked like someone who could snap at the simplest thing and beat the ever-loving crap out of you. Again, this assessment would be correct.

"No. I really don't," Ryker responded, sounding bored.

I knew better.

"Sprig." I pointed to my bag. He stuck his tongue at me.

"I am going to call security if you don't leave the premises," the man spoke with false authority.

Ryker emitted a deep laugh. "Those rent-a-cops? *Please* do."

I had to stop this from escalating.

I pointed again for Sprig to climb in. He sat back on his heels with his arms folded across his chest. "No. I am tired of being in there."

"I don't have time for this." I turned to the door. Sprig jumped on my shoulder the moment I opened it. The movement of the door caught the man's eye.

"Hey, what are you doing?" It was enough of a distraction for Ryker. His fist came up, punching the man in the face. The man went down in an instant.

"Was that necessary?" I exclaimed.

"If you hurried like I asked, then I wouldn't have had to hit him."

"So this is my fault?"

"Pretty much." Ryker stepped across the man, walking away.

Sprig leaped off my shoulder onto the man's chest. The man's lids fluttered, opening wider when he saw the monkey. "Ha! He just went ape-shit on your ass!" Sprig grabbed his collar. "You get it? Huh? *Ape*-shit?"

"Sprig," I warned.

He giggled and hopped on my bag and pointed to the man. "Don't mess with a Viking and his monkey."

"Where do you learn these things?"

"Bravo TV." He shrugged before crawling inside.

I snorted, then took off after Ryker. Hopefully the man wouldn't remember any of this, and if he did, he would chalk it up to a hallucination.

# EIGHTEEN

Ryker found an empty hotel room on its upper floor. It had a big patio/balcony, which made a good observation point. A lot of the rooms were being used, but as long as they didn't bother us, we wouldn't disturb them. I doubted anyone even knew we were here. We snuck in the back and saw no one as we made our way to the top. You could escape from the ground level better, but people could also get to you easier. The top gave you time and a better view.

Sprig found a drawer to crawl into for the night. I noticed he liked to sleep in safe confined spaces. I wondered if this was something he acquired at DMG. He could fall asleep anywhere, but if he was intentionally going to sleep, he picked "protected" places.

Ryker took extra blankets from a cupboard and made a bed on the floor. Dark soon coated the room, telling us it was time to go to sleep. Back in the day when they had no electricity, you could see why they followed the sun, going to bed early and rising when it did. No TV or things to do turned the evening into an early night.

My body was exhausted from nearly getting hypothermia, making my lids close quickly.

*When I opened them, I was standing in DMG's training room.*

*"Did you ever really love me?" a voice spoke behind me. I spun, already knowing who I'd see. He was dressed in his training attire. Black sweats and T-shirt.*

*"Daniel." My lips formed the word with so much joy and happiness. My feet wouldn't seem to take me any closer to him even though I wanted nothing more than to run into his arms.*

*"Did you, Zoey?"*

*"Of course." It was the dumbest question he could have ever asked me. "I loved you so much."*

*"Ah. Past tense." Anger flashed in his eyes. Something I had never seen directed at me.*

*"No... no." I shook my head. "It's not what I meant. I love you."*

*A frown creased his forehead. "If you really loved me, how can you be with him?"*

*I knew the "him" he was referring to. "It's not like that," I denied.*

*"Really?" His eyebrow hitched.*

*"Daniel, you know it's not. I'm stuck with him. I love you. Since the day we met, I fell head over heels for you."*

*A cruel smile twisted Daniel's mouth. "You have betrayed me."*

*"No!" I struggled to move to him, desperation blazing in my veins. Daniel walked backward, away*

*from me. "No, Daniel. Wait. Don't leave me. I love you."*

*"Keep telling yourself that," he said as he dissipated before me.*

*"Nooooo!" I screamed.*

"Hey. Wake up." Someone shook me. My eyes popped open to Ryker standing above me, the night rich and dark around him. "You were screaming so loud you could have woken the dead."

I pushed away from him and ran for the sliding glass door, yanking it open. Cool air washed over me, chilling the beads of sweat trickling down my face and back. Tears stung my eyes, but I didn't let them come. I felt too much pain to cry. *It was a nightmare, Zoey. Simply a nightmare.* But it felt so real. If I turned around, Daniel would be standing there again. The ache in my chest doubled me and made me gasp for air.

Slowly, I straightened and went back into the room. Ryker was again lying on the floor, his arm draped over his eyes, the blanket barely covering his shirtless chest. Seeing his naked, taut physique only sent waves of hatred through me. Everything Daniel accused me of or hinted at dug into my soul. Thorny weeds of hate pricked at the open sores.

"Are you all right?" he mumbled from under his arm.

More anger boiled under my ribs. "Fuck off, fae."

He dropped his arm, staring at me.

I stomped back to the bed and threw myself on it. I was angry, embarrassed, and disgusted.

I just didn't know at whom—Ryker or myself.

It took me a long time to fall back to sleep, but finally exhaustion took me. The nightmare still hung in the background of my new dreams, swirling with explosions and death.

When I woke again, silence cloaked the room in an eerie humming. I twisted, looking at the glass doors. They were wide open; a nippy breeze flapped the curtains, billowing them into parachutes. The sky was turning a dim shade of gray with morning light. I shifted off my belly, onto my side. The cool sheets tangled around my legs; the comforter sprawled on the floor in a heap. I shivered.

"Ryker?" I leaned forward to where his makeshift bed lay empty on the floor. The memory of the night before and the harsh way I yelled at him after he asked me if I was okay came flooding back. I was so angry and upset, and I took it out on him.

My toes curled as they gently touched the icy floor. "Ryker, where are you?" The only response was Sprig's heavy breathing coming from the cupboard, confirming I was not alone. "Ryker?" I climbed from bed, padding to the bathroom. Empty.

What if he had enough? What if he took off? Nervousness escalated the steady rhythm of my heart. Would he leave me? Even though I was sure he would never ditch his powers, which included me, the thought of him abandoning me fluttered the air in my chest. I should have been used to being discarded, but it hit on a childhood issue of being left or disposed of too many times. The guarded nightmare I kept hidden in the depths of my soul crawled its way up my throat. Most people's emotions would gradually grow from worried to terrified, but mine were instantaneous, a physiological switch permeating every muscle and fiber in me. Air filtered shallowly in and out of my lungs. He never let me out of his sight. If he hadn't left, the other option was he had been kidnapped. Killed.

"Ryker!" I broke into a run, moving toward the open doors. My hand landed on the frame, and I stopped. A gasp crammed itself in my esophagus, causing a traffic jam of air wanting to move.

Ryker stood at the far end of the balcony, dressed only in his jeans. His knees into a deep lunge; his arms swept above his head. Sweat glistened off his chest as his physique moved in quick fluid motions. Graceful and strong, he seamlessly transferred into a new position. Jumping, kicking, spinning, his form danced soundlessly across the wood planks.

I had taken several different classes in martial arts and recognized some of the methodical movements. His were somewhat different than any I had seen. They seemed more ancient, barbaric, and beautiful, as if his body was telling a story—a legend from another time and place.

He was mesmerizing to watch. His muscles moved obediently under his skin, recognizing each harmonizing movement. Powerful, strong. I shifted back on my heels, looking away from him. My arms clutched my stomach as I cleared my throat.

There was only a slight pause in his sequence, noting he heard me, before he continued the fluid routine. When he finished, he stood straight and took a slight bow. I could see his chest expand as he drew a deep breath, then swiveled to face me, his jaw already locked in a tight line.

"You should be sleeping." His voice was clipped. "You tossed and turned most of the night." He snatched his shirt off the deck lounge.

My arms compressed harder across my stomach in defense. "I woke up, and you were gone." I didn't venture on, now embarrassed for my impulsive reaction. My dream had rattled me, leaving me vulnerable and sensitive. *It would be anyone leaving me, not him personally.*

Ryker strode to me. Fae did not seem to understand personal space even when they found you repulsive. His bare feet skimmed the tips of mine, and his staggering height loomed over me. His proximity made me extremely aware I was only in my underwear and thin tee, a shirt that left nothing to the imagination. I shifted my arms, crossing my chest.

"I figured being right outside the door was still in the zone." He didn't retreat an inch; if anything, he leaned in closer.

I wiggled my toes, watching the early morning light glint off the chipped lacquer. Lexie was the one who painted them. It was before one of my late-night meetings with Daniel.

*"Zoey, most men have a foot fetish. They find red toenails sexy and enticing. Like you'll be red-hot in bed, too."*

*"Jesus, Lex. You're twelve. Where do you hear this shit?" I lay back on the rug with a huff. Lexie had the*

*foot pampering stuff in front of her on the floor. With her hands, she tucked her lifeless legs tighter underneath her.*

*"How have you not?" She rolled her eyes. "God, Zoey, no wonder you haven't pulled him yet."*

*"Hey!" I sat, leaning back on my arms.*

*Lexie grinned. "I've heard you on the phone with him. You change. You become so goody-goody. I've never heard you ever utter a bad word or disagree with anything he says."*

*"He's my boss."*

*"No." She shook her head. "That's not why. You become a different person around him." An impish grin twinkled up to her eyes. "If you want to get into his pants, you need to show him the true Zoey, the sexy dominatrix side."*

*"Dominatrix Zoey?" I laughed. I would look good in leather. "And how is painting my nails red showing him my S&M side?"*

*"Oh, it comes with whips, chains, and some spanking. But that's all up to you. I can only help so much. You need to have everything in your favor." Her shoulder hitched in a shrug. "Who knows? This might be the thing to set him off. Cause him to teeter over the edge. He could be like, 'Nah... oh, wait, her toes are painted red. Now I want to fuck her!'"*

*"I swear I am never letting you leave this house again. The shit coming from your mouth." I groaned. "What about him liking me for me?"*

*"Oh, please." She swished her hand. "With your personality?"*

*I leaned over and swiped at her. She burst into a fit*

*of giggles, causing me to pounce on her and tickle her relentlessly.*

Her giggles and pleas for me to stop faded away as pain stabbed my chest. I hadn't accepted either of their deaths yet. The day would come, and it was going to be gruesome and horrible. I swallowed the memories, looking at Ryker. Mistake. He was far too close—his unclothed ribcage and abs only inches away from the thin barrier covering my breasts. I tried to shuffle back, but rammed into the frame of the door.

"Don't tell me you were worried something happened to me?" Ryker crossed his arms, his tone gave away nothing, but a slight smirk curved his top lip. This was the perfect time for him to mention the night before, but he didn't. For this I was grateful. I wanted to forget everything about it.

"Hopeful was more like it," I grumbled.

His mouth stayed closed, but his eyes glinted with an uh-huh-not-buying-the-bullshit look. I shifted under his gaze and nodded to where he had been.

"What were you doing?"

His gaze followed mine, his jaw clenched. "Why?"

"Just curious. Looked like a form of Taekwondo."

"Something like it," he uttered and brushed past me.

"Seriously, you can't even tell me that?" I threw up my hands and twisted, following him into the room. "You fae are so secretive and over the stupidest things. You think I am going to go tattle about how you learned martial arts?" I clomped to my neatly folded clothes, snatched them, and headed for the bathroom.

"It's not Taekwondo," Ryker uttered, his back to me. I stopped. "It's Kalaripayattu. It's an ancient martial art from India. My father taught it to me. It keeps me calm and centered."

My limbs were frozen in place, scared to move an inch. I wanted him so badly to continue, to learn more about his past. When he didn't, I gulped, knowing opening my mouth could result in a full retreat from him. I had to take the chance.

"Your father?"

"Dhir was my adoptive father. He led a tribe in a remote village of Nepal."

*Adoptive?* How come he never mentioned it before? It was something we shared, could relate to. Oh, right. Because he didn't want to bond or care. I was human, beneath his esteem. "What happened to your real family?"

Ryker whirled, his eyes in narrowed gaps. "They were my *real* family."

"You know what I mean."

His jaw clenched together. "They *were* my true family. They took me in and raised me like their own. They knew I was different, but they were aware of fae. Father was the one who told me I was a Wanderer and trained me."

"Wait? You said they were aware of fae?" My brow furrowed. "Are you telling me you were raised by—"

"Humans. Yes." He cut me off.

My mouth dipped open. "But you despise humans? I don't understand. If humans raised you...?"

His shoulders rolled back, his chest straining. "It's a long story."

"But I don't understand why you hate us so much."

He ground his teeth back and forth, fury lighting the tattoos across his torso.

"Tell me. Jesus, Ryker, tell me something. Anything!"

His head jerked back to mine. "Because humans are weak. Their lives are as fragile as a soap bubble." His fist throttled the shirt in his hand.

A heavy silence pervaded the space between us. I hadn't moved an inch from my spot. My eyes were still fixed on Ryker. He shifted under my gaze.

"I'm going to go look for food." His voice sounded like a military sergeant, brusque and commanding. "We're going to lie low today." He then turned and stormed from the room, slamming the door behind him.

Surviving here was precarious. A teeter-totter. And it could easily tip to the wrong side. We constantly had to move around, skirting our enemies so they'd never find us. Staying off the streets and out of popular areas was vital. Food and water were our top motivators to move. Only the Red Cross had shelters with running water. Keeping a stock of food, painkillers, and a first-aid kit for Ryker and me were other high priorities. Today I felt grateful for Ryker's decision to stay put. Being on the run was exhausting work.

I never considered the houses I lived in to be home. Walls and a roof meant nothing to me. It was Lexie who gave me a place to belong. But I had to admit I was jealous of kids who lived in the same house their whole lives. The memories they had: Christmases, birthday parties, prom photos in front of the fireplace.

Most of all, I envied the feeling of being safe. The family inside the four walls gave you a sense of comfort and belonging. Even when you didn't get along with your parents, you knew they loved you. You would never be given back to the government because you made them mad one too many times.

I tucked the comforter around me tighter. The breeze from the open doors prickled my skin, but I liked it. Soft pebbles of rain struck the wood deck in a soothing way. Rain made me feel alive and refreshed. My legs curled underneath me in the large chair, Daniel's book on my lap.

Ryker was still gone, and Sprig couldn't handle sitting still for more than five minutes before he got the zoomies. Then he'd collapse under the pillows on the bed. The silence was heaven. Well, it was until the empty space became occupied by horrific images of Lexie's and Daniel's deaths. Lexie was the worst because my mind filled in what I didn't see or know: her crying for me, her pulling herself across the floor, her trying to get to the door before passing out from smoke inhalation.

My fingers absently rubbed at the base of my neck for comfort, my head shaking. "Stop, Zoey."

Daniel's book was the only thing that might occupy my mind, get it off my vivid depictions. I carefully opened the cover, the spine cracking like bones of an old man. The pages still felt damp from the trip into the water. Some were drying, crinkled, and more transparent than they had been.

My fingers wrapped around the edges. Tears pricked at my eyes. Daniel had touched this last. I petted the well-worn leather jacket like a lover. I snuggled deeper into the chair, preparing to read. I flicked through the first couple of pages when something caught my eye. Markings I hadn't seen before now appeared on the thin paper. I grabbed the candle next to me, holding it to the other side. Under random letters were dots.

I sucked in my breath and ran my thumb along the edge of the pages, flipping through them quickly, going from back to the front. It was sporadic, but on every few sheets the same kind of dot formations appeared.

My stomach tightened. I knew it was a code. Daniel had taught it to me. It was his altered version of an encryption he learned in the black ops. I never questioned learning it. I figured it was part of the training. Now thinking back, I wondered why I never did. Why would a collector need to break a code or know one?

I scrambled from the chair, book and candle in hand. My sudden movement startled Sprig. Pillows fell from him as he sat. "What? What's going on? Are the butterflies drunk again?" He looked around, a faraway haze clinging to his features.

"Go back to sleep, Sprig." I went to the desk and pulled the drawer open. "Yes." I snatched the notepad and hotel pen.

"But the turtles need me. They are losing in strip poker against the tree sprites," he said, clearly still half asleep.

"Then you go back and help those turtles. No one wants to have shell-less reptiles." I went to the bed, grabbing one of the pillows.

"Yeah... yeah." He lay back down. "Would rather have the bunnies lose."

I clicked my tongue and placed the pillow over him. "Naked bunnies, of course." I shook my head and returned to the desk. I sat, reopening the book. What would Daniel write a code for? Why in this book?

Using the program Daniel taught me, I went through the book writing the correlating letter that went with the symbol. This was only the first part. The letter he wrote the cipher under was used as a number telling me the order the letter went in. It was a giant puzzle. To anyone who didn't know it, it wouldn't make any sense. Daniel had spent countless hours teaching, drilling, and testing me on it. A voice in my gut was now telling me he had done it for a reason. Did he want me to find this book? He forced the connection I had to it. It was the one he carried everywhere with him, pushed me to read, quoted it daily. Of his entire library or any book in the world, he would know I would pick this one. It represented him. The paper and leather engulfed Daniel's essence. It didn't seem a coincidence.

It took a while, but after I got all the letters, I started on the order.

The world tilted on its axis, affirming what I had felt in my gut to be true. The first word stared back at me, sweat dampening the back of my neck despite the chilly rain.

The candlelight flickered across the first word I decoded.

*Zoey.*

Holy hell. My breath quickened. I rose from the seat, needing to move. It was like his ghost came back through the pages, speaking to me with a kiss of a word. Zoey. Daniel had written this before he died and hoped I would select this one and see the code. But I wasn't sure I would have ever noticed if the book hadn't gotten wet. There was no way he would count on an incident like taking a plunge in the water. It was a very lucky happenstance.

Frantically, I worked at placing the next letters. It was time consuming and my patience was skeletal.

*Zoey do not trust...*

"Jesus, Daniel," I whispered. I could feel him wanting to tell me so badly, but the words would not come fast enough.

It felt like forever, but I finally worked it out. The sentence stared at me. Taunting me with its cryptic meaning.

*Zoey do not trust not what it seems find my father he will help he is why it all began.*

The last person I thought Daniel would be mentioning in a secret code was his father. What did he have to do with anything? And why did Daniel want me to go see Daniel Senior? Wasn't he in some home with most of his mind and memories ripped away? What would he be able to tell me?

Don't trust who? The only thing I could think of was him warning me of the DMG. When he wrote this, he couldn't have foreseen what would happen to me or DMG would turn against one of their own. By now I was well aware they were not as ethical as they once appeared. Or maybe my ethics were changing.

Daniel took the time to write a code in this book, hoping I'd find it. If he wanted me to find his father, there was a good reason. I needed to locate Daniel Senior. I pulled on the knob of the bottom desk compartment, revealing a phone book. Would Alzheimer's facilities even be listed in the yellow pages?

This seemed another clue showing me there was more to DMG than I formerly believed. And it seemed connected to me. Kettenburg solidified the notion. The DMG knew who I was before they ever recruited me. How would they know what I could do? Why were they watching me and for how long? I learned early to hide or pretend I didn't have the sight. So why did they ask Kettenburg to watch me? They had him teach every course in psychology so he could keep an eye on me? Why?

I couldn't make the connections yet, but it was clear. They had been lying to me since the day I walked through their doors. I needed to figure out the reason.

It was late evening by the time Ryker returned. He walked in while I was lying on the floor, Sprig sitting on my back, holding a flashlight, as I circled places in the phone book.

"What about this one?" Sprig stabbed at the page with his long finger.

"No." I bit the end of my pen. "I'm sure Daniel mentioned driving to see his father. I don't think he's in the city."

"What is going on?" Ryker shut the door; a paper bag clutched in his other hand. The smell of French fries and hamburgers wafted deliciously into my nose. My mouth watered, and I bolted. Sprig clung on like he was in a rodeo, then pulled himself onto my shoulder, his tail wrapping around my neck.

"Do you have fast food?" I went for the sack in Ryker's hand, seeing the familiar emblem displayed across the bag. "No way. How did you get it?"

He pushed past me, walking to the desk. "I ventured a little beyond town so I would have less chance of being recognized. There are a few restaurants in the northern suburbs using generators to open for a few hours a day."

"Oh my god. You have no idea what I found." I picked up *The Art of War* and held it to my chest. "Daniel left me a code in this book." He placed the bag down and turned to me. "Daniel taught me this comprehensive encryption system..." I waved my hand. "But that's not important. Look!" I slammed the piece of paper on the desk and held the flashlight on it.

Ryker leaned over and read the words. "Okay, so we find this guy's father."

The wind in my sails fluttered down. He was not as excited by this discovery as I was. "Yeah, but come on. This is a huge thing. He might be able to tell me something. Tell me what is going on." If he wasn't having a bad day and knew his own name. The probability of me finding out anything from him was slim, but I was going to take the chance.

I told Ryker about the night Mr. Kettenburg stopped me. So much had gone on since then, I had forgotten. Again, he wasn't as thrilled as I was about the news.

"Zoey, this is your fight. If he can tell me where Garrett is hiding Amara or how I can get my powers back from you, then you will see me eager about going to see a human or the fact the DMG was stalking you in your preteen years."

"I was in college."

"Same difference."

My nose scrunched in frustration. "You're right, Sprig." I peeked at the animal on my shoulder. "He really is a *Viking*."

"To the highest degree." Sprig nodded.

"If that is supposed to upset me, it doesn't."

I watched him pull items from the bag. The aroma of the food quelled my anger and turned my focus back to my stomach. My tongue ran over my lips. "Smells amazing."

"I didn't know what you'd like, so I got a few things." He continued to withdraw more paper-wrapped grub.

My head tilted, and I peered at him. "You didn't pay for this, did you?"

"They received payment."

My hands went to my hips, an eyebrow arching.

"Or so they believed." He smirked. "We don't have money. You want me to take it back?" He grabbed for a hamburger.

"No!" I snatched it first.

I was in no place to judge and cared even less when the warm burger hit my taste buds. Flavor sang in my mouth after weeks of the bland and tasteless.

Saving the candles and flashlight batteries, we sat on the floor, leaning against the bed, consuming the bag of food. The night was pitch black, the storm clouds covering the sky in a thick murky cream. I could barely distinguish Ryker's profile, but his bulk was solid next to mine. The heat permeating from him warmed me.

Sprig curled on the bed right by my head after eating half the bag of fries, the food coma luring him into slumber.

"He's like a puppy. Go-go-go. Then, *bam*, asleep." I petted his soft fur.

"If he poops on the rug, you're cleaning it up."

I smiled, my gaze returning to Ryker. His glowing eyes flicked to mine, then back out the doors. We sat for a while in silence. I rubbed at my full and happy stomach, listening to the rain pelting down.

Ryker adjusted next to me, and finally he spoke. "My past is a sensitive area for me, and I'd like to leave it in the past."

I pulled my knees to my chest. "I completely get that. I understand about wanting to forget or not wanting to relive your past." I put my chin on my knees. "Believe me. There is nothing in mine I care to remember, and most of it I would like purged from my mind forever."

"Like?" he replied.

"Now who's being nosy?"

He nodded, stuffing the last fry in his mouth.

What gave me the urge to talk, I can't say. The need probably had been sitting on my chest for years, but I never spoke a word of it to anyone, especially Daniel. I hadn't wanted him to look at me differently.

I never had any real friends, no one who went beyond the superficial level. You had to trust and let someone in for you to really be friends. I doubted it was ever going to happen for me. Where I was from, trust was a sacred thing and could easily be used against you. The person who knew me best was Lexie, and still she was unaware of most of my past. I kept the ugly stuff from her. She was way too young to know the full truth. She didn't need my crap on her, too.

Telling Ryker seemed strangely appropriate. I knew he didn't care enough to think differently of me and even less to use it against me. It was like talking in an empty confession booth. It felt good to let it out, giving voice to my horrors, which lived inside me, tearing slowly at the cage I locked them in.

Ryker listened to it all: the beatings, drugs, alcohol, stealing, and the abuse. But he stiffened when I told the story about one of my foster fathers and the countless times he came to my bedroom, starting at the age of nine. Until I shot him. It was only in the leg. I was aiming higher, but I was young and didn't know how to handle a gun very well. After the failed attempt, I learned. I would not miss again.

DMG had their employees go to therapy, but I was good at getting out of talking in detail about my past. I would invent stuff or gloss over it. Some hoity-toity bitch with coiffed hair and a clipboard was not going to get me to bare my soul.

"Did you ever tell anyone?"

"I tried, but I discovered my nine-year-old voice was not strong enough against an adult's. He was good at making me the liar, and his wife was even worse. It didn't matter if she knew the truth. She backed her husband 100 percent. I was the ungrateful brat. He would punish me even more for saying something, so I stopped talking after a while and took it, half believing I deserved it in some way. After all, I was the girl no one wanted..." My voice quivered, and I coughed to clear it. "Whatever he did was clearly my fault, and I must have deserved it." I was speaking from my nine-year-old thoughts and not what I presently believed.

"Where is he now? Was he ever caught?"

"Not that I am aware of." I hugged my legs tighter. "It's what eats at me. He probably continued to do it to the next little girl they took in. I was eleven when I left their home, and I wanted to forget it. Now I feel horrible for letting it happen to some girl after me because I didn't try hard enough."

"You were a kid."

"Doesn't matter."

"You are remaining the victim."

"What?" My spine straightened, and I whirled to face him.

"You are blaming yourself instead of putting it where it should rightfully be. He was a grown man, a repulsive human who took advantage of an innocent little girl. He is the sick fuck. You are not to blame."

"I know."

His eyes pierced me. "Do you?"

My lower lip quivered, but I kept my gaze on him. I hated the man who took my innocence. I did blame him, but I blamed and hated myself almost as much for letting it happen. Somewhere deep inside, I still thought I somehow deserved it.

"Zoey?"

I blinked and looked away. My jaw clenched. "I am not weak."

"Weakness has nothing to do with it. It doesn't make you vulnerable to admit you had no control of a situation. What makes you powerless is putting the blame on yourself and easing it off the culprit. To take on what he did and make it your own." His voice stayed deep and soothing. He remained matter of fact, but the words struck me deeply. "And you are one of the toughest humans I ever met. You are anything but weak."

It was like the rain opened up on the desert. The simple but needed words, especially from him, broke me. He sat in obvious discomfort, watching me cry before he finally pulled me into his arms. My tears soaked his shirt. His hand slid over my head repeatedly, trying to calm me. My crying freaked him out, but he didn't tell me to stop. I could feel the weight of my tears. The things I went through would not heal immediately, but by letting them go for the first time, I felt there was a chance. Someday they wouldn't control me.

My sobs ebbed to sniffles. I pushed away from his chest, but his hands stayed on either side of my face, cupping the weight of my head. "Thank you," I uttered.

He watched me, his eyes roaming across my face. My eyes locked on his, and I couldn't seem to look away. My heart leaped into my throat and hammered in my chest.

Suddenly a rumble came from the bed, and we jumped a part. A putrid smell wafted to us. Sprig released a contented sigh in his sleep.

"Oh my god." I laughed, my nose scrunched, and I fanned my hand in front of me. Another wave of gas fluttered from Sprig.

"He's not getting fast food again." Ryker jumped, moving toward the fresh air.

I followed Ryker to the open doors.

"Damn." Ryker held his nose in his arm, shaking his head at the figure on the bed. "How does something so smelly come from something so small?"

I pushed away the odd moment Ryker and I almost did or didn't have. A strange moment meant to be ignored. The saying "saved by the bell"—well, we were saved by monkey farts.

I couldn't be more thankful to Sprig and his indigestion of greasy processed food.

# NINETEEN

The morning brought more rain. *Seattle.* Some days I thought I'd lose my mind if it rained one more minute, the clouds working as a co-conspirator and hiding the sun. Other times, mostly when I was warm inside looking out, I loved it. Today was not one of those days. I reached my peak of being cold, wet, and dirty.

Ryker seemed especially silent and Sprig overly chatty. Both were driving me nuts. For once I didn't feel anger bursting off Ryker, but he was in an odd mood. I couldn't pin it down. I would find him covertly glancing at me, but I could not decipher the meaning in his looks.

The trek was long to the care facility where Daniel Senior lived. As we traveled, I noticed the number of homeless seemed to be growing every time I turned my head. Groups of people were huddled in crude shelters they had erected. They were digging through trash or trying to set traps for rats and pigeons as food. The Red Cross shelters had only so much room, and some people preferred not to go there, wanting to fend for themselves.

Help could already be seen in the downtown area. Fire departments and volunteers worked different areas, and dogs hunted for live or dead bodies under buildings. The need was still too great and not enough hands or money. Sadly, the poorer the area the less likely any help would be coming for them, not for a long while anyway.

We walked through several tent cities on our way. People huddled together under tarps with fires they built in whatever could hold it without burning itself up. They stared at us, leery of why we were traveling through. Some ignored us, and others came out to us, like guard dogs, telling us to continue—there was no place for us here.

The other things I noticed throughout the city, especially downtown, were the memorials laid out. Flowers, pictures, or some kind of mementos were left in the place where a person lost a loved one. The pictures of children stuck in my mind the most. From the last report I heard, the death toll had risen. During the last few weeks, the lists of missing switched to accounts of the dead. Watching firemen pull body after body from collapsed buildings sent more chills along my spine.

It was crazy that one storm could cause so much devastation. The fae who created this destruction, I wanted to hunt down. But killing them would be too good or easy. This fae did not deserve a quick death. I wanted to shoot them in the legs with fae bullets and watch the Otherworld metal slowly poison them.

After hours and hours of walking, we finally made it to the facility where Daniel's father lived. "There." Ryker pointed to the one-story accommodation but steered us in a severe curve, heading for the back. I could see security and nurses milling around the front.

There was no electricity here, but this facility had huge generators, keeping most things going. My eyes widened when I saw they were government issued. Normally, it wouldn't have fazed me, but I felt it wasn't a coincidence. Every other place we saw in the city or along the way worked without auxiliary power. Why would a place way out here have it and not the ones in the city? My intuition told me it had to do entirely with who was being kept here.

"It's up to you to get in and find him without being caught. I figure most of the people living there will have a bedroom window. Sprig will go in with you. He will come find me to let me know where you are. I can sense you but won't be able to pinpoint the exact room." Ryker and I walked to the rear of the property. It had a tall wooden fence with a wire wrapped around on top surrounding the backyard. It was probably enough to keep the type of clientele they had inside. To me it was laughable. "I don't have a good feeling about this place. And I'd like to keep you in my sight."

I nodded, preferring him to be there. I had a bad reaction to the facility, as well. Its vibe felt odd. My intuition pricked the hairs on my arms.

"Let's do this. Ready, Sprig?" I opened my satchel.

He covered one eye and saluted me. "Eye, Matty."

"It's aye, matey."

"Then who is Matty?" He angled his head.

"There is no Matty. Or an eye."

"Of course, Matty has no eye. He's a pirate." Sprig rolled his eyes like *duh*.

I blew some air, looking at the sky. "Cutting off your TV."

"Simpson says what?" he screeched.

"*Simon* says..."

"Who is Simon?"

"Stop. Both of you." Ryker interrupted my reply. "Get going." He nodded toward the fence. We selected a spot near a tree. It would disguise us as we climbed over.

We moved quietly to the building. We snuck along the back till we found a window cracked open. The room was dark and vacant. I pushed up the glass. "Okay, Sprig, as soon as she locates him, come get me." Ryker spoke sternly to my bag.

Sprig was about to give Ryker a hand gesture before I closed it.

Ryker lifted me and helped me slide through the upper window. I landed on the other side, keeping low. I gave Ryker one last look before I slipped from the room and down the hall.

My awareness was high and fixed on every noise, every squeak of someone's shoe on the laminated flooring. In the first room lay a woman, at least in her seventies. She stared into space. Vacant. In the second room rested an old man. I knew from Daniel's picture on his shelf what his father looked like—very similar to his son, even the piercing blue eyes.

A squeak of a cart came from the hallway. *Hell.* I ducked into the nearest room, closing the door.

"Who are you?" I swung around. A gray-haired woman sat in the bed staring at me. "Are you my daughter?"

"No, ma'am," I whispered, shaking my head.

"I don't know you." Her voice went louder. "You're not my nurse. I know my nurse. Are you my daughter?" Her hands twisted around a cloth handkerchief. She became more confused and anxious.

"No—"

Her scream cut off my answer. "Nurse," she shrieked.

Holy shit! I needed to get away from here. I'd never been comfortable with older people. Kids, fine, but old people made me uncomfortable. Her shouting only heightened it.

I could hear commotion from the hallway. I took the opportunity and darted across the corridor and into a janitor's closet, closing it as I saw figures come around the corner.

Pressed together, my lips held back even a trickle of air. A sliver of light leaked around the edges of the door. Sprig popped his head out, and I rubbed his soft fur, more to soothe me than him.

"What's wrong, Mrs. Thorn?" A woman's voice tried to speak over the woman's shrieks. "You need to be calm."

"Someone was here. I did not know her."

"Okay." The nurse was not really listening, only trying to get her to settle down.

"I didn't know her," Mrs. Thorn repeated, letting out a shaky breath.

"It was probably our new nurse, Stephanie. Remember I came in here with her yesterday?"

It broke my heart to hear this woman. She babbled on for a while, not sure anymore what or who she saw.

The nurse finally left in search of some medication to help her sleep.

I slipped from the closet and ran, shaking from the experience. Alzheimer's was a horrible disease—soul sucking for both sides, whether it happened to you or you were watching it happen to someone you loved.

I snaked along another hallway. Two rooms in, I found who I was searching for.

Daniel Senior sat in a wheelchair staring out the window. His hair was still thick and white, kept well clipped and smoothed back. You could see he had been quite handsome when he was younger. Now, it appeared no one lived inside.

"Sprig," I whispered. He came out of my bag and hopped to the floor. "The room next door is empty; go out the window there."

He chirped and took off.

I needed Mr. Holt to be as coherent as possible. Not sure if seeing a monkey would help or hurt my cause, I needed to be on the safe side.

"Mr. Holt?" I took a tentative step into the room. I didn't want a repeat of Mrs. Thorn. "I'm a friend of your son, Daniel." He continued to stare. I took another step, shutting the door. "Mr. Holt, do you know who Daniel is?"

His neck turned to me. "I had a son named Daniel... no, David." He rubbed angrily at his forehead.

I grabbed an empty chair and pulled it to him. "My name is Zoey, Mr. Holt." I sat. "I knew your son."

"I had a son?" He slanted his head. His memories seemed to be drifting in and out, none landing securely in his mind. How horrid to lose yourself this way: to slowly misplace your memories and the ability to recognize your own family, to not even remember your own name or if you liked ice cream.

"You had two sons, Mr. Holt." I placed my hands on his.

He stared at my fingers touching his before he looked up. Crisp blue eyes, Daniel's eyes, stared into mine. Recognition took over the vague emptiness that had filled them only a moment before. "It's-it's you." His voice was barely a whisper. "I can't believe this. I would know you anywhere."

"Who?" I leaned forward in my chair. "How do you know me?"

He continued to stare at me before his interest vanished out the window, watching the small birds twitter and fly.

"Mr. Holt, who do you think I am?" I touched him again, wanting to draw his attention back. It didn't work. Frustration crept along my spine. It was not his fault, but time was limited, and I needed to understand why Daniel had sent me here. I squeezed his fingers. "Mr. Holt?"

His head whipped around, shifting up higher in his chair. "Doctor. Doctor Holt. I am a much-acclaimed doctor."

"Okay, Doctor Holt. Please, I need to know why Daniel told me to come here. What do you know about DMG?" Three letters. This was all it took to claim his attention.

His eyes widened, and his shoulders rammed the backrest of his wheelchair.

"No." He peered around nervously. "Never say their name. They are always watching. Always listening."

The burden expanded in my stomach like soap bubbles in the laundry. "I don't understand. How are you connected to them?"

Fear seemed to stabilize his wandering mind. His focus sharpened. "You don't have much time. You should not even be alive. Get away from them while you can. Daniel never listened to me. He didn't want to leave you."

"What do you mean?"

Dr. Holt gripped my hands painfully. "I am very sorry. If I knew what they really wanted to do with you guys... you were only babies." He swallowed, his jugular throbbing. "In my youth, I had been cocky and reckless. I was one of the best in medical research. I-I didn't see what I was really getting into. After you, I wanted out. I destroyed all the DNA codes. I wanted to tell the world what they were doing." Liquid lined the rim of his lids. "They had my David killed to keep me quiet and prove their hold over me. After my wife's death, they put me in here and recruited Daniel as an agent." His lips quivered. "I *am* sorry."

Muscles in my chest clenched, letting only a sliver of air into my lungs. DMG murdered David? Daniel told me his brother was killed in combat. Was he concealing the facts, or was it something he thought true? If Daniel knew or not, David's death wasn't why I was here.

"What do you mean, 'after' me? What were they doing?"

"I am extremely sorry, Zoey. Please forgive me!" He looked stressed, his eyes bugging out.

"W-what?" I stuttered. I gulped, my throat tightening. "What are you sorry about?"

A tear slipped down the old man's face. "I-I can't... everyone I loved is gone. They are stealing my mind..." His eyes clouded, a void growing between his mind and reality.

Hell, I was losing him.

"Mr. Holt." My tone was approaching anger. "Tell me about the DMG."

His lids drifted close, and for a few moments I thought he had fallen asleep. His tongue dampened his bottom lip. "I named you. You were almost lost, like the rest of them. But you were strong and determined to live. Zoey means life." He touched his throat, his voice thick. "Only a few of you survived."

"You named me?" What was he talking about?

He rotated his head to look outside. Drifting.

"Doctor Holt. Sir." I pulled on his arm.

"You lived." He sighed, his lids floating shut briefly.

"What do you mean I lived?" I asked.

"You are special, Zoey. Daniel stayed there to protect you while he found a way to destroy them. They are not what you think." He twisted, scratching at the drawer at his bedside table. He opened it and lifted a false bottom. "Here." He picked up something and shoved an object into my palm. I opened my hand. A small key sat there. "Quick. Hide it before they see." He anxiously watched the door, his hands shaking with distress. I slipped it into my pocket, which made his anxiety lessen. "I was good. I remembered." A little boy smile full of pride widened his expression. "Daniel would be quite pleased with me." He seemed like a kid, basking in the glow of a father's pride, instead of the other way around. Though it had been many years, the roles had reversed, and Daniel Junior was the father and Senior was the child. Did he even know Daniel was dead?

He closed his eyes again. "You'd be so proud of me, Danny. I did what you asked," he whispered quietly.

"What does the key unlock? What's it for?"

Daniel's lashes flicked up, his expression blank. At seeing me, worry consumed. His eyes darted nervously. "Who are you? Nurse!"

"It's me, Zoey." I placed my hand on his.

He jerked out of my grip, his body wiggling fretfully. Agitation had him rocking in his chair; a soft whimper escaped his lips. It was awful to watch the decline of the man sitting across from me, to witness the deterioration of his mind. He no longer recognized me. I was a stranger. I could not imagine how Daniel felt every time he visited his father, how horrible it must have been to go from son to a stranger. To see the man you had admired as a boy, the strong military doctor, reduced to a frightened child.

Footsteps clipped the cheap tile floor before a heavyset nurse stepped into the room. "I'm here, Mr. Holt." She froze at seeing me. A tray teetered in her hands at the sudden stop. It was filled with a cup of orange juice and various medicines. "Hey! Who are you? What are you doing? You shouldn't be here." Her authoritative voice echoed off the blank walls. "Guards!"

*Damn it.*

I hopped up, rushing to the window, my only exit. My fingers dug into the frame as I tugged at the ledge. Voices heightened around me, and more footsteps pounded the hallway. I tugged forcibly at the glass. It didn't budge.

Ryker's face popped into view. His eyes widened, responding to whatever stood behind me. "Back up!" I did what he said.

A blade slammed into the window, cracking the glass into tiny veins. Ryker's axe crashed again into the spider web of shards. The glass shattered, spraying into the room like rain. I ducked, covering my head against the blizzard of pieces. Nicks of pain hit my hands and cheek. Blood burst from the cuts, dripping down my arms and neck.

"Zoey!" Ryker's voice boomed from the other side of the window. I dropped my arm and saw the nurse and guards still cowered in the corner, protecting their faces from the flying shards. I didn't hesitate. I dashed for the hole in the window. More pain ripped through me as small pieces of glass slashed through my clothes, slicing me.

Ryker stuffed his axe behind his back in its holder, his arms reaching to help me through the opening. His hands fit under my arms, pulling me up. A guard sprang toward us, snatching something from the floor and going for Ryker. The glass glinted in the outside light as the man turned his wrist toward Ryker's neck.

*No!*

The word shot through my mind, but didn't make it out of my mouth in time. Ryker swiftly jerked out of the man's way, but I was still in his arms. Caught off balance, Ryker let me go and fell back. I tumbled over the sharp debris across the casement and fell on him. The guard jumped on the ledge, then to us.

"They warned us someone might come here for him." The tall dark-haired man re-gripped the large fragment of glass. He didn't say anything more. He didn't need to. It seemed clear they were told to dispatch whoever came to speak to Daniel Holt Sr.

My reaction was slower than Ryker's, which cost us. He tossed me from him, rolling from underneath me. The guard's arm went back and fell heavily, the shard aiming for Ryker's heart. Ryker barely had enough time to twist, his side taking the brunt of the attack. Blood sprayed, coating my face like icing. The man grabbed another chunk of the window, peering at me. "I can't let you escape."

Out of nowhere, a little brown object leaped on the man's head. Squealing and hissing, Sprig clawed at the guard's face. The guard's arms flung widely until he hit Sprig, knocking him off his head. Sprig flew across the lawn.

A roar rumbled from Ryker's chest. He jumped up, hauling his broad axe out in one fluid motion. The weight of the weapon put speed into his swing. Like chopping a juicy watermelon in half, the guard's head severed from his neck with little effort. It tumbled onto the dirt before his body followed. A high-pitched scream pierced my eardrums. The nurse, still hunched in the corner, screeched like a howler monkey.

Ryker shoved his weapon into its case and spun to me. He tore the glass sticking out of his side with a firm yank. He swore and mumbled a few things in another language. His breath was ragged. "We have to go."

My feet were lead, cemented in the ground. My eyes regarded the man's head.

"Zoey," Ryker growled and grabbed my chin with one hand, smearing the dots of blood on my face.

My neck snapped up, his white eyes burrowing into mine. They no longer intimidated me. They now were my lifeline, bringing me back to earth.

"Yeah." I breathed heavily.

His hand dropped from my face, leaving tingles behind. His fingers curled around my hand and tugged me. He began to jog, and I followed numbly behind.

"Sprig," I called. The little monkey-sprite ran for me and leaped on my arm while I opened my bag. Then he climbed into his protected pouch.

Ryker and I scrambled over the fence.

And ran.

# TWENTY

It wasn't till we heard the sirens did my shock fade and my survival skills kick in. We weaved through suburbia, a blur of fences and cookie-cutter homes. He skirted along a lane, dipping us behind a hedge.

The trauma of the afternoon sent Sprig into a deep sleep. His soft snores could be heard from my bag.

"Ryker, we need to go underground as soon as we can. We're too noticeable out here." That was an understatement. On a normal day, Ryker would never be able to "blend." Normally I could, but today we were both covered in blood, and we were running from police who surely had our descriptions blasted all over their channels.

Ryker turned to face me. "As soon as we get close enough to the city, we can go into the sewage tunnels. Until then, we have to use streets," he spoke through gritted teeth. His forehead dripped with sweat.

His demeanor sharpened my notice of him. His shirt was drenched with blood, which also soaked the top of his jeans. I saw a gash through the rip in his shirt. I couldn't help but reach out. He took a step back, away from my touch.

"You're really hurt." Dots of red fell onto his boots, splashing to the ground. I peered behind us; large drops of blood trailed our steps like breadcrumbs. "I thought fae healed quickly?"

"I will eventually, but you have most of my fae powers. I've noticed I don't seem to mend as fast as I used to."

"Shit, Ryker. We need a place to hide until you heal. Right now you are leaving a path right to us."

"They won't be able to detect me, and Earth canines don't have a strong enough nose for our blood."

"The drops will still lead them to us." I frowned. A sound of a siren in the distance brushed along my spine, giving me goose bumps. "Plus, you are in no shape to run. You look like you're going to keel over. You won't make it back to Seattle." His lids narrowed, and his arms folded across his chest. I mirrored his actions. "Don't fight me on this. Let's find a place for the night so you can rest."

He rolled his head back, looking at the rain threatening sky. "Bossy and stubborn."

"But right." I grabbed his arm and pulled him deeper into the yard where we were hiding. "Now, let's find a house which isn't occupied."

Locating a vacant house became easier than I thought. Only a couple blocks away, we found an empty residence. Cars were gone, along with most of the stuff in closets. The stale air in the home told me they had been gone for a while. They probably left right after the Electrical Storm and never looked back.

Fear was high around the outskirts of Seattle because raiding and squatting in homes were growing rampant. People who lost everything or, like me, didn't have much to begin with, understood houses in the suburbs were the perfect place to stock up. No electricity, but there was a roof, walls, food, and beds to sleep in.

As soon as we closed every blind and secured the doors, I scoured the house for rubbing alcohol and any sort of needle and thread. The house was in shades of green, beige, and mauve. Ornamental taupe wallpaper covered the living room walls; the sofa was decorated in floral pillows. It was clear an older couple lived here. They had pictures of themselves on cruises and what looked to be their grandkids, but it was only the two of them who occupied the two-bedroom house.

"I think Grandpa and I would get along." Ryker opened the sideboard in the dining room. Bourbon, vodka, and rum bottles lined the shelves. He snatched a bottle of bourbon, twisted off the lid, and took several swigs. He didn't even flinch as the harsh liquor drizzled down his gullet.

There had been a time when I was the same way. When I was fifteen and going through the "I hate the world" phase, beer and shots of cheap whiskey had been my "escape." It took me a while to realize it didn't drown out the bad things, which had happened to me or the anger I felt. The alcohol actually caused more problems. I let myself become very accessible to men, thinking sex meant they cared, and I was worth something. In truth, it was the opposite. Lexie woke me up. She got drunk one night on something Jo had left in the cupboard. When I yelled at her, she came back with "you do it." From then on, my actions changed—at least in front of her. I wanted her to be better than me and to get out of the hellhole where we were living. I wished it for both of us.

I was no saint, and I enjoyed drinking, but my reasons for doing it had changed. And my worth came from me, not anyone else.

I located the woman's sewing kit in a basket by the sofa. "Bring your friend with you." I nodded to the bottle clutched in his hand.

He took another swig. "Won't be leaving my side tonight." He tilted it toward me. "Calms the nerves."

"You really want me to have some before I sew you up?" My eyebrow cocked up.

He whipped it back to his chest, flinching at his rash movement. "You're not touching me."

I sighed and without a word ripped the bottle from his hands. I wiggled it back and forth, taunting him. "Come on. If you want this..." Once I got him into the bathroom, I leaned him into the counter.

"I'm fine." He batted at my hand.

"That's Johnnie Walker Black Label talking," I said, ignoring him and reaching for his torn T-shirt. "Let me look at it."

He jerked back before my fingers could touch him, pushing farther into the counter. His guarded expression cautioned me to step away.

"Ryker, you have been stabbed, actually *impaled* with dirty glass. You don't have your fae powers to protect or heal you as rapidly. It could get infected." My manner was matter of fact. "Let me look at it."

His nostrils flared, and he looked away. It was the closest to a "go ahead" I would get.

I lifted his shirt. I had probably touched him hundreds of times. Mostly him pushing me somewhere or grabbing me out of danger, but this felt different. Before it was in the moment, usually under perilous circumstances. This time I was purposely touching him. Suddenly, I became very aware of the unlit bathroom. The only light came from a frosted window across the room.

"Take it off." I motioned to his top. It was dirty, ripped, and saturated with blood. It would only infect the wound. His arms bent to grab the fabric and tried to tug it over his head. A hiss came nosily through his teeth as he stretched. "Here, let me help you." I stepped closer, gripping the ragged material in my hands. I tried to ignore the closeness of our bodies—the fact I was undressing him, how his breath trickled my neck, and how my knuckles slid across his abs as I drew the shirt up. His toned stomach rippled under my touch. I kept my eyes off him, but I felt his gaze burning into me.

"Lean down." My voice came out a hoarse whisper. He curled forward, and I tugged the cloth over his head. A grunt hummed close to my ear as he stood. "Sorry," I mumbled, tossing the shirt into the bathtub.

"No, you're not."

Finally seeing the wound clearly, I bit my lip. Blood oozed out of the open gash, the torn skin jagged and raw. Muscle, veins, and guts poked through the gap every time he took a breath.

"What?" Ryker's lips were closer to my ear than I expected.

"I didn't say anything." My heart slammed into my chest, unnerved by his proximity.

"You didn't have to. You have the look. It's your 'fuck, this is not good' face."

Something about the fact he knew my facial expression was jarring. "You sure this is not my 'you're a jackass' look?"

"No. I know that one very well."

I grabbed a fresh towel from the shelf and doused it with the alcohol. A sharp, smoky aroma immersed the room, spinning my head. "This is gonna hurt," I said and pressed the cloth into his side. I was ready for him to squirm like I electrocuted him, but his only response was to grip the countertop so tightly his knuckles turned white.

He took in a deep breath. "This isn't my first time being stitched up."

"Yeah, but normally you fae heal quickly." I continued to clean out the wound. Good thing I didn't have a weak stomach. Blood and open cuts didn't faze me, probably because I had seen a lot of it in my time. Mine and others.

"Yes, but the length of time for us to heal depends on how bad we've been hurt."

"And when was the worst you've been hurt?" I peered at him through my lashes.

He cringed again as the towel in my hand moved closer to the tender gash. He stayed silent for a few moments before his voice came out quiet. "One time I was burned so badly I didn't come out of a coma for a month."

I straightened up. "A month?" For a human it would be normal. I couldn't imagine a fae being hurt so badly it would take him a month to heal. "What happened?"

"How did you get burned?"

His eyes drifted to mine then went toward the door, looking out into the rest of the house. "Trying to save my family."

He had given me a very brief account about losing his family. His *human* family. "What happened?" It was not a demand but more of a request. He was such a mystery to me, so private. I wanted to be let into some part of his world.

His lids narrowed, and his body tensed under my touch. He stayed quiet so long I figured he disregarded my entreaty. He took a swig of the brown liquid.

"I didn't know my true parents. I was young when my Wanderer magic came to me. We are rare, and not much is known about us. Normal fae don't really develop their full magic potential until later in childhood or puberty when they can understand what is going on and can control it." He breathed out. "I wasn't so lucky."

I listened to every syllable he uttered but continued with my work as if it were any other story he was telling me. I threaded the black string I found and pinched his skin together. He grumbled as the needle pierced his skin and broke through, lacing the edges together.

"I was only three when I first jumped. I didn't know how to get back or exactly how I even did it. It seemed when I got extremely emotional, it would happen without me trying. I think I jumped several times before I went to the Tamang family. They lived in a remote village in Nepal in touch with the earth. They understood its magic and were raised on legends of the 'magic ones.' They took me in and nurtured me. My father, Dhir, eventually learned what I was and trained me to manage my powers. He tutored me in everything, teaching me different languages, history, martial arts." Ryker shifted his footing, taking another swallow from the bottle.

"Don't move." I tightened the string, keeping together the part I already sewed. He placed the bottle on the counter, gazing at the ceiling.

We were silent for a few beats before he spoke again. "I was returning home from a hunting trip. It would soon be winter, and we wanted to stockpile before the first snow. From a distance I saw the smoke, could hear it... the fire roaring, the screams. When I jumped back to the village, it was too late. The whole thing was in flames. Some neighbors were running away, and when I asked what happened to my family, they pointed to the house. It was in the middle of the blaze, but it didn't stop me. I popped myself inside the house.

"Fire and smoke consumed me, but I pushed through the blaze trying to find them. I saw my mother, father, and my little sister being burned alive. I tried to save them, but it was too late. I don't remember escaping. I must have passed out from the pain, but I woke a month later in Africa. The villagers near where I woke said I had appeared from nowhere. They thought I was some sort of god or devil." He uttered a tortured scoff. "In their land, either can be respected and feared."

My motion stopped. "You had a little sister who died in a fire?"

Our gazes locked. His eyes grew soft, in a mutual understanding. We had been through a similar experience. Knowing our loved ones die, horrifically, burning to death, and we were too late to save them.

He nodded. "Her name was Madhuri. She was only ten." He shook his head and seemed lost in memory. I was afraid to breathe, worried any noise or movement would halt his confession. "Madi had this habit of coming to the loft where I slept every night and snuggling next to me. She said she could feel the magic coming from me, like the stove, and I kept her toes and heart warm." Ryker blinked, his face going hard. "They all died. I could not save any of them."

"Why didn't you tell me?"

He cocked his head to the side. I glanced at my feet. *Right. Why would he tell me?* Humans shared stories to bond, to understand each other. He hadn't wanted to connect with me, a human, on any level.

"The night of the storm when I found you..." He tapered off. His Adam's apple dipped as he swallowed. "It angered me."

My teeth skimmed my bottom lip. It angered him because he felt he was reliving it.

He shrugged, and the harsh exterior plunged back over him. "It only re-emphasized humans are fragile, and they would have died eventually. Feeling love for them is pointless."

"Is this why you hate humans?"

His face turned to mine. "I could live forever. Your kind won't."

I pinched my lips and nodded. "Maybe we are feeble compared to fae, but I would rather live a short time and let myself love someone than live thousands of years and be alone."

We stared at each other for a long time. Slowly a grin curled his lip. "Who says I haven't let myself love? I just cut out humans."

His statement irritated me more than it should. I flicked my eyes to the side with annoyance, returning to my needlework. "Then I'd say you would be missing a lot." I was really talking out of my ass since I acted no different. There was only one man I ever loved, and he was dead. I didn't let anyone in, human or other. I used sex as a substitute for love. It didn't strike me how sad and lonely it sounded till now.

He stayed quiet; his stare remained on me as I knotted his guts back inside him. The tension of his gaze curling around me, igniting my skin, felt uncomfortable in our silence. "So you're learning my expressions, huh?" I changed the subject.

He snorted. "It's easy. Humans wear their emotions on their sleeves." Ryker hissed as I yanked hard on the thread, tying it off. "See." He chuckled.

I couldn't fight my smile as I looked at him. He stared at the floor, his warm breath fluttering between my breasts. The light from the window glinted off his pale eyes. Our gazes fastened on each other. Air stopped in my lungs, and a quiver went through my stomach at the intensity of his strange eyes.

I broke away and turned my head, stepping back. "I'm gonna go see what they have in their pantry. You should find a shirt... and probably rest."

He grabbed my arm, pulling me to him. Suddenly I couldn't seem to get enough air; my lungs inflated like huge balloons, expanding my chest. His hand came to my cheek. His expression was penetrating, causing heat to consume me. My lips parted, pulling in more air. His finger skated along my cheek.

"You have a deep cut on your cheek." Both his hands slid underneath my arms, grazing my boobs as he picked me up and tossed me on the counter.

I blinked several times, sucking in a deep breath of air. My hand went to my face. "I'm fine. I'm used to wounds."

"Yeah." He touched his knitted skin. "You seem to know what you're doing around a needle."

I let my legs swing back and forth. My long brown hair dangled to hide my face. "I used to be a fighter. Besides robbing houses, it was how I got money."

Ryker's eyebrows arched, a grin hinting at his mouth. His gaze covered me from the top of my head to my toes. "A fighter? You?"

I sat straighter. "Yeah," I responded defiantly. It felt like I was letting him see me naked. I never even told Daniel what I did before I started DMG. Not in detail. He knew I used to get into fights but not to what lengths it went or the fact they were organized in a seedy, dank alley with gang and drug money being used to place bets for or against me. He would have never approved, and I didn't want to see the disappointment in his eyes when he saw the dark, corrupt side of me.

It would have made a great story if I had been forced into it to pay my foster sister's medical bills or some bullshit like that. But I wasn't. The state covered most of her expenses. Not all, so the money was a great perk for extra items and special medication for Lexie. But she wasn't why I fought. I simply loved it. That changed when I met Daniel.

"A street fighter *and* a thief." Ryker's eyes shimmered with amusement. "Think we have more in common than I thought." He skipped the biggest one of all: the losing-sisters-in-a-fire bond. He grabbed the cloth and dipped the rag in more bourbon. The hefty fragrance clouded my thoughts. His hand came to my cheek. Now it was my turn to hiss from the stinging pain.

"I don't do it anymore."

Ryker tilted his head, his expression critical as he watched me. "Is it because you wanted to stop, or you thought you should?" My mouth opened and closed. "How did you get into something like that?" He continued to clean my cut.

Memories flipped back to my first paid fight. "In foster care you learn fast how to protect yourself, but I liked it more than most. Maybe because of the money or my true nature or possibly because I didn't look the part. To see the shock on the faces in the crowd when I kicked the shit out of someone a foot taller and fifty pounds heavier than me. I don't know... it got my blood boiling. It was the one time I didn't want to be anywhere else or be another person with another life. It made me feel alive." I blew out, cringing at the sting of the alcohol. He used the saturated cloth to wipe the rest of my face, clearing it of the dried blood left from him. "I liked the tangy taste of blood from my lip or dripping from my eye and the adrenaline pounding in my veins." My gaze drifted to my knees. I couldn't believe I was telling him these things I kept secret.

"Yeah, you're a biter." He smirked.

My cheeks burned with embarrassment. "I lose myself completely and animal instincts kick in."

"Like a feisty kitten."

"More like a Tasmanian devil."

He smiled. "Sure. I'll let you believe that."

He set the towel on the counter and placed his hands on either side of me, his thumbs brushing the outside of my thighs. "You'll have a scar there, but it should heal."

I shrugged. "I'm used to scars." My butt slipped off the sink, causing our bodies to touch. I figured he would shift the moment he felt me move.

He didn't.

His arms caged me between the vanity and his hips. The heat from him infiltrated my clothes and skin.

"*Bhean?*" I heard a small voice come from the living room. "Where in the suburbia hell are we?"

With one word, Sprig broke the trance, which incinerated the bathroom. Ryker jerked like he had been electrocuted. He straightened, grabbed the liquor bottle, and strode into the other room.

"Don't think for a moment I'm going to play family pet and curl up at the end of the bed. Or eat dog food... Wait, does dog food have honey in it?" Sprig blathered on.

I heard a cabinet door creak open and Ryker grumble.

"Do they have any honey?" Sprig's voice carried. Ryker mumbled something again. "Jeez, Viking. All I asked for was honey." It probably irritated Ryker that Sprig picked up on my pet name for him.

I took in a breath, held my shoulders and head high, and walked out. *Nothing happened.* And it was exactly how I willed myself to act.

When I entered the living area, Ryker leaned against the cupboard, already starting on another bottle of bourbon. Sprig had climbed inside the cabinet, tossing stuff on the carpet. "Yuck. Ick. Blah." One by one, more bottles fell to the floor. "Don't they have anything with honey? Is it too much to ask?"

My feet took me to the kitchen, and I rummaged for a few minutes before I found what I was looking for. "Sprig?" I held up the plastic honey-filled teddy bear.

He chattered with excitement, racing to me. He jumped on the counter and tugged it out of my fingers.

"Take it easy. Don't drink yourself into a sugar coma." I knew my warning was worthless as I watched him suck the thick syrup. "You fae and your sweet tooth." I shook my head, strolling into the living room. I stopped as Ryker took another swig of alcohol, his eyes on me.

Ignoring the race in my pulse, I walked to the shirtless man, taking the bottle from him. His side puckered from where I had sewn him up, looking red and angry. The owner's face watched my every move. I took a gulp and handed it back. Our eyes never left the other. He studied, explored me. It was too much, too intense.

"Maybe Grandpa has a shirt you might fit into." My legs were already moving in the direction of the bedrooms. Any reason to get away from him worked for me. I wasn't thinking clearly, the liquor mucking up my rational thoughts. Whatever moment we had in the bathroom was caused by the whiskey. Between the liquor and the day we had, my emotions were all over the map, unsure and nervous, looking in all the wrong places for comfort.

First priority. Getting the well-built man dressed.

The farther I stepped away from the heat of his body, the better I could breathe. It was growing dark, the clouds obscuring the corners. I searched the back bedroom, finally finding a closet with a few things appearing to belong to a son or older grandson. I took the shirt and headed for the front room. The smell of burning lumber and paper curled into my senses. Ryker poked at the flames growing in the fireplace. The warm glow washed across his features, glittering off his eyes.

"Here." I tossed him the white T-shirt. "It's all I could find that might fit you."

He took it and stood. My gaze watched his torso coil and shift as he pulled the shirt on. It curved over every muscle like a second skin. It was tight, but it fit well enough. I shifted my head and went to the kitchen. Sprig passed out on his back, drooling. Honey trickled from the side of his mouth. "What'd I tell you?" I sighed and opened a cupboard, examining whatever food they left behind. "Pringles!" I fumbled with the lid, trying to remove it. The sour cream and onion chip lay on my tongue, and my lashes fell. "God. So good."

I felt heat, his body behind mine. His hand came over my shoulder and grabbed the container. He took a handful, stuffing them into his mouth.

"They're good, huh?" I mumbled through bites, rounding to face him.

"I've had them before, you know."

"Well, I don't know what you fae eat."

"I've been around for a while, mostly on Earth. I've had things you've probably never tried."

"You'll eat anything. Except if they touch. Got it," I jabbed.

He ignored me and jammed another chip into his mouth.

"How long have you been around?"

"A long time."

I rolled my head back. "You won't even tell me how old you are?"

"It was before your great-great-great-grandparents were even a twinkle in their parents' eyes." He tossed another chip into his mouth. "I think we have more important things to discuss than my age. What did you find out from Senior?"

The Pringle canister stayed firmly in my hands while I grabbed a bag of generic corn chips from the cupboard and walked past Ryker, snagging the bourbon from his grasp. I traveled to the sofa and jumped on the cushions, snuggling into the corner. I took a long swallow from the bottle. My eyes watered at the harsh liquid. Ryker followed me, sitting on the loveseat diagonally from me. He slid off the settee onto the carpet and leaned back. I set the bottle on the coffee table and pushed it to him. I also threw the corn chips on the table but kept the Pringles. Sharing was one thing, but there was no reason to get all crazy.

I placed another salty piece of heaven in my mouth before I started talking. I revealed everything Daniel Senior had told me, as scattered and unreliable as it was. "He said he knew me and had named me." I folded my legs, tucking them underneath me. "I don't know. He spouted about DNA and if he only had known what DMG was up to." With every minute away from the old man, his words seemed more and more like talk of a crazy man.

"This guy is in a special home. You're really going to believe what he says?"

I shrugged. "He sounded so sure. I don't know what to believe anymore. Daniel sent me to his father for a reason... and he recognized me. He knew me. It was strange." I dug into my pocket. "And he gave me this key. He seemed really agitated, as if he didn't want anyone to see him give it to me. I think Daniel gave it to him to hold." I showed him the tiny metal object. Ryker swiped it from me, examining it closer. "I have to find what it goes to. I feel in my gut the answers I need might be connected to this key."

"There are numbers on it." Ryker rubbed his thumb across the metal.

"Numbers?"

"I know what they mean."

"What?"

"They are bank numbers. Every bank has its own. Like a code. If this key is lost, it will be returned to the right bank."

"How do you know this?"

Ryker handed it back to me. "You learn things when you steal from enough of them."

I took another drink. "You were a bank thief?" It was more in surprise than judgment.

"Typically, it was to steal from a particular vault, something my client wanted, an object of some sort. Not usually money."

"Like the stone?"

He nodded in response. "We need to find which bank these numbers coincide with. I know of a few people who might know."

"Really?" I regarded the figure before me. He was going to help me again?

Ryker pressed into the sofa and stretched, his arm propped on his knee, the bottle hanging from his fingers. "When we return to the city, I'll try to contact them."

The fire warmed the room. Between the heat of the flames and the alcohol, I felt myself slump heavier into the cushions. I finished the chips and lay on my stomach, elongating myself over the sofa. I tucked the pillow under my head, staring at the dancing flames. "A month ago did you ever think you'd be in cahoots with a human and a narcoleptic monkey-sprite, and you'd be running from dark fae and human scientists through a demolished city?" I couldn't stop the giggle at the ridiculousness of it all.

Ryker twisted his head to peer at me. The liquor was causing his lids to go half-mast. "No. Nor did I believe a fae storm could transfer my powers to another. Or my girl would be kidnapped out from under me." He bowed his head. He never let on, but after the night on the roof, I could see how guilty he felt for letting Amara be taken. There wasn't much he could do, but logic didn't curb you from feeling responsible.

I shifted my head on the pillow. "I never thought I'd lose the man I loved and my sister in a matter of hours." Staring at the fire kept me from making eye contact from Ryker. "I was supposed to go to South America with him, open a place for foster and abused kids. A place they could feel safe. Lexie would help me, especially ones who were disabled or had special needs." My mind filled with the fantasy I had developed during the years, so detailed it felt real. "On nights off, Daniel and I would head to a bar, play pool, and get drunk on cold beer. Have amazing sex."

Ryker was quiet before he asked, "Your sister was disabled?"

"Yes. Her mother was a junkie and didn't stop even though she got pregnant. Lexie would have been sequestered to a wheelchair for the rest of her life," I replied. "She was a huge reason I wanted to join DMG. If there was any way I could help her, take her pain away, I would do it. If it meant testing on fae so my sister could walk again... I didn't even think twice about it."

"And now?" Ryker's stare dug into me. It was not angry or accusing. He seemed generally interested in my response.

"There isn't much I won't do for the people I love, but things are different now. My eyes have been opened."

His Adam's apple bobbed as he swallowed, and he looked at the floor. "Maybe someday you will go to South America, get drunk, and take some hombre back to your place." He took another drink of bourbon, the liquid swishing in the bottle. The light from the fire turned it a deep molten gold. "Open your facility."

"Yeah." No matter if I went, my dream, my plan was forever altered. It would not be the same. The man I took there to have wild, hot sex with was supposed to be Daniel. The dream was now lost, and it broke my heart to dwell on it. I tucked tighter into the pillow, my lids growing heavier. "Right now, tomorrow is all I can focus on."

"We'll head back to the city in the morning, and I'll the track the guys who might know something about your key."

I didn't respond right away, letting the silence build between us. The crackle of the fire and Sprig's snores occupied the room. Finally, I took a deep breath. "Thank you for going with me today... for everything."

His gaze darted to mine. He watched me, the tension jamming in the space between us. "Go to sleep, Zoey."

It was like my body had been waiting for permission. At his request, my lids dropped closed. The warmth of the fire pulled me under.

*"Zoey!" My name rang out. I stood in DMG's training room. The black fighting mat stretched before me. My hair was tied in a ponytail, but instead of wearing training gear, I wore jeans and a top with blood drops sprinkled across the top. "Zoey."*

*I twisted around to see where my name came from. A man stood across the room, his back to me. "Daniel?" The man didn't respond to my call. "Daniel!" I ran toward the figure I knew better than my own. He turned enough his profile came into full view.*

*"You disappointed me, Zoey." His pupils shone with disgust and ire. His muscles strained along the ridge of his shoulders.*

*My legs stopped short. "What?"*

*"You let me die." His lips hitched up. "Your hands are covered in my blood."*

*I glanced down, bringing my hands up. Thick red liquid coated them, dripping in globs. Horror constricted my throat. "I-I..."*

*"You let a fae kill me. How could you do that?"*

*"Daniel, I tried to stop—"*

*"Don't lie to me. You stood there and did nothing,"* he snapped.

*He was right. It all happened so fast. I did stand there and let it happen. Could I have stopped it? I could have at least tried.*

*"I am so sorry." I held my arms against my chest. The blood did not leave my hands. It only stayed on them, like they were gloves. "I would have done anything to save you."*

*"But you didn't." He rounded, facing me fully.*

*Words caught on my tongue.*

*"And you claimed to love me."*

*"I do! I love you so much."*

*He scoffed. "I never loved you. How could I ever love someone like you? You are trash and will never be anything more." He regarded me with revulsion.*

*I choked back a sob.*

*"You've only proved my point by falling in with a fae. I wasted my time on you."*

*"Daniel... please." My chest ached by the overwhelming pain his words caused, weighing me down. "I'm sorry."*

*"Save your apologies for her."*

*"Who?" He pointed over my shoulder. I swung around to see my sister sitting on her bed. We were in the bedroom we shared. The blood was gone from my*

hands and clothes, replaced by fallen ash and black charcoal smears on my fingers.

"Lexie?" I took a few steps toward her. She sat on her bed; her face contorted in pure hate. "Lexie, what's wrong?"

Her lip twisted up, scrunching her nose. "You let me burn."

Blades ripped at my heart, a lump of shame curling in my stomach. I stood by our shared dresser, a picture of the two of us sat on top. The glass crackled and popped and burst into flames.

"You let me burn," Lexie growled again.

I turned away from the picture and back to her. "I am so sorry. I tried to get to you. I did..." My feet moved to her but only got halfway before they stuck to the floor, unable to move. I tried to raise my feet, but my muscles wouldn't listen. Panic and fear crawled along my spine.

Her eyes flashed. "You. Let. Me. Burn!" In a flash, flames engulfed her, searing away her flesh. Shrieks of agony broke out in a chorus. They surrounded me, pounding till I was on my knees.

# TWENTY-ONE

"Zoey, wake up." A voice spoke through Lexie's cries. "Wake up." My eyes opened, and I shot into a sitting position. Sweat poured down my face, my chest heaving.

The room seemed dark and unfamiliar. I lay in a full-size bed, smelling of a flowery detergent and rose perfume. It took me a moment to remember where I was and who I was with. I had fallen asleep on the sofa, not in a bedroom. I was also clothed, but now I only wore my underwear and tank top.

The moonless night and lack of streetlights kept the room almost pitch black. The only thing I recognized was the person sitting on the bed next to me. Ryker's shadowy outline dominated the space. He only wore his boxer-briefs. The black string of his stitches across his stomach caught my eye.

"Another one?" His hand pressed into my leg on top of the bedspread. He must have brought me in here after I fell asleep.

I nodded. My breath still struggled to remain even; the images of my dream hung heavy on me, ready to return the moment I shut my eyes.

Ryker didn't say anything else, but his hand grounded me and bought me back to reality. *It was a dream, Zoey, only a dream.* Daniel's and Lexie's distorted expressions of hate blistered in my mind. The guilt was all consuming. I understood I was the voice behind the rage—my subconscious blaming me. It wasn't actually them, but it didn't shake the chills out of my soul.

My legs pulled up to my chest, and I laid my head on my knees, the tension along my back relaxing. The weight on the bed shifted, the frame creaking as Ryker stood. His silhouette moved for the door. Terror jolted me straighter.

"Wait," I whispered. He stopped and half turned. "Stay." I couldn't be alone. The nightmares were waiting for me to lower my lids, impatient for a chance to attack again. Having someone there felt like a barrier between sleep and terror. Ryker was my shield, keeping them at bay.

He stayed in the doorway, looking like he was debating.

Desperation to not be alone, to have him next to me, rooted deep within me. "Please."

He shifted his weight and finally nodded. He came into the room. I scooted to the far side of the bed. He lifted the covers and crawled in. Fear does funny things to your walls. Tomorrow in the daylight I would probably care, but right then—in some stranger's bedroom in the darkness—I didn't. The moment he laid back, I turned into him, curling into his chest. My head fit perfectly in the crook of his arm. The warmth of him was like taking an Ambien. He hooked his arm tighter around me, pulling me into his side. I carefully skimmed my hand over my needlework, his skin bumpy where the string tightened.

Another impression dented the bottom of the bed, and I lifted my head to see a small figure of a monkey crawl onto the bed. He didn't say anything, but I felt his need not to be alone. He curled by my feet. It discharged any lingering feeling of fear or uneasiness. A smile snuggled over my features, and I tucked into Ryker even more. Drowsiness engulfed me, tugging at my conscious mind. My mouth and mind were no longer connected because I suddenly uttered, "Your sister was right. You keep toes warm."

I could have sworn I heard him utter, "And what about your heart?" But sleep took me under its wing, taking all comprehension between reality and the dreamworld away.

Sunlight streamed into the room, bringing me into consciousness. My head lifted off the pillow. I lay alone in the room. The vagueness of the night before caused me to doubt it happened at all—the whole thing a distant dream.

In the morning light, I could make out the room better. Large palm tree wallpaper covered the wall in a false tropical theme. Wicker chairs and gold fixtures only solidified it as an older couple's home. It was like stepping into a *Golden Girls* episode. There was so much rain and cloudy days in the Northwest I could see why they wanted to pretend they were somewhere warm and tropical.

The fragrance of the sheets mixed with the woman's perfume. I rubbed at my nose as the irritants continued to waft up my nostrils. I hated flowery smells, though they had to be better than how I smelled. The need for a shower hit an all-time high. A visit to the shelters should be on our to-do list for the day. They were the only place you could get a warm shower.

Images of tropical plants covered the bedspread, which fell to the rug as I rose to my feet and stretched. I hadn't slept so well in ages. It felt nice to sleep in a bed again. My dirty jeans lay across the arm of a chair in the room, and I pulled them on. I felt slightly shocked Ryker undressed me for bed. Since he was one guy who would probably not try to get a peek at me naked, I wasn't disturbed by him removing my clothes. Again. It was nice he did.

The soft beige carpet cushioned my feet while I padded to the bathroom. I avoided peering into the mirror as I made my way to the toilet. It was too early to take on the horror that would stare back at me. I did find an extra brush left in a drawer and tried to detangle the knots coiling my locks.

"Ouch." The brush tugged at the ratty mess, and I found it pointless. Too much dirt, blood, and sweat coated the strands. I stared longingly at the shower before heading out to the family room.

Ryker and Sprig were in the kitchen. Ryker sat at the dining table, staring outside. He leaned on one elbow as his fingers tapped at his mouth. Sprig sat on the tabletop next to him, contentedly eating dry cereal off the counter. The open box of Honey Nut Cheerios sat between them, looking like they were sharing them. Something about the scene triggered a smile. *This would be Ryker's version of getting his kid breakfast.*

Ryker's head twitched. He knew I was there but

didn't look at me. Our wall that had come down the night before now stood back in full force. It put me on guard. I crossed my arms and walked into the kitchen.

"*Bhean*," Sprig called to me with a mouth full of Cheerios.

"Hey." I pulled out a chair and sat at the other end of the table.

"Want some?" Sprig held a handful of gummy cereal. I shook my head.

"You'll need to eat something," Ryker said. His voice was cold and packed with displeasure.

"Yes, Mom."

His eyes peered at me with annoyance before returning to the window.

Today was going to be one of those days.

I settled in the chair. "So what is our plan this morning?"

Ryker's curved finger tapped one more time against his chin before he exhaled and turned to me. "We travel into the city. I need to find the people who can help us with the key."

"How are we going to locate them?"

"There is no 'we.' Only me."

"What do you mean?" I sat up, leaning forward.

"These men do not like humans. It is better if it's only me. They will not take kindly to me bringing a human along. And they aren't the kind you piss off, especially when you need their help."

Frustration singed at the edges of my patience. "Fine." It wasn't fine. "What should I do while you track these guys?"

Ryker shrugged.

I ground my teeth. "Sprig and I will go to a shelter. I need a shower anyway." I stood and moved to a cupboard. There was nothing much in it except for stale bran cereal. Cheerios it was. I poured my own mound on the table and munched quietly.

Ryker got up, shaking his arms in irritation. "When you're done smacking your lips, I'll be outside waiting." He strapped on his harness and inserted his axe. His boots beat the floor as he stomped through the sliding glass door.

Sprig's head rolled to me. "Wow. Viking's in a pissy mood this morning. What'd you do? Give him blue balls?"

"Sprig!" I choked on an oat loop. "I didn't do anything."

The monkey's little eyebrows hooked up.

"I swear."

"I saw you two last night. Don't tell me nothing is going on."

"You know nothing went on. You slept with us," I exclaimed. "Plus, eww."

Sprig rolled his eyes. "Deny it all you want. And I wasn't talking about you two doing the hokey-pokey. It's more than that."

"I don't want to talk about this anymore." I got out of the chair, grabbed my jacket, and slipped it on. I lifted my bag from the counter and threw the strap over my head.

"Why? Hitting on a nerve?"

"What will it take for you to shut up?"

"This is fun."

"I will get you a dozen granola bars when we get to the shelter, the ones with honey."

Sprig tilted his head. "Shutting up now."

I stuffed whatever I could into my bag: medicine, Band-Aids, rubbing alcohol. There wasn't much. Whoever lived here did a good job of clearing out. "Sprig." I pointed to my bag.

"Am I really so noticeable?"

"A human girl, a talking monkey, and a Viking look-alike? Yeah, we stand out no matter what, but you will cause panic if you open your mouth."

He humphed, shoveling a last handful of cereal into his mouth before crawling into the bag I held. He settled at the bottom, wrapping around his goat.

"By the way, how do you know about blue balls?" He opened his mouth to speak, before I cut him off. "You know what? Don't tell me."

"But—"

I closed the top of the bag, drowning out Sprig's response and headed after Ryker. I was better off not knowing about Sprig's understanding of blue balls.

We trekked back to the city toward the Red Cross shelter residing in the northern part of Seattle. It had only been a day, but the city looked in further disrepair. The air held hopelessness. All promise and faith were buried along with the dead. People milled around, homeless and idle, waiting for something to happen. The county, the state, and local volunteer services tried their best, but with so much devastation, it seemed impossible to help everyone. There were so many layers needing attention. Where did you start? The crumbled buildings, the electricity, the water, the homeless people, the dead, food, homes, medicine, or the people still alive under the rubble, if there were any living? It was all desperately needed. It would take years to get this city on its feet again. Until then, for those who couldn't get out of the city, they hung around—waiting.

Ryker did a full sweep of the area before he found me a less populated tent.

"I need the key."

My finger felt for the object in my front pocket, tugged it out, and placed it into his palm. A lot of trust went into my action, but what could he do with it? This was not his mystery to unravel but mine. I had to believe he was doing this because he wanted to help me.

He coiled his fingers over it and shoved it into his jeans. "Don't leave here. I'll be back as soon as I can." His gaze darted around. I could tell he was not happy about leaving me alone, but there wasn't much else to do if I couldn't go with him.

"Well, I thought about going shopping, then maybe a movie or something."

He stared at me, unamused. "I'm not kidding. Stay put."

"Yeah. Yeah. Where am I gonna go?" I opened one of the candy bars we stole from storage and shoved it into my bag. A happy groan emanated from the inside. "I'm going to take a shower and relax. Something I recommend you do when you get back."

He didn't stink, he actually smelled incredible—a clean, earthy scent. Like the air before a storm over a vanilla field. It was strange and slightly sweet but still woodsy and masculine. Most fae had various ranges of this scent, but Ryker's affected me differently and in ways I didn't want to think about.

"Keep your guard up. DMG and Garrett are still out there, searching for us." His head was positioned deeply into the hood of the sweatshirt he took from the house where we stayed. He tried to remain hidden as much as he could, but no matter what, the man could not disguise his daunting form or distinctive looks.

"I know."

Ryker inclined his forehead, almost touching mine. His hood sequestered us, blocking out the rest of the world. He breathed in, his mouth compressing into a thin line, then pushed away from me, walking away. I watched his noticeable shape exit the room, and I wasn't the only one. More than a handful of women observed the Wanderer leave the room as if he were a magnet, most keeping a close eye on the man's ass.

The feeling of being deserted rushed to the surface, plopping me on my cot. *He'll be back. He's not leaving you, Zoey.* I was aware of my abandonment issues, but there were very few times they had reason to surface. Most of the time, I didn't let people close enough for it to be an issue. So how and why did a fae stir these emotions in me? I recognized we had been through a lot together, and I had no one else now. All the other people who could manifest these reactions in me were dead. *I am projecting,* I reassured myself. *Simply projecting.*

Opening my bag, I saw Sprig fast asleep, hugging Pam. He usually napped after he ate. Or anytime, really. I grabbed him, the travel-size shampoo, and the towel they issued every cot and took off for the shower. He would most likely stay sleeping, but I'd rather him be with me in the shower than leave him unattended on my bed. Someone could search for money and freak out when they found a monkey instead.

I hung the bag from the hook where I could keep an eye on him and got under the warm spray of water. Washing the dirt and blood out of my hair and the layer of grime from my skin felt like heaven. The water stopped after my allotted time, but I stayed till the last drop. I helped myself to clean underwear and socks from the Red Cross supply closet. Clean undies were a must. When I climbed into my clothes, it dampened my exhilarated mood. Dirty clothes on a clean body were not ideal, but at least I smelled a lot better.

Sprig stirred as I finished dressing. "Stay put," I mumbled, shoving my feet into my boots and wrapping my wet hair in a bun. I slid my jacket on and left the shower tent. When Ryker said "stay put" I figured it meant within the shelter area. At least it was how I took it.

The mess hall looked set for lunch. Small sandwiches, bottles of water, chips, and more granola bars lined the table at the far back. The sight of the bars made me ill, but my finicky appetite was put on hold when hunger struck. Several sandwiches went straight into my pouch. Actually, "pouch" was the perfect description—like a mother kangaroo keeping her young fed by stuffing food into her protected pocket.

"You good, Joey?" I patted my bag lightly. He wouldn't get it, but it amused me.

Walking back to a table, I started to take a bite of my food when the ground felt like it gave way. Fae auras came into the tent, glowing with energy. Every once in a while I would sense a fae aura around the shelters, probably feeding in their own way, but these figures came with names. Garrett and Maxen, the man who killed Daniel, stood at the entrance. Their eyes scanned the room.

"Shit." I dropped, hiding myself behind a table. A sharp squeak came from my bag. "Sorry, Sprig, but Garrett's here," I whispered hoarsely. A few people sitting around stared, watching the crazy lady talk to her handbag.

Alarm rose as I watched them walk farther into the room. *Dammit!* I wanted Ryker to be with me, but at the same time I was grateful because he was the one they were after, and he was much easier to spot. There was a chance I could get by unnoticed. Didn't we all look alike to them?

Maxen passed a piece of paper to Garrett. He took and examined it.

I could see it was my picture. *Not good. Really not good.*

He placed the paper on the table, his voice and face filled with worry and love. "Excuse me." His accent floated to me. "Have you seen her? She is my sister, and I am so worried about her. Our whole family is." The charm oozed from him, appealing to the ladies. They tilted their heads in concern.

"Oh, you poor dear." One lady patted his arm. Whether he was using glamour or simply the power of his Irish accent, it worked. They were smitten.

One of the ladies studied my picture. "I recognize her. I swear I feel like I just saw her getting a sandwich only a moment ago." She pointed over her shoulder at the food table.

*Shit.* Panic swaddled my lungs, wringing them. If they caught me or even saw me, I was done. They would use me against Ryker, and he made it clear he would not let them have the stone, no matter what. He would have traded Amara for the stone already if he were willing to be threatened. He certainly wouldn't trade it for me.

I drew my hood over my head. They advanced toward the far end of the room, studying everyone as they walked. I took the opportunity to start walking to the front. Keeping my head lowered and shoving it in my sweatshirt, I proceeded to the exit. If I walked too fast, I would call attention to myself; if I walked too slowly, I might be caught. My heart thumped out of rhythm with my steps. I tried to keep my strides steady and paced, while the beat of my heart pommeled my ribs.

The entrance of the tent seemed to grow farther and farther away, and my legs itched to run. Finally, I reached the opening and made it past. The sight outside the tent stopped my steps, a shriek vaulted around in my mouth. I chomped hard to hold it in. The area brimmed with fae. The glow of their auras colored the gray of the day. Garrett's men swarmed the vicinity, going in and out of the dozen tents located on the premises. All the guys held my picture. My teeth ground together, keeping the fear inside. I ducked my head and turned away from them. *Don't see me. Don't see me*, I chanted in my head.

"Hey," a voice called. I stiffened, solidifying in place. "Have you seen her?" I peeked from my hood. A blond fae walked to a man exiting the tent near me.

"No, sorry." The man peered at the picture and shook his head.

The fae proceeded in the opposite direction. Hot relief limbered my muscles and allowed me to move again. *Holy shit. Much too close. Why didn't he approach me?*

I didn't have time to care. I quickened my stride, distancing myself from the throng of pursuers. Following the tent around, I moved to the back of the shelter, away from the people and toward the park across the street. Trees equaled protection. At least I could disappear easier. With a glance over my shoulder, I looked to see if any of the fae had noticed me leaving. The men in the distance moved around searching for the girl in the picture and did not seem to notice the real one slip through the trees.

Getting away from them shouldn't have been so easy, but I wouldn't question my stroke of luck. I still wasn't clear of them.

The moment I hit the tree line I ran across the park and into a neighborhood. The area had been hit hard by the ES. Every few houses were burned or in pieces. I sprinted till my lungs ached. Finally my legs slowed, protesting the intense pace. I folded over my knees, taking in gulps of air. "You all right, Sprig?" I asked between breaths, opening my bag.

"Yeah. I feel a little jumbled but not much different than some of the experiments I went through." He poked his head out.

It stunned me when he made comments like this. I was such a hypocrite. Before I had no problem with DMG running tests on fae. Now it bothered me. One big reason was because Sprig had become personal to me. He was my friend. It changed things.

"I hope Viking boy sees them before he goes traipsing through yelling for you."

"Won't he sense them or something?"

"What do you think? We smell each other or something?"

"Don't you?"

"Some species do, but those are mostly shifters. They take on their animal instincts. If their animal is better at hearing or smelling, then that's what they are like in their person form, only heightened. Sprites don't have a nose, we have intuition." He tapped at his chest. "Most fae are aware of other fae, but we don't know what they are or anything like that. It's not like we wear club pins or something."

"It would be handy if you did."

"No kidding."

"Do you think Ryker will be all right? How will he find us? We can't go back there."

"His instincts are better than anyone I've ever met. He will sense something is strange." His little monkey mouth opened in a yawn. "And he will find you. No matter where you go. Believe me..." Sprig's sentence trailed off. His head fell on the ledge of the bag, soft snores escaped his chest.

I snickered and tucked him into my satchel. I placed Pam next to him and closed the flap.

Ryker told me he would be able to find me because I held his magic. So far he had an excellent record, and I was going to believe this time he would be able to again. Before I didn't want him to, now I did.

I continued to make my way through the city. I had no specific place in mind to go, since venturing to another shelter would be suicide. Garrett either had it covered already, or he would be going soon. Going to Elthia would only put her in danger, and without Ryker's presence, she probably wouldn't be so pleased to see me standing on her doorstep. My brain mulled my minuscule option list.

"Well, well, well... look what we have here, boys." A man stepped out, cutting me off. I identified his face instantly. Sleek black hair, dark brown eyes, olive skin. The night we crossed paths in the warehouse was corroded onto my retina.

Marcello.

My defense had been active and sharp but for the wrong threat—fae, not man.

Marcello rubbed his hands together, scanning my body. "I remember you. Where's your boyfriend?" The leader of the gang looked around for Ryker. "Did he leave you all alone? Such a pretty thing like you should never be left unattended."

An old reflex coiled. Fear of men, ones who wanted to dominate you, could never be unlearned. I spent too long fighting, defending myself. Humans were as dangerous as fae, a different danger, but probably even more terrifying.

Instead of ripping my guts out, he would tear my soul.

I sensed his men coming around the back, surrounding me. Impulse overcame me, and my legs darted for the widest opening in the group. They were on me in a matter of seconds. My fist cracked into a man's face. I twisted and kicked, hitting the groin of another. He fell to the ground, spitting saliva and swear words in my direction.

I grabbed another guy's arm and flipped him over my back. If there were only three or four of them, I would have been fine. I could handle myself in a fight, but there were at least twenty men. What really stopped me was the gun being shoved into my temple, the hammer cocked back.

The gang leader took a step toward me, clapping his hands. "A feisty little thing, aren't you?"

Dozens of hands and arms held me in place, the gun a strong reminder I was no longer in control.

"We've been searching for you and your boyfriend." He grabbed my face. I struggled against his grip. "You came into our house, ate our food... and how did you repay us? Three of my men are dead and five of them are in intensive care."

"The blame for one of those dead men can be laid at your own feet," I spit at him.

His fingers squeezed harder, hurting the bones along my jaw. "Yeah, about that. We don't really like witnesses. Now where is he?"

I didn't respond.

"We only want to return the favors. Show him the same hospitality he showed us." He put his face only an inch from mine. "If you don't tell me where he is, then you will become the reason he finds me... and he might not like the condition you are in when he does."

I tried to smile. "You won't get him." No matter what, I would not have told him anything, but I didn't have a clue where Ryker was.

Marcello stepped back. "Oh, I think I will." His eyes traveled over my body. "I think I have something he really wants." He pivoted on his heel. "Time to get comfy in your new accommodations, Goldilocks."

The gun slammed into my temple and everything went blurry before I blacked out.

# TWENTY-TWO

"I told you to stay put," a husky voice murmured in my ear. My lids flew open, and promptly, the throbbing in my head sent shockwaves of pain through my skull.

I cringed but kept my focus on the man kneeling in front of me. "Ryker?" White eyes met mine, an eyebrow curving up. He found me. Everything inside me wanted to react, to cheer in happiness.

"Do you ever listen?" He worked at the rope tied around my wrists, attaching me to the railing of the stairs.

"Garrett's men came. He had my picture."

"I know." Humor hinted in his eyes.

"Really? You enjoy giving me a hard time now?"

"There isn't a time I don't relish it."

"You shouldn't be here." I blinked, clearing my vision. "Marcello has been searching for you. He is really pissed. They're gonna try and kill you."

"Let the humans try," he scoffed.

"Ryker," I hissed at him.

"You want me to leave you here?"

He was taking this too lightly.

I glanced around, scouting for Marcello's men. It was another warehouse. A different one than the one we had been in before, but it appeared similar in the way it was designed. The large space stood empty, but it looked like it once housed large items for boats, like propellers, or engine parts. Hefty chains hung from the rafters, ready to crank up heavy machinery.

What bothered me was this warehouse was silent. No one was walking around or guarding me.

"This is a trap, Ryker. *I'm* a trap!"

"I know."

As soon as the words left his mouth, fifteen or more men appeared out of nowhere, surrounding him. He came in knowing I was bait—but he did anyway.

Ryker jumped and swiveled around, withdrawing his axe. His arms twitched as the muscles coiled, the blade swinging.

*Crunch.* The cleaver hit a guy in the head. His body flew, knocking several of his fellow comrades to the cement. A voice yelled and more men came from behind us. There were now more than thirty of them. There were too many men coming at Ryker at once, and Marcello's men were more prepared for Ryker's speed and strength. Marcello wanted to make sure he would not lose this time.

"Ryker, watch out!" I screamed as five men carried a thick chain connected to the ceiling in his direction. My warning came too late. The group ran for Ryker, tangling him in the cables.

"Now," a man yelled. More than five men jogged to the crane and cranked it by hand. Ryker fought and struggled against the thick boat chains. He roared with fury, his eyes burning brightly. They could only pull him a couple of feet off the deck.

"It's a shame," Marcello's voice came from the stairs above me, "what a fine pair of tits and a cute ass can do to a man. Women are like kryptonite. But we can't seem to help ourselves, huh? Even knowing this was a trap, you still came for her." Marcello sauntered down the steps, straightening his sports coat. He wore a nice suit, his expression full of haughty arrogance. He had the upper hand and loved proving to his men who was the "real man."

Ryker growled; the ire in his face and muscles twitched with the need to tear into Marcello. If the leader was afraid, he hid it under his ego. He smiled and walked to where I was tied. He watched me for a while. "Even with a lump on her head, she really is beautiful. I can see the draw." He nodded to one of his men and strutted to a table. "Untie her."

Three men were on me, unfastening the rope. They stood me and dragged me to Marcello. My eyes caught the object on the table Marcello touched.

My bag.

*Sprig!*

"Lose something?" Marcello seized my carrier and held it up. "Have to admit, I was surprised by what I found inside. Of all things I expected to find, it was not a sleeping monkey."

"What did you do with him?" A wave of sickness rocked my gut. The thought of him hurting Sprig sent bile up my throat.

"Why do you have a primate in your bag, *Zoey*?" He

said my name with smugness. "That is your name, isn't it? It's on this piece of paper I found tucked in a book with an adorable picture of you and another man. *The Art of War*? Interesting choice of reading material. These aren't things you normally find in a girl's purse."

He was leader for a reason. He was smart, and he knew things didn't make sense when it came to Ryker and me. We didn't fit the norm, and to people like him, if you didn't make sense, then you were a threat.

"What did you do with him?" I scowled.

Marcello smiled, his white teeth in contrast to his dark skin. "He is safe for now. I will decide what to do with your pet later. Right now let's focus on this one." He rotated to stare at Ryker. The chains twisted around Ryker's neck, cutting into his flesh. "How would you like your lover to die?"

Loathing gripped my air passage so tightly I became dizzy.

"I'll take your silence as you're open to anything." Marcello went for Ryker's axe, which had fallen on the floor. His forehead strained as he pulled on the handle. He tried to cover it up, but it was obvious he couldn't lift it. Ryker let out a deep laugh. Being embarrassed invoked Marcello's fury. He pulled the gun from the back of his pants and emptied the magazine into Ryker's gut. *Boom. Boom. Boom*. The gunshots continued to explode in what felt like an endless stream before the slide on Marcello's gun locked.

Screams ricocheted off the walls. My screams. The men took on my weight, my legs giving out. It didn't matter if logic told me he was fae and these were human bullets. When you watch the blood of someone you know spray across the room and pour out of his body, it sends logic out the door.

Ryker's head fell forward, his body going limp. One of Marcello's men yanked on the hand crank. The chains jerked under Ryker's weight. His body slipped, wrapping the shackles around his neck, pulling it in an unnatural angle.

*Crack.*

The loud snap bounced off the walls. Ryker's legs went limp, dangling, as his body hung from the noose.

Ice poured into my feet and bubbled along my spine like blowing into a straw.

Ryker was dead. Deep in my gut I felt it.

Marcello grinned. "I would normally say it wasn't personal—merely business. But this one is personal and even more gratifying."

Shock took over my thoughts and reactions, shutting me down. Anger bulldozed across my heart, minimizing all emotion except rage. My teeth clenched, my shoulders drawing back.

"I am sorry you had to watch that, but you need to know who runs this town. I will not be made a fool of." He ambled to Ryker, wiping one finger across his boot, catching the blood dripping out of the hole in Ryker's stomach.

I wanted to kill Marcello. I wanted to tear him a part. "Fuck you."

Marcello shook his head in disappointment and strolled closer till he stood in my face. "What did you say?

"I. Said. Fuck. You," I spit out. His hand struck my face. Spots of light blurred my vision, my cheek

Stacey Marie Brown

stinging and pulsing in agony. I spat saliva thick with blood. "Do your worst. I have had crueler men than you try to break me."

"Look at you. All tough talk. You know, it only causes this to be easier." He tucked a piece of hair behind my ear and leaned in. "And it's only making my dick harder."

Here stood another man who perceived me a certain way, underestimating me because of my appearance. Looks could be so deceiving.

The glint in his brown eyes told me exactly what he thought. My stomach rolled into a knot. I had seen the same look on other men many times in my life, including one of my foster fathers, a sick twisted prick with an inferiority complex. Seeing someone weak or in their control gave them pleasure. Metaphorically and in actuality—a hard-on.

Marcello was no different. He wanted nothing more than to put me in my place and show me and everyone around who was boss.

His smile curled up his face and into his eyes. His finger came to my chin, his minions gripping me even tighter. Knuckles stroked my cheek, leaving a trail of blood in its wake. Ryker's blood. "Seattle and everything in it is under *my* control. I regulate what comes and goes in this city. I run this town." He straightened, his gaze searching mine for a reaction. Did he expect my panties to drop at his declaration? All I could think was, *What a fool*. If he only knew what really controlled this city, he would be the one wetting his pants. His empire would soon fall. Unfortunately for me, it would not be soon enough. "And I will enjoy fucking the spirit out of you."

I kept my face frozen. I had not yet been broken. This asshole would not be the one to do it now.

Even with what would happen to me, I couldn't stop my eyes from looking at Ryker over and over again. Blood dripped, pooling on the concrete below. He hung in the chains like a scarecrow in a desolated cornfield. I searched for any flutter of his chest. Nothing. He could have survived the gunshots. But not this, not his neck snapping. He was dead.

I was alone once again. It was my fault since I stupidly let myself get attached and allowed myself to depend on someone else. With my past, I should have known better. I would not be making the mistake again.

I pressed my lips together, my attention going to the "prince" of Seattle. I always got myself out of my own messes. This was no different.

Knights in shining armor or the last-minute saves in movies were not real. After too many nights, when tears had long since stopped, did I understand life was cruel and ugly. It took my innocence and incinerated it, burning blisters into my soul. But I was a fighter. Whatever happened, whatever he did to me, he would not break me. I would live, and I would get out of this.

"Take her upstairs." He nodded to the men behind me. "Make sure she is secured." Marcello turned, his arms going up, and motioned at Ryker. "And take care of this mess. The cops keep sniffing around this area."

My muscles reacted out of instinct and wiggled against the men's hands as they escorted me to the stairs. Realizing it was a waste of energy, I let them guide me to the room at the top of the landing.

A desk faced the door against one wall, with files stacked on it. There was a chair for the person sitting at it, but no other pieces of furniture were in the room. A map of Seattle hung on the wall, stabbed with red pushpins. It didn't appear anyone, including Marcello, spent a lot of time in here. He could position himself above others to literally look down on his minions.

They pushed me through the office to the rear, which appeared to have been a storage area at one time, but now it acted as another type of holding room. For people. Broken zip ties sprinkled the area, suggesting I wasn't the first one held here. The thought of girls before me, who no longer occupied the space, sent a chill across my heart. What happened to them? Where were they now?

They dragged me to the radiator and pushed me to the floor. A dark-haired boy grabbed a few zip ties from the pile on the shelf. He had a deep cut in his top lip, which hitched the skin, never letting him fully close his mouth. The hitch-lip boy, who couldn't have been older than seventeen, laced my wrists through the plastic and looped them through a metal strip on the radiator. The ticking sound of them tightening hammered in rhythm with my heart. He pulled the ties, crushing my wrists as he strung both my arms high above my head.

"Remember me? You kicked me in the *cojones, puta.*" Another dark-skinned guy leaned in with a sneer. "When the boss isn't here... I will be." He shoved his hand under my top, wiggling past my bra, grabbing one of my breasts. My whole body howled to respond, to snarl, bite, and kick, which is exactly what he wanted from me, to react, to show my fear. I blinked, keeping my face void of any emotion. *Keep it together, Zoey.*

Hitch-lip smacked his buddy. "Back off, you sick bastard. She belongs to the boss."

The sick fuck dropped his hand from my chest and stood. He waited for the other three guys to leave the room before he turned to me. "*Te la voy a meter de mira quien viene.*"

It took everything I had to keep my face void of emotion. Vomit gurgled its way through my throat, burning holes in my esophagus. My reaction could no longer be held in. "Only way to get laid is to rape them, huh? Yeah, I can see why." My jaw set as I looked at him with disgust. I knew what was coming, but I couldn't help myself. It usually only pissed them off, making them even more determined to have you under their power, but the vileness in my chest was too much to contain.

He didn't disappoint. He grabbed my hair with a severe yank, his eyes shining with rage. "I will show you, bitch, until you are screaming." His hand gripped the top of my head and slammed it against the metal.

Blackness poured into my vision, tugging me in its grasp until I was again lost in the void of nothing.

# TWENTY-THREE

Slowly, I became aware of my surroundings before the sharp thumping in the back of my head started. I cringed, wanting to soothe the pulsating pain, but my hands would not cooperate with my mind. Then I realized I didn't feel my hands. I only felt a dull ache in my arms. My lids fluttered as they tried to open. The only thing telling me my eyes were open was a slight glow where the door stood open. The light came from someplace in the warehouse.

My arms dangled from the radiator, numb with blood loss. My ass wasn't feeling much better. Neither one of those body parts held a candle to my head. The sharp metal corner, which the bastard hit my head against, left a pain so indescribable I could barely keep my eyes open. My stomach rolled with nausea.

Things were not looking great. I was bound and probably about to be raped and murdered. Ryker was dead, and Sprig was locked in a cage, most likely to be traded in the black market or eaten for dinner.

Anger flared. This was not how I was going to die. I still had to find out who I was. What was the secret the DMG, Daniel, and Daniel Senior concealed from me? The strange hints both Daniels left me were highlighted in my thoughts with red marker. Dying this way was not going to happen. Fuck these assholes. I had tougher guys wanting me dead or tied in a room. This commonplace gang was not going to take me down.

I sucked in a breath and tugged at my restraints. They only tightened more, cutting into my skin. *No. Plastic was not going to be my downfall.* I fought against the cuffs. A trickle of blood slid along my arm, soaking into my top.

"You are only going to hurt yourself more," a voice came from the door. Marcello stood, his outline filling the jamb. He walked to his desk with very little light guiding his way. The sound of a match striking perked my ears. A glow flickered in the kerosene lamp, igniting the space. I flinched, my eyes closing against the brightness, rejecting the sudden brutality. It was like someone twisted the nerves and blood vessels in my head, which pumped and throbbed with sharp twinges of pain.

"You've been out for hours." Flames shimmered in his dark cold eyes. "I had words with Pedro. None of my men will touch you again." He took slow calculated steps before squatting to my eye level. His hand came to my hair, slithering down to touch my face. "That is my job."

My chin moved away from his touch. He might try to come across like a gentleman, but he was as vile as his men. Anybody who sexually abused someone to show control and authority was the lowest scum on Earth.

He only smiled at my reaction. "If you are curious about your boyfriend, he is now at the bottom of the ocean, being chewed on by sharks." He winked.

A stone fist punched through my chest at hearing the finality of Ryker's death. My heart felt both heavy and empty at the same time. I had gotten used to the fae being there, annoying the hell out of me. But he had been there the night when the nightmares hit strong, his warm body next to mine. I had felt safe. The few smiles I ever got out of him flickered in my head, wrenching my gut. Now I felt truly alone, but being solitary was something I was used to. It was better this way; all I had to worry about was me.

"And your circus monkey would normally go for a high price on the black market, but Seattle's priorities have shifted a little. I'm still going to put the word out. See who is interested." Words were coming out of his mouth with no emotion, but fire burned deeper in his eyes as his fingers trailed along my neck to my collarbone. "I think we'll both enjoy this."

"Doubtful."

He stood abruptly, his fingers working at the button of his slacks and taking the gun from the back of his pants. He tipped the safety off. "If you use teeth, I have no qualms about shooting you. You're pretty but very replaceable." He tapped the muzzle on my head. I fought back the gut-wrenching terror wanting to break forth. My past was revisiting me.

He shifted closer. He pushed at his pants, letting them fall around his ankles. He tugged down his boxers. His expression became distant and full of desire. He licked his lips, pushing his erection toward my face, the gun pressing into my temple.

"Marcello?" A girl's furious voice rang through the iron building, echoing off every wall.

Marcello let his head fall back in a sigh, swearing under his breath, then grabbed his pants, pulling them up.

The sound of mumbling voices floated up. "I don't care if he said not to disturb him." The girl's voice went high and whiny. "Marcello!" Heavy footsteps pounded on the metal stairs.

Marcello stuck his gun back in his pants and walked to the door. "Jesus, Maria. Shut the fuck up. Your voice is like eating glass."

"Screw you too." A silhouette of a girl lined the other side of the door. She looked to be a little younger than me and my height but much curvier. Not fat, just very filled out. Her naturally curly brown hair hung to her boobs, which were on display in her low V-necked shirt. She wore tight leggings and gold heels. I was enough in the dark and balled in the corner she didn't seem to notice me. "We have a problem. The Scorpions have taken the northern gate of the city. They have a place there where they are stashing the stuff coming from Canada."

Marcello grunted and rubbed his head. "How do you know?"

The shadows covered her, but I could still see a sly smile widen her red lips as she tipped her head to the side. There was something in the taunting stance that struck me. A memory. It flittered something in the back of my brain, but the feeling was gone before I could grasp it. "I have my sources."

"You mean your pussy has sources."

"Works, doesn't it?" She shrugged, not seeming to be bothered by his crude words.

Was she a girlfriend? An employee? He seemed all right with her being with another man.

Marcello shifted his shoulders back. "We're gonna have to show those fuckers who controls what goes in and out of this city."

Maria put her hands on her hips. "Do you need the girls? They'd love to show those dicks who has balls."

"No. I don't need females to help me fight. What kind of *pussy* do you take me for, Maria?"

Her fingers dug into her sides. "A big one. You don't get all sexist when you make money off them. They fight for you, and they can take out any guy. Hell, they could crush you."

"I still don't need any girls fighting for me in this. I need them to stay out so I can *keep* making money off them," he growled, moving farther in the room.

"The Scorpion leader, Du, is no longer afraid of you. Not after we lost so badly last time. I mean, Crazy Kat didn't simply knock Bethany out. She killed her."

He moved around the room, lost in thought.

Maria's eyes landed on me, and they widened. "Marcello, who the shit is this? What have you done? Are you kidnapping girls off the street now?" She stepped into the room, moving closer to me. Her eyes narrowed, taking me in. "Holy fuck! Is that who I think it is?"

My back tensed as I pressed into the heater.

Maria leaned closer, peering at my face. "Holy shit! It is!"

"What are you talking about, Maria?" Marcello's interest went from me to her. "Who is she?" He looked confused, irritated, and slightly intrigued. I couldn't deny there was something familiar about her. The tickle in the back of my brain moved to my chest and dropped.

"How do you *not* know? Why else would you have the legendary Avenging Angel tied up?"

Air was sucked out of my lungs. My past came from the depths, finding its way to the surface, burying me. The name brought back all the memories I had repressed for so long. For more than three years, I had been free of the street-fighter life. I had cut all ties and left behind all acquaintances and associations a short time after I started with DMG. Every day with Daniel I felt the other life becoming a distant dream. Some other girl's life. In a way it was the truth. I was another person then.

"I fought this bitch." Maria tilted her head. "Remember me? You gave me this." She pointed at the scar at the corner of her eye. "I almost went blind."

Oh, yeah. Now I remembered. She had been new to the scene, and I was not kind. If I believed in karma, I would say it had just bitten me in the ass. Good thing I didn't.

"No way." Marcello walked next to Maria. His head shook, refuting the declaration. "*This* girl is not the Avenging Angel." Seeing them side by side I had no doubt they were brother and sister. The shape and color of their brown eyes, their mouths, and cheekbones were too similar for them not to be. "Not a chance."

A deep-seated arrogance pushed to the surface. I felt offended. It wasn't like I got fat and old in the last three years. If anything, I was more fit from my training. But I had lost my blood lust, the feral aura that made my opponents afraid. Not many fought because they liked it. At the time, I did, and it showed.

"It is." Maria crossed her arms. "Tell him," she demanded, acknowledging me. His head swiveled, locking on me.

I kept my chin level. "I have no idea who she is talking about."

Maria's features pinched, and her eyes flashed with anger. "You bitch." She leaned over and grabbed the collar of my jacket. "Don't make me look like an idiot. I know you. You think I could forget the face of the girl who put me in the hospital for four days?"

"I am not a street fighter." Anymore. "But it sounds like this girl really kicked your ass." A taunting smile curled the corner of my mouth. "And enjoyed every moment of it."

The slap came quickly, but I was expecting it. I remembered her anger was predictable. She lashed out with her emotions. A good fighter learned an opponent's weaknesses. A great fighter learned how to manipulate them and turn them against their owner.

"You whore!" Maria came for me again. Marcello grabbed her by the arms and pulled her back. "It's her, Marcello. I know it is."

"I believe you." His beady eyes drilled into me. I could almost see his brain churning. He was planning something—involving me. This was bad, and I wasn't the only one who saw the glimmer burning in his pupils.

"What? What are you thinking?" Maria stepped out of his grasp, facing him.

A slow smile parted his lips, his gaze never leaving me. "If the Scorpions want a fight for the northern boundary, we'll give them a fight."

*No.*

Maria studied Marcello, then me. "What are you saying?"

"Contact your source. We are going to arrange a match. Winner takes all," he responded.

"Takes all?" Maria waved her arms. "Are you insane?"

Marcello's attention on me finally broke, his jaw set as he glared at Maria. "If you're right, we can't lose. The draw of her name will bring in a lot of money. You think Du would pass up this opportunity? If he does, he is a coward. If he takes it, he has a chance to take me. I know him too well; he will not keep away. He will not let the Scorpions appear weak." Marcello bent, clutching my chin between his fingers. "I knew there was something special about you, but I never imagined your taut piece of ass was such a meal ticket."

My teeth clamped, fear and anger puffing at my lungs with shallow gulps. "And what if I am not this girl?" I uttered. Almost no emotion leaked into my words. The years I pushed down and the person I used to be were not enough to dissolve the instincts. It was part of me and a piece I denied for a long time.

"I think we both know you are." His index finger again slithered along my neck to the hollow area at the base of my throat. "But if not? Then you die. No real loss to me."

"Are you willing to lose everything if I don't win?"

"Oh, the fight is simply a front. While you are

providing an exciting distraction for the masses, some of my men will be retaking ownership of the northern gate." He inclined forward, his mouth brushing my ear. "You are going to make me a rich man while I get back what is rightfully mine. Fate brought you to me, and I will not let this chance go to waste." He nipped at my ear, and I jerked away. He smirked and rocked back onto his heels. "I really hope you live through this, because I want to continue to make money off you."

My options here sucked. I either died or became his property, which probably included providing sexual favors. Death was looking like the better option.

Marcello turned his head to Maria. "Tell them we want a match Friday night. And make sure you leave hints as to who we have but don't actually confirm it. It will drive people out in force to see if the rumors are true."

She nodded. Her regard flickered back to me. "After the fight, let me have my turn. I want a chance with this bitch again. Show her who the better fighter is now."

"Yeah, so fair. After I've already fought a full round? I think it will only prove once again you are a mediocre fighter with a premature right hook and predictable reactions," I snapped.

Maria let out a wail and leaped for me. I tucked my head, waiting for her blows. Marcello jumped between us, grabbing Maria. "Whoa, sis." He pushed her back, putting distance between us. "Wait till after she fights. I'll give you one round with her. I need her to stay alive. She's worth too much money to me." He clutched Maria's shoulders and twisted her to face the door. "But now you have a job to do. Go earn your keep."

Her glower full of hate and promise of what was to come reached me. Then she gave him a nod and stomped out of the room.

Marcello stayed watching the door until he heard her walk down the stairs. Shortly after, there was a loud bang of a metal door clanking shut. He let out a choppy sigh and turned back to me. "If I didn't know for sure you were the Avenging Angel, I do now." He chuckled softly.

I shifted but stayed silent.

He walked back, put his hands on his hips, and stared down at me. "You're good at pissing people off, aren't you?" I was pretty sure it was a rhetorical question. "I should be more disappointed you aren't some pretty girl who could suck me off right now, but you are going to make me far too much money to be upset. Actually, the thought of all the money you will bring in makes me much harder, but I will wait till after your fight. I know how keyed up you girls get after a match."

My insides twisted with crushing hate.

"My girls help me, and I help them. We scratch each other's backs around here."

"Sounds more like forced prostitution," I snipped. "Oh, except prostitutes get paid for demeaning themselves."

"My fighters get paid." He tilted his head. "I run an operation here."

"I wasn't talking about fighting. That part I'd do for free."

His fists clenched at his sides, his nostrils flaring.

"Like your sister, you're just a mediocre game player with an inferiority complex and mommy and daddy issues."

I should have been playing the damsel, the weak-willed girl who didn't have much fight in her. My mouth would only cause his retaliation to come back tenfold. He was going to work extra hard to break me. Normally, I was good at acting and doing what I needed to get by, but after hearing about Ryker, something in me snapped. I no longer could pretend. I was a ball of fury and fear. The Avenging Angel would come out with her talons sharp and ready to attack.

Marcello did not trust the Avenging Angel to not break free of the plastic binds. He had me dragged to another portion of the warehouse. It was arranged like a cell, bars on the window and a metal door. One of Marcello's minions dug out handcuffs from his pocket, chaining me to the exposed water pipes. My arms hung from above, and my feet barely touched the concrete.

"This should put you in your place." Marcello sauntered to me, grabbing my face. "But if you try and break free, your punishment will be beyond anything you could ever imagine. You will beg me for death."

I kept myself blank.

Marcello stepped back, a snarl on his mouth. "You pretend to be tough and aloof. We'll see." He turned to the man who bound me. "Undress her."

A sickness rolled my lids shut but only for a moment. My jaw clenched.

Smartly, the man didn't say anything, but he smiled evilly when he faced me, his back to Marcello. He sliced my shirt open with a knife and slowly pulled my pants off.

I focused on the window above where pigeons lined the cell, pecking and squawking, oblivious to me. I let my mind slide so far back I was not even aware of my body. It was a trick I learned when I lived in the foster home with the vile dirtbag. I could make myself disappear, not even feeling anything going on—a pocket in your mind you could disappear to, where things were pretty and people were kind.

I was only semi aware Marcello left my underwear and bra on. It was the small blessings, I guess. It was a power trick. He wanted to demean me. Take my power away and leave me vulnerable in every way. Having me tied almost bare had nothing to do with the naked form. It had everything to do with power and control, to show his dominance over me.

His mouth was moving, but it was a buzz in the background. I was no longer there. I didn't even feel when he slapped me, but my head jerked to the side, his hand by my face, so I knew he must have. Then he stormed out of the room.

Time here meant nothing. People came in and out. It didn't matter. I stayed tucked away in my safe place, digging my heels in deeper. Becoming a vacant shell.

Leaking water from the old pipes dripped on my shoulder, trying to keep me in reality, thumping a constant beat, like seconds on a clock. After a while, even it blended into the background.

Then something changed. I could feel it even before the girl stepped into the cell. She looked familiar. She spoke to someone behind me for a while before my brain could focus on her words.

"What the hell were you thinking, Marcello?" The buxom brunette flung her arms toward me. "You expect her to be ready to fight in this condition?"

Maria. Right. Now I remembered.

Marcello walked around, examining me. "She needed to be taught who the master is."

"So you make her useless to fight?" Maria put her hands on her hips. "Are you an idiot?"

"Hey, I—"

"No." Maria raised her finger, rolling her head. "You were thinking with your dick and your ego. She pissed you off, and you wanted to beat it out of her. But it's the exact quality she needs in a fight." Maria let her head fall back. "God, you are so stupid."

His face turned a bright shade of red.

"Get her down. I only have a few hours to prepare her," Maria demanded. Marcello appeared to want to tell her off, but she stomped her foot. "Now!" He nodded and did what she said. As my cuffs were unlocked, my body fell to the floor with a thud.

"Go get me one of those boosters and some water." She sat next to me. Marcello huffed and stomped out of the room, slamming the door. "He is such a stupid fuck. Good thing I pretty much run the girls. He wouldn't know what the hell to do with them." She spoke to the room. It was humorous to watch the siblings. Maria seemed to be the only one who could tell Marcello what to do. It didn't surprise me. With tough guys like him, they usually did fear the women in their families who dominated the house.

Marcello came in and left as soon as he gave Maria the items she asked for. She tipped a bottle of water into my mouth. I was so parched it took her several times to get the liquid beyond my dried lips. Once the water flowed, I couldn't stop drinking.

Maria cradled my head. "Did I ever think one day I'd be holding the Avenging Angel in my lap like this?" She shook her head, chuckling. "Of course, if you weren't about to bring in a ton of money for my family, I'd probably enjoy kicking the shit out of you right now. But I can see clearer than my brother. His ego controls him."

She took a cloth and wiped at the dried blood at the corner of my mouth. "The buzz about you on the streets right now is insane. Even the hint you might be fighting tonight has brought people out in droves. Girl, you have caused an uproar in the underground community. You've brought it back to life right when people needed something else to think about and to be part of when our world is in turmoil. Even broke and poor, people will find the money somewhere when they need something to forget their troubles."

I swallowed, my voice breaking. "H-h-how long was I here?"

"Two days," she growled. "If I knew he was stringing up our prized fighter like a carcass in a meat house, I would have shot him. Now, instead, I have to pump your system full of drugs to get you to the fighting level we need."

"W-what?"

She clasped a needle and shoved it in my arm before I could blink. "It's only vitamins." She smiled wickedly. It wasn't simply vitamins. Oh, please, don't let it be heroin or any addictive drug.

I had seen it happen so many times. "Nooooo." I shook my head violently, trying to sit.

"Don't worry. It's not anything *too* bad." She pushed me off her and stood. "It will give you some extra energy for tonight. Now, get up. We need to get you dressed and ready to go. You are the main attraction, and we need to present you as such." She moved to the door, beckoning me to follow.

I still felt woozy, but I forced my legs under me. Warmness slid along my arm. I couldn't think about what she gave me. Whatever it was, I would deal with it later. Right now, surviving this fight was my main focus.

I inhaled and followed Maria.

My fate was taking me along a path I thought I left behind. The past was coming back, even though I thought I buried it—obviously not deep enough.

# TWENTY-FOUR

White feathered wings adorned my back, shooting in the air like steeples. They were only for my entrance. Marcello and Maria wanted it to be spectacular and give the crowd what they wanted. The mask framing my eyes was dramatic—eyes of an angry angel, heavy with black makeup. They wanted to strike fear in my opponent when in actuality, I felt more like a Victoria's Secret model. I bobbed up and down; whatever Maria injected me with pumped intense energy through my veins, making me aggressive and needing to move.

A couple of stolen generators lit lamps around the open stadium parking lot. The arena itself had been destroyed, so Red Cross could not use it as a refuge. The lot was mostly untouched. It was a perfect place for an underground fight ring.

Hundreds and hundreds of people filled the area, chanting and screaming. Maria and Marcello hid me in a tent till I was introduced, keeping the suspense growing as people continued to flood in. I admit I was pretty well known by the end of my time. I brought in my fair share of fans, but this was ten times anything I had ever seen. People were desperate to have something to redirect their sadness, fear, and loss. The crowd's energy only upped my adrenaline, keeping me hot and twitchy. I was only in a thin white T-shirt and black stretchy jeans Maria had gotten me, but I was boiling. My boots were the only familiar clothing I wore. I was sure Marcello would have loved me in some sexy outfit, but Maria insisted on something I could fight in and still keep me protected against the asphalt.

She did seem to be more of the business person when it came to organizing a match. Marcello wanted the big show but didn't care about the details. Maria was all about the fighters, helping them so they could give their best performances.

There were smaller warm-up fights set before the big match. The Scorpions' lesser-known girls against Marcello's, like an opening act before the headliner.

"All right, girl. You are next." Marcello came into the tent. He was dressed in a black suit with a white tie, and his black hair was slicked back. Even with all the turmoil going on, he wanted to present the finest and best. His eyes roamed over me. "If you even think about throwing this fight, I will slice you in such small pieces you won't die for a long, long time. Then I will find your family and do the same to them."

His threat meant nothing. I had no family. I didn't even have Ryker or Sprig anymore. When Maria moved me through the gang's warehouse, I tried to search for Sprig. I found nothing, and no one would tell me anything.

What I did see was Ryker's axe on Marcello's desk. Seeing it made his demise much more real. From then on, I *wanted* to fight.

I wanted to *kill*.

The old feelings of fighting came back. My blood boiled with life. I felt alive, and I couldn't wait to taste this girl's blood. We lived in a world where boys could say these things but girls shouldn't. I adapted to what people would accept. After the one woman gave me up over the bike incident, I pretended to be what they wanted. I played the role. With everyone. Even Daniel. With Ryker, it didn't matter. With him, I could be myself and spill my deepest, darkest secrets.

I actually missed him.

The declaration was jolting, but I couldn't deny it. I hated he was no longer around. My stomach felt sick with the thought I would never see him again. I shook my head and turned my attention back to the roar of the crowd and let it release more adrenaline. He was gone, and there was nothing I could do.

"Is the northern side secured?" Maria asked.

Marcello smiled. "Like taking candy from a baby. I knew this would work."

"Yes." Maria turned to me and rolled her eyes, letting him pat himself on the back. She was the one who told him what was going on and got it organized, but she let his fragile male ego believe it was all his doing.

Marcello offered his arm, as if he were escorting me to prom. I wanted to slug him, but I placed my hand on his sleeve instead. There was no point in combating something so trivial. I needed to get through this, and I would deal with him after. Right then, all I wanted was to fight. It was crazy how fast my old ways came back. I used to crave this high, and like a junkie, I returned for more. Even after being clean for years, it was still in my blood.

A microphone screeched feedback. I wondered if this electrical equipment comprised more items Marcello's men stole from the Red Cross.

"Ladies and gentlemen," a voice boomed. The chanting voices of the crowd quieted to a hush. "You may have heard the rumor flying around that a legend has come back to us." The crowd howled in response. "Our world is around our ankles... our town is in ruins... our hearts and souls are adrift. We have lost too many and have suffered so much." The announcer was going to milk the moment. "In a time when we feel all is gone and no hope is left, we need something to believe in." The crowd was chanting louder now. "A miracle has come to us. As if it had *fallen* from the sky and answered our prayers." *Jeez, seriously?* "Ladies and gentlemen, it is my proud honor to welcome back the one and only... AVENGING ANGEL!" The masses went into hysterics when their hopes were finally confirmed. The tease was not merely gossip.

Marcello pulled me forward. The sheet was drawn to the side for us as we walked out. The amount of energy that hit me almost pushed me on my butt. I never had this kind of response. I usually arrived, and a few men organizing it would keep me guarded from any opponent's threats before the fight started. After the contest, I would go home. I had fans before, but this was insane. This had to be because of what happened in Seattle. People were reaching for something familiar, a time before the ES.

Fans wore shirts with my moniker or wings. Signs bounced through the crowd as I descended to the improvised ring. Deafening wails burst against my eardrums. Marcello's back couldn't go any straighter, his pride booming through his puffed chest. He had the prize, and he wanted everyone to know it.

"And on the other side is the ruthless, merciless Crazy Kat!" Two figures came into the ring. The man escorting the girl must have been Du, the leader of the Scorpions. He was a skinny Asian man, but his face held a cold-blooded power. I had heard a lot about their triad here in Seattle. You did not get anywhere near them. Hard and merciless. I gulped, realizing who I was really fighting. It wasn't the girl on his arm; it was the Scorpions.

The girl was tall and lean except for her defined muscles. She was of Asian descent as well. Her sleek black hair was pulled into a tight bun, and her face was decorated with a mask, a black cat. Through the mask her dark eyes found mine. There were pitiless.

A few people cheered, but most booed her. You could see it startled her. Before my return, she had probably been the girl on top.

Falling from grace was hard.

Marcello stripped the wings from my back while I slipped off the mask, handing it to one of his bodyguards. "You are avenging one of our own. This is a fight to the death." He leaned in, kissing both my cheeks for show. "You better win." His tone left no room for debate before he waved to the crowd and left the ring.

*Fight to the death?* I wanted blood, but I didn't want to kill anyone. One thing I learned on the streets was kill or be killed. I had tried to get away from this life.

But standing here, seeing the horde of Scorpions across from me, Marcello's men behind me, and the hatred deep in her eyes, I knew she would not hesitate to kill me. There was no longer a choice. It was down to survival.

I stretched my arms and legs as my challenger had her last pep talk with her "manager." Vitality spread through me, ready for the fight to start.

Finally she turned to me, her face bare of decoration, and the announcer rang a bell.

Fight on.

I tuned out everything around me, and she became my only focus.

"So... you are the fearless Avenging Angel?" Crazy Kat taunted. "You look like nothing more than a pathetic little sorority girl." She examined me, laughing.

Goading was a big thing in fights. You found out soon who could handle their temper, and who let it control them. She was trying to learn me.

I smiled.

We danced around each other.

She kept sending out insults, including my white race and small size. I realized the more I didn't talk, the more it made her babble. She was probably used to being provoked right back. She had learned to keep her temper if they insulted her. But someone not talking, not taking her bait, unsettled her.

She had been fighting amateurs.

Finally, between the booing at her and my silence, she stepped into my space first, lashing out with the first hit. I almost wanted to laugh. This was too easy.

I twisted out of the way, using the angle to make my first strike. My fist hit her side, causing her to stumble. The crowd cheered. To them, the fight was finally underway.

She immediately bounced back at me and cracked her hand across my cheek. Her other hand hit my eye. Fire burned in my face, my insides simmering with anger. Blood gushed from my wounds.

Okay, she could rebound fast, and she struck hard. Her getting a hit on me wasn't my plan, but sometimes letting your foes land a few let you learn a lot about their style. She was not about flourish and show. She was to the point—probably why she was on top. Most got absorbed in the show of it, the performance.

She darted for me, and I jumped to the side, digging my elbow into her back as she passed. She fell to the cement on all fours. Already understanding her style, I knew she would be up quickly and be coming back for me. I was faster. My fist slammed into her cheek. It was my first really good hit, and I was expecting the high feeling to kick in. Usually, I went to a whole other level, and my adrenaline would sharpen my concentration and bring the animal out. Except it didn't come.

The hesitation cost me.

Her knuckles slammed into my ribs so hard I heard the snap of bone. Pain rocked to the core, doubling me over. She drove her elbow into my back, and I hit the pavement. She jumped on me. Her hand seized my hair before she slammed my face into the concrete. Blood pooled from the open wounds.

Something flared in me.

The crowd disappeared. My pain dissolved.

Like a robot, I threw her off my back and climbed to my feet. My senses stripped. I knew I was going to kill the threat. Something must have changed in my face because her dark eyes widened.

My arm struck like a snake. It was so fast she didn't see it coming. It collided hard with her face and swung her around. My foot slammed into her back, sending her flying onto the cement. The kitty cat tried to roll over, but I grabbed her and flipped her before jumping on her.

My fist struck her face over and over again. Blood sprayed from her nose and mouth. Red bubbles slid from the corner of her lips as a gargled cry emanated out of her throat. I didn't stop.

The cheerleaders circling enticed the violence in me to finish her off. I had never been consumed like this. It took me prisoner, stripping me of any humanity. Everything became white noise in the background. I was a good fighter, but I could feel something was different in me, giving me more strength and stamina.

*What in the hell did Maria give me?*

"Kill her! Kill her!" Chants traveled through the crowd around me.

My arm primed for another hit, when I felt eyes on me. There were hundreds watching us, but this was different, like fingers grazing my skin. My knuckles paused midair, and I looked up. The sea of undistinguishable faces blurred into a hazy outline. The only thing I saw clearly was a pair of glowing white eyes under a dark hood staring back at me. It was a gunshot to my soul, my emotions swirling. I gasped for air and fell off the girl.

Ryker.

A soft cry splintered out of my mouth. Relief flushed through me and snapped the last bit of strength and fire from my muscles. My head fell back onto the pavement; my lids blinked the tears and blood from my eyes.

"Stand up!" I heard Marcello scream at me. "Finish her off!"

I ignored him. A tear squeezed from under my lashes. *Ryker is alive.* He came back for me. My joy was diminished by the budding disgust in myself and the hatred I felt for Marcello for what he had done to me. Loathing sprouted in me like weeds, wrapping their way around my heart and squeezing. I was about to take a life. The only reason I didn't was because of Ryker. Losing him was the reason I wanted to destroy everything in my path. Seeing him made me stop. Having him alive changed everything.

I had worked hard to keep this part of me concealed. I almost believed she had disappeared, but in one day she came barreling forth as if no time had passed. She had been waiting quietly and patiently but always there.

"Get up, bitch! End her!" Marcello screamed again, his arms flying about in a fevered motion. He came close and kneeled next to me, pointing to the girl. She was almost unconscious, choking on her own blood. "Now." He seethed through his teeth, his eyes bright with anger. This fight was to the death. If I didn't kill her, then Marcello would lose face. Even though his men had taken back the north area, he didn't want to be defeated in any way. Crazy Kat had killed one of his girls. Eye for an eye. Losing on the streets was a billboard sign displaying a weakness others could exploit. It was also an ego thing. I had fallen trap to both so many times, but my fights in the past had never been to the death.

Mortality was different to gangs and street kids. You lived every day with the thought it might be your last, which made you cold and cut off, treating others' lives with the same flippancy. I probably would have followed the same road if it hadn't been for Lexie. She came into my world when I needed to learn how to respect and cherish life. That was why it scared me I wanted to kill this girl. The feeling melted away the moment I saw Ryker. But what if he had never arrived? What would have happened?

I lifted my head, blood slipped off my chin, falling on my shirt, which was already soaked with a mixture of our blood. My spine cracked as I stood.

"Come on." Marcello eagerly tugged on my arm to help me. He had the illusion I was following his demands. My shaky legs pushed me onto my feet. I wobbled a bit, my eyes finding Ryker's again. His attention was directed on me, unrelenting and unemotional. Still, his eyes seemed to give me strength and comfort. Marcello wiped the blood from my eyes. "That's my girl. Let's finish this. You and I together. Show them who rules this town."

When I was young, I would have fallen for his false encouragement. He was putting us together as if we were a team. I knew now it was bullshit. Later he would show me he was the only one in power, and I was merely a piece in his game. I no longer wanted to be controlled and told what to do by anyone: not the government, foster parents, poverty, and certainly not by this asshole. I was sick of being defined by someone or something else.

I ripped my arm from his hold. "No."

His head did a double take. "What?"

"I said no. If you want this girl dead, you do it. I am not your pawn." I turned and limped away, toward the throng of people.

Marcello grabbed me and whipped me around to face him. His jaw twitched, and his eyes widened with fury. "Get your ass back in the ring and finish the fight."

My legs could barely hold me, but I forced my chin higher. "No." Determination hardened my one-word answer.

Rage blazed in him. He clamped my shoulders and shook me so violently my teeth clattered. "I own you. If I tell you to bark, you better fucking bark!" He flung me to the hard surface. Grit and fine pebbles tore into my palms.

I had been determined before. Now I was pissed. My face turned back to his. "I am no one's to own."

He stepped over me, his legs on either side of my body. Marcello leaned and grabbed my chin. "I own you and your sweet pussy. Now get up."

"Fuck off!"

He bolted upright, his foot swinging back before it slammed into my gut. Pain snapped the air from my lungs. My already splintered ribs howled in excruciating agony. I gasped as his foot came at me again. I heard a roar in the foreground so deep it rattled my bones. Vomit burned my airway, and spots impeded my vision. Red-dyed saliva slipped out of my mouth onto the black pavement. The pain was too much for me to handle. My body curled in a defensive position, ready for the next attack, but it never came. Out of the corner of my eye, I caught movement. Fury rolled off a figure as it came at us like a speeding train. The blunt, thick end of a battle axe swung, striking Marcello's skull. The man looming over me went flying, his body tossed into the crowd like a ragdoll. Marcello's men responded promptly, coming at the attacker.

Ryker let his hood drop, his stance widening, the axe swinging in anticipation. Gasps and screams traveled through the group.

"You're supposed to be dead," one of Marcello's men cried. It was Pedro, the one who shoved his hand down my top.

"You're not very good at your job," Ryker's voice growled. "However, I am." He leaped for Pedro. The axe in his hand twirled so fast the human eye could barely see it. Like bowling pins, Ryker knocked several men off their feet with only a couple of swings. Pedro skidded across the cement. Blood poured from a gap in his chest.

Groups of men fell, groaning as the blade made contact with their heads, stomachs, and chests. Under the lights from the generator, Ryker's eyes and his tattoo, scrolling up his neck, smoldered bright. An internal neon sign burning from the inside.

In less than a minute, the first line of threat lay scattered; the second string took one look at the furious Wanderer and stepped away. It was not hard to see there was something strange about him. If I didn't know him, I would have been cowering in the corner. Rage expanded his chest, spreading his shoulders and adding to his intimidating stature. His face was stone, but the fury burning in his eyes was something I had never seen. He rotated, facing the circle of humans, pointing his blade at everyone. In unison the mass stepped away from him.

Adrenaline was leaking from my veins, and my eyelids grew heavy, but my pain level spiked higher.

Movement from a lump lying at the feet of the crowd twitched. My eyes landed on Marcello. His chest slowly rose and fell. He was alive, but the side of his head was caved in. It created a ghastly deformed outline. This time vomit made its way through my throat and out.

Ryker was at my side, his arms scooting underneath me. He huddled me close to him as he rose. He let out a warning growl to anyone thinking about challenging him. When no one moved, he took steps out of the circle. The throng parted, forming a vast space for us to walk through. No one uttered a word as we passed. They kept their distance; fear rooted deep in their eyes.

On the other hand, I felt safe. I burrowed my head deeper into his warm chest. Ryker was here. He was alive. For the first time since we'd been separated, I took my first real breath of air.

# TWENTY-FIVE

I figured Ryker would take us as far from the fighting ring as possible; instead, he ducked into a restroom off the street near a park. He held me with one hand while he locked the door behind us. "Are we safe here?" I gazed around the dirty community restroom.

He walked to the counter and placed me carefully there. "No one will follow us." His tone left no room for doubt. He took off the cloak and threw it on the floor. It hit with a heavier presence than a cape should. He stepped to the counter, taking my gaze away from the item on the ground. "Is anything broken?" He placed his hands on my shoulders and methodically slid the length of my arms, his fingers investigating my torn skin.

"A few ribs." I grimaced from trying to sit straighter.

He didn't look at me, but his hands went to my ribs. "Do you mind?" He nodded to my shirt. I shook my head. The white shirt was soaked red and ripped in so many places it was almost pointless.

I struggled to lift my arms. He bunched the fabric on my torso and then slipped it over my head. A gruff inhale came from Ryker's nose. A frown etched between his brows. The tips of his fingers glided over my painful skin. I peered down and let out a chirp. My stomach and ribs were already turning a deep purplish-blue. He pressed harder, concentrating on each bone. It was painful, but his touch also warmed my muscles, creating a tingle to run through them.

"None feel broken, but some may be cracked." He let his hand drop. This news felt odd to me. I had heard them break like a snap of chicken bone. But when I placed my fingers along my ribs, I knew he was right. They were all intact. Sore and painful as hell but unbroken.

His gaze seemed to be fighting for a place to land. Being in my bra in front of a guy was no big deal. I had done it a dozen times. With him several times. But something about this time felt different. I felt naked. "We'll need to find a wrap to bind them."

"And strong painkillers," I mumbled, fighting the urge to fold my arms over my chest. I wasn't huge, but I definitely wasn't small. Right then, I felt my breasts were parading in front of his face. Ryker stepped back and pulled at his shirt. His muscles flexed and rippled as he yanked it over his head. My eyes felt locked on the deep indentions on his torso, the V-cut hinting at the top of jeans. I quickly looked away, pressing my legs together.

"Put this on." He tossed the shirt at me.

The top was still slightly damp and smelled of seawater and Ryker's familiar smell. It drifted over me as I tried to stuff my arms through the sleeves. My ribs ached from the movement, and I squeaked in pain.

Ryker strode back, taking the shirt in his hands. He stretched the neck wider and settled it over my head. It was big enough so I could keep my arms low while he opened the sleeves for me to put my limbs through. The collar of the neck, dipping low, almost didn't cover my boobs, which was amusing because it was the point of me having it on. My breath sharpened when he moved closer, pulling the shirt around my waist, and his knuckles grazed my tender skin.

He paused for a moment before he turned and went to the paper towel dispenser. When he came back, his shoulders and neck were clenched.

He tilted my head, and a rough paper towel dabbed at my lip. The pad of his fingers pressed firmly along my chin line. His breath fluttered over me, and I finally realized how much lighter I felt. I didn't think I would be so grateful to feel his touch again, but it meant I was not alone. I hadn't let myself dwell on his death. My own survival had been foremost on my mind, and I hadn't wanted to contemplate what his absence would have meant to me.

"You came back," I whispered.

He paused before the damp paper patted my mouth again.

"Oh, right." I locked on the flickering generator light pouring brightness into the room. Of course. He returned because of his powers. I was a walking, talking lockbox holding his prize possession.

We stayed quiet as he cleaned my wounds.

"I knew a regular bullet wouldn't kill you, but I didn't think fae survived their necks being snapped." I swallowed. "I thought you were dead."

He huffed, picking out the gravel embedded in my cuts. "Believe me, I am almost impossible to kill. Better men and fae have tried before, and they didn't succeed." His eyes rolled under in a slight frown. "It did take me longer than I thought to heal and swim back. I should have been here sooner. I apologize."

He'd been shot a dozen times, his neck broken, and was dumped in the middle of the Pacific, but he was apologizing because he didn't get back fast enough?

His arm dropped from my mouth and went to the cut near my temple. "Close your eyes."

I gratefully did what he asked, his chest being far too close for comfort.

"Well, I'm glad you came back," I blurted without thought.

Silence.

Finally he spoke, a slight teasing in his voice. "The Avenging Angel, huh? You told me you were a street fighter, but I didn't realize you were infamous."

I peeked at him through my lashes. "My return kind of sent it into overdrive. But yeah. I was pretty well known. I started at fifteen, and I was good."

"I think you forgot to emphasize how *good* you were. Some of those people had tops with your nickname on it."

"Because you're so forthcoming with me," I responded.

A scowl creased his forehead, and his mouth thinned.

Humming from the outside generators and voices from the dispersing crowd seeped into the dark room. "Thank you again for coming for me. I mean, I'm glad you were there to stop Marcello from killing me... or me killing her." Admitting aloud I was going to murder her struck me.

Frantic realization shot through my chest to my head. I jerked from Ryker's touch, my eyes wide with awareness. "God." I squirmed in my seat, suddenly uncomfortable in my skin. "I was going to do it. I really *wanted* to kill her." My lungs surged in and out in sporadic gulps, triggering my chest to ache more. I had done a lot of bad shit in my day, but murder was not one of them. Fighting was something I enjoyed, but I had never wanted to finish off any of my opponents so literally.

My hand slammed into Ryker, pushing him away from me as I hopped from the ledge. I gritted my teeth in agony, but my mind moved my wobbly legs in frenzied steps across the tiles. My one hand went to a loose piece of hair, stroking it between my fingers, trying to soothe the hysteria spreading through by body. The other arm wrapped around my stomach, trying to press away the pain pounding in my torso.

"What is wrong with me? I was going to beat her to death!" I could hear the wail in my voice.

"Zoey." Ryker took a stride to me.

"No," I shouted. "Seriously, tell me what is wrong with me." He pressed his lips together, watching me. "I didn't even think about it. I was simply going to do it." Liquid filled under my lids. My one arm stayed locked around my middle while my other hand rubbed at my face and hair. "Something is very wrong with me. I've denied it for so long, but it's always been there. It's why the little old lady got rid of me. She saw it. She knew I was not right." I rubbed at my chest, pulling at

Ryker's shirt. "Daniel Senior hinted about DMG doing something to me. What if I'm not natural..." I let my sentence trail off. Tears clouded my vision, a few escaping and falling down my face. "No one normal wants to feel someone's bones crunching under a fist or to taste their opponent's blood."

The tears now plummeted from my cheeks. "What did DMG do to me? Did they make me evil, or is it simply me?" I pleaded, knowing fully well he couldn't answer my question. Logic didn't matter; I needed someone to help me, to carry some of my burden. Everything came rushing back to me: the years of keeping everyone else together; trying to be responsible and in control; never asking for help even when I felt myself drowning. A choked cry tore from my lungs, my legs giving out, and I went to my knees.

Sobs I had held back since I was a child came gasping to the surface, denied too long. I had only cried in front of two people my entire life. *Really* cried. Once was when I was five, and a foster "grandma" slapped me hard across the face and told me to suck it up and get thicker skin. The other person stood beside me now. Even if those tears were well deserved, I didn't like showing my vulnerability. Daniel hadn't even seen me cry, and already this fae had seen it a couple of times.

The Wanderer bent, his large hands grasping my shoulders. It was what I wanted, someone to touch me, to hold me. But the need for not only someone—but specifically *him*—sent my fury into overdrive. A crazed wail clogged my windpipe, my arms striking out, hitting anything they could. I no longer felt the pain in my body. Everything in me turned off.

"Maria injected me with something..." *Whatever she*

*gave me did something to me.* I clung to the thought, grasping at straws, but this excuse wouldn't stick. It was me. I had wanted to kill the girl.

"Zoey," he said firmly, his voice calm.

"Don't touch me." Abhorrence and fear blasted over me, and a dry heave rose from my abdomen. I tried so hard to be the woman Daniel would love and be proud of. Now look at me. In collaboration with a fae, the very thing he trained me to capture and despise. The girl he cared about was a lie. She never existed. The truth hit me deeper than anything else. I actually believed I had changed and I could rise above the foul life I was born into. But I hadn't. I played the part, but the only person I deceived was myself.

Ryker held me tighter against him. "Stop."

I spit at him, my nails clawing for his arm and face.

"Zoey..."

"Fuck off, fae!" He had called me human for so long. I should have done the same and kept him in his rightful place. Far away from me. I hated him and everything he represented. "You left me!" The words flew from my mouth. "You left me alone. I was better off without you. I wish you never came into my life."

With a growl, he latched on to my biceps and lifted me. His jaw was locked; his eyes glowed in the dark room. "Enough!" He slammed me into the wall. My head bobbed off the tile, creating a vehement hiss. My dangling legs kicked wildly to hit any part of him I could. "STOP!" he bellowed and threw me back onto the counter. He thrust himself between my legs, pressing my arms back into the glass. My ribs suddenly came back to life, protesting the harsh movement.

I took a gulp of air, squeezing my lids together. The throbbing made my head spin. I took another choppy inhale through my nose. He slid my arms down the mirror but didn't let go. He moved them closer to my chest so I wasn't overextended. The hurt was still there but lessened a bit.

"Are you calm now?" His gruff voice forced my lashes to lift.

His lips were only inches from mine. His face was tight, but his eyes glowed intensely. Air pumped at his bare chest, highlighting his toned muscles. Desire unexpectedly consumed me—the primal yearning to forget myself in someone. To let go and feel pleasure.

He adjusted his grip, pressing closer. The friction brushed against my inner thighs. My mouth opened, breath sucking through my teeth. The overpowering need to pull down his jeans and feel him slide deep into me wrapped around my lungs, limiting their motion. As if he could sense my thoughts, he tensed. The tattoo on his neck flickered. His lids drifted half closed, and his attention was drawn to my lips. The heat from his mouth reverberated off mine. Our deep breaths bounced off the four walls, pounding in my ears. Neither of us moved. Ryker stayed pressed against me, and I felt every inch of him. A drop of blood from my sliced lip seeped along my neck, trailing between my breasts. His eyes followed it.

My head suddenly spun. Lust and need kindled hot, inciting my nerves. My muscles trembled. I could hear his breath falter in my ear, becoming sporadic.

*Holy shit, Zoey. What are you thinking? He is fae.* A voice came thundering into my head. I'd heard in heightened situations you felt emotions you normally wouldn't. This had to be the reason. Besides, he had a girlfriend, and I was still in love with Daniel. And bottom line: I hated fae, and he despised humans.

Ryker's hand clenched mine. Then he was gone. He retreated across the room, his back hitting the toilet stalls. My arms slowly fell back to my sides. It was a long time before either of us spoke. Finally, his deep voice broke the uncomfortable silence. "You are not evil or wrong."

My tongue dampened my lips, wiping the blood away. I wanted to speak, but my voice couldn't find its way out.

"You act and pretend, only showing certain aspects of yourself to please others. There is no good and bad. Only you. And you have to accept all parts of yourself. The more you push away or deny who you are, the more intense the various sides will be when you let them slip."

I sat taller, looking at my dangling legs. Protectively, my arm wrapped around my middle again. "But what if I don't want to?"

"Then you will never truly be happy." His gaze finally met mine. Steady but distant. "You are a survivor. You do what you need to stay alive. Don't be ashamed of all the different aspects of yourself."

"I was going to kill her."

"Yes."

"I was going to beat her to death, Ryker."

"Do you think I feel sympathy for that human?"

I scoffed. "No. You're fae. We're nothing to you. You care nothing about human lives."

He stood straight, his shoulders ramming back. "I care about one."

Breath caught in my chest. Blood rushed to my cheeks. *Stupid, Zoey. Of course he cares. He cares about what you carry inside.*

I pushed myself off the counter, needing to change the direction of the conversation and emotion in the restroom. "We should go. We need to get Sprig. Marcello still has him imprisoned at the warehouse. Oh my god. My bag. Daniel's book and..." I freaked.

Ryker peered at the ceiling, taking a huge breath. He grabbed an object under the cloak on the floor. "I got it. I went back to the warehouse before finding you here." Of course, Ryker had to go there to get his axe. Last I saw, it was on Marcello's desk. "Sprig was gone."

"What? Gone?"

"The cage was sitting on a desk in one of the rooms, but the lid was open." He curved slightly forward and pushed himself off the stall. "He wasn't there."

A dagger stabbed my heart. I might not particularly like fae in general, but the little bugger had grown on me. He showed me all fae weren't bad. "Are you sure?"

"Yes." Ryker tilted his head, annoyance rippling over his features. "If he is free, he will find you."

I hoped with all my heart Sprig escaped and was on his way to us now.

"We have to keep moving forward. I know what bank your key belongs to."

With everything going on, I had forgotten about the reason Ryker and I had separated. Daniel's key. "What? Where?" I exclaimed. "Do you still have the key?"

"Bellevue." Ryker pulled at a black cord around his neck; the key dangled from it. It had slipped around and lay on his back when he took off his shirt, hiding the object from my notice.

"Bellevue?" The excitement deflated. It was not far if you had a car or could take a bus. By foot, it would take at least half a day, and walking left us vulnerable.

"We'll find somewhere safe to spend the night and start out in the morning." Ryker bent and lifted the cloak he had been wearing earlier. "Put this on until we find new clothes for you. Your pants are still covered in blood, and Marcello's men will be looking for you." He threw the scratchy cover at me.

"And a shirtless Viking with white eyes won't stand out?" I circled the cape about me, pulling the hood over my head. I grabbed my bag, already missing the weight Sprig produced.

"I am still fae. I can be invisible a lot easier than you," he retorted. When Ryker was satisfied the blanket covered me head to toe, he turned for the door. Unlatching the lock, his hand paused on the knob. "With or without the powers, I would have come back for you." He yanked open the squeaky door and slid out into the dark night, leaving me gaping at his exit line.

# TWENTY-SIX

"We'll stay here tonight." I think my limping finally got to Ryker, but I had to admit I experienced a lot less pain the more I walked. Exhaustion was tiring me more than movement.

We made it a little past Sam Smith Park before he had enough. We would cross over the Murrow Bridge in the morning, leading us to Bellevue. It took Ryker longer to find us a place. Less damage had been done out this far, so more people stayed locked in their homes. We finally found a studio across from a little Italian restaurant off Interstate 90. Once I broke into the spot, he secured all the doors and windows. There was a musky, foul smell coming from the refrigerator. Whatever was in there would stay enclosed. Everything would be rotten by now, and it would only let out the rank odor.

Ryker lit the last of the candles in my bag, giving the five-hundred-square-foot apartment a glow. I wandered around the space. It had windows on the street side. The bed was on the opposite wall with a small sofa at the foot it, facing the TV. The bathroom and small kitchen were on the far side. The style was clean with a touch of eclectic. Un-frilly, but clearly a girl lived here: fashion magazines on the table; pictures of friends decorated the walls; heels lined her closet; and funky outfits mixed with sleek office-style suits. The place was tiny but cute and functional. I was envious of whomever lived here. This was what I imagined my first place to be like. Minuscule—but all mine. The dream of owning my own apartment seemed hopeless now.

In the kitchen, a calendar was pinned to the wall. I ran my fingers over it, touching the day when my entire universe changed. The woman had written "Leave for Hawaii" two days before Seattle exploded in flames. At least I knew she was alive and in a warm, secure place. Far away from this mess.

"Do you know what day it is?" I asked.

Ryker was lowering the shades in the living space. "No." He paused, peering at the ceiling in thought. "Wait. I think it's Thursday, April 18. It's what the fliers for the fight on Marcello's desk stated."

I touched the date and let out a sad chuckle.

"What?"

"Today's my birthday," I said quietly. A few weeks ago the date held so much hope. Daniel was going to take me out. I felt in my bones things would have changed in our relationship. They were slowly beginning to—before he was taken from me. I think he knew it, too. It's why he asked my plans for the day. My birthday was the pivotal night, and he would have finally let his guard down.

I can't say my birthday had ever been a happy event. Most of the time, it was ignored. But between Lexie getting old enough to really understand other people's birthdays and Daniel coming into my life, things were changing. I looked forward to them. It brought me one year older in Daniel's eyes to be more a "suitable" age.

"Happy birthday," Ryker said awkwardly.

"Don't they celebrate birthdays in the Otherworld?"

"I'm sure they do, but I never lived in the Otherworld. And I've never celebrated my birthday."

"Why not?" I turned to look at him through the kitchen pass-through.

"Do I look like the type to have birthday parties?"

"No." I smirked. The visual of him with a party hat on, blowing out candles was almost too much.

"I also don't know what day it is." He shrugged, finishing securing the blinds.

"You don't know when you were born?"

"No. I went to the Tamang family when I was three. I don't remember much before."

"Much? At three, most wouldn't remember a thing."

"It's more impressions. I can't see anyone's face, but I remember my mother was tall and beautiful. Her hair was the color of sunlight."

"And your father?"

"All I remember is in contrast to my mother, he was dark, and I feared him." Ryker rubbed his temples, turning his back on me. He didn't want to talk anymore about his first family.

Silence grew between us.

"Thank you." I cleared my throat.

He stopped and looked over his shoulder. "For what?"

"For telling me." I motioned to him. "For saving me today. I would be dead right now or a murderer or forced to be Marcello's next sex slave." I shivered at the thought. What he would have done to me after the fight would have me wishing to have died in it.

"I should have made sure I killed him. Slowly." Ryker's eyes flared bright. "Did he do anything to you?"

There were a lot of close calls, and he did enough, but I didn't feel like telling Ryker any details. He couldn't do anything about it now anyway.

"No." I shook my head, leaning against the sink and bringing the subject back to safer ground. "It's funny because at one time, all I wanted to do on my birthday was fight. I can't say there isn't a part of me that still doesn't enjoy it in some way, but it didn't feel the same. I finally realized how much my past was controlling me the night I told you what happened to me. I was letting it run my life. It consumed me, eating slowly at my soul."

Ryker stared at me, not moving or speaking.

"Well, anyway, thank you again. I can honestly say you've been the only thing to make this a pretty good birthday." I chuckled. "It's the simple things, right? I lived without being killed or raped. It's a good day."

The muscles along Ryker's neck and jaw tightened. I was thankful even with the candlelight it was dim, and he wouldn't be able to see the deep red blistering over my cheeks. Why did I tell him those things? What was it about him that made my mouth open and shit fall out—stuff I never told anyone and the vulnerable side I let no one see?

Ryker's boots clomped toward the door. "Lock this behind me; I'll be back soon."

"What?" I sprang off the counter. "Where are you going?"

"Just lock it behind me," he repeated. He then slipped through the door, leaving me standing in confusion.

Since none of the absentee resident's clocks worked, and even the one with a battery seemed to have decided to call it quits, I didn't know how long Ryker was gone. It felt like forever. To keep my mind off his absence, I flipped inattentively through some of the woman's magazines, the candle wax dripping on her glass coffee table.

It bothered me I was so restless because he was gone. My heart leaped every time I thought I heard movement coming up the stairs. After a while, I was sure my mind was imagining every little sound.

The void left by Sprig bothered me as well, though missing him didn't trouble me like Ryker. Sprig was a little fur ball of attitude and hilarity. I worried about him being on his own and who had him. I hoped he was smart enough not to open his mouth. That would be bad. My instinct to protect him and need to have him safe with me was new. It was a cross between having a kid, little brother, and a pet. Never having any of them, I imagined this was what it would feel like. Now I sympathized with Andrew losing his dog. They did become part of your family. With Sprig gone, I understood the deep loss experienced.

For the twelfth time, I peeked out the blinds before slumping back on the sofa. I was twitchy. And even though it was cold outside and in the apartment, I felt hot. *It has to be whatever drug is in my system working itself out.* Waves of heat spiked, and I tore off the cloak. Ryker's shirt clung to my chest. The smell of him grew intense. I became more sensitive to its touch by the minute. Like a cat in heat. I always got stimulated after a fight, but what I felt now was extreme.

Then a tap sounded at the door, striking three times. *Ryker!* I jumped off the sofa and hurried to it, unbolting it and swinging it open.

The large Wanderer stood on the other side, a bag in his hand. "Don't ever open it without looking first."

"I knew it was you."

He scowled and stepped in, shutting it behind him.

"And how do you know I didn't check?"

"I know." He moved to the kitchen.

"Where have you been? You were gone forever." I landed next to him, feeling the warmth come off his body, which only upped mine.

I reached for the bag.

"I'm not as good at breaking and entering as you are," he grumbled, smacking my hand away from the sack and going to the sink.

"I could have gone with you."

"That would have ruined the whole point." He peered over his shoulder, studying me closely. "Are you all right?"

Okay, embarrassing. He could probably sense or see the flush, which covered me from head to toe. It only turned higher the moment he walked in the door.

"Yeah. Just hot. Might be getting a fever or something."

"You said Maria injected you with something? What was it?"

"I don't know."

He watched me.

"I don't!"

He nodded, still staring. "Go sit." He indicated the chair on the other side of the counter.

"Why?"

He grabbed me by the shoulders, twisted me around, and walked me to the stools on the other side of the breakfast bar. "Sit," he demanded.

I watched him skeptically but sat on the stool.

"Close your eyes."

It took a beat before I let my lashes fall.

"Keep them closed." His voice was gruff and demanding, but for some reason, I found it endearing.

My ears sensed a movement, paper crumpling. Then I felt heat before he said, "Okay, you can open them."

Slowly my lids lifted.

A loaf of sourdough bread with little squares of butter, dried salami, and a bottle of wine sat before me. They weren't what made my eyes tear and my heart twist with emotion. Stuck in the middle of the loaf of bread was a burning candle.

"It's all I could find across the street to eat." His voice went unemotional, dismissive.

My eyes blinked over and over, my throat tightening.

"Anyway. Happy birthday."

I would not cry. I would not cry.

*Shit.*

A single tear escaped, but I quickly wiped it away.

Ryker rolled his eyes. "Fuck sake, Zoey. I was getting us something to eat anyway. I happened to run across a drawer with candles in it. Seemed fitting for tonight. So blow the damned thing out."

He was lying. You didn't simply run across candles unless you were searching for them. I worked for a minute as a waitress. I was fired after the first week because of my attitude, but I knew most places kept this type of stuff by the hostess stand.

I would play his game. I closed my eyes and blew out the flame. I swallowed my emotion and reopened my lids. "You better have stolen a wine opener, or I'm sending your ass back."

He smirked and grabbed the bottle. "Twist off."

I grinned. Most likely the girl who lived here had both wine and an opener, but it was the thought that counted. I collected the bread and meat. "Grab a knife."

I set the food on the coffee table, sat on the sofa, and freed my feet of my boots. Ryker followed with the wine, grabbing cups and a knife out of the drawer.

The bread was stale but still tasted good. Salami was not one of my favorite meats, but it was heaven tonight. Everything tasted amazing, especially the wine.

After we finished all the food and were down to the last swig of wine, Ryker grabbed my legs, stretching them over his lap. "How are you feeling?" His hands prodded at the cuts in my jeans and nodded toward my ribs.

My heart thumped like a rabbit's foot.

"Surprisingly well." I lifted my shirt a bit, the bruising was still purple and blue, but it hurt a lot less. "I mean, I'm not going to do any gymnastic routines, but I thought I'd be in a lot more pain."

His brows tightened, his hand touching my stomach, feeling the ribs underneath. I had been warm earlier; now the room was stifling. Beads of sweat dampened the back of my neck. *Shut up, heart.* The damn thing was broadcasting my emotions. Was I so lonely that a simple touch from a man would send my heart into cardiac arrest? Okay, he wasn't a normal guy. This one was so intense, so sexually masculine, even if he weren't necessarily your type, he would be. At first I hadn't thought of him "in that way" or even imagined him having sex. After the night he confused me for Amara, I was fighting the fluttering in my heart, pushing it away. Sitting next to him on a small sofa, my legs across his lap, his fingers tracing my ribs, it was all I could think of.

Oxygen. I needed oxygen.

I bolted off the sofa. He leaned back, looking startled.

"Sorry. Have to pee." I escaped into the restroom, shutting the door firmly behind me. My hands gripped either side of the sink, my head lowered as I breathed in deeply. It was almost pitch black in the small room, but the moonlight let in enough glow so I could make out my outline in the mirror. Turning my face, I caught a glimmer of my eyes reflecting in the glass.

"You are simply lonely. You've been stuck with him in some intense circumstances... that's all," I berated the image in the mirror, my voice an angry whisper. "You don't actually have feelings for him. You're projecting." See, I did learn something from my therapy.

*Shut it down now, Zoey. Shut those pesky feelings off.*

Taking another deep inhale, I straightened myself and walked back to Ryker. He sat on the edge of the sofa, his head in his hands, shoulders hiked to his ears. He rubbed fiercely at his temples.

"I'm tired," I stated and walked to the girl's dresser. She wouldn't mind if I borrowed something for the night, right? I needed to get out of my bloody jeans and Ryker's T-shirt. His smell was too close, suffocating me. I grabbed a pair of pajama bottoms and a tank and went back to the bathroom.

In a cabinet I located some face wipes and cleaned myself the best I could. The dirt and blood covering my body was more than skin deep. I could feel it soaking into my skin and coating my insides. Perspiration dotted my forehead as I struggled to get on my tank and pants, but there was no way I would call Ryker for help. Finally dressed, I plopped on the edge of the tub, exhausted. Was it possible to age years in a month?

"Do you need help?" Ryker knocked. He was asking, but his tone was hoping my answer would be no.

"No." I glared at the door, my words snapping through the barricade. "I can pee by myself. Thank you."

"Good." My lip rose in a snarl, annoyance covering my limbs. With effort I stood and swung open the door.

"It's all yours. Unless you already used the sink as your toilet."

His chest filled with air. "No. Viking. Peed. On. Floor," he replied, clearly getting my insult.

"Thought you weren't a Viking."

"Like it matters to you what I am." He brushed past me and slammed the bathroom door behind him.

Arrgg! Fae. Wanderer. Viking. Pirate. Asshole. Check all the above for the pain in my butt. I stormed to the bed and flipped down the bedding, crawling between the sheets.

*Oh. My.* I had slept chained to a water pipe in Marcello's hideout for the last several nights. The mattress and quilt swallowed me, wrapping comfy arms around me. Finally Goldilocks found her "just right."

"Whoever you are. Thank you." I spoke to the spirit of the woman who lived here. I silently sent her appreciation vibes, directing them to Hawaii. I didn't know her, but I was happy she was safe. There was a good reason she was not currently living here, and it didn't include the words *dead* or *in the hospital*.

Jeez, when did I get so sentimental?

The bathroom door creaked open. For as big as he was, his footsteps were practically silent if he wanted them to be.

Anger had dissolved the moment I sank on her mattress. It felt too good to be mad at anything.

Ryker grabbed a pillow and a blanket off the settee and tossed them on the carpet.

"Oh, jeez, Ryker. You don't have to sleep on the floor. It's not like we haven't shared a bed before."

He surveyed me with mistrust. Like a typical woman, my moods changed in an instant. This unsettled most men. They weren't sure if they trusted this new mood, or if we were going to strike the moment they put their guard down.

To be honest, it could go either way.

Whether I actually wanted him next to me, or if this was my way of showing him it wasn't a big deal if he slept in the bed with me, I didn't know or didn't want to know.

I rolled my eyes. "Get in." I flipped the bedding on his side open. "Seriously, you will thank me. I want to marry this mattress." I snuggled back in, wiggling with happiness.

He walked over and sat at the end of the bed, pulling off his boots.

*Shit!* What did I do? I rolled over and faced the opposite wall. I heard him take off his harness and unzip his pants before his jeans hit the floor.

I squeezed my lids together. What the hell was I thinking? An almost naked man was lying next to me on my birthday when I was extremely lonely, a little tipsy—and let's be honest, horny. When was the last time I had sex?

No! No sex thoughts. Bad sex thoughts.

The bed dipped as he climbed in next to me. His heat hit my back like an explosion, adding to the fire already inside me. I felt his bare skin taunting mine. His leg brushed against mine, and I bit hard on my lip.

This was a very bad idea.

My arm ached, but I didn't move a muscle. I took shallow breaths, trying to convince my mind to sleep. It laughed at me.

I could feel the tension. Neither of us moved. It wasn't natural. Only three nights ago, I slept in his arms with no problem. I wanted to scream, to sit and demand we get over whatever this was, to go back to us disliking each other. Loathing was comfortable for us. It made sense.

I heard him let out a staggered breath, and the bed moved as he rolled onto his side, his back to mine.

Eventually my body beat out my mind in the need for rest, but it was only surface sleep since my brain mixed Daniel, Lexie, and Ryker in a stream of cruel and mocking images.

# TWENTY-SEVEN

"Wakey-wakey." Something patted my face. My lashes lifted to a furry brown creature not even an inch away. I jerked, my eyes blinking. "Looks like not being here last night was a good thing." His eyebrows wiggled, nodding toward the object beside me.

My brain felt so confused and sleepy, but the feel of Ryker pressed against my back, his head tucked into my neck, shot adrenaline through my veins. My brain suddenly cleared, reality zooming in distinctly. "Oh my god, Sprig!" I sat, causing Ryker to jump. He looked around, puzzled. "You're okay!"

"Of course, *bhean*." Sprig hopped on my knee. "It took me a while to find you, but never doubt I will."

"I don't doubt you. I only thought Marcello did something to you. Sold you." The sheer panic of it clipped my heart. I hadn't wanted to think about him being hurt or sold off, because I couldn't have handled it. I released a long breath. He was here and all right. I grabbed the furry little beast and hugged him.

"Wow, you get frisky in the morning." He smirked. "He didn't tire you enough?" I ignored his jabs, not caring what he said. The possible loss of him set in. I needed to hold him near me. Relief washed over me, a smile growing on my face. The sun crept through the blinds, adding to my cheer.

Sprig's safety was another perfect birthday present. "I'm so happy you are safe. I missed you."

"I missed you too." Sprig reached and patted my face again, wiggling under my grip.

I finally let him go, and he bounced all over the bed like a windup toy. "So what are we doing today? Huh? Huh? Do you have any more of those granola bars? I'm starving. Oh, do you think there is one of those honey bears here?" He was already off, racing to the kitchen.

I didn't think my smile could grow any bigger. I looked at Ryker, and he also watched Sprig with amusement.

"Wish you could bottle his energy, huh?" I kept my eyes on the monkey crawling in and out of the cupboards as he continued to chatter.

"Or strangle it." Ryker snorted, pushing the covers off. From the corner of my eye, I watched his back muscles flex as he stretched and stood.

Heat flooded my cheeks when I saw it wasn't the only thing standing up.

"Coffee... maybe she has coffee." I scrambled from the bed and went to join Sprig.

The room spun, and I grabbed the back of the sofa. Heat exploded inside, expanding to my fingertips. Perspiration dampened the back of my neck and brow. "Whoa." I held my head, remaining in place.

"What?" Ryker turned to me. Everything about him stood at full attention.

I forced myself to continue my journey to the cupboard. "Nothing. I rose too fast." The fever I hoped would break overnight didn't. It felt worse this morning. Maybe this was what coming down from a drug high felt like. Whatever Maria gave me was still working its way through my system. "I need caffeine." I really wanted to crawl back in bed and stay there all day.

"What are you going to do? Lick the beans?" Ryker said. I could hear him pulling on his pants. Good.

It took me a moment to realize even if she had coffee, beans or ground, it wouldn't help me. No water, heat, milk, or ice.

"I am so over this storm thing. I want electricity. I want a good warm caramel latte from Starbucks." I would sell my soul for one if someone offered.

Sprig pouted on the counter till I removed a granola bar and handed it to him, rubbing his head as I did. Damn, I loved the little guy. Opening one of the cupboards, I found a bag of coffee beans. I opened the top and took a deep breath. "Oh yeah." I felt my eyes roll back in my head with ecstasy.

As he walked to me, Ryker tugged on the shirt I had thrown across the sofa arm. "Should I leave you two alone?"

I took a bean and plopped it into my mouth.

"You're not going to like it." Ryker shook his head.

Immediately, I opened my mouth, letting the acrid bean fall off my tongue. "Ick."

"Told ya."

"How can something so awful taste so good brewed in a cup?"

"Because of the caramel, sugar, and milk."

Okay. I wasn't a purest.

Sprig finished his bar and jumped off the counter, chirping and running and jumping about the studio like a crackhead. Mid-leap from the sofa to the bed, his condition kicked in, and he face-planted on the bed. Snoring.

I couldn't stop laughter from bubbling, along with fierce feelings of protection. I would never let him out of my sight again. No one would hurt him.

Ryker spoke after I stopped laughing. "We have to get going. I want to cross the bridge early. We are very exposed there, and I want to get it behind us."

I agreed and moved to the woman's closet. Along with the pajamas I *borrowed*, I would be stealing other clothes. Pants and a top were a necessity. Blood covered my jeans, and Ryker took back his shirt.

By the look of her clothes, she was tall and lean, so I had to take a pair of leggings. They still were long on me, but they fit my ass well. I grabbed another tank top and sports bra. It felt nice to be rid of my dirty garments. She had good taste, and I couldn't help myself from snagging a cool brown faux leather jacket and a hoodie. Maybe I should leave her a thank you letter. No. It would probably be too creepy. Ignorance would be bliss.

While dressing, I realized the bruising along my ribs turned more yellow, and it didn't hurt as much to lift my arms. My ribs hadn't been fractured. I had cracked them before, and the pain was severe and lasted forever. It didn't make sense. I had heard them crack. I thought they were broken. Even the bruising should have been hurting me more. I felt stiff and sore, but not even in the realm of what I should have been.

Slipping back on my boots, I lifted Sprig and held him to my chest as I walked back to toward the kitchen.

Ryker leaned against the counter, staring at me.

"What?"

He lowered his head, shaking it. "Nothing."

I looped my purse over my head and put Sprig at the bottom. Reuniting him with Pam. The book and picture of Daniel and me were tucked underneath him. All my most prized possessions. I was so grateful Marcello left everything untouched.

Ryker withdrew bottles of water and more bread from the bag he brought the night before.

"Anything else hidden in there? Like a lasagna? Cannoli?"

"You are lucky we got stale bread for dinner." He stuffed the items in the empty compartment in my bag and moved to the door, grabbing his axe and makeshift cloak. "You ready?"

I nodded and followed him outside.

Whatever lay ahead of us, we would deal with it. The three of us.

Okay, Sprig would sleep through most of it.

Three and half hours later, we made it to the bank without incident, which had to be a record for us. We could see a little damage across the bridge, but not nearly what downtown suffered. Still, most of the businesses on the Bellevue side were out of electricity and seemed to be abandoned. At least for now.

We found the bank in the upscale part of Bellevue, sandwiched between Mercedes and Porsche dealerships. Smart move to have a bank in the middle of those two.

Ryker took us to the front doors, both of us on high alert for anything not feeling right.

"Great." I motioned to the pristine large double white doors. The bank appeared so pretentious it had no name on the front, only an address gold plated on the side. The chains hanging off the door handles protruded like sore thumbs. Several types of locks fortified the front door. Someone at least knew this would be a hotspot, and they were trying to prevent it from being robbed. But we weren't planning on taking a dime.

"Sprig?" I quit trying to keep him in my purse along the journey. If people saw us, they would think me a crazy lady with a monkey on her shoulder. My fever seemed worse. It rolled inside, pushing through my skin, keeping me splotchy and lightheaded. Sprig tried to keep my mind off it with his constant jokes, mostly about sprites or monkeys. Ryker gave the impression he wanted to silence him for good, but he didn't say anything.

"Yes?" Sprig responded. His tail curled around my neck. It made me even warmer, but I stayed quiet. I wanted him close.

I nodded toward the locks. "Go to it, monkey-man."

He chirped happily and jumped off my shoulder, plying his magic on the locks. One by one, the latches fell open as he worked through them.

"I really love you." I unhooked them from the door. "Seriously awesome."

He smiled. His little face lighting with pride.

Ryker didn't wait for Sprig to finish with the main lock. Ryker twisted the knob till it shattered inside. He opened the door, motioning for us to enter. Sprig scuttled in before I slipped in after him. Ryker closed the door, looking around for something to block it. Money saturated the building and not only in its vaults. Elegant crystal chandeliers and white leather sofas and chairs decorated the lobby.

"Nice." My eyes took in the place. It made me feel like a vagabond—probably the intent of the place.

Daniel came here? If the security was as first class as the décor, then I could see why he did. Though it probably wasn't prepared for a fae storm to destroy the cameras and electronic security.

Ryker pulled a sofa across the entrance and pushed it firmly against the door. It wouldn't hold people back for long, but it would give us warning.

We wandered the hallway lined with locked doors. Each one, Sprig unlocked for us. Most were offices or storage rooms. Finally, we found what we were looking for—the room storing the safe deposit boxes.

"Holy shit." My eyes widened, taking in the metal-lined wall where boxes were inserted. Each had a number and lock on the front, and a key would release the box from the wall. There had to be more than three hundred of them. The numbers on the boxes appeared to have no rhyme or reason to them. Normally, the bank employee would retrieve your box for you. They certainly did not want to make this easy for people coming in like us, trying to find a particular box.

"We have a lot of boxes to cover and little time to do it." Ryker stepped to the wall.

"Sprig?"

"Go keep guard?" Sprig finished my sentence.

I smiled at him. "You're a rock star."

"Actually, I played in a band before my capture. Every other night The Honey-Dew's performed at the village tavern. I played the flute, and I—"

"Sprig," Ryker warned.

"Right. Going now." He ran from the room.

Ryker turned to me and pulled the key from under the collar of his shirt. "The first part of the number tells what bank it's from. The second part is the box it coincides with." He yanked at the cord, breaking the bind holding it there.

"Look for chest 79X3W."

My finger scanned the line of coffers. We were going to be here a while.

Ten minutes later, Ryker pronounced, "I found it."

He pulled the bin and set it on the table and handed me the key. Apprehension chilled the back of my neck. Was I ready for whatever this strongbox held? In my core, I felt it would change my life. Would I be better off not knowing?

Sensing I needed a push, Ryker cupped his hand over mine and led it to the container. Together we unlocked the chest. He lifted the lid, and I almost stepped back, thinking something would jump at me.

I peered in the box. Two thick files sat underneath a handheld video camera. I grabbed the camera, holding it in my hands for a while, debating. What I might find terrified me. I wanted to believe Daniel Senior was a crazy old man, and no truth existed to anything he told me. If I hit the switch, would everything change?

*No point in stopping now.* I pushed the button. The light on top turned green, the batteries holding enough energy to turn it on. A sharp inhale halted the air in my lungs as an image of Daniel came on the screen. I stared at him, not able to move. He was dressed casually in jeans and a T-shirt, an outfit I had seen on him many times. The same room we sat in appeared as the backdrop for his video. I fell into the chair, the same one he used. I felt frozen, locked on his face.

"Are you going to watch it?" I could tell Ryker was anxious. We didn't have a lot of time before someone noticed the building was broken into, but I couldn't move. "Do you want me to do it?"

I nodded.

Ryker leaned over and pushed play. Daniel cleared his throat and shifted in his seat. My heart lurched to see him alive. Had it been a day we had spent together before he taped this? Did he just drop me off at my house before he came here? Pain and sadness engulfed me, triggering my tear ducts. I squeezed my lids shut to keep the water back.

Daniel's eyes were locked on the camera. "Zoey, if you are watching this, then I am either dead or DMG has discovered what I know, and they have taken me prisoner. Knowing DMG, it is probably the latter, as they will try to torture me for information first. Either way, I'm as good as gone. I know how these things work." He took a breath, folding his hands and placing them on the table. His voice saying my name ripped at my heart. One hand went to my mouth to keep the sobs back, and the other one went to screen to touch him. It might have seemed silly, but it let me have him back for a moment. "There is much I need to tell you. I wish I could have told you this in person, but for your safety, for my father's, I needed to keep the facts away from even you. I am sorry for this. I hope you can forgive me. Because I do love you. I fought it for a long time, but I fell in love with you anyway."

I could no longer hold back the cry that came from my soul. These words were what I had wished to hear for so long. Words that would have changed my life but were never said. It felt even more painful to hear them now. It was too late. Our love would never be realized. It was now only a wish or dream—*what could have been.*

Daniel's voice continued. "It's why this is hard to say. I fear your feelings will change the moment you know how much I kept from you. But if you're watching this, then it is probably a moot point anyway." He shoulders fell in a sad shrug. "Before I begin, remember I did this because I care about you. Keeping you safe became my only concern." He took another long breath before he talked again. "If you are watching this, then you found your way to my father. I am glad he was lucid enough to remember the key I hid with him. I'm not sure how much he could tell you. DMG is keeping him almost incoherent, so I will try to explain it all.

"The DMG originally came together to tag, study, and experiment on fae. Dr. Rapava's initial design of the group might have come from good intentions... to save human lives. It is how they still portray themselves, how you know them. Sadly, like many government agencies, DMG soon became corrupt with money, power, and knowledge. Dr. Rapava quickly realized humans were outnumbered and outgunned. We had no hope to fight against the fae if they ever decided to invade us. People with the 'sight' or seers comprise a low percentage of the human race. The DMG didn't feel they could get a handle on the fae population. Not unless we produced our own seers."

My back went rigid, and I jolted away from the camera screen. Daniel's father's voice came back to me. *If I knew what they really wanted to do with you guys... you were only babies.* I felt as if I were about to step into a minefield. My whole world was going to explode, no matter where I trod.

"My father was a top molecular biologist, and they recruited him to generate human babies with the seer gene." Daniel's hand went to his mouth, rubbing absently before he let it drop again. "You are an experiment, Zoey. You were one of those who came from my father's experiments... Daniel's Kids."

*What? An experiment? What did that mean?*

"If you ever wondered about the coincidence of your last name and my first, don't worry. We are not related. The name originated from the experiment you came from." He coughed into his hand and took a drink of water from the bottle next to him. "Each child was created in a petri dish with an egg and semen from strong seers all over the world. They tweaked and played with the DNA code, trying to strengthen and perfect the seer gene.

"While playing with genes, DNA made a lot of mistakes. Most of the eggs did not make it. And sadly, most of the babies died. Only a few of you survived."

*There were others?* My mind was having trouble grasping the full truth of what he was telling me. I existed because of a lab project.

"Being scientists, they were curious of the effect of nature versus nurture, wanting to see which child would develop into the stronger seer. Out of the kids who survived past a year, two stayed with DMG, five were placed with families, and six got the unfortunate alternative of being put in foster care." Daniel's lids flicked, his eyes burning into the cameras. "Think we know which hand you were dealt. DMG kept a close eye on all of their subjects as they grew, but they never interfered unless it became a matter of life and death. With all other things, they turned a blind eye."

I felt the tears threaten again. I understood what he meant. Raped, beaten, drugged. All had happened, and they never interceded. They probably were more curious on how those incidents would develop my character or my seer sense than protecting the loss of my soul.

"Then something started happening to the surviving test subjects. They began to die. You were all made from different specimens but created from the same testing batch, so you share the same weakness. DMG would have kept creating babies like you, who would only die, if my father hadn't stolen the DNA codes. Over the last fifteen years, eleven of the subjects died of the same sickness. Twelve years ago, my father finally discovered the strand of DNA that was defective. A weakness you all have. By then it was too late. It's only a matter of time." Daniel's throat bobbed as he swallowed. Sadness seemed to cause his shoulders to droop. "Your headaches. The nosebleeds. I knew what they meant—what was slowly happening to you. It made me realize my true feelings for you, to know I had little time with you left." Air stilled in my lungs. "You've actually lived longer than my father estimated, but... you are dying, Zoey."

# TWENTY-EIGHT

*You are dying, Zoey.* The words repeated over and over in my head.

Coldness blew into my soul like an Arctic wind, icing my throat. It felt like Death stood behind me as the tip of his scythe skated the length of my spine. My limbs and lungs froze. No air circulated. Ryker stood next to me like a statue, no response showing on his face.

"I am sorry. I can't imagine how you feel at hearing this news, and I hate not being there for you. Every time I dropped you off, I felt scared it would be my last day with you. I wanted to tell you, but in a way I knew it was better you didn't know." Daniel glanced away, his lids blinking.

"After finding this fault in the DNA, my father wanted to get away from the DMG. He destroyed some of his work and set the lab on fire. He did not want them to keep recreating more subjects, more innocent children who would die. They tried to force him back, but he refused. Let's say his retaliation did not go unpunished. We will never have conclusive proof, but a note left to my father about having his older son join his youngest was enough for both of us to know David didn't die from a random car bomb overseas. They killed him. I am sure they murdered my mother, too, but again we will never know for sure.

"When they recruited me after David's death, I understood it wasn't a choice. I decided to play the good soldier, pretending to hate my father, while finding enough proof on them to close DMG. Then they brought you in, and everything in my world changed. I still wanted to take them down, but protecting you became my main focus, to spend every moment with you I could."

I felt Ryker stir next to me, his hands flexing open and closed.

"As you've probably deduced, there are still two of you alive. The other girl was raised with a family in Seattle, also very unaware of where she really came from and DMG's true link to her creation." Daniel looked at the ceiling, a glimmer of a smile on his face. His eyes came back to mine. "You are going to love this, but the other kid is Sera."

My jaw unlatched and fell open. "Sera?" I sputtered. But she had a family.

"Sera's parents never told her the truth about her being adopted." Daniel clutched one of the folders, his fingers curling around the edge. "But it's true. It's all in this file."

*Sera adopted? She was like me?* I understood we weren't really sisters, but I felt like I learned she was. The girl I couldn't stand shared something with me no one else in the world did—a strand of DNA that bonded us, making us more than sisters. Another thing bonding us was the nosebleeds. She would die from the same thing as me—a flaw in our DNA.

It shouldn't have surprised me about Sera. She was a strong seer. It made sense why she and I were more powerful than any other seer DMG ever had. Though, if we were made in the same test tube, wouldn't we be the same age?

"But..."

My rejection of his theory stopped as he continued. "I know what you must be thinking. She is actually younger than her birth certificate states. DMG wanted no connections between their subjects. In case you were placed in the same school, they made all of you different ages. They had her a year older and you a year younger than your actual age."

What? So I was actually twenty-four now? My one-year age jump felt like the least of my problems. If I were a test tube baby, did I even have a *birth*day?

"Again, I am extremely sorry for what I kept from you, but I was only thinking of you. Any more information you need is in the yellow file." His hand patted the folders next to him, which now rested on the table in front of me. "The green one is the information you will need to close the DMG. I couldn't acquire all I need, but this is enough to threaten them. They are running experiments on animals down there you could never imagine. I saw firsthand the monsters they created with animal and fae parts. And humans... Dr. Rapava must be stopped. You will need more evidence, and I hope you will be able to succeed where I failed.

"The agency is not what it seems. They have been working again to recreate the DNA codes my father destroyed. They are planning to make even stronger, more powerful humans, using fae parts and human DNA. This information is what's in the file." He tapped at the green one. "Do not let them get their hands on it, Zoey, whatever you do."

He took a breath. "I've noticed in the last year something has changed. Rapava is getting more anxious and desperate. He no longer cares about helping to cure humans. He wants to create weapons against the fae. This leads me to believe he feels there is an invasion coming. I've also noticed a change in the fae. There are a lot more cases of them being on Earth, and they are getting bolder. Because of this, I cannot say Dr. Rapava is completely wrong. Fae will only use and kill us. We must fight against them, but his method is no longer right."

He took in a shaky breath. "I wish we got a chance to do this together, but it seems it was not in the cards for us." He gripped the documents. "Crush the DMG and find a way to live. You deserve the best this world can offer you. Take Lexie and live the fullest lives you can. Love and have lots of babies. I want all your dreams to come true. If anyone can survive a weakness in her genes, it is you. You are too much of a fighter." He took a gulp. "I love you, Zoey Daniels, no matter how you came to this Earth."

"I love you too," I whispered back, reaching for the screen.

Ryker shut it off, the display going black.

There were two resounding truths: I was a lab experiment, and I was going to die. At any moment, my brain could decide it was time and kill me—the weakness in my genes finally taking over.

"Breathe," Ryker's voice mumbled next to me. He squatted next to my chair, one hand on my thigh, the other on my back.

I released a breath I didn't know I held and gasped for another. His hand rubbed my back in slow methodical motions. I was only twenty-three as of yesterday—actually twenty-four—and I only had months, maybe days, or minutes left to live. The sudden wish to join Daniel and Lexie didn't sound as appealing as it once did. The need to survive grew in me like a wildflower. "I'm going to die," I said, turning to Ryker like I was informing him of news.

His eyes, the color of white foam lying over a stormy ocean, gazed back into mine. "I heard. We'll find a way to fight it."

"No. You don't understand. I am dying." I pointed at myself frantically.

"I heard him, Zoey."

The need for him to understand what I meant took hold of me, and I leaned over him, clasping his face between my hands. Pulling him closer, I peered at his striking features. He stiffened under my touch but did not move. "No. You are not getting it." My eyes darted back and forth between his. "I can die at any moment."

Finally, the understanding of my meaning hit him, and he bolted from my grip and to his feet. "You die, so do my powers."

I nodded wildly.

He stared at me; his expression worked itself into a stone sculpture. "You are dying, and you're concerned about me getting my magic back?" His face grew red, muscles in his jaw clenching with rage.

"Yeah," I whispered, confused by the wrath coming off him.

"Zoey—"

"*Bhean.*" Sprig cut off Ryker's sentence as he raced into the room. "They're here."

"Who's here?" I sprang from my chair, facing Sprig.

"DMG. They found us."

I glanced back at Ryker.

"They must have this place monitored or equipped with some kind of detection device. They somehow knew you would eventually come," Ryker said.

"They were ready for us here because they slipped in without me detecting them. They have us surrounded. They are coming. Run!" Sprig chattered, his voice hitting a higher frequency. Not a good sign for him. Before I could tell him be to calm, he jumped on the table, bouncing frantically. "I have failed you. I. Have. Failed. You!" And then he keeled over. Splat on his back with his limbs stretched in a star formation.

"Fuck. I hate when he does that." Ryker swiped him up and placed him at the bottom of my bag, next to Pam. He fitted the straps between his fingers and slipped it over my head. He stuffed the video of Daniel and the files into the part of my bag Sprig didn't occupy. "Ready to go?" He asked it like we were having a relaxing time at a restaurant or something. He focused solely on me. My heart caught in my chest as I got ensnared in his eyes. I went stationary under his gaze. I didn't want to move. I wanted to stay exactly where I was.

A loud crash of wood and glass from the hallway shattered the hold he had on me. "Yeah. I think I am ready." I nodded.

A hint of a smile grazed his mouth. He whipped me around and pushed me in the direction of the exit. It opened to a long corridor, sprinkled with doors. I peered down one end of the hallway and then the other. Voices and more loud bangs echoed off the walls, making it hard to decipher which way our enemies were coming. If they had us surrounded, no choice was good.

"This way." Ryker tugged at my jacket, taking me the opposite way we came in. Without question, I followed him.

Shouts and pounding footsteps sounded behind us. "Stop!" a man yelled. His demand only caused us to increase our pace. Gunshots rang out. The draft caused by a bullet whizzed past my head, and it embedded into the wall beside me. With a cry, I curled forward, my hands covering my head. What little good it would do. "Shoot him, not her," another man yelled. A rock dropped into my gut. The voice was one I knew well—a voice belonging to a man I used to admire and respect—Dr. Boris Rapava.

He didn't ever leave his lab and never went on a hunt. His presence unsettled me beyond what the man with the gun did. There were only two reasons he would be here: for me or for the information Daniel had about them. Two very good reasons for him to want to intercede.

Ryker tore through the passage, turning along another seemly random corridor. We slid as we rounded the corner at a sprint. An exit door sat at the end. My heart lifted with the idea we might possibly get away.

I should have known it would never be so easy.

We pushed through the door to the hazy afternoon glow. Freedom so close. A body slammed into Ryker's from above, taking him to the gravel. I barely turned my head before I saw another figure jump off the roof, heading for me—Sera.

I dove for the ground, rolled away, and tossed my bag from me so I didn't squash Sprig. It skidded toward Ryker, the files spreading all over the asphalt before the bag settled next to a cement parking block.

*Noooo!*

There wasn't time to think about the papers as Sera landed where I stood a few seconds earlier. We were trained to react in a moment, and neither of us took more than a breath before we were going for each other. It had only been a day since I had fought Crazy Kat. My muscles and bones still ached, but adrenaline helped coat the pain and push me on.

I jumped as Sera's foot struck at me. I twisted, and my leg swept in a roundabout kick. She rolled to the ground and back up in one fluid movement.

"Sera, I'm not the enemy. You don't know what they've done to us."

"What? Trained us to fight filthy things like you? Do you know how thick your fae aura is now? It makes me nauseated to look at you," she seethed. We circled each other. "You are worse than fae. You willingly fuck them." Her lip coiled in disgust.

They all still thought I was pregnant. To them, it could be the only reason my aura would be fae. True, I held a fae essence, but it wasn't a baby.

"DMG is not what you think." I motioned between us. "*We* are not what you think."

"I am *nothing* like you."

"We were experiments, Sera. You have to listen to me."

"No, I really don't, you crazy bitch." She snarled and rushed at me, her elbow digging into my gut. Pain shot along my ribs. Biting through the agony, I wrapped my arm around her neck and shoved her onto an abandoned car in the parking lot. I didn't want to hurt her. I wanted her to understand. But with every kick or punch, she made it harder and harder. My anger tingled around my shoulders, causing me to tense.

"Listen to me," I hissed into her ear from behind, keeping my arm tight.

"No!" Her head knocked back, but I had been ready for her. I kept my face to the side of hers. She fell heavily into a car hood, bringing me with her. We rolled off the hood onto the ground, hitting the brick wall of the building. The moment let me take in my surroundings. Two more hunters who I had once called friends jumped in to help Liam. They were highly trained to fight fae, to wrestle someone like Ryker. They would not be as easy to fight as a group of gangsters who had no real training or experience with combating fae.

Sera and I clambered to our feet, circling each other like sharks. Dirt and blood covered her face, and a snarl bowed her lip, hatred deep in her eyes. She wanted to hurt me. Probably even kill me.

The commotion behind Sera captured my attention.

Hugo came around, kicking at the tendon in Ryker's back leg, as Peter and Liam barreled into him. Peter held a knife in his hand. It was Peter's favorite weapon to use when a hunt went wrong and killing became the only option—a fae-welded dagger. This blade would kill Ryker with a simple flick of Peter's wrist across his throat, and just a slice of it across Ryker's skin could paralyze him, making it easy for the group to overpower him

"Ryker!" The words arose from my mouth, the need to warn him hot on my tongue. It was all it took.

It was stupid. I broke one of the major rules of combat. Chapter Three in *The Art of War*: never let yourself get distracted. Daniel had been very clear about this rule. You needed to be highly aware of everything going on around you in case another threat came at you. But you never, never let yourself get diverted by it. Your head had to be in the game. The moment you broke this, the game was over. Your opponent, especially a highly trained one like Sera, would take advantage of the half second and pounce.

A foot collided into my chest, and I flew back, skidding across the blacktop. My chest had been healing, but the fracture getting a direct impact sent bile up my throat. A faraway roar permeated the air, stirring the blood in my veins. Warmness swirled in my gut, probably a bleeding liver or kidney.

Sera came into view. She said something, but I couldn't understand. My ears hummed. Figures and voices boomed around me, but nothing made sense. The warmness in my stomach moved to my limbs and into my chest, numbing them. My head rolled to the side. It took several blinks, but Ryker on his knees finally came into view. All three hunters held him. More men, at least a dozen, exited the building and came from around the corner. Guns all turned on Ryker. But he paid no attention to them. His focus locked on where I lay.

The back door of the bank opened, and Dr. Rapava exited. "Good job." He nodded approvingly at Sera and Liam. He went to my bag and seized it. He snapped his fingers at a man to retrieve the files. "I cannot let you have this information, Zoey. What we do is for the best. I am disappointed you no longer see it. What is in here will only help us in the battle against fae."

I wanted to argue, to say something. The burning in my body kept me locked in place. The fever I felt for the last day consumed every fiber of muscle. The warmth turned to blistering heat inside, and I could not even open my mouth to scream.

"Your lover has been a thorn in my side." Rapava turned to face Ryker. "I wish I could run tests on you. You are a rarity, even in the fae world, but you are regrettably not my problem."

Ryker's lip hitched, a snarl escaping him, his eyes still on me.

"I made a deal." Rapava sighed as if he lost his favorite toy. "Sera?" The doctor turned and nodded for her to step forward. Sera pulled a gun from her halter. It looked different than the weapons we were issued, but I had no time to analyze or even think. All I understood was she would shoot Ryker. If it happened, alive or not, our chances of escaping went to zero.

The thought of him getting hurt again twisted my gut. The heat that had been incinerating me flamed till I almost passed out. Then it broke, and a cold river washed through me. I gasped for air. My limbs became moveable.

Sera pointed the muzzle at Ryker's heart. My frame vibrated with strength. Energy burst through my muscles like an explosion. I sprang to my feet. I felt no pain, only searing anger shooting into every crevice of my being. They would not touch him. I would keep him and Sprig safe.

The gun discharged its bullet, heading for Ryker's chest.

*No!*

Everything happened in a split second as I barreled toward him. I would protect him somehow. I could not let them hurt him or take him from me. Every moment we shared, every memory flashed through my mind: the time he covered my torso with his own to keep hypothermia from taking me; stitching his wound in the bathroom; the first time he dressed me; the time he undressed me; and the night we talked about how I wanted to follow my dreams to South America and open a refuge for disabled children in orphanages, to relax at a local dive bar, drinking cold beer on a hot humid night. This vision had been my lifeline, always thinking I had time to fulfill my dream. The fantasy disintegrated between my fingers, like crumbling clay. I only wanted us to be far away from here. Spend my last days alive on some warm beach, drinking with *him*. I was going to die without ever leaving the invisible borders of Seattle.

I slammed into Rapava, pushing him out of the way. The action hooked my arm through the bag handle he held and yanked it from his grip. With tremendous force, I crashed into Ryker. The Wanderer fell backward, taking us both to the ground. I could only see his chest as we dropped together. Heat jolted through my nerves, my vision spun, and air rushed by my ears as if I had stuck my head from a speeding car. His back collided with the terrain, jarring me as we slid several feet before something stopped our movement.

Silence became the first thing I noticed. I only heard his breath next to my ear. It shouldn't have been this quiet. They would be coming at us. Yelling, feet thundering. But there was nothing. The second thing was the stale stench of beer and cigarettes.

I slowly lifted my head and blinked, then blinked again, looking around at the chipped walls adorned with red and white flags, dilapidated wood floors, and an old jukebox in the corner crooning a Latin ballad. The bar appeared lined with stools, which you could barely see through the dim light and haze. A pool table leg pressed into Ryker's shoulder, the object that had stopped our movement. A Hispanic man stood in a doorway next to us, a case of beer in his arms. He peered at us with his mouth open.

"What the...?" I couldn't seem to grasp the dingy, shabby hole-in-the-wall bar surrounding us. It reeked of smoke and booze.

Ryker stirred underneath me. When I looked, his eyes had grown wide.

"Are you all right?" I examined him to make sure he was in one piece.

"Yeah." His intense gaze turned back to me. Suddenly, I could feel every inch of his torso beneath mine, and his strong arms around me. One wrapped around my waist, his hand on my butt. The other hand clutched the back of my head, holding me tightly to him. Air evaporated, my chest tightened.

"You know you saved a fae." His voice low.

"I saved *you*."

He sucked air through his teeth, but no other emotion came to the surface. This close, I saw the outline of his eyes weren't as pure navy blue as I thought. They had specs of silver running through them like a map of a river. They seemed to drag me in, taunting me to fall through them.

He licked his lips, drawing my attention to them. They were all I could see—damp, full, beautiful, and seemed to be calling for mine. My head lowered as he tilted his.

"*Qué demonios?*" The man still stood in the same place. Shock widened his eyes and mouth. "El diablo!" The box fell from his hands, slamming onto the floor. The shattering sound of glass inside jolted me away from Ryker's mouth. Liquid leaked onto the wood planks. The smell of beer swam into my nose, suffocating my senses. The man continued to speak Spanish as we scrambled to our feet.

My bag lay on the floor next to us. "Sprig!" I opened the top, leafing through it. Snuggled at the bottom, a monkey-sprite lay sound asleep still curled around Pam, a book, and Daniel's video camera. My shoulders sagged with relief. *How the hell did he sleep through that?* He had saved the camera from going into Rapava's hands. The doctor had the files, which was extremely bad. I hadn't even had a chance to go through them, but whatever was in them, Daniel had hoped I would keep it away from DMG. I failed him. Still, we had Daniel's video. The thought of losing the last bit of visual and audio piece of him destroyed me. Sprig's toes clung to it for dear life, like he had fallen asleep doing so. I felt so glad the little bugger was here and unharmed.

Fevered Spanish circled around me, drawing my attention back to the stranger. The dark-skinned man stood flinging his arms around, pointing at us with fear and suspicion. His Spanish was accented. It didn't sound like someone who came from Mexico. My eyes examined the room, my brain trying to understand. The Peruvian flag hanging on the wall confirmed our true location and shoved the whole "how the hell are we here?" to the forefront.

"How—" Was all I uttered before Ryker cut me off.

"You." His head turned, taking in the bar. Late afternoon rays streamed through the musty window by the front door. The sun looked a little lower in the sky than a moment earlier in Seattle. "You caused us to jump." He turned to me.

My head shook automatically, wanting to deny this statement. But I felt deep in my gut he was right. This tavern appeared so close to the place I envisioned in my head before I tackled Ryker. I jumped us to South America. His magic existed, alive in me. It had been growing for a while and now flamed wildly. The powers had come alive to protect their home—the man they belonged to. It was the fever, which had been growing in me, the unbearable heat I felt when lying on the ground. His magic helped me heal and defend its owner.

My hands went to my stomach and moved to my chest. Before the jump, I felt it was contained to a small area in my gut, but the energy had broken open, and now it flowed everywhere. The warmth that immobilized me was his power coming alive.

Ryker's face appeared hard, his focus laser sharp on me. The Latino man continued to wail in Spanish, spouting about how two people crashed into the bar from thin air. There were a lot of Hail Marys entwined in his rants. I understood him, but he wasn't a priority. He finally ran, choosing to fear us from outside the walls of the cantina.

"Why are you looking at me like that?" The way Ryker's jaw clenched, I knew he wasn't happy. But I saved his life—both of ours—and had gotten us far away from DMG and Dr. Rapava. Why was he so upset?

"What?" I demanded.

"They are adapting to you. Your system is no longer foreign to them."

"What are? Your powers?" I asked. "What does it mean, adapting to me?" Fear coated my throat.

He folded his arms; anger burned under his words. "It means I might never get them back, and you will become one of us."

Time stopped. Sound dispersed. Only the thudding of my heart rang in my ears. "Y-you mean I will become fae?"

"Yes. Part. You are stealing my powers, who I am." Every word was shot at me like a bullet, digging into my gut.

This could not be possible. Actually, it could be, but I didn't want it to. I had been taught to despise fae, everything they were. Now I was becoming one.

Ryker's expression faltered. His stare zeroed in on my face. "Zoey...?"

As soon as he called attention to it, I felt the warmth sliding to my top lip. I touched the spot. My fingers came away with red liquid. The pool of blood dripped from my hand onto the floor.

*Nosebleed.*

*Experiment.*

*Dying.*

Ryker grabbed a napkin off the bar and handed it to me.

"Is it too late?" I whispered, placing the paper under my nose.

Ryker stood for a moment before he shook his head. "No, but it won't be long."

"We have to stop the powers from acclimating to me." I looked at my shaking hands balled around my nose, streaked with fresh blood. "Before... before..." I couldn't finish the sentence, but we both knew what I meant.

If what Daniel said was true, then I was a ticking time bomb. At any moment my defect could kill me. Ryker's magic would be lost in me forever.

Only a few months ago, I was a collector. I hunted fae.

Now, I am the one hunted.

If death didn't beat them to it first.

*Thank you to all my readers. Your opinion really matters to me and helps others decide if they want to purchase my book. If you enjoyed this book, please consider leaving an honest review on the site where you purchased it. Thank you.*

*Want to find out about my next book? Sign up on my website and keep updated on the latest news.* www.staceymariebrown.com

## The Barrier Between (Collector Series #2)

The hunter has become the hunted.

**Zoey Daniels** is on the run for her life. Hiding from the very people she used to work for. She just found out her whole life was a lie, a science experiment of DMG. One with a fatal flaw—one that could kill her—taking Ryker's magic with her forever.

With their relationship changing and their shaky alliance growing into something more, they are in a race against time. Ryker, Zoey, and a narcoleptic monkey-sprite, Sprig, set out to find a way to transfer his powers back before it's too late. Their journey takes them to the rainforests of South America, dealing with those who are after something Ryker possesses and who will stop at nothing to obtain it for themselves.

What Zoey and Ryker discover could destroy them...tearing them a part for good.

### Book #2 Available Now!

# Acknowledgements

To my readers: You are the only reason I can follow my dreams. I hope you enjoy these new characters and story as much as you loved the Darkness Series. Thank you for opening your arms to me and the crazy voices in my head... which are real!

To my mom: Thank you for being my front line and for being my sounding board, reader, critic, and giving me advice and support. I don't know what I would do without you. I love you.

To Hollie: Working with you has been incredible. I am so happy you are in my life. There is no getting rid of me now! http://www.hollietheeditor.com/.

To Judi at http://www.formatting4u.com/: Thank you! You have made the stress of getting my books out on time so much easier.

To all the bloggers who have supported me: My gratitude is for all you do and how much you help indie authors out of the pure love of reading. I bow down. You all are amazing!

To all the indie/hybrid authors out there who inspire, challenge, support, and push me to be better: I love you!

And to anyone who has picked up an indie book and given an unknown author a chance. THANK YOU!

# About the Author

Stacey Marie Brown works by day as an Interior/Set Designer and by night a writer of paranormal fantasy, adventure, and literary fiction. She grew up in Northern California, where she ran around on her family's farm raising animals, riding horses, playing flashlight tag, and turning hay bales into cool forts.

Even before she could write, she was creating stories and making up intricate fantasies. Writing came as easy as breathing. She later turned that passion into acting, living and traveling abroad, and designing.

Though she had never stopped writing, moving back to San Francisco seemed to have brought it back to the forefront and this time it would not be ignored.

When she's not writing, she's out hiking, spending time with friends, traveling, listening to music, or designing.

# To learn more about Stacey
# or her books, visit her at:

**Author website & Newsletter:**
www.staceymariebrown.com

**Facebook Author page**:
www.facebook.com/SMBauthorpage

**Pinterest:** www.pinterest.com/s.mariebrown

**TikTok:**
https://www.tiktok.com/@staceymariebrown

**Instagram:** www.instagram.com/staceymariebrown/

**Twitter:** https://twitter.com/S_MarieBrown

**Goodreads:**
www.goodreads.com/author/show/6938728.Stacey
Marie_Brown

**Stacey's Facebook group:**
www.facebook.com/groups/1648368945376239/

**Bookbub:**
www.bookbub.com/authors/stacey-marie-brown

Made in United States
Orlando, FL
21 April 2023

32334148R00224